My Daughter's Boyfriend

D0670983

MY Daughter's Boyfriend

Cydney Rax

FINKELSTEIN
MEMORIAL LIBRARY
SPRING VALLEY, NY

3 2191 00973 1752

Dafina
Books

Kensington Publishing Corp.
http://www.kensingtonbooks.com

DAFINA BOOKS are published by

Kensington Publishing Corp.
119 West 40th Street
New York, NY 10018

Copyright © 2004 by Cydney Rax

All rights reserved. No part of this book may be repro-
duced in any form or by any means without the prior written consent of the Publisher, excepting brief quotes used
in reviews.

If you purchased this book without a cover, you should be
aware that this book is stolen property. It was reported as
"unsold and destroyed" to the Publisher and neither the
Author nor the Publisher has received any payment for
this "stripped book."

All Kensington Titles, Imprints, and Distributed Lines are
available at special quantity discounts for bulk purchases
for sales promotion, premiums, fund-raising, and educa-
tional or institutional use. Special book excerpts or customized printings can also be created to fit specific needs.
For details, write or phone the office of the Kensington
special sales manager: Kensington Publishing Corp., 119
West 40th Street, New York, NY 10018, attn: Special Sales
Department. Phone: 1-800-221-2647.

Dafina and the Dafina logo Reg. U.S. Pat. & TM Off.

ISBN-13: 978-0-7582-8023-7
ISBN-10: 0-7582-8023-8

First Kensington mass market printing: March 2013

10 9 8 7 6 5 4 3 2 1

Printed in the United States of America

To my mother
Margaret,
who is not just a mother,
but also a friend;
great, supportive, and loyal.

And to the memory
of my father,
Oscar (1939–2000).
I know you're
watching over me.

I

Tracey

It was the second Thursday in November. It was also the day that my daughter, Lauren Hayes, turned seventeen. As soon as I thought she'd woken up, I burst into her bedroom with a card, a glass vase stuffed with pink spray roses, and a tiny rectangular birthday cake punctured with a single burning candle that spelled out the word CELEBRATE. We ate one thick slice of her favorite, German chocolate, and my daughter then informed me that the festivities would continue that night. She'd been invited out for a bite to eat.

Later Lauren was surging through the apartment looking for her sling-backs and fussing with her French twist. And because I like to cool down after putting in my eight hours of workplace labor, I started my weekday ritual. As soon as I get home, I close the blinds and disrobe—my way of enjoying my world in comfort and without distraction. This particular evening I had on some white lace panties and a matching bra.

I was passing through the dining room, which has a

mirrored wall. Everything was fine until I noticed my reflection. For most people there's always one body part or another that they don't like, and I'm what some might consider "thick," but even so, I'm proud of my creamy-looking legs and voluptuous thighs.

I was captivated by my appearance, but felt annoyed when I caught my daughter staring.

"Don't you have to get ready, girl?" I asked her from the mirror.

My daughter, five-seven compared to my five-five, inherited her daddy's fair complexion and long skinny legs. Although several people accuse Lauren of tinting her hair, those reddish and blond roots come natural. She has a mole above her lip. And she is blessed with some Beyoncé-type eyes: wide, exotic, and sparkly. In spite of Lauren's cockeyed stare and her mouthing off that "Ugh! Nobody wants to see you half-dressed," I was too unnerved to admonish her for her ill manners. She shoved a red T-shirt and some black leggings in my hand, and stormed off to her bedroom. I slipped the T-shirt over my head, but thought it was too warm for the leggings, so I laid them on the brown leather sofa.

Once Lauren disappeared, I stole a look at my surroundings. Under normal circumstances our apartment was low-maintenance and free of excessive clutter. But tonight the place looked jacked. Piles of T-shirts and musty-smelling jeans made a trail from my bedroom to the living room. Dirty plates and crusty silverware littered the kitchen counter, and I wanted to start organizing the magazines that had multiplied all over the front area.

There's a wide column of built-in shelves that take up a wall in my living room. I was crouched in front of it, busy doing my domestic thing, back turned, when I heard this voice rush from behind.

"Well, hellooo, Mrs. Davenport."

I turned my head so sharp I heard a bone pop. A flush of heat penetrated my face from the inside out. I had on the T-shirt, but he could still see my panties, and my legs were uncovered. I didn't know if I should excuse myself, or skip the apologies and shove a huge throw pillow against my lower half. But, paralyzed as I felt, all I could do was stare.

Even though he'd been dating my daughter for quite a few months, it was always hard to catch him for long stretches of time; it seemed he and my daughter were always running in and out of the apartment to be with each other.

But tonight, Aaron Khristian Oliver hovered over me dressed in a wine-colored suit and a multicolored necktie. In some ways his looks reminded me of a tall version of the actor RonReaco Lee. His dark wavy hair, lightly trimmed mustache, and athletic body made it difficult to deny that Aaron Oliver put the "hot" in "hottie." His hands were shoved in his pockets and he tried to play things off, raising his eyes a little, but I knew he noticed my legs.

I turned from Aaron and my mind said, *What the— okay, don't say nothing, just leave the room, no, no, his staring feels kinda—but this ain't cool, Lauren's only a few steps away . . . what if she . . . oh God, Jesus God.*

Once those thoughts vanished, I felt a teensy bit tensed, but managed to sigh like his standing near was no biggie. I don't like letting any guy intimidate me, even if he does intimidate me. But just when I thought I was the one who controlled my world, I heard Aaron say real low yet audibly, "Mmm, mmm, wow."

At first his flirtation seemed silly. *Yeah, right, he's gotta be kidding,* I thought. *Young fool, he's just messing with me. Ha ha ha, funny, funny funny.*

I started to go on about my business, but Aaron wouldn't stop staring. Usually when men stare, I get annoyed and want to look anywhere except at the man whose eyes won't let me go. But with Aaron, this was different. I felt myself blushing, wanting to smile almost. Yet something screamed, *He's crossed a line. Perform tongue-fu on him. Tell him his ass is grass and you're the lawn mower.* But then another instigating inner voice said, *Eat it up, Tracey Lorraine Davenport. It's okay for him to stare.*

It felt weird to admit that I liked the way he lifted me. And after what I'd been through on my lunch break that day, hearing a long whistle and assuming it was a man, just to find out it was a bird, this was definitely an upgrade.

I turned and smiled at Aaron as widely and sweetly as possible. His body was so close he could have reached out and caressed my arm. I felt frozen to the floor.

"Mmmm, you look . . . never mind," he said in a low voice. Then he made a what's-the-matter-with-me groan and looked at the ceiling, at the floor, then back at me. I waved my hand at him so he could keep on talking, but without warning, he gave me a hardened stare and backed away.

Can you believe I felt a tiny stab of loneliness, just that quick? From enjoying the highs of feeling like an "it" girl, to being so-last-year, just that fast?

I stood only a couple feet away from him, but it felt like he was on the other side of the earth. He was standing next to the door, mumbling what sounded like "damn," and he was clutching and turning the doorknob.

"Hey," I said, stepping close to Aaron and forcing him to look at me again.

Aaron lifted his head and opened his mouth, but instead of hearing his words, I heard, "Mom, what are you *doing*?"

Right then I felt like the child and not the mother. I jumped back from the guy far enough to create some innocent distance between us. I covered my thighs with my hands, then grabbed a few magazines and placed them in front of my crotch with an overdue "This is so embarrassing. Aaron, don't you know how to ring a doorbell instead of just walking in here?"

I glanced at Lauren, apologized with my eyes. Her terse expression softened a little, but not enough to make me feel totally at peace.

The entire atmosphere shifted, the tantalizing moment escaping with few promises of a return. I even retrieved the leggings from the couch and scurried to my room and slid my legs inside them. Once my hands stopped shaking, and when I felt calm enough to emerge, I rushed past Aaron and resumed stacking magazines.

Aaron hung around for a little bit longer, until Lauren was ready. She grabbed him by the hand, snatching him through the door and toward the safety of the outside world. Yet before they left, and all the time he was standing there, I never made eye contact with him again. But I'd bet a hundred bucks, even though all three of us were in the same room, that my daughter's boyfriend sneaked another peek at me.

She didn't have to worry, though. I liked his attention, loved how good his stare made me feel, but after thinking about things long and hard, I decided I wasn't going to be a fool. Once I knew they were gone, I said out loud to the mirror with a strong voice, "Aaron is just a kid. And I don't do kids."

2
tracey

Once Aaron and Lauren departed for her birthday outing, I was moping around the apartment waiting for my honey, Steve Monroe, to call. He and I have been seeing each other going on seven months. Steve is thirty-eight, six-foot-two, and a thick-bodied type with muscles that ripple like waves on the ocean. Most days he wears his thick brown hair in a neat-looking ponytail, and he has a fondness for stylish eyewear.

Steve is a manager in the shoe department of Foley's at Memorial City Mall. He loves his job and works long rotating hours, but he always tries to check in when he gets a free moment. So there I was, sitting on the couch and watching the telephone. It was mocking me, *No, he has not called yet, and staring at me won't make him call any sooner.*

I turned my head away from the phone and retreated outside. When I want peace of mind, some nights I sit on my balcony for hours, lifting my head toward the sky, examining the shape of the moon, counting stars, and trying to figure out the shape of my life.

"Thirty-one, thirty-two . . ."

The phone began to ring, and I lowered my eyes.

"Shoot!"

I glanced one final time at those blinking stars and ducked through the tiny crevice left open by the sliding glass door. At the third ring I pounced on the phone before the answering machine could do what I purchased it to do.

"Hello!"

"Hey, babe, Daddy's home."

I smiled into the phone and collapsed on the couch like a teenager in love. Nestled my head on a couple of oversized pillows and propped my feet on one end of the couch.

"Can Mommy come see Daddy?" I cooed.

"Uh, sure. Give me a little time, though. Gotta take a shower and relax a bit. Those customers 'bout drove me nuts today."

"Mmmm, I'm sure, with y'all having that forty-percent-off sale. You lay aside any shoes for me?"

"You know it. Picked out a couple just for you. Looking at 'em right now. They'll be waiting on you when you get here. But I gotta go now. Pager's going off. Hear it?"

I frowned.

Gripped the phone a little tighter. I hated when I did that, hated when my insides reacted to any adverse information Steve told me. Out of the five lovers I've had since the age of fifteen, Steve Monroe is the one who rates the best. So far, he's the only man who can make me shake, rattle, and scream like my butt is on fire. Finding a man whose prowess can make you scream is about as rare as finding a five-hundred-dollar bill on an inner-city park bench. So you can guess that having Steve in my life is a top priority.

"Steve, Steve," I said sitting up. "Do you really have to get off the phone right now? Why don't you call whoever that is later?"

"Ahhh, baby. You want to see me that bad?"

I settled back and resumed resting my head on the pillow.

"Hey, tell you what, Tracey. Give me a half hour. Let me return this page and get myself situated. And, uh, don't bother coming out tonight. I'll call you before I swing by your place. How's that sound?"

I hoped he didn't perceive my frown. Hoped he couldn't feel my heart drag like time had doubled. I wanted to say, "Does *everything* always have to go your way?" But fear imprisoned my question and instead I offered a languid "No problem. Sounds good. See you soon."

I hung up without hearing if he ever said good-bye. The fact that he seemed to brush me off made me feel bad. In the past he'd given me a lot of attention, but recently, and without a clear-cut warning, the attention vanished. That made me wonder. Was there anything about me that turned Steve off? What could I be doing that made him not want to hold me like he used to?

Last time we did anything worth screaming about was damn near five weeks ago. Oh, believe me, I've gone without for a lot longer than five weeks. But that was when I was between relationships. Going without because you don't have a man is one thing. But when you have a man, or think that you have one, and you're still going without, well, that makes you tend to question everything. From your personality to your looks, you start questioning your value, your appear-

ance, and your existence. You start comparing yourself to the shapely, light-skinned sister in the grocery
store, the one with the flawless skin, good, long hair
that cascades down her back, and who always seems to
have on the classiest outfits and is unaware that dozens
of men, black, white, and Hispanic, are taking longer-
than-necessary looks at her. Trying to look their way
into an introduction and trying to stare their way into
her future. I look to see the woman's reaction and
abruptly turn my eyes away, pretending I'm interested
in the price of artichokes. I don't give a foo-fee-fang
about artichokes, but no one would know that. I'm
touching and caressing, sniffing and rubbing the arti-
choke as if my whole life depends on it, yet my mind is
taking me back to Steve. Does he look at these types of
women when I'm not around?

The ringing of the phone pulled me back down to
the realities of the earth.

"Hello!"

"Lauren there?" he asked.

I raised my eyes to the ceiling. "Whatever happened
to 'Hello, how are you?' "

He didn't say anything.

It isn't hard to sigh. "No, Derrick, Lauren's gone.
It's her birthday and she's out on a date."

"I *know* it's her birthday, Tracey. That's why I'm calling . . . to wish her a happy birthday and to see if she
wants to do something either tomorrow or Saturday
night."

"How freaking thoughtful of you to want to take
your daughter out one to two days after her birthday.
I'm sure she'll be thrilled."

"Look, Tracey, you told me Lauren's on a date. How
am I supposed to take her out if someone else already
has?"

"Plan ahead, Derrick. Call her a month in advance and secure this date so she won't have to choose to go out with someone besides her father."

"Uh, well, I . . . I didn't think about it like that . . . but if she's not busy this weekend, I'll make it up to her."

"Well, last time I checked, I wasn't Lauren and I can't speak for her. I don't know what she has planned for tomorrow. But thanks for call—"

"Hey, Tracey. Don't hang up. I'm not done. What's up with you? You sound like you're a woman who hasn't had any decent dick in a while. At least not one that has a man at the other end of it."

I stood up.

"What did you say?"

"You heard exactly what I said. That's why I hate calling over there, because every time I do, you have that stank attitude. Take it from me, Tracey, no man is going to want a woman with a piss-poor attitude."

"Derrick, when I want your advice, I'll give it to you. And furthermore, you have a lot of nerve. Ain't no telling when you last had a woman."

"You're right about that. I'm not telling. If it weren't for you, neither of us would be going through this mess."

"Derrick, don't drive us down that street again. *Please!* You're almost forty, but no one would ever know it. It is *not* my fault that we have a daughter, it is *not* my fault you had to drop out of college to get a full-time job, and it is *not* my fault you never married."

"Yeah, yeah, yeah. I've heard that BS before. But you know good and well what I'm talking about. Seriously, Tracey, if it weren't for you—"

"Derrick, why—how can you still . . . you know it

isn't even worth talking to you. Your life is your life because of *you,* not me. So get over it!"

Slamming the phone down, my hand was shaking as if I had Parkinson's disease. I wondered how I could let a man I don't even like, let alone love, get me all riled up.

Derrick Patrick Hayes, my baby's daddy, also happens to be the man who took my virginity. He and I met while he was a sophomore at Texas Southern University. He was nineteen. I was fifteen. I don't know why I liked him, because he's a high yellow guy, and I don't really like high yellow guys, but for some reason I liked him. He was tall, intelligent, a little bit on the nerdish side, and he didn't get frustrated or threatened when I argued with him.

I consider Derrick my first real boyfriend. Back then my mom, Grace Davenport, didn't approve of me seeing someone so old. But the more she and I butted heads, the more determined I was to hang out with him.

"Tracey," Derrick said one Saturday night when we were wrestling on the floor of his brother's van.

"What?" I said barely able to see because for one thing it was dark as hell and for another, his soft hands were caressing my legs, thighs, and very sensitive booty.

"Will you let me make love to you?"

Nobody had ever said that to me before. Hell, it made me blush and feel like I was special. So I said what any other warm-blooded person with a smack of sense would've said.

"When? Where? What time?"

Derrick smiled broadly, like I'd just announced he'd won a full scholarship or something.

That weekend, when my mother was away at work,

Derrick came by smelling different than I'd ever known him to smell.

"You didn't have to drench yourself with cologne, Derrick. I wasn't going to change my mind," I told him.

He laughed. Thought I was so cute.

Derrick spread my favorite quilt on the bed and forced me to put on a Prince record—which one I can't remember, they all sounded outlandish to me. I thought all that ceremonial stuff was cute but such a waste. What? Would listening to Prince help Derrick get a higher rating?

Then we got totally naked. Well, not quite. I left on one sock. For some reason I didn't think losing my virginity would seem as bad if I left on one article of clothing. Derrick stretched out next to me and started kissing me the way I like to be kissed. Lots of tongue, spit, and sucking and stuff. He'd just finished drinking a cold glass of lemonade and his tongue tasted like fruit, which to me was even better, because regular tongue tasted boring.

Okay, long story short. The guy humped me like a coyote in heat, and I felt as woozy as a senior citizen on roller skates. First time I ever screamed because something good happened. We pounded against that bed like horses running around a field. I'm screaming, he's moaning, pulling, and tugging at my hair. Had to slap his hands a few times because I definitely wasn't turning into Baldy Locks just so he could get his. By the time we were done, Derrick was singing like he just got back from happy minute. I was perspiring, sore, and sleepy but I had no doubt that we were going to be doing the nasty again and again.

Well, as you might have guessed, after doing it using part-time contraception, you're going to get full-

time pregnant. I found out I was expecting when I noticed I was yawning and wanting to crash at eight every
night. And, of course, the clincher was the fact that my
period did a disappearing act. Although I always hated
when my cycle came, boy, did I ever wish that sucker
would hurry up and make an appearance back in
those days.

But nothing happened.

At least nothing that I wanted to happen.

I remember the night I called Derrick. It had been
difficult trying to get in touch with him. He was busy
catching up on his studies after returning from a week
in Corpus Christi. "Spring break," he claimed. Anyway,
once I finally caught up with him, I was so scared. Part
of me wanted him to share the fear I was feeling. The
other part of me wanted to see what he was made of.
Would he run off like he was being chased in a man-
hunt, or would he hang around and be a man?

"Derrick, I got something to tell you," I said with
caution.

"What's that, baby?" he said with a smile in his
voice.

"I think I'm . . ."

"You think you're what?" he asked, smiley voice
gone.

"The 'P' word."

" 'P' as in . . . popular?" he asked, sounding dumber
by the minute.

"Ha! I wish. Keep going."

"Pretty?" "Hey, I think I rate a little bit higher than
pretty. One last guess."

"Look, Tracey. I'm drawing a blank. Why don't you
help me out?"

"Shoot, that's what I need to be saying to you, because I'm going to have your little bambino in eight months or less."

"You—you—you—you, what did you say?"

"I—I—I—I said you and me are going to be a daddy and a mommy."

Silence.

"Hello?" I clicked the line to see if he was still with me.

I was feeling tense because I'd heard about girls who'd have these guys all hot for them until the girls tell them the bad news. Suddenly those hot guys get real cold and swear "it's not mine." And this claim would be made even after these dudes had been freaking the girls like freaking was going out of style.

I couldn't imagine Derrick switching out on me like that. Not him, no way.

"Derrick, you're *scaring* me."

"Well, *you're* scaring *me*," he finally replied.

"And why is that?"

"Because this wasn't supposed to happen."

"News flash, Derrick: I came, you came, and now the baby's coming." He went on and on about how his plans didn't include a child, he wasn't ready for this, and was I sure it wasn't anyone else's? Just a bunch of defensive crap that wouldn't change anything about what was happening. I was so mad I felt like slamming down the phone, but instead I kept listening.

"You tricked me."

"Ha ha," I screeched with my that's-so-ridiculous laugh.

I'd heard it all, and at that point I didn't care anymore.

As book-smart as Derrick was, I guess he hadn't fig-ured on becoming a co-parent with his teenage girlfriend. But once he got over the initial shock, he seemed to accept that he was going to be a daddy, and our daughter was born later that year.

In the early months of Lauren's life, Derrick hung around like a man in love with the female version of himself. That is, until I filed for child support. Worst thing a woman can do to a man is file on him. It's like you've taken an already sharp knife, sharpened it again, and wedged the knife dead center in his heart and somehow, some way, the blade reached his wallet too. And, of course, the wound in his wallet hurts far worse than the one in his heart.

I thought that after Derrick became accustomed to a few months of regular payments, he'd lighten up on the grudge-holding bit. But that was seventeen years ago and he rarely speaks a kind word to this day. I really don't care. Don't have time. Derrick is a long-ago history lesson.

'Cause, see, although I was sixteen with a kid, the river of life never stopped flowing. I still managed to earn my diploma. I worked here and there, changed diapers, took a few dead-end college courses, trained Lauren to ride a tricycle, then how to put on a pair of panty hose. I went from twenty-something to thirty-something, kicked a few guys to the curb, got kicked back, and for the past few years I've been employed as an office coordinator at the University of Houston.

Seems like I've spent half my life raising Lauren and trying to be a good mom. But many days I realized just how difficult that was . . . trying to be good *and* a mom was just a hard, hard gig. Especially when you're actively involved with guys, and screwing around with screwed-up men like the ones I'd known.

And the fact that Derrick Hayes had called but

Steve Monroe hadn't called back created a lethal combination in my mind.

I shuddered and ran my hands through my hair. Glanced at my watch. A good thirty minutes had already snuck by. I went and changed out of the T-shirt and leggings into something loose: a long-sleeved, dark brown silk shirt, matching slacks, and some leather pumps. Then I debated whether I should call. Most men don't like when you push and squeeze too hard. I'd been there too many times before not to know that if you pressed too hard, you'd force the man right out of your life and into some other woman's. Whereas women think a man would be flattered to have so much attention, in reality he's thinking an altogether different thing. And I long since had learned that men's thoughts rule the world.

James Brown, the King of Soul, was right. It *is* a man's world.

So much time had passed it made me nervous, my mind headed in unhealthy directions. If Steve was coming, wouldn't he be here by now? Or was he putting me off again, something he'd done before. After a couple more minutes of debate, I grabbed my purse and keys and closed the apartment door behind me.

The man who I was waiting on—well, his world was about to be entered.

3
Tracey

The longer I waited for Steve to call, the more I got the urge to see him. That pretty much sums up why I was flying down the street in a car that has no wings. I'm not an idiot, and I knew it would mean trouble if I showed up at his place feeling discombobulated. But when your heart is involved, logic ceases to have a voice, and the only thing I could hear at that moment was the cry from my soul, the frightening moan that senses when something just ain't right.

The normally twenty-minute drive took half that time. I swerved in front of Steve's town house. My car stretched across two parking spaces.

I noticed the vehicle right away.

A black baby Mercedes sat under the streetlight like a trophy. I saw the string of Mardi Gras beads dangling from the rearview mirror. Noticed the Louisiana license plate and the pink-and-green bumper sticker. All things that I'd seen before.

"Ain't that nothing?"

The owner of the vehicle was Lelani Thibodeaux, a thirty-something woman Steve used to date. She was originally from New Orleans, but had been living in the Houston area for the past few months. Called Lani for short, she was the classic Louisiana babe: long, wavy hair that rested against her back, huge breasts, shapely hips, and enough booty to go around for months; the very type of gorgeous woman you'd see in the grocery store, except Steve's town house was hardly Pak 'n' Save.

Feeling for my purse, I dug up my Nokia and had to start over three times before I could accurately dial Steve's digits. I hung up after three pointless rings.

Then Steve's front door opened.

Yep! It was Lani. Even though it wasn't that cold, she wore a floor-length coat. Her hair was flowing down her back as if she were a movie star. All he had on was a pair of dark slacks and a damned terry-cloth bathrobe. It was probably the one I bought him for his last birthday. Well, make that *charged* to my Dillard's account—I hadn't even paid the thang off yet.

They stood in front of the doorway, spooning in an upright position, like they shared the same bones. In each other's universe. A comfortable closeness that should not have been. I couldn't believe him. How could Steve be so hugged up with her like that? Why wasn't I on his mind? Didn't he just call me "baby" an hour or so ago, or was I the only one who remembered things like that?

Steve turned Lani's chin toward him and kissed her on the lips.

I damn near wanted to shriek nonstop, even though it felt like doing so would be meaningless, but instead my hand fumbled until it gripped the door handle.

When Steve went back for seconds, I brushed my fingers across my lips and then . . . I opened the door and my heels hit the pavement.

I clanked up the walkway, not caring how I sounded or looked.

Lani raised her head. She grinned, but it wasn't an I'm-happy-to-see-you grin. It was more like an I-got-him-and-you-don't smirk.

"Stacey Davenport. What *you* doing over here?" she said.

That heifer knows my name ain't Stacey.

My eyes vaulted over Lani's phony smile to Steve's troubled expression.

"Oh, don't worry, Steve. I didn't come over here to join the drama club. Just explain to me why you lied."

Lani folded her arms across her size 40C breasts. As I tried to step closer to Steve, she positioned her leg in front of me.

I paused.

"Do you mind?"

"Yes, I *do* mind, Stacey. You have no business over here. Quit chasing Steve and get a life."

"What?" I said. "Steve, did you hear what she—"

He looked straight ahead, standing mute like Jesus on Golgotha. Except the only thing Steve has in common with Jesus is long hair. And I doubted that the Messiah would have been wearing tortoiseshell glasses.

"Look, Lani. Steve and I are in a re-*la*-tion-*ship*."

"Were," she told me.

"E-excuse me?"

"You *were* in a relationship with Steve, but all that's over now because he's back with *me*. He was supposed to call and tell you."

"He *did* call me, but what he said didn't sound anything like this."

Steve acted like her cat had his tongue. And the worst part was he wouldn't look at me. It was bad enough to be released without advance notice, but I felt he owed me enough courtesy to tell me himself.

Lani rolled her heavily made-up eyes and grabbed Steve by the arm.

"Come on, baby," she told him. "Let's go."

"Go where?"

"Let's *go*, Steve!"

She aimed her remote-access transmitter at the Benz. The locks unsnapped. She gave me one last sneer and her body began its swivel walk. After not hearing footsteps following, Lani stopped and turned around.

"Steve, don't tell me you're having second thoughts. Now if . . . if you thinking 'bout changing your mind, you need to let me and that bitch know."

Now I know I can be a bitch sometimes, but I sure didn't want Lani to point out that little detail.

With both Lani and me staring Steve down, he looked like he wished he could melt right into the pavement and evaporate like a dispensed raindrop. That's what I didn't understand about some men. Lots of them had the hard body, the height of gods, the strength of mules, but regardless of the physical stamina, deep inside, some were weak, lost, and unable to make sound decisions, like their inner man didn't match their outer build.

I watched Steve. Even behind the glasses, his black eyes seemed to tighten, as if that action would mercifully erase all the tension. And after what felt like forever, he cleared his throat and stepped closer to Lani and whispered in her ear. She frowned but walked a few yards away, and he turned to face me. And from the look he was giving me, I had a feeling he wasn't exactly about to ask me if I wanted to become Mrs. Steve Monroe.

"Tracey, this is how's it laying tonight. Lelani's the head, you're the tail."

"What in the hell you mean, I'm—"

"Look, you aren't stupid. I meant it just how I said it. This shit's not working out."

I slapped my hand on my throat as if that action would prevent all the air from escaping my wounded soul.

"Well, well, why weren't you talking about heads and tails a few hours ago when you, when you, you called me and—"

"Old news is no news."

I panted and stared in the eyes of one who suddenly resembled someone I wasn't sure I knew. But I *knew* I knew Steve. But who exactly was he right then?

"Steve, how can you stand up here and make a decision like this? Something's not right, here." I sliced the night air with a few waves of my hand. "This is not even like you. I know you wouldn't—I *know* you wouldn't do me like this."

"Never, ever second-guess what a man will do, especially if that man is me. Now please leave. Go on and get your ass away from here," he said, and rejected me with a counter-wave of his own hand.

Everything I was seeing made me feel like I was sinking, like I was falling, and it seemed I'd keep on falling until I crashed. And the thought of crashing made me afraid. And when I got afraid, I got weak, and when I got weak, I got tired. Standing there with my mind numb, I felt *so* tired, so sick of losing out and knowing I was losing, but not able to figure out why I couldn't seem to win.

"Wait a minute," I told him. "You cannot, you *will* not, stand here and drop this garbage on me like that. This is bullshit."

"Look, how many times I have to tell you? You're through!"

I clenched my jaw and looked at Steve like he was hate personified. How could he embarrass me in front of Lani, and play me like I was some kind of nothing? For a while I didn't know what to do, what to say. And in spite of his damning words, Steve kept flicking his eyes at me like he was confused himself, but then he half-smiled at Lani and turned away from me. At Steve's facial affirmation, Lani raised her head and sashayed to the car; then she took one last intense look at Steve and drove off.

As soon as her taillights disappeared, Steve rushed to place his arms around my waist, hugging me tight like he wished he could squeeze away the last few moments.

"Baby, baby, baby," he said, shaking me hard with each word he spoke. "It's not what you think."

I stared at him, my mouth wide open as if to say, "What the hell am I *supposed* to think?"

"Look, Lelani paged me and came over here demanding that I hook up with her again. She put me on the spot. I didn't feel like arguing, so I let her go on and on, and that's when you showed up."

He kept sputtering one tired excuse after another, but by then my anxiety had drowned out his voice. Everything happened so fast I didn't have time to think about what I was supposed to do about what they were saying.

"Tracey," Steve said, shaking me and looking deep in my eyes, "say something, baby. Talk to me."

"Wh-what do you want me . . . what do you expect me to say, Steve? I'm not in the mood for any games y'all trying to pull. She telling me this, you telling me that."

"Tracey," he said, looking directly in my eyes, "I don't care what Lelani said. You know you're my baby, the only woman for me."

His words caused my heart to warm. I found myself smiling a smile I didn't all the way feel. On the one hand, I detested what had just taken place, but on the other hand I'd hoped Steve would come through for me—that even though Lelani was strong-willed, his feelings for me should have been stronger.

We stood there for a few moments clinging to each other, he kissing strands of my hair, my cheeks, and even grazing his soft lips across my neck. Neck-kisses are my weakness. So I closed my eyes and shivered, absorbing the warmth of his body, and was reminded of how much I yearned to be with this man.

Yes, the sex was unparalleled. *Yes,* I liked how he'd sometimes make me laugh with his corny jokes. *Yes,* I enjoyed sitting across a table from him, sharing a meal, and dissecting a conversation.

The sight of blaring headlights intruded upon my thoughts and my heart leapt when I saw it was the second coming of that Mercedes with the Louisiana license plates.

"She's back," I said lifting my head. "You need to tell Lani that she's old news."

When Steve looked up and saw Lani's vehicle pull into a parking space, his eyes enlarged and he jumped back like he was trying to escape gunfire. At first he grabbed his hands, which were shaking in tiny jerks like he was being swayed by something I could neither see nor feel. But then he hid his hands behind his back, lifted his chin, and looked away from me, effectively shortcutting all connections between us.

Ooooh. Ugghh.

I bent over.

Uggghhhhh.

I placed my hands on my throat and gently squeezed; a thick and harsh bile climbed swiftly up my throat, hot stinging tears filling my eyes with blindness. My guts were being ripped from my body, Steve's actions a dagger mauling my already bruised heart. Taking no time to think, no moment to rationalize or surrender, I lunged at him and palmed the side of his face.

"Who the hell you think you are, dammit? How you trying to play me, huh, Steve? You will *not* disrespect me. Not today." I ground my teeth, hitting, slapping, absorbing every heated sting from pounding his hardened skin, and with each punch, I felt tears spill from my own eyes, as if to hurt Steve was to hurt myself. And I was surprised yet saddened that instead of stopping me, he let me strike him again and again.

One frustrated slap later and Steve's glasses flew off his face, the force so great that they veered toward a nearby bush. He pinched his jaw between his fingers, eyes bulging, nostrils flaring, and looked at me like he didn't know who I was or what I'd turned into.

Chest heaving up and down and sweating, I clenched and unclenched my fists and began pacing the front walk in small, jerky steps. When I turned back toward Steve, Lani, who'd watched from her car, ran straight at me. I moved away from her, but she jumped at me from behind and bashed me hard in the back of my head with something so thick it felt like a damned hardcover dictionary. I blinked a couple of times and turned around, but was met by her long fingernails flailing wildly at my face.

The strength in me rose up and I blocked her twice, but she nicked me on my neck and I took one deep breath and, shoving with every ounce of power I possessed, I rammed her voluptuous ass right into those skin-piercing bushes. She began shrieking.

"Three words, Stacey. Watch your back."

I glanced bitterly at her and then at Steve, who was diligently pulling aside branches.

Wiping my eyes, I got in my car and burned rubber driving away.

4

Lauren

It was just like Aaron to have me get dressed up for my birthday, just to take me to Pizza Hut. We were standing at the front of the lobby, waiting for someone to show us to our seats. Aaron had this mischievous grin on his face and I felt embarrassed for wearing my long gold-layered dress, which was cute but seemed to clash with the atmosphere.

"Aaron, is this your idea of a joke?" I asked.

Aaron's answer was a gentle kiss to my cool lips. I raised my face to meet his, closed my eyes, and let our kiss last longer than normal. But I pushed him off me as soon as I felt a familiar stirring that reminded me things were progressing beyond my control.

"Lauren, no joke. Just wanted to see what you'd do."

I blushed and inhaled the aroma of tomato paste, pasta, and grease. Since it was a Thursday night, the place wasn't crowded. Following the female hostess, I slid my butt in the nearest booth. Aaron sat across from me and smiled.

"Everybody loves pizza, Lauren," he continued, "and I know you do."

"Yep, I love pizza, but I don't know that I want to eat it wearing this dress."

"Believe me, the pizza does not know and it won't care. So don't be worried about how you're dressed. You're looking fine and you're with me."

"Gracias."

"Voy a ordenar la pizza, mi amor, espereme aquí?" he told me in Spanish, something he'd speak occasionally to try to help me out with my language class, just one of my courses at Sharpstown High.

" 'I'm going to order the pizza, my love, wait for me here?' " I smiled.

"Muy bien," he agreed with approval.

"Very good to you, too," I said and waved at him while he went to get our food.

Aaron Oliver and I first crossed each other's paths at my part-time cashier's gig at McDonald's. It was during the weekday lunch rush and there were already twenty or so people in my line. This irate customer was yelling at me because his order wasn't ready and Aaron, who was standing in line behind him, calmed the man down, paid for his meal, and talked so soothing to me I couldn't help but melt under his graciousness. He told me about himself, that he was a student and a part-time employee. After revealing more info about his background, he asked for my number. I told him no. He returned to my job a few weeks later, talked real sweet, gave me a five-dollar tip, and asked for the number again, which I reluctantly revealed. Aaron and I started out talking on the phone every few days, with me warming up to him as time progressed. Then once my mom met and approved of him, he and I would either go to the movies,

Astro World, the malls, or swimming at the beaches of Galveston Island. That was several months ago and we've been love connecting ever since.

Aaron returned to our booth bringing a sample of every type of pizza on the buffet, breadsticks, lasagna, and tossed salad.

"Aaron, I can't eat all this," I laughed.

"I know, Bunny. I just want it here for you in case you're hungry."

"I'm not *that* hungry."

I gave him a flirty, sexy look, the one where my mouth is partially open and my chin is uplifted. He stopped what he was doing to zero in on my facial seduction dance, and I shook my head.

"Uh-oh. Better stop this. We came here to eat, celebrate, and get away from the house."

"Hey, Lauren. Don't think that *this* is the highlight to your birthday."

"You mean there's more? What else you get me?"

"As soon as we're finished eating, you'll find out what your gift is."

I shoved my plate to the side. "I'm done."

A half hour later we were headed toward Aaron's apartment. Transportation was provided courtesy of his five-year-old black-and-gold Acura Legend, a decent-looking ride that his parents bought him when he graduated from high school.

"Let's go," Aaron ordered after we pulled into his reserved covered parking space. Aaron's home is in the Parkwood West Apartments, on the southwest side of town. For the past year and a half Aaron has lived there with his roommate, Brad McMillan, who's originally from Detroit. Aaron, a native Houstonian who decided to remain in state to attend college, met Brad in a sociology class at the University of Houston.

Aaron and Brad's apartment was very different than most of the ones I'd been in. You walked in the door and located directly to the right was a hallway that had two bedrooms and a full bath. If you kept going straight you'd come to the dining room, the kitchen, and then the living room, which was in the back of the apartment. There was a nice-sized balcony, but it was full of junk: mountain bikes, snorkels, tennis rackets, and other sports equipment.

After walking in Aaron's home, I clutched my purse next to me and sat on the edge of the couch. On the other hand, Aaron had removed his coat, his suit jacket, and even his shoes. He went into his refrigerator and poured us sparkling white grape juice in champagne glasses. I smiled when he handed me a glass. I crossed my legs and reached to take a small sip. After one soothing taste I ended up guzzling a little bit more. Then I emptied the glass and placed it on a wooden coaster on Aaron's cocktail table.

Meanwhile, Aaron seemed to be in his own world, moving about the apartment, pulling out various CDs and placing them in the disc changer: Brian McKnight's *Back at One,* Mariah Carey's *Rainbow,* and Maxwell. I watched him standing by the speakers. His eyes were closed and he was swaying to Maxwell's distinctive high vocals.

A minute or so passed, but I refused to remove my coat.

"Hey, Bunny, you all right? Why you still got your coat on? Is it too cold in here?"

"Huh? Oh no. I'm okay."

"Sure? I can turn up the heat."

"Oh no. D-don't do that, Aaron. I'll take my coat off in a few."

I yawned hard enough to make him yawn too, and leaned my head against the big cushy pillows.

"Is it okay if I take off my shoes?" I asked.

"Nope, it's not okay. I know your feet smell like hell."

"Well, if you already know that, then it shouldn't be a problem," I said, and slid my feet out of my slingbacks.

"Fortunate" happened to be both Aaron's and my favorite slow jam. When Maxwell's screams filtered from the CD player, it was a matter of seconds before Aaron extended his hand and I stood up. Aaron slid my coat off my shoulders and dropped it to the floor, but I ducked down and placed the coat on the recliner. He smiled at me and held out his hand, and I put my hand in his and we walked to the open space of the living room.

I loved slow dancing, loved it so much that I did not complain at all when Aaron grabbed me around my waist and started rocking. I love to tilt my head and look in his eyes, and he really gets on my nerves because *he knows I love looking into his eyes,* but he closed them, so I ended up pinching his waist until he opened them again. So we kind of held each other, bodies merging into one another, and rocked to the music. And when the song ended, I wasn't surprised when I heard Maxwell start screaming again. I figured Aaron had put the song on repeat, and I didn't know if I wanted to repeat the same dance steps over and over again. I knew something had to give, I just wondered what and when.

Aaron took that moment to wet his lips and placed a smooth, warm, and oh-so-tantalizing kiss right on my neck and I wanted to melt like butter on a scorching griddle.

"Bunny?"

"Y-yeah?" I said in a soft, petrified voice.

"Ready?" he half-whispered.

I stiffened. He acted like he didn't notice my reaction and kept rocking. His lack of response irked me.

"Hey, Aaron," I said, but he shushed me.

The dress I had on was one of my favorites, but right then I wished I hadn't worn it because it had a zipper in the back and I could feel Aaron's hands on the zipper and yep, you guessed it, I could hear the doggoned zipper being unzipped and frankly I didn't know what to do. So I didn't do anything and before I knew it, my dress had been slid over my hips and down my legs and then it was crumpled around my feet and I knew I didn't buy that dress just to have *that* happen.

"Uuhh," I said in a scatterbrained tone, "Aaron, wh-where is the gift you said you got me?"

"This is the gift, Lauren. Making love with your man is the gift."

I sighed and kind of hoped Aaron didn't hear my sigh, yet I hoped that he did because maybe my sigh would say what my words could not.

By then Aaron's hands were sliding up and down my nervous and twitching back. He was rocking back and forth and we were still twirling around the living room and that's when I noticed something that gave me the jolt of reality. Aaron's erection talked to me. I had its complete attention and it was indeed rare that my body felt something as hot and aggressive as that and why was it so close to me and did it have to be so obvious by prodding and poking my thigh? In all the time I'd known Aaron, we'd kissed and caressed each other's shoulders and arms, but he'd never gone this far, never held me this close.

A shaky "I gotta go," was released from my divided

soul, and I pushed him off me. Even though our bodies were no longer in contact, my mind still latched on to the memory of how warm and snug Aaron had felt against me. I shuddered, bent down, and pulled up my dress over my shoulders, and I didn't care if my dress was zipped or not.

Aaron looked at me and had this messed-up expression on his face, like I was trifling and I had some nerve. I averted my eyes and slipped my feet inside my shoes and clutched my coat and walked around the corner and stood at the front door.

The music stopped playing and Aaron approached me and I was too afraid to look up at him, so I looked at the floor.

He stepped to me, waited a while, and lifted my chin.

"Let's talk!"

He grabbed my hand and we returned to the breakfast bar. I sat down while he leaned against the counter.

"What up?" he asked with a look of confused hurt on his face.

I swallowed what little spit was left in my mouth.

"Aaron, we—we've been over this before and I know what you want, how you feel, but I just don't think I'm ready to accept your gift." I laughed, hoping he'd join in.

He stared at me like not a damn thing was funny.

"Um, I care about you. I want you, even, but I'm . . . I'm still not ready, Aaron, tooooo . . . have sex with you."

"So, when will you be ready to . . . to make love with the man who wants to make love with you?"

"Ewwww," I said, feeling hurt and humiliated. "Why'd you have to put it like that?"

He just gave me a lingering look that made me feel even more uncomfortable.

"Well, Aaron, to be honest, I don't know when that time will be. Soon, maybe, but I just can't say."

His eyes grew so dark that I stood up. "I am *sooo* sorry about all this. My birthday has been really great and I thank you for the pizza, and the money you gave me when we were in the car, but I just want to go home . . . right now."

I flashed him a look of assurance that I didn't feel, and headed toward the front door.

"Are you done?" he said. I felt him behind me, his breath humidifying my neck.

I swallowed hard and turned to face my beau.

"Aaron, all I know is I do want to be with you and when I'm ready I know it'll be for the right reasons and at the right time," I said, hoping he'd believe me and know it was the best I could give.

He narrowed his eyes and paused a moment.

"Tell you what! Give me a rain check and I'll wait on you."

"You will?" I exhaled and stepped closer to him.

He nodded and grabbed me around my waist and pulled me against him so close that my chin smashed his shirt collar. At that moment I knew beyond a doubt that I'd made the right decision.

5
tracey

The only place I knew I could go unannounced at ten o'clock at night was my friend Indira Collier's house. I'd known Indira for almost eight years. We talked on the phone at least once a week and occasionally met for dinner. More important, Indira and I used to belong to the same worship center. And last year, after I elected to leave Solomon's Temple, she was the only church member who behaved like I still existed.

Indira, a forty-year-old native Houstonian, was a widow whose husband, Malcolm, had died of lung cancer. Malcolm owned a successful architectural firm at the time of his death, and he was wise enough to leave Indira with several hefty insurance policies, enough to quit her florist job and burn the mortgage on their quarter-million pad in a fancy southwest subdivision.

I made a left turn toward Indira's cul-de-sac and pulled in the circular drive of their two-story peach stucco home. Took me a few minutes to punch in Indira's phone number on my Nokia. She answered on the second ring. Moments later I saw her slightly open the front door and wave me in. Wearing a royal blue lounging gown, Indira grabbed my hand and we retreated to the game room, a gathering place that featured a wide-screen television, an oak wall unit with a DVD player and sound system, and an off-white Italian leather sofa. I sat on the sofa under several studio lights that glowed from the ten-foot vaulted ceiling.

Indira is five-foot-eight, has broad shoulders, long eyelashes, and a small but consistent smile. That evening the front of her hair was set in large pink rollers; the back portion was braided and rested at the tips of her shoulders.

"Something to drink? Eat?" she asked while she waited to play hostess.

"No, I'm—I'm okay for now."

She knelt and settled on the floor next to my feet. Patted my thigh.

"Tell me what happened, Tracey. Start from the top."

I recounted the night's events to Indira and dared to look in her eyes.

She flashed me a "been there" look.

I fumed about how I didn't appreciate Steve telling me one thing, but backing off it when Lani reappeared.

"That pissed me off. I mean the fact that, first of all, he barely acknowledges my presence until after she's left. What was that? He made me feel as if I was delusional about being in a relationship with him. All these months of spending time together and that's how it's laying? You don't even treat a dog like that, you know what I mean?"

Frowning, Indira waved at me. "I know. Keep going."

"And don't even get me started on Lelani. Talking

about *I* need to go and get a life. She barely graduated from college, her parents buy her everything she wants, and *I* need to get a life? Can you believe that?"

"I hate to say it, but based on what you've already told me about Lani, heck yes."

"Then he totally confuses me. He goes from saying 'Lani's the head' to 'You're the only woman for me' in less than three minutes. Does the brother know what he wants, or what? Make up your mind. I can take it."

"I know that's right," Indira said, pumping her fist in a display of female power.

"It's either me or Lani 'cause it damn sure as hell can't be the both of us."

"He may want to have his cake and eat it, too," Indira said pretending like she was holding a fork.

"Well, which one of us is the real cake?" I asked with a horrified look.

"Girl, you got me," she grunted. "So what's next?"

"I don't know, Indy. I mean, I've had run-ins with Lani before, and Steve would always take my side. But this . . . this is something different and I don't know . . . I don't know if he was showing off because she was there or what. But I made sure and put some serious whip-ass on him just in case."

Indy looked at me strange. "Mmmm, I won't ask," she murmured. "Well, what's up with Steve? Why would he string you along if he knew he wanted to be with her?"

I stared at Indira, answerless. I couldn't believe I was even going through this. It's a trip to wake up in the morning and think you'll know what's gonna happen by the end of the day, just to find out there's no such thing as a sure thing.

I swallowed deeply.

"I don't know, Indy. I think I'm starting to learn

that no man over the age of sixteen is truly single. I mean, they *say* they're single, but . . . all men either have a bed buddy, an ex-wife, a former shack-up mate, or some drama-queen residue somewhere in their lives."

"I'm telling," Indira laughed, yet her eyes twinkled with a knowing sadness.

"What can you tell me?" I sniffed and looked at her, hoping she'd have some type of wisdom since she'd been out there, hubby-less and alone, for the past couple of years.

"Well," she said, her smile disappearing, "these days being single don't mean what it used to mean back when I was in my twenties, which was a good hundred years ago."

I smiled and popped her on the forehead.

She swatted me in return. "Back then it meant totally solo, no girlfriend, no lover, nothing."

"Right," I told her. "Fast forward to now. Men hallucinating and talking 'bout 'Yeah, I'm single.' Interpretation: 'I got somebody, I'm just not claiming her right now,' or telling you, 'Yeah, I'm single,' but he's really sleeping with two, three women who he don't plan on marrying, so . . ."

Indira and I gave each other a been-there-done-that nod and kinda reflected on what was instead of how we wished things could be. The weird thing about it was even though I saw how dreary the man situation looked, I knew that the desperate and egotistical parts of me would still bend in spite of circumstances. It seems when you don't have much to start off with, you might be open to doing all kinds of things to make up for what you can't have. Realizing that scared the hell outta me; my lack of good alternatives invited parts of me to emerge that I really wouldn't know about other-wise.

"Tracey, do you have any personal belongings at Steve's?"

"Uh, probably. He said he had a couple pair of new shoes waiting for me over there."

"Ha, girl, you can kiss those shoes good-bye if there really were any shoes," she said, and waved bye-bye with her hands. "Anything of relevance?"

"Oh, I have several photos over there that I've al-ways wanted to get back. And I did loan this punk some money a couple of times, but I'm not worried about that."

Indira hooted, laughing with mouth wide open like it was Saturday night at the comedy club.

"Oh, you never told me you loaned Steve money."

"Because I knew what you'd say. He's a grown man working, and if anything he should be giving me money. And he *did* sometimes. But then he'd turn right around and borrow it back."

Indira yelped with laughter again, this time louder, shaking her head and apologizing to me with her eyes. It was like we were sitting in her game room at eleven o'clock in the morning instead of late at night. I hoped Regis, her fifteen-year-old daughter, couldn't hear us.

"Where's Miss Regis?"

"With her relatives. One of her cousins is having a sleep-over, so she's out of my hair probably, hopefully, until Sunday," she said, smiling and popping her fin-gers.

"Good for you," I said.

"Which reminds me," said Indira. "Regis is having her own little slumber party in a couple of weeks. I'd planned on mailing the invitations tomorrow, but since you're here . . ."

"Indy, you mean to tell me I'm not worth the price of a stamp?"

"Oh, for heaven's sake. I'll make sure and put a stamp on the doggoned invitation before I hand it to you."

I laughed and thought about how glad I felt to be with Indira and how grateful I was to count her as a close friend.

I sat up in Indira's house until a minute past midnight, talking in spurts and trying to force genuine laughs and smiles. And I did all this without being upset by the lateness of the hour. I figured that Lauren was out with Aaron. They'd gotten my permission to be out beyond curfew in the past, and most times I didn't worry. But after becoming a bit sleepy, I stood up. I gave my friend a tight hug, and began making my way home.

The night air was brisk, and the November darkness erased Houston's skyline. The engine of my two-year-old white Chevy Malibu made soft tapping sounds as I drove through the front entrance of Williamstown's Apartments, our home of the past several years. Located near the busy intersection of Bissonnet and the Southwest Freeway, it's an enclosed community of blacks, whites, and a ton of Hispanics.

Our apartment unit is at the far end of the property. After driving past the guardhouse, I made a sharp right and then headed left until I reached my building. Aaron's Legend was backed in so that the rear of his vehicle rested near a rickety wooden fence. Looking up at my apartment's windows, I shivered when I noticed all the rooms seemed pitch dark. When I got to the door, I made sure to rattle my keys, sticking them in the lock and twisting and turning the key as loud as possible. The darkened apartment was cold and smelled musty, like soiled laundry. After two flicks of the light switch, I saw Aaron's burgundy suit coat resting on the arm of the couch. Lauren's slingbacks and purse were abandoned in the middle of the floor.

"Oh no, God. Please, please."

I squeezed both sides of my face until it hurt, and forced myself to step out of my shoes. Waited another couple minutes before I tiptoed down the hall to Lauren's bedroom. The apartment layout is split: my bedroom is on the right, the living room, dining room, and kitchen are in the center, and Lauren's bedroom and the main bathroom are on the left.

Standing outside her room, I wanted to tap lightly but said, "To hell with that." I opened her door, turned on the light, and saw a lump in her bed covered by a queen-sized comforter. When I went to her bed and pulled back the cover, the only thing I saw was a balled-up blanket.

Backing out the doorway, I stepped into the hall and heard voices coming from inside Lauren's bathroom, which was directly across the way from her room.

I cupped my right ear and pressed it against the door.

"Mmmm, no, stop. Remember, rain check?"

"What's wrong?" I heard Aaron say.

"Stop," she pleaded.

"What's wrong?" he asked again.

"Stop," I called out, and rattled the doorknob. All

conversation ceased. I heard nothing except the drip-drop of a leaky faucet. The dripping stole away the noises of what could have been, yet it sounded empty, making the moment appear innocent.

I forced myself to step away from the door and wrung my hands, hoping that whatever I couldn't see wouldn't betray me. Then I wondered if my past conversations with Lauren, my insistence on her remaining a virgin, had created a bigger problem. I hated second-guessing my decisions when it came to her, but after all I'd been through as a teen mother, I knew I had to make the tough choices and stick to them.

I went to my bedroom dragging my feet and leaving tiny imprints on the carpet. The sounds of doors opening and closing held my rapt attention. I sat on the edge of my bed, eyes shut and toes curled so tight they clustered upward as if they were bruised and swollen.

After a while I heard a tap on my door.

"Who is it?"

"Aaron, ma'am."

I snorted and opened the door to the degree that my eyes could only see his. He pushed his head through the crack as much as the tiny space would allow. His lips and mustache were inches away from my own lips.

I sniffed, not the I'm-about-to-cry kind of sniffing, but the kind that your body allows when you want to inhale the scent of a man who doesn't belong to you but that tiny detail still hasn't registered.

For a second something inside asked me, *Why do you insist on checking out Aaron? Does the name Steve Monroe mean anything to you?*

Why should his name mean anything? I thought, and winced at the memory of Steve's sorry-ass tactics.

I squinted at Aaron, who had a blank yet sexy look on his face.

"What you guys doing?" I asked in a low, deliberate voice.

"Nothing," he said, looking straight in my eyes, "Ab-so-lute-ly nothing."

"Wh-where's Lauren?" I questioned in a hushed tone, and tried to peek through the door just in case itching ears were near.

"She's in her room." He shrugged. "Her door's closed," he said, still eyeballing me.

"Oh."

He kept staring and I didn't know how I was supposed to react. My legs twitched every few seconds. Even though I was nervous, I looked back at Aaron. I didn't want him to think he could intimidate me, but right then, our staring at each other felt bizarre yet soothing.

I can't do this. I can't do this. Tell his ass to go home. Tell him.

My heart sank like a million gallons of tears weighed it down. I swallowed real hard, hoping that all my illicit thoughts might drown within my body, disappearing, and canceling out whatever bad-girl things I was thinking at that time.

What exactly had Lauren and Aaron been doing behind closed doors? I pictured this guy sucking her lips and fondling her tiny breasts. And for just a second I wondered if he'd enjoy the experience better if I was my daughter and his hands were all over me.

Stop that, Tracey. Stop.

"Hey, uh, I need to get something, please?" Aaron said, and snapped me out of my mental bondage. His voice sounded more normal, more sincere.

"From here? You need something from my room?" I asked.

"Uh, yeah."

"What is it? I'll get it," I snapped.

"My paaaas," he mumbled.

"Speak up, what did you say?" His tongue got in the way of his words, and he was acting strange, a little too annoying for my tastes. I couldn't wait for him to get whatever he needed and then get on out.

"Pants," he said, his voice laden with edginess.

I whirled open the door, smirking in doubt, but sure enough the guy only had on a white undershirt and a pair of tight-fitting BVDs, but no pants.

How utterly stupid, I thought, looking from his eyes to his midsection to his eyes again. *He could at least have the brains enough to let Lauren sneak in here and get his pants.*

I widened my door and let him brush past me and he retrieved his slacks, which were crumpled on my bureau.

I kneaded the corners of my forehead with my fingers. It was one of those moments when a parent knows she should ask, but just doesn't want to hear the details right then. I just didn't want to know.

Moving my hands from my temples, I stood there looking at him yet not really seeing him, but he waved his arms at me rapidly as if to say, "Do you mind?"

Appalled, I spun around, heard him slipping his legs inside his trousers, zipper zipped, and he brushed past me like a whir of light once more. I didn't say good-bye, didn't want to. He didn't say anything either. I followed him to the door and locked it behind him. And in his departure I sniffed again, battling the unsettling feeling he gave me, then taking in a long, deep breath.

In Aaron's absence, and with the settling down after all the drama that just happened, I noticed how my body ached, how my muscles felt tender and sore, how my throat was parched, and how it felt like everything hurt, on the inside and out. I stepped back inside the doorway of my bedroom and it seemed all my movement came to a complete stop the second I detected the tantalizing scent of a man's cologne *talking to me.*

6
tracey

"Mom, how old was you when you started having sex?"

"Hmmm. I know where this is going, and the answer is no."

"But, Mom—"

" 'But, Mom,' my butt, Lauren. We've been over this far too many times for us to even be having this discussion, and I just don't wanna talk about it."

It was Saturday evening, and Lauren and I were in the car on our way home from shopping at the IKEA on the Katy Freeway. Recently my collection of books had been growing, growing, growing. I had some extra cash and decided to pick up two sets of bookshelves. But soon after writing the check, I thought about how I just wasn't in the mood to assemble them.

"But, Mom, this isn't fair. You started having sex with Daddy when you were fifteen."

"I wish I'd never told you that," I said, trying to fuss and drive at the same time.

"And I'll probably be on Social Security by the time I find out—"

"Believe me, it's overrated. These music videos and movies and *Dawson's Creek* stuff makes your little hormones think they're missing out. But you aren't missing a thing."

"Oh, I'll bet you weren't thinking that when you and Daddy conceived me." I could feel her staring at me from the corner of my eyes.

"Look, Lauren. Only reason I'm telling you this is because I've been there and done what you think you want to do. Now, I hope you and Aaron haven't gone there yet—"

"No, we have not, thanks to you."

"You oughta be thanking me. I'm trying to save your life, girl."

"I don't need my life to be saved."

"Lauren, at this point you don't know what you need and I'm not down for you crawling in some guy's bed when you're just a teenager."

"So it was good enough for you to know about sex firsthand at a young age, but not me?"

I didn't say anything. What could I say? I'd already told her a thousand times how it was for me. How my body was never the same after I'd had a child. Belly puffed out like a loaf of bread, no amount of sit-ups ever making any worthwhile dents. And all those nights my mother and I were forced to rush Lauren to the hospital because her four-year-old self would be running around and boom—she'd slam into the corner of a table and then yell, scream, and suffer scrapes and bloodied gashes on her forehead. Just little things here and there which advertise the fact that you're a youngster raising a youngster and trying to survive in a grown-up world. As far as I was concerned, I only wanted to tell my daughter about those types of experiences; she shouldn't have to live through them herself.

"Mom," she said, with hope lifting her voice. "What if we use a condom? I don't even think you and Daddy used one."

"Now hold up. You can whine and state your case all you want. The bottom line is, safe sex isn't even an option for you. No sex is more like it."

"Well, what if I sneak and do it?"

I laughed. "Ain't no such thing as sneaking. Parents always find out stuff sooner or later."

She groaned and turned away from me. "I guess my stuff will be found out later, huh, Mom?"

"I guess so," I replied in such a way that she knew the conversation was over.

We rode along in silence for a few miles, but then turned into the parking lot of one of those Burger King combo gas stations and drove up next to the take-out speaker.

"What you want, Lauren?"

"Onion rings. Fish sandwich. And a large cola."

"Hmmm, okay. I think I'll just get a strawberry shake."

Five minutes later we arrived in front of our apartment unit. I grabbed my shake and Lauren reached for her soda.

I paused.

"What about the rest of your food? You gonna bring that in the house? You know I don't like you to leave half-eaten food in the car."

"Okay, okay, okay," she mumbled and reached for her paper bag.

* * *

At midmorning the next day, Lauren's dad picked her up fifteen minutes late to take her to worship service at Solomon's Temple. Lauren had on a cute little beige pantsuit and was tossing keys, a pen, comb, and some cosmetics into her church purse.

"Have a good time. Say a prayer for me," I called to Lauren, who hustled through the front door.

It was nearly twelve o'clock. Overcast outside as well as inside my mind. I had nothing on my agenda. No plans for lunch, no prospects to be sitting on some guy's lap. Feeling abandoned and restless, I glanced at the unopened boxes of IKEA bookshelf materials and felt a familiar lump of loneliness in my heart. No matter what bad things go down between a man and a woman, she's always good for remembering the times. And at that point my mind was clogged with memories. And minutes later those recollections had me snatching my handbag and locking the front door.

During the well-traveled route, my ears burned and my heart screamed. *Yes,* I remembered what happened the other night. *Yes,* I knew I'd smacked him across his lying face, but if he was self-introspective, maybe he'd realize he deserved it. Better yet, maybe he missed me.

Besides, I had those bookshelves and I needed a handyman.

Twenty minutes later I came to a stop in front of the town house. The tan brick building with yellow and white shutters looked peaceful and clashed with the emotions that raged inside me. With my heart thumping like a time bomb, I plodded toward Steve's door and tapped. Several minutes passed before a guy I didn't recognize opened the door and peeped through a slight crack. He yawned, then cleared his throat.

"Yes?" he mumbled, like talking was a struggle.

"Steve here?"

He frowned and thumped his fingertips across the back of the door, then let me in.

I tiptoed into the living room, observing every piece of furniture: the sectional that I helped Steve pick out a few months ago; the thirty-two-inch console we used to camp in front of like TV was going out of style. Then I spotted the fish tank and shuddered at the memories of what Steve and I used to do next to his big aquarium. Running my fingers against the chilled glass, I wondered if the fish remembered me.

"Steve's upstairs. I'll go get him."

The guy turned and paused. "I'm Joseph, by the way. Steve's second cousin."

"Oh yeah? So glad to meet you," I said, but actually I could care less.

I inhaled when I entered the kitchen. No female aromas here.

I allowed myself a small grin . . . especially when I noticed a gray box of Aerosoles.

Were these mine, I wondered. Running my hand across the box, I lifted the lid. Hmmm. Cute shoes. Replacing the lid, I blushed and raised the box.

Size eight? My feet can't squeeze into a doggoned size eight. I dropped the shoebox and sat my dejected butt on the couch. I felt like a stranger in his town house, a place I'd been to that used to feel like home. Parts of me wanted to run from there as fast as my pride would allow, but the stupid and insecure parts of me won out, and I remained cemented to my seat.

It took ten nail-biting minutes for Steve to bound down the stairs. He wore no glasses, was dressed in a wrinkled gray muscle tee with black running shorts, and his beloved ponytail was as wild-looking as an un-tended lawn.

"What you want, Tracey?" he asked, standing near the television.

Even though my mind told me to walk, I half-ran toward him. "Hey, baby—"

"I'm not your baby," he said. When I tried to reach for him, he stepped aside.

I felt dumb and dumber and wasn't sure how to handle him. Maybe I shouldn't have come to see him. Maybe I wasn't trying hard enough.

I softened my voice. "Steve, I—I know you may be pissed about what happened, but I've had some time to think. I want to make sure you meant what you said the other night."

"What you talking about? I said a lot of things."

"I'm not talking about the bad stuff, Steve. I'm referring to the good stuff."

"Why'd you think I meant that?"

"Because you put your arms around me as soon as Lani left . . . and you told me I'm the only woman for you." Men are *so* forgetful.

"And so?"

"And sooo . . . I was thinking I must've meant *something* to you for you to even do that."

"You're grasping, Tracey," he said with this satisfied smirk.

"Steve, this isn't . . . this isn't grasping," I said. Couldn't he tell this wasn't grasping?

"You know, with everything that went down, I can see me and you aren't going to work out . . . so too bad you wasted your gas driving over here because . . . it *is* over."

"But it doesn't have to be. I didn't mean—"

He groaned and looked unimpressed. "Look, I'm getting a little bit tired of repeating myself, but if necessary I can do it again."

"It's not nec—"

"For the last time, Tracey, you are through."

"Steve, don't *be* like this," I whisper-pleaded.

A ringing noise screeched through the air.

We both looked up.

"Tracey, start making your way outta here," he said in a don't-fuck-with-me voice.

"But all I want—"

"Hey, Steve. Phone," yelled Cousin Joe from the second floor.

"Be right there," Steve shouted, then turned to look at me.

"It's over, it's over," he said, shaking his head matter-of-factly.

When I failed to make my way out, he looked at his watch, then at me, and asked, "Anything else?"

I cleared my throat. "Since you claim we're through, I—I was wondering if I could get the clothes I left over here. And the photographs . . . and the two hundred dollars I loaned you."

"You know, I *hate* women like you," he hissed, and shook his fist. "I'm about to go upstairs, and by the time I come back down, you'd *better* be gone."

He headed upstairs without a backward glance.

I stood frozen to my spot, blinking. Every time my eyes snapped closed, I pictured myself in his arms.

Steve loving me. Caressing me. Him saying how I was the bomb while a tidal-wave orgasm ripped through my body and his.

I walked toward his front door but turned to look

up those stairs. Strained my ears to hear Steve's voice one more time. To hear him say, "Hold up, don't go." Or hear him admit he didn't mean what he said.

But after waiting so long, I heard nothing, except the tragic thumping of my own heart.

7
Tracey

It's been two full weeks since I last talked to Steve, seven weeks since I was held in his arms. I often think about what happened when we were at his town house. It was all so embarrassing, dramatic, and unnecessary. I wish I could receive closure. The things that went down remind me of the numerous other times that my exes cut me loose.

Poncho sent me a "Dear Jane" e-mail that had a virus attached to it. Poncho said he finally knew what he wanted in life, and it wasn't me. Slick Rick decided it was time to get a new unlisted phone number; he never bothered to tell me. One day I dialed Slick's old number and caught the hint. And good ole Badman called and said, "I don't want to be in a relationship with you," but he wouldn't explain why. He told me don't come by anymore, and if I did, he'd apply for a restraining order.

At first I cried from the pain of how my ex-boyfriends treated me, but then I grew depressed.

Wondered what was it about me that caused these guys to have such disrespect that our relationship couldn't end in a civilized way. Wondered if their past claims of loving me were lies because if they really cared, wouldn't they break up using a method that was a little more tender, a little less humiliating?

This is the way my father, Reynaldo Davenport, did my mother, Grace. Dad married her, gave her a baby, acted like he was in love with her and me, and years later announced that his job was moving him to another state and no, we weren't joining him. Then he deserted us without a backward glance. Although it was Mom who was married to him, it felt like my dad divorced me too.

These are the things I dwelled on when it came to the Steve Monroe situation. I hoped he'd handle things better, but Steve turned out to be an identical twin of all the other cowardly nonconfrontational men who were so inept at communicating their feelings. As far as I could tell, most women are so much braver than men. We're fighters, survivors, and far more honest with our emotions. And because some men can't verbalize their feelings, they're threatened by women who do. And what happens? If the man can't deal with it, women get punished and the gender gap widens. These realizations were something that drove me into an overall sad frustration.

On top of all that, I just cannot deny that Steve was the best lover I ever had. No one could do me like him. I missed that part of our relationship like a diabetic misses sugar. Sugar might not be good for you, can even be dangerous, but it may not stop you from wanting it.

So when you add up everything—the fact that Steve

wasn't trying to get back, the fact that I had no other prospects, and the fact that I loved sex—well, things were bound to happen.

It was a Saturday. I decided to skip out to Katy Mills. Katy Mills was the largest off-price retail mall in the Houston area. It had more than two hundred stores and restaurants and was the hot spot for shopping till you dropped. Last time I'd been there was in October, during the grand opening, and I'd been itching to go back.

I gassed up my car and arrived around five that evening. Since it was a few weeks before Christmas, traffic inside the mall was mega-congested. Folks shuffling their feet, elbowing their way through. I thought I'd just get lost in the crowd, venture into my favorite stores, grab a bite to eat, and head on home. But just when you think you've figured out your schedule, you realize there's no such thing as a schedule.

I had shopped for a half-hour when . . .

"Mrs. Davenport?"

I looked up at hearing Aaron's voice.

He was by himself.

Since the last time I'd saw him, I thought about how I behaved, relinquished my pride, and asked God to forgive me for even allowing my mind to go there. And since then, I'd made sincere attempts not to dwell on those encounters, but now that Aaron was back in my face, he brought back memories. And the fact that I could check him out again, up close, and minus the presence of Lauren, well, it floored me to realize I felt a little bit nervous yet excited at the same time.

I smiled and checked out his attire. He was dressed in a black leather jacket, which covered a pale yellow shirt. The blue jeans and a neat pair of loafers completed his ensemble. And I noticed an energy that surrounded him even though he wasn't moving.

"Hi, Aaron."

"You here alone?" he asked, his eyes darting about like men's eyes tend to do.

"I'm as alone as alone can be."

He smiled and looked at me with kindness.

"Why would someone who looks as fine as you be all by yourself on a Saturday night?"

I opened my mouth in shock, but laughed. "If you're trying to make me feel good, you've done your job. But you know, Aaron, there comes a day when everyone must spend some time alone. We don't always have to be up under somebody. That alone shouldn't validate a person."

He blinked his eyes like I'd given him too much information.

"Sorry. It was one of those weeks," I stated.

Without specifically agreeing to do so, we walked side by side. I heard the noises of crying babies, laughing children, and loud teens that swarmed around us, but it was like they weren't even there. Compared to Aaron, those people looked like a blur.

While making our way through the mall, I was surprised but pleased that Aaron kept a respectful distance. When I'd come a little too close to him due to the crowds, he'd slow down, or spread his hands and point the way so I could pass through. I looked at him in admiration. He noticed my intense stare and had the nerve to blush. I *love* it when men blush.

"So, how are things going with you and Lauren?" I asked with a tease of a smile.

"Th-they're going."

"That bad, huh?"

"They're okay," he hedged.

"I'll bet I have something to do with how things are going."

Instead of responding, he turned to gaze at the mechanical alligator in the man-made pond outside the Rainforest Café, near the front entrance of the restaurant, which boasts a jungle theme complete with towering trees, massive leaves, talking birds, resembling an indoor safari. We laughed at the dozens of children that pitched quarters, dimes, nickels, and pennies inside the roaring alligator's mouth.

"Hey, have you eaten here before?" I asked.

"Nope."

"Want to join me? I'm hungry."

He looked at his watch.

"Well, I guess it'll be okay," he said.

"Why are you hesitating?"

His facial expression froze, so I smiled and pulled him by the arm.

"Come on, son. You're practically my son, anyway. It won't hurt you to join me for dinner. Lauren will have a fit when I tell her I ran into you at the mall."

He exhaled and didn't move away when I grabbed his arm. After we were seated, we placed our order, sipped on lemon water, and nibbled on chicken breast strips dipped in honey mustard.

"You doing a little last-minute Christmas shopping?" I asked.

"Yep, I already bought Lauren's gift. Now I need to find something for my parents."

"Your parents? How are they?"

"Doing good. Except Dad's sugar's been getting to him. Other than that, they're well."

"I've never had the pleasure of meeting them. Maybe you could bring them over one day." I was trying so hard to be good. Trying so hard to maintain my feel-ings.

He hesitated, then said, "Sure."

"You have a problem with that, Aaron?"

"Oh no, no, no. It's cool. My folks are, well, they're getting up there in age."

"Do they like Lauren?"

"They don't care who I date, Mrs. Davenport."

"I really wish you'd stop calling me Mrs. Davenport. I'm not a Mrs. Never married."

"No?" Aaron asked. "Would it be prying if I asked why not?"

"Well, it's not like I didn't want to get married. Just never met the right guy."

"And Lauren's dad, apparently he wasn't right for you?"

"Oh, hell naw."

He grinned in a way that could rival Chris Webber's smile.

"I don't mean to make it sound so bad, but ulti-mately all we did was get together and conceive a baby. At least that's what it boils down to, in my assessment. Now, if you asked Derrick, he might have a different take altogether."

"Was it worth it?" he probed.

"What? Having the baby?"

"Not just that, but having a relationship with Lau-ren's dad?"

"I've never really thought about it. At the time we met, I'm sure I thought it was worth it. And I definitely can't imagine Lauren not being in my life. So, in ret-rospect, I guess I can say it was worth it—just to have Lauren, it was."

"And her father? How does he fit into the picture these days?"

"You should know the answer to that. You see how he keeps in touch with Lauren. You and Derrick have been around each other much more than you have been around me."

"Yeah, I've hung out with Mr. Hayes a little bit. He seems protective of Lauren, nice, but distant sometimes."

"That's Derrick."

"I hope you aren't offended when I ask this, but I take it Mr. Hayes used to be your type, but isn't . . . anymore?" he said.

I hesitated, but admitted, "You take it correctly."

At my revelation, Aaron's eyes penetrated mine to the point that I felt outright uncomfortable. It seemed he was loosening up a bit and roles were being shifted. I didn't know if I liked that or not. Wondered what it meant. Having no answers, I downed the remaining half-glass of lemon water, then signaled the waitress for two more glasses. Mouth felt that dry.

"So, what kind of man is your type?"

"Is there a reason for these questions, Aaron? Feels like I'm being interviewed."

He snickered like he enjoyed the fact he could do things that made me put up my defenses.

"Say, Tracey. Dang, calling you that sounds so strange."

"Get used to it."

"Hmmm, okay. Like I was saying—what was I saying?"

"Don't know. You tell me."

"I don't remember what I was going to say, but I will say this. I—I think you're a highly attractive woman, you seem like a good person to talk to, and I think any guy who has you in his life should consider himself fortunate."

I thought about Steve and said, "I don't know about all that," and shifted in my seat.

I swiped the menu from the center of the table and scanned it with such intensity that even if the ghost of Marvin Gaye floated in, I wouldn't look up. I pulled the menu close to my eyes like I was nearsighted. But even while I was reading, I was wondering if Aaron was wondering about me. It seemed he'd go from being timid to aggressive, and his mood shifts intrigued me. Messed with me.

I set down the menu.

"Aaron, why would you say something like that about me? Why?"

"Something like what? That you're attractive?"

"Yes, that."

"Uh, I don't get it. What? You want me to lie to you? Tell you something that's not true?"

"Oh, so you're saying you don't lie?"

"I'll say I don't make a habit of lying to a woman. Not if I can help it."

"That's a lie right there."

We locked eyes. Mine misted. I don't know if his eyes misted or not, but I know for a fact they stayed glued to my face. Felt strange to be scrutinized, yet I liked to be looked at by someone who was good to look at. I mean, most days I thought I looked as fine as Vivica A. Fox, but other days I felt I looked just okay, and I was always suspicious if a man told me I was *extremely* attractive. I wanted to believe him, but it was tough to accept a compliment at face value, no matter how great the words made me feel.

When Aaron finally stopped staring, I noticed how his hair smelled so fresh and looked so moisturized. His fingernails were clean, and professionally mani-cured. And since mustaches are my weakness, I stared at the hairs above his top lip. Stared until I found my mind going there once more. My soul warned "no," but my bold mind was uncooperative. Imagining. Wondering what would've happened if he hadn't left my apartment that night. Could something have gone on between Aaron and me?

Nah, I thought. *I doubt it.*

Fantasizing is wonderful, and at this point that's all it was, I reasoned, pure fantasy.

We started eating our meal, and the conversation came to a temporary halt. He didn't seem to mind the silence. Buried his face in his plate and put the "pig" in pigging out, chomping on food and smacking his lips. Since I had nothing better to do, I looked around the restaurant while I ate. A few women, black and white, cast rude stares toward our table.

"Hmm, Aaron. Check out the looks that we're getting."

"Oh yeah?" He raised his head from his plate to observe his observers.

"Wonder what they're thinking?" I said, starting to feel self-conscious.

"I don't give a damn what they think."

"And why is that?"

"For all they know, you could be my sister, my cousin . . . or my girl."

I bit my bottom lip. Damned eyes misted once more.

"But then again, Tracey, you got somebody already, right?"

"Funny you should ask. I—I recently got out of a relationship with my ex, Steve."

"Hmmm, sorry to hear that."

"Why would you be sorry?" This I had to hear.

But he set down his fork and asked, "What happened that y'all broke up?"

"You're something else, Aaron."

"Why you say that?" he asked, taking a sip of his drink.

"You're kind of blunt for somebody so young."

"And so?"

"Well, usually men get blunt as they get older. Time is shorter, and they've got no time to waste by mincing words."

"Well, I'm young, but I've lived long enough to speak what I know. And to me, that's key, that's the principal thing. Nothing wrong with that, is there?"

I smiled. "Okay, put it this way. I'm not sure it's politically correct to even go here with you, but because I don't really know, then I figure I won't be intentionally doing anything wrong . . ."

He said nothing. Only tilted his head and stared intently at me.

"A few weeks ago, Steve Monroe and I broke up over something so foul."

"What?"

"Take a guess."

"Another man?" he asked in all seriousness.

I nodded and burst out laughing at the same time.

"Stop lying," he frowned.

"No, seriously, it was a woman."

"Cheated on you?" he said like he couldn't even imagine.

"Well, I don't know that for certain. See, he had this ex-girlfriend named . . . well, that's not important, but anyway, this woman was always lurking in the background. Steve gave me plenty of attention, *most* of the time, but I figured she was somewhere in his proverbial closet. I thought she'd just go away. If he was with me, why would he want her, you know what I mean? But this broad never went away. And I think she pushed herself up on Steve so tight that he . . . well, we're not together anymore."

"So, you think if it weren't for this other woman, you and Steve would still be together?" he said.

"Absolutely. Things were fine till she popped her neck through the door."

"Are you sure?" he asked.

"Huh?"

He leaned forward.

"Tracey, are you positive that this lady—"

"She's not a lady," I said, and shook my head like nothing could be more doubtful.

"—was the only reason you broke up? Could there have been other warning signs that you just didn't notice?"

I set down my fork. "What? Look, I don't know what you're implying, but things between Steve and me were wonderful, okay? He gave me all kinds of shoes when he could. He loved my cooking and that's saying a lot. He'd take me on drives, spontaneous ones sometimes, and we'd talk and just be together. And the sex—you haven't had sex like that."

Finally, Aaron flinched. He sat back. Thought.

I thought, too. Maybe I'd said too much. How did I know I could trust Aaron with this kind of information?

"I'm glad to hear that you considered your intimacy with Steve to be—"

"Freaking hellified."

He smiled, but I didn't.

"And that's what makes me pissed, excuse me, Aaron, for going there, but hey, we've been going all afternoon, so why quit now? Steve was thick and solid in the intimacy department. And now since that whorish ghetto-fabulous wannabe snatched him—"

"Hey, hey, calm down."

The ladies in the restaurant had stopped eating and were staring at us. I hadn't realized how loud I'd gotten and how unnerved I felt. My hands were trembling and my mind felt clogged, like all my thoughts were crashing together and letting me know just how deeply this whole incident had affected me.

I leaned toward Aaron.

"You know, I'm glad you asked me these questions, because now I realize those things that I hadn't come to terms with."

"Uh-huh. I'm listening."

"Now that I think about it, Steve *wasn't* always there for me. He was only there when it was convenient for him. Hurts to admit it, but I put my life on hold just to be available for the moment that *he* could be available. He never went out of his way to meet my schedule. What schedule? *He* was my schedule, dammit. And I did everything I could, sacrificed time with Lauren, friends, job, personal interests, to be with his ungrateful ass."

Aaron covered my shaking hands with his steady and warm ones. My torso and legs shook as if I were standing outside naked in the kind of weather that makes you crave warmth, or that makes you wish you had a covering.

Exposed.

That's what Tracey Davenport was. Not Steve Monroe, but me, because I could finally stop lying to myself about how great our relationship supposedly was. Instead of stretching the truth, I could stare truth in its face, an unflinching, uncompromising reality that forced my heart to see what it never before wanted to acknowledge. That what Steve and I had was just barely okay, and when you wanted more, okay just wasn't good enough.

"Hey," Aaron said, staring into my face and shattering my thoughts. "It's okay, okay?"

I reeled back from his words and did not speak for a few minutes. But when I did, I got up and sat in the empty chair next to Aaron.

"What up?"

"If you don't remember anything else, Aaron, remember this—women have a strong need to be cherished. If you don't cherish her, be prepared to lose her."

He had a blank yet serious look on his face. I couldn't quite interpret it, so I left it alone.

I hated to disclose so much of my feelings to him like that. On the one hand the revelations seemed too much, too fast, and I wasn't sure he'd be mature enough to do anything worthwhile with them. But I realized I had so much inside of me and was at the place where I craved that male point of view. I knew it was risky to lower my guard and expose my hurts, but right then the hurt seemed so mountainous, what difference did it make? What good would it do to suppress the pain of Steve not valuing me the way I felt he should have?

Several moments later, Aaron paid the tab over my protests, and led us back into the shopping crowds. This time when we walked side by side, he bumped into me without apology. Shoulders rubbed shoulders. His presence invaded my comfort zone, making me feel comforted.

"Books-A-Million? Sure, I'll go in here with you," I said to Aaron, and trailed him through the store's front entrance. "Hey, you might even find a gift for your folks. It's one of my favorite stores in the mall," I added.

"I thought so." He winked.

Displays of the hottest books filled every conceivable space: T. D. Jakes, John Grisham, Sue Grafton, and more were vying for customer attention.

We walked around the store in a slow trot. Incredibly relaxed. No rushing. No other place to be, except with each other.

"Tracey, what about some Iyanla Vanzant?"

"No. Too deep. Your folks might appreciate something lighter."

"Okay, I'll keep looking."

When he left my side, and I found myself alone in the fiction section, I felt my heart tug. Felt ashamed for becoming attached so fast. Wasn't good to get attached too fast.

After unsuccessfully trying to get myself interested in some discounted calendars, I swung hesitant fists at my conscience and sought Aaron.

"Hey, now, coffee-table books are always a good choice," I called to him. Thick hardcovers on every topic you could imagine were stacked on a dozen bargain book tables. We pored over just about everything, from exotic cookbooks to celebrity biographies.

"My dad wouldn't want to read about Paul Reiser."

"How do you know?" I asked.

"Because Paul Reiser is not Aretha Franklin." He smiled and held up the Queen of Soul's autobiography.

"Okay, now, what about this book on the history of African-Americans? It has some fabulous photos. And look here, your mom might like this one on decorating."

"Okay," he said and grabbed the books.

I was shocked, embarrassed. Acted like I was picking out gifts for my own folks, but Aaron didn't say a word. We waited in line until he got rung up; he signed the credit card slip, and grabbed his merchandise.

"Now what?" he asked, looking at his watch.

"You got to be somewhere?"

"Nope. You?"

"No," was my gentle reply.

"Then let's go around the corner and check out a movie. Come on, let's go," he said.

"Aaron, I don't know about that, it's—"

"It's time out for excuses, Tracey. I want to cheer you up. Get you away from it all, from sitting around the house hoping that Steve Monroe might call. Steve ain't gonna act right. Bump Steve."

"But Lauren—"

"Lauren ain't thinking about you or me. She's at the sleep-over having fun and hanging out with Regis and her crew. Ain't nothing wrong with us going to the movies. I mean, if there is, let me know and we can part right now. I'll go back to my lonely apartment and hang out with my roomie Brad, if he's even there. And you'll just go home and look at sad-ass tearjerkers on cable."

I broke into a grin and gave a swift and unbelieving shake of my head. And even though I was sure he saw me shaking my head, I wondered if he could tell that my soul was also shaking from deep within.

Ten minutes later I was so nervous I didn't notice what movie he picked. Even though I wasn't hungry, he took the initiative to order hot buttered popcorn, a large Coca-Cola, and plenty of Good & Plenty. Aaron led us down the aisle and let me sit in the chair near the wall in a dark movie theater. The film had started fifteen minutes before, but Aaron kept glancing at me. Made me blush. I liked that attention, yet I felt weird being with him. I wished I could totally relax, but I really didn't know how to achieve that.

If only this were Steve sitting next to me, and making me feel the way he was supposed to, the way he used to, then maybe I wouldn't have felt so edgy, and maybe I could let go of fear.

Aaron didn't seem to be having as tough a time as I was. While he looked at the movie and laughed or commented to the screen, I just sat there going through the motions. I was in the movies, yet I wasn't. At that point, where we were didn't seem to matter.

About halfway through the flick, at the part where a couple began making love, my hands started perspiring. I cast my eyes away from the screen to the chair in front of me. Aaron glanced at me again. I felt his arm go around the back of my chair.

"You doing okay?"

"I—I'm fine."

"Yes, you are," he said with gentle respect.

"Aaron," I objected, but warmed inside at his wonderful attention.

"I'm not flattering you. Just telling you the truth," he said, like he could care less about my little protests.

I felt foolish. Wouldn't hurt to be gracious.

"Well, thanks. I need that."

"Hey, did you guys come to the movie to watch it or to hold a conversation?" remarked a loudmouth moron sitting behind us.

Aaron draped his arm across my shoulder and smiled me into a smile. He then surprised me by giving me an exaggerated hug. I'm sure he did it to annoy the people behind us, but I was also wondering if he put his arm around me because he simply wanted to.

Once the movie ended, he walked me to my car. I drove him to another area of the parking lot so he could get his. I wasn't surprised when his car followed mine to my apartment. But I was surprised when I allowed him to come in.

After putting away my packages, the first thing I did was look at caller ID. Lauren hadn't phoned. That was good, yet bad. Good if it meant she was so busy having fun that she wouldn't call. Bad if she decided to take that moment to phone home. What if she asked what I was doing?

The thought of having to make a confession made me want to die.

Aaron, not yet having said one word, made himself at home. He went to the fridge and poured a three-quarter glass of fruit punch. Then he took a seat and wasted no time gulping his drink. His silence unnerved me. It was as if he looked forward to being alone with me in the apartment. I felt warm and warmer. I decided to go change clothes when I felt the wetness of my shirt clinging to my breasts.

I held up a finger. "Be right back." Aaron nodded and rested his arm against the back of the couch. He looked relaxed and content.

At first I started to throw on my hokey PJs, the ones that cover all your skin, the kind that good ole grandma would wear. But I opened my drawer and retrieved a Victoria's Secret black satin lace-up gown: High slits with lattice tie-ups on the side, plunging V-neck to showcase the prominent cleavage.

Hey, Aaron had already seen some of what I had to offer. I believed he appreciated what he saw, and the more I thought of Steve's trifling ways, the less I cared about what I was doing.

So caution was thrown to the wind, completely forgotten.

"Hey now," he said when I entered the room. I took slow steps; paraded in front of him, twirled around with my hands outspread. Felt myself perspiring. It would have been a great time to blast the air conditioner, but I didn't think it would make a dent.

He stood up, appraised me up and down, and grabbed both my hands.

"See, I wasn't lying, Ms. Davenport," he said with softness. "You *do* look good. Hell, you look damned good."

I raised my eyebrows.

"Ms. Davenport?" I asked, pulling my hands from his grasp and placing them on my hips.

Aaron blushed as embarrassment scrambled across his face. He stepped back and returned to the couch.

I looked at the ticking clock mounted on the living room wall.

It was eleven-forty.

"Hey, got any good music?" he asked.

"I'm sure I have something you might want to listen to."

He removed his jacket, exposing his smooth and toned arms. Winked at me and smiled.

I swallowed deeply. Felt a stirring between my legs that couldn't be denied.

"Let's see what you got over here," he murmured, approaching the stereo.

"Hey, Aaron. Lauren tells me you have a lot of CDs. My little collection pales compared to yours."

"Don't feel bad. I'm sure you have something we can both enjoy."

We.

I warmed again. Wiped my eyes. Felt weaker. Especially when he slipped on the Isley Brothers' *The Heat Is On* CD. Loved that music when I was younger; still loved it now that I was older. The wailing of "For the Love of You" inducted us into a different realm. He grabbed me and I didn't stop him. Let him grab my waist, pulling my cleavage against his scorching chest. Felt so bad, so confused. He may have been young, but I swear his body didn't know it. I laid my head against his neck, enjoyed the strength of his body, and rocked with him.

Outwardly I was acting like everything was legit, but deep inside a battle ensued. For a second I thought I was lapsing into mental instability. I'd go from realizing how great it felt to be in this handsome guy's arms, and seconds later I'd think of Steve and how he'd brought this on himself. And much less often I'd think of the young lady I'd given birth to, believing that my being with Aaron wasn't newsworthy. Since Lauren claimed that she and Aaron hadn't consummated their relationship, she couldn't miss what she'd never had, right?

Or could she?

Because we were in the living room, every once in a while I'd hear noises outside the door that sounded like several footsteps coming up the landing. I knew Lauren was at the slumber party and wasn't about to come home, but that little fact didn't make me feel secure.

Aaron pulled me against his chest, pressing his cheek against mine. God, his skin was *sooo* soft, so warm, it felt like our bodies were melting together, two entities becoming one.

I heard the patter of footsteps outside, and stiffened like inertia was setting in.

"Are we sure that it's okay to be doing this, Aaron?" I asked, my voice quivering.

"Ms. Davenport," he murmured.

"Please call me Tracey," I said, still swaying.

"Tracey," he said, and pressed his face against my hair, while his hands gripped my ass. "A dance is just a dance."

"You sure about that?" I uttered, saying words that didn't have to be said.

"Why are you afraid?" he asked, and moved his hand to my shoulder, caressing it with one strong fingertip.

"Aren't you?"

"Nope," he said. He sounded like he meant it.

"You *do* lie," I replied. How *could* he mean it?

"No, I'm not lying. I can honestly say I'm not afraid because I know we're just cool like this. I date your daughter and I'm keeping you company while she's out tonight."

I froze.

"So if she were here, none of this would be happening would it?"

"I doubt it," he said, his body still moved by the classic Isley wail.

"Then it must be wrong. If it's something we can't do in front of her face, it's wrong," I said, more for my sake than his.

I felt his embrace weaken, preparing to give my body back to me.

"Aaron, did I strike a nerve?"

"Nothing's struck, at least not with me. I'm not worried about me. I have self-control."

"Oh, really now?"

Seconds later he stepped completely away from me, his touch now in the past.

"Yep, I do, Tracey. I'm personable, but I'm not crazy. You're an attractive woman, but that's as far as it will go. Maybe I should leave."

"Wait a minute, wait. Let me think."

I cleared my throat and looked at my clothing. Who was I kidding? Giving the poor guy mixed signals. Loving the feeling of him holding me in his arms, yet wondering what would happen if Lauren saw us. I felt awful, like a tease that might not follow up.

"Yep, you're right. I think you should leave," I said.

He had already grabbed his keys. That made me mad.

Don't grab your keys until I say it's all right to grab them.

"You know your way out."

"Tracey, it's a small apartment. Of course I know my way out."

"Well, goodie for you."

He stared at me for a minute, then turned to walk out the door, closing it without a sound behind him.

8
Aaron

When I got home and turned on the lamps, my roommate Brad had a rhythmic snore going. He sounded like an eight-hundred-year-old man. Under ordinary circumstances he's a normal-looking guy: complexion the color of maple syrup, thick waist, round legs, and a robust build. On most days, Brad's short Afro had an uneven look and he'd wear a metal pick lodged in the back. Oh, one more thing: one of his eyes was bigger than the other, which made some folks think he's crazy, but that was debatable.

Tonight it looked as if he'd crashed and burned on the living room couch, stretched out lying on his belly with his lips spread apart, a small pool of saliva resting on the corner of his mouth. VH1 was playing music videos for the ultimate insomniac. I grabbed the remote, aimed it at the TV, and increased the volume to maximum.

"What, who, what—?" Brad mumbled, shifted his body to the side, and kinda thumped, then rolled to the floor.

"Man," he said, opening and closing his eyes like a newborn baby adjusting to its first day of life, "what in the hell is your problem? Turn that thang down."

I muted the volume. "Hey, Brad, sorry 'bout dat. I—I need to talk," I said, standing over him.

"You need to do what?" he asked yawning. "Sound like my sister."

"I'm not your sister, but I do need to talk."

"Damn, man, what time is it?" he asked, his stomach still pressed to the floor.

"Don't matter, sit up, Brad, man." I urged him up with both of my hands, "Get up, this is serious."

"Ah, hell. I didn't know paying half the rent here would entail all this." He mumbled a few other things that weren't decipherable, but I tuned him out and stretched out on the couch. Brad squatted on the floor Indian-style and leaned his shoulder sideways against the couch.

"Okay, okay, Aaron. Whassup?"

"It's this . . . this *woman*."

"Uh-huh," he replied, digging underneath his finger-nails. "So I take it you're not referring to Lauren?"

"I said she was a woman."

"Well, who is she, Aaron?" he asked, looking bored.

"She's, she's, uh, I can't say," I told him firmly.

"Damn."

"It's like that right now. Thing is, I haven't admitted it to her yet, but I'm digging her big-time. She's more mature but sexy as hell, and man, we have this chemistry."

"So what's the problem?" Brad asked, yawning once more and rubbing his eyes.

I winced. "I—I want to get with her, but it might be the wrong move."

" 'Cause of Lauren?" he said, pointing his finger in an I-think-I-get-it way.

"You got it."

"If you want her that bad, sneak some but don't tell Lauren," he replied, and placed one foot on the carpet like he was about to get up.

"Sit back down, Brad. It's not that simple."

He groaned, but repositioned himself by leaning against the couch. "Why not?"

I looked at the floor. "Sh-she lives near Lauren. Too risky." I looked at Brad. "Not out to hurt my girl."

"Then don't do it. Or bring the woman over here," was Brad's brilliant response.

"Hell, naw," I said, but still picturing myself bringing Tracey over. Getting her alone. Helping her to release both our frustrations.

"Damn, man. Who is this mystery babe?"

"Take a guess."

"Who is she, Aaron? Tell me."

Should I or shouldn't I tell?

"She's . . . uh, better not."

"Tell me, or I'll tell Lauren you're cheating on her," he said like he was serious and wouldn't hesitate to do just that.

"But that's the thing, I'm *not* cheating on her."

"But you're thinking about it, right?" Brad said, and stared so intently I thought he was trying to see through me, trying to break me down.

I scratched the side of my face and patted down my hair. What was I doing? Sometimes things happened in such a way that it seemed I wasn't taking time to evaluate what I was doing. Guess I never did feel comfortable thinking about stuff too much, seemed like that always made things too hard.

"Yep, you're thinking about it," Brad said with a sat-isfied grin, like he was a freaking relationship guru who could figure everything out in ten minutes.

"Why you say that?" I said in such a serious tone that my earnestness canceled out his grin. He pondered his words for a moment and shrugged. "Getting with somebody always starts with a thought. Apparently you've been thinking about this. Only a matter of time before you're acting it out."

Hmmm, is that right, I thought. All you gotta do is think about something, then you'll be doing it? Hey, let me think about being a millionaire and watch the money roll in.

Yeah, right.

I looked pointedly at Brad. "Well, she's been some-what on my mind lately, but today was when I really started thinking about her."

"Why today?"

"Saw her at the mall and . . . we hung out," I said, holding on to the most treasured parts so I could savor something for myself.

"Oh yeah? Well, how she feel about you?" he asked, wobbling his legs up and down like he was starting to develop a cramp.

"I think I've hooked her and she tries to fight it, pretending like I don't affect her. But I know she feels the vibe," I said, surprised to hear the admission my-self.

"Maybe y'all pulling each other, man."

"I don't know what it is, but whatever it is, it's pow-erful. Plus some other things are going on that I don't want to get in to, but I gotta—I need to do some-thing," I told him, rubbing the soreness that was throbbing and humming on my neck. I couldn't be-lieve how exhausted I felt, mentally and physically, and it seemed *something* was definitely affecting me in multiple ways.

"What? You thinking about dumping Lauren and hooking up with old girl?"

"I can't hook up with Tracey," I tried to mumble.

"Oh, *that's* her name? How old is Tracey? Where'd you meet her?" His black eyes sparkled and he actually smiled at me in a more genuine, less BS kind of way.

"Damn. Hey," I said standing up. "I think this is a good time for you to take your exhausted self back to sleep. Maybe you'll forget we had this conversation."

"I will go back to sleep, but I doubt I'll forget. Good luck, my brother," Brad said, this time laughing a bit, but then he clumsily lifted himself to his feet just to spread back out on the couch with a dull thud.

I escapted to the privacy of my bedroom, firmly locking the door behind me. Dozens of unopened CDs lined the bottom of one wall. The other wall lodged my chest of drawers, a small oak desk and chair, and a portable stand with a combo TV/VCR. I slid out of my leather jacket, shirt, jeans, socks, shoes, and boxers, and crawled on top of my queen-sized bed.

Ever since I'd been with Lauren, I'd forced myself to hold back, trying to wait on her and thinking she'd be worth the wait. But sometimes when a man misses the touch of a woman, waiting takes a backseat. I hadn't had any loving in so long, I was scared to even try and remember. I wasn't used to that. Being around Tracey, drinking in her feminine aroma, and brushing against her curves reminded me just how long it had been. I didn't know if that was a good thing or a bad thing.

I sighed, slipped underneath the bedcovers. I reached

over to pull out an ancient pornographic magazine from between my mattress and box spring. Instead of browsing the mag from the beginning, my fingers fumbled right to the centerfold. Mmmm, yeah. An interracial cutie from Baltimore. I smiled at her. She smiled back at me with her gorgeous brown eyes. I traced my trembling finger across her thick lips, pouty and sensuous. Zeroed in on her legs, which were covered with lavender lace, and that got my mind imagining all types of things. And I studied her breasts, which were suck-happy huge, as big as watermelons. I took one final look at my new friend and clutched myself, stroking to rock hardness. I shut my eyes and pictured myself banging Lauren's innocent vagina like I was a drill sergeant trying to drive home my point. Something I'd been aching to do for months.

By the time I entered my pleasure zone, shuddering like a satisfied fool, Lauren wasn't on my mind anymore.

A couple hours later I woke up slimy, groggy, and crusty-eyed. It was two-thirty in the A.M. I sat in silence for a while, and once the drowsiness cleared from my head, I dialed Lauren's phone number.

"Hel-lo," a gentle voice breathed.

"Did I wake you?" I asked.

"Nooo, I was looking at Oprah and folding laundry," she said sarcastically. "Who is this?"

"Tracey, it's Aaron," I replied in a soft voice. Hoped she wouldn't be mad.

"Oh," she said, sounding surprised yet nonchalant.

"Uh, did Lauren ever call?"

"No, Aaron." She coughed and cleared her throat. "You worried about her?"

"No."

"Then why would you call here at two in the morning, wanting to know if she's called?"

"Well, I also called to see if you're okay, Tracey."

There.

I said it.

She knew it, I knew it, now what was she gonna do about it?

"I'm not okay," she told me.

"I'm sor—"

"I'm *asleep*. Or at least I was."

"Sorry 'bout dat," I said, and looked at the mag once more before sliding it under a pillow.

"Don't be. I wasn't sleeping all that great anyway. After you left, I felt kind of regretful . . . and abandoned, you know what I mean?"

"I know," I said, voice thick.

"Mmm-hmmm," she moaned. I heard a little movement.

I could imagine her tossing and turning in her bed. Solo.

"Hey, you want some company, Tracey?" I blurted.

"Right now?"

"Yeah."

"And you're serious?" she said, like my request was just so fanciful.

"More than very."

"Aaron, you're *crazy*."

"Oh, you don't have to go there. Just asking," I said wondering if I was making a mistake, wondering if I ought to leave this appealing yet dangerous woman alone.

"What are you doing? What are *we* doing?" she asked with a less sluggish, more awake voice.

"Just wanted to see you. I enjoyed hanging out last

night," I said, grabbing two pillows, and pictured myself holding her tight in my arms again.

"Mmmm, same here, but as enjoyable as it was, we can't make a habit out of that, now can we?"

"No, we can't." I paused. "Well, we could, but we shouldn't, right?"

"Right." Her voice was husky.

I stroked myself again. Imagined my hand was Tracey's.

Didn't feel the same.

"Tracey, people always do what they shouldn't do. Why should we be any different?"

"Sounds like you're grasping, Aaron."

I didn't say anything for a while, and she didn't either. The fact that she hadn't ended the call gave me hope, and that was key.

"Do you want to be with me?" I blurted.

"Mmmm, I—I can't answer that. I mean, I appreciate your attentiveness toward me tonight. Your listening ear. That was very sweet. But, well, we probably shouldn't forget that you are dating my . . . my daughter," she said in a breathy whisper.

"Ehhh, yeah, I know," I half-laughed. "You're right. Makes no sense." I turned over in bed.

"Life hardly ever does, but . . ." she said, drawing her words out like she was singing.

"Yeah?" I told her, my body rigid.

"Well, maybe we can talk about this again sometime. Need time to think."

"What's there to think about? What are you getting at?" I asked, sitting up in bed.

"Well, the way things are going, I think it would be good to . . . to talk," she said like she was sorting through her thoughts. "When? Where? I'm not sure.

But I'll get back with you, Aaron. Better go now. Good night, morning . . . or whatever the hell it is."

She hung up.

I abruptly let go of my limpness.

Reluctantly let go of her voice.

9

Lauren

When I showed my face at the slumber party, no one else had arrived. Miss Indira, Regis's mom, conned me into toting party grub from the kitchen to the dining room. They set up a buffet that made me want to kiss Dennis Rodman: Buffalo wings with horseradish sauce, sliced pineapples and jumbo strawberries, tiny little egg rolls stuffed with shrimp, ice-cold beverages, and a slew of other goodies.

Miss Indira rushed around, giving orders like I was the hired help. I didn't think so. Last time I checked, I was a guest. But since this was my mom's close friend, I put a clamp on my tongue. Plus I didn't want to miss out on the eats. I couldn't wait for this party to start.

"Where's Regis?" I asked, after placing the last of the appetizers on the buffet.

"She's upstairs getting ready," her mom said while she hovered over a large tin pot of simmering meatballs. "You can go up there. People should be arriving any minute."

Getting ready, I thought as I ran up the stairs. *It's her party, she shoulda been, been ready.*

I knocked on Regis's door twice, then tried to open it, but it was locked.

"Let me in, Hooch," I yelled.

"Screw you, Heifer," she yelled back, and swung open the door. She winked at me and went and planted herself in front of her usual stomping ground, the mirror.

Regis Collier has distinctive features: she's ten shades darker than me and has these wide eyes, thick lips, and one of those descendant-of-the-Motherland noses. For the past couple of months she's been sporting these beautiful long braids that are always covered by a colorful headband—you know, the kind that hides the crown of your head and then lets the rest of your hair peek from underneath. With these headbands, Regis resembles a teenage Jamaican queen; she walks with her head up and stares people in the eye. And Regis is petite, but I don't think she knows it.

"Damn, I look good," she said, and applied a few coats of grape-toned lipstick to her pouty lips. She pressed her lips together and dabbed at the corners of her mouth with a tissue. I rolled my eyes and watched in her shadows.

"Don't I?" she asked, looking at me in the mirror.

"Regis, don't start. I'm not in the Regis Collier fan club, remember?"

"Girl, what you mean you not in the Regis Collier fan club? Shee-it, you the founding member."

"Oh, pu-lease." I sat on her bed and looked around. You'd have thought we were at a movie star's house. Her queen-sized four-poster bed was arranged with at least eight pillows of all sizes, and matching pillowcases, a bed skirt, shams, and a comforter. Even with all her hardwood furniture, she still had room for a thirty-two-inch TV, DVD, stereo system, and an oak bookshelf (even though she doesn't read books all that much).

"So, what you wearing, Lauren? I'll bet you brought your jammies over in a duffel bag, didn't you?" she chided.

"Yep."

"I *knew* it. Too scared to wear your PJs over here. Nobody trying to look at you, chile."

I didn't say anything. Instead I stared at a wall and pretended to be captivated by a D'Angelo poster.

"Well, check out mine," she said.

She went inside her walk-in closet and soon brought out a red and black satin baby-doll nightie with spaghetti straps.

"*That's* what you're wearing?" I asked.

"Yep," she said, holding the outfit against her. "Something wrong?"

"No, it probably will look cute."

"Damn straight it will. Too bad no guys will see me in it, though."

"You mean to tell me this will be a strictly female slumber party, Regis?"

"Hey, I tried to convince Moms to let me invite guys, but she wasn't having it," she explained, and tossed the nightie on her bed.

"Hmmm! Wonder why," I mumbled.

"Smartass," she said, and started getting undressed right in front of me. She wiggled her hips and scraped off a pair of jeans. Short as she was, Regis still sported an ample chest. After she pulled off her shirt, her tits were released from their one-hundred-percent-cotton prison.

"Lauren, you think I should leave on my panties?"

Within seconds, I escaped to the other side of the room.

"Yes, Regis, I think that would be a good idea."

"You do? Hmmm. That settles it," she yelped. "Off they go."

She slid off her underwear, standing naked. I turned my back.

"Oh, hell," she hollered and came and planted herself in front of me.

"Lauren, what is your problem? We girls. All this is here, is some meat," she said, rubbing both hands across her breasts and stomach. "Can't hurt you."

I raised my eyebrows.

"Oh, I get it. You think I like girls, don't you, Lauren? Humph! If you don't know, you better ask somebody!"

"No need," I replied, and shooed her away with my hands. "Please leave so I can get dressed. I heard the doorbell ring. Aren't you going downstairs now?"

She looked at me like I sniffed permanent markers.

"Chile, when I do join the party, I plan to be the last one there, you hear me?" Regis announced.

She stood there gaping at me. I stretched my hand toward the door until Regis threw on her nightie and left the room.

It was going to be a long night.

After everyone had arrived and when all seven of us girls were in place, Miss Indira hung around trying to make sure we were having a good time. Her presence actually prevented us from having any fun because no one dared cut loose. But she looked startled when we started talking about our favorite Old Testament scriptures and quietly left the game room. By then it was a little past eleven o'clock. Now the fun was really about to start.

Besides Regis and myself, the other slumber party attendees were Charisse Youngblood, Regis's seven-teen-year-old neighbor from across the street, Lia Brock-ington, Justine Knight, and Zoe Brand, classmates of Regis; and Hope Barnett, a cousin on Miss Indira's side.

Charisse's doe eyes were covered with pink glasses; she was wearing a pink-and-white short set. Lia, who's on the plump side, wore a sky-blue gown that allowed her toes to peek from underneath. Justine, tall and regal, had her hair tied in a gold silk head wrap that matched her gold cat suit. Zoe had on a polka-dot boxer-short set, and Hope, the shortest one of all, wore a violet sleep shirt with bunny rabbit house slip-pers. I wore some checkered pajama pants and a black halter.

Lia snapped her fingers and said, "Cool, Miss Indira fiiinally got the hint. Let's get this joint *started*."

Hope replied, "I know that's right."

"Ah," Regis scowled and pursed her glistening lips, "y'all shut the hell up. You coulda talked in front of my moms."

"That's a lie," Lia protested. "If your wild butt held back, where does that leave the rest of us?"

Regis shrugged, "Y'all just scrubs. Scared to talk. If you gonna be in my crib at my party, you better show your ass 'cause I'll sho' be showing mine."

Justine replied, "You don't mean that literally, do you, Rege?"

Regis smiled and shifted her eyebrows up and down in a silly manner. Then she lowered the straps of her baby-doll nightie, exposing her thick shoulder. Charisse's face turned red. "No, Regis didn't mean it. I *know* that girl doesn't mean that."

"Okay, okay," Regis said, waving her hands, "I won't get naked right now. But we playing strip poker later. Y'all game?"

Everybody murmured, "Sure, Regis. Yeah, yeah, yeah. Whatever."

Lia's thick lips spread into a wicked grin, "Let's do some girl talk. Okay, which of y'all is sexing?"

"Which of us ain't?" That was Regis.

Mostly everybody laughed. I started fanning myself and felt relieved when Regis dimmed the lights. She motioned for everybody to sit in a circle.

Regis cleared her throat and said, "Okay, I'll answer Lia. This easy." She looked around the circle at each of us, pointing as she talked, "I know my neighbor Charisse not screwing."

Charisse adjusted her glasses and lowered her head, but didn't say anything.

Regis continued, "I know my cousin Hope screwing, with her whorish ass. She only thirteen, y'all. Ain't that a shame?"

Regis acted like her announcement was a news flash, but there was nothing new about that flash. She'd already given Justy and me the scoop about her cousin. Regis said Hope had slept with so many boys, the only part of her body that hadn't been felt on was her tonsils.

Fiery yet modest, Hope's eyes enlarged and her mouth flew open. "Regis, don't be telling all my business." Hope reached across Zoe to smack Regis, but Regis raised her hand and grabbed her cousin real quick, then pretended like she was going to twist Hope's arm.

"Chile, please," Regis laughed, and rolled her eyes, letting Hope go. "I don't even have to say nothing. You can look at Hope and tell she screwing. She got that gap between her legs. You know the kind of gap that look like a girl been riding on a horse."

Lia yelled, "Hi-ho, Silver!"

Hope squirmed, yet managed to giggle. "Oh, y'all got jokes."

Responding with an easygoing chuckle, Regis said, "Put it this way, my guess is that seventy percent of the girls in this room is getting some loving, okay?"

"Are you one of the seventy, Regis?" That was Lia, as if she had to ask.

Looking at this group of girls, I couldn't believe how bold everybody was. I hoped they wouldn't ask me any in-depth questions. If they did, I guess I could lie, say "no comment," or crack some joke. Letting the crew know the four-one-one about my love life would be too humiliating.

"Is Regis one of the seventy?" Zoe huffed. "Don't ask stupid questions, Lia. We're talking about Regis Collier here."

Regis burst out laughing, and shook her braids with wildness. And when all eyes settled on her, she said, "If anybody sexing, you *know* I am."

I couldn't believe she was giving herself big ups.

Regis waved her arms and rocked her butt, even though she was sitting on the floor. "How y'all think my ass got so big?"

I doubted this seriously, but blurted, "Stairmaster?"

Regis said, "Negative. *Dickmaster,* girlfriend."

Both Zoe and Lia were like, "Ugh! Yuck!" I was thinking the same thing, but said nothing. Couldn't believe how gross Regis could be. Didn't know what she was trying to prove.

Regis continued, "No, for real, y'all. My man Sporty does my body *sooo* good." She shuddered like that eyeglass-wearing male dancer in the *Beat It* video.

Lia waved her decaled fingernails. "Give us the details."

"Okay, okay, okay." Regis smiled, lifting her eyes toward the ceiling. "Okay, I'll tell you about one time when we did it." She looked around the circle. "Oooh, it was *sooo* good. Happened last summer. My moms went on the church picnic, but I was sick that morning so I asked if I could stay home alone."

I asked, "And she believed you?"

Regis rolled her eyes. "Anyway, I started feeling better around noon. So I paged my baby, Sporty, and asked if he could swing by. First he said no, he had thangs to do. But when I said nobody was home but me, he said he could be there in a couple of hours. He was an hour late and I was pissed, but once we started kissing, I got so worked up you couldn't pay me to remember why I got pissed in the first place."

I couldn't see how Regis could admit all this. If and when I did start bumpin', would I tell a bunch of broads my play-by-plays? Weren't some things considered special enough to be private? If this was the way it was supposed to be, I had to get used to it.

Zoe leaned toward Regis. "What else happened?"

"Don't rush me," Regis snapped. "I'm getting there. Soooo, then we went to my bedroom and I closed all the drapes and blinds and stuff so it could seem dark. He took off his clothes, then I took off mine. We started kissing and stroking each other's body. I looked at his thang and he asked me what I thought. And I asked him, I said, 'This here pretty big, but, uh, could you super-size it?' "

Hope smirked. "Ooooooo-wee. I'm feeling you, cousin."

"Then what?" Zoe wanted to know.

Regis's voice lowered. "I started licking and sucking him till it grew even bigger and harder, just how I like it. And . . ."

Lia leaned in. "What? Tell us."

"I put his nozzle in my gas tank and *he started pumping*." She screamed with laughter.

"Regis Collier." Justine scowled. "You are one sick puppy."

Regis lifted her fingertips and panted, "Arf, arf."

Lia sprawled out on the carpet, screaming and flailing her legs in the air. Hope high-fived Regis, and the rest of us just looked at her in amazement while she bunched her shoulders up and down in an impromptu dance.

Charisse stared at Regis like she'd just met her, or never knew her true nature until just then. "Regis, does your mom know that you're having sex?"

Regis stopped cutting up and got serious. "Duh, Charisse, I don't know what my momma know. Hell, she might, but she ain't never said nothing to me. Maybe it ain't none of her business."

"As long as you're living—"

"Under this roof, blah, blah, blah. Hey, I heard it all before. You ain't telling me nothing new. But this is life, Charisse. Most teens banging, you know?"

"Doesn't mean you have to do it because everybody else is."

Regis sighed and rolled her eyes. I felt sorry for her. It wasn't often people stood up to her antics, especially when she was around several of her friends.

In a gentle voice, Justine asked, "Do you use protection, Regis?"

"I ain't dumb. I always make Sporty put that body bag on."

Zoe's eyes widened. "Well, what if he forgets? You not on birth control?"

"You on crack? My momma would stab me if she found some birth-control pills around here that ain't got her name on 'em."

"So," Charisse said in a soft but firm voice, "Ms. Collier doesn't know you're having sex, and she wouldn't approve, would she?"

"You know, I'm about to throw your corny ass out my house, Charisse. I *told* my momma not to invite you. Charisse Youngblood, the moral conscience of New Territory subdivision."

Charisse lowered her head and whispered, "Sorry."

Justine spoke up. "Okay, Regis, chill out. We're just talking. Charisse, I don't know you very well, but you seem like a concerned friend. The reality is that it's too late for Regis and Sporty to go back to hand-holding."

Regis's cheeks spread out into a grin. "Thank you, my sista."

"But on the other hand," Justine said, looking straight at Regis, "with HIV and stuff, doing the do these days is no game, you hear what I'm saying?"

Regis's smile disappeared. "Chile, quit tripping. I ain't no lesbo. Plus I'm only fifteen. I can't catch no disease like HIV."

"Look here, Miss Smartass. Age doesn't matter. The number of people who are infected is increasing, especially with heterosexual African-American females."

I wanted to smile but didn't. And inside, my heart was screaming, *Go Justy!*

Zoe joined in. "Regis, Justy's right. That killer disease doesn't care how young you are or the fact that your butt prefers dick."

Since the others had spoken, I felt safe adding, "I heard that." Hell, why should I be afraid to speak up? Right was right, wrong was wrong. Even though this crew seemed like a bunch of nut cases, I was relieved a couple of them seemed to have some sense, that they weren't totally out there. Maybe they could influence Regis. Maybe.

Even Lia pumped her fist. "I heard that, too. Preach, Justy and Zoe."

Hope just looked and listened for the longest, not saying a word. With her furrowed brow and serious look, she didn't seem like her usual smart-aleck self. I wanted to ask her if she used protection, but didn't think it would be a good idea.

Our teenaged voices became murmurs for a while, whispering as we thought about what Justine had said. Listening to her, in a way I was glad I hadn't start having sex yet. I mean, I wanted to, but it seemed too complicated. Besides, it was one thing to hear my mother give me her warnings of sexual doom and quite another to hear it coming from my peers. But even though I wanted to be cautious, not just because of diseases I didn't understand and babies I didn't want, even so, I yearned to be with Aaron, if only just to have him snuggled next to my side. Holding hands and helping me to feel protected at a moment when I didn't feel all that sure anymore. Yet with all my desire, I knew that when I finally did decide to have sex, it would be for the right reasons, and at the right time.

10
Tracey

It was approximately one o'clock on Sunday, my normal day to wash clothes. I had lugged a few baskets of dirty laundry to the complex's on-site washateria. By the time I'd started a few loads and eased my way back toward the apartment, Lauren had returned home from the sleep-over. She was standing on the second-floor landing in front of our apartment door and inserting her key when she spotted me.

"Hi, Mom," she called.

As soon as we made eye contact I stopped walking. I felt my face warm by several degrees. I allowed myself to walk up the stairs before I answered her.

"H-hey, didn't know you got back."

"Yeah, Miss Indira took home Justine, then she dropped me off. What's for dinner?" She entered the apartment and plunked her duffel bag on the floor next to the fireplace.

"Oh, I haven't cooked a thing. Mmmm. Maybe we could have dinner at Luby's," I suggested.

"Bet," she said, and disappeared into her bedroom.

Soon I heard the bumpity-bump of music blasting from her room. For once I didn't mind how loud it was.

I scoped our apartment and it seemed untidy. Grabbing a broom, I furiously started sweeping the kitchen. Whish, whish, whish, I was calling all dirt from the corners of my kitchen. Was so absorbed in what I was doing that I didn't notice Lauren standing in the doorway looking at me. She clutched Aaron's black leather jacket in her hand.

"Aaron came to see me yesterday?"

"What? He left his jacket, huh?" I asked, blushing and hoping I was a pro at looking surprised.

She pressed the jacket against her nose and sniffed.

"Mmmm, smells just like him, too. I miss my honey. Gotta give him a call," she replied, heading toward the phone.

"I wonder why he rolled by," she yelled from the living room. "I told him I was going to the sleep-over. Guess he didn't believe me, huh?"

I busied myself sweeping the nasty dirt into the filthy dustpan. I really needed a new dustpan. Maybe I could run to Walmart real quick, before all the church folks got out of worship service.

"Hmmm! Mom, I see he called yesterday, too."

Damn caller ID. I could've choked my own neck for not remembering to delete incoming calls like any normal person would.

It seems like when you're caught up, your mind isn't thinking about all the evidence that could link you to a certain indiscretion. And even though I didn't believe Aaron and I had done too much to feel ashamed about, guilt shook its finger at me.

She returned to the kitchen holding the portable phone.

"You must not have been here when he called, or else why would he come over? He must've really wanted something. But I just got through calling him and there's no answer. Mom, could we skip Luby's? I'll just boil a few hot dogs. I want to stick around in case my honey calls."

I didn't speak or look at her when I dumped the kitchen's dirt into the garbage container. Too much damned housework to pay attention to what she was saying.

Lauren retreated to her bedroom. I heard the thumping bass of the radio blast even louder.

Dr. Dre was sounding good to me.

For once rap music sounded real good.

When the doorbell rang around four o'clock that afternoon, I headed straight for the main bathroom and grabbed three magazines on my way. The commode in the master bedroom wasn't working properly, so Lauren's bathroom would have to do. I slammed and locked the door. The lid was down and I sat on the stool like it was a chair. I skimmed through a couple pages of Today's Black Woman, but when I heard Lauren's voice nearing the bathroom, I sat up and opened the lid. I pulled down my panties, sat on the toilet, and grunted.

"Hey, Mommy, Aaron's here. We're going on the balcony, in case you're wondering where I am."

"Ugh, okay, Lauren," I called out. As soon as she left, my stomach started hurting for real. Mild diarrhea. Couldn't believe it. My prolonged visit to the bathroom lasted about thirty minutes. Would've stayed longer but I heard a sharp knock on the door.

"Ms. Davenport?"

Damn! What did he want?

I squeezed my thighs together. "I'm indisposed right now."

"Well, I need to use it as soon as you're finished, please, ma'am."

"Be right out," I said, and rolled my eyes like he could see through wood.

I flushed the toilet and nearly injured my finger trying to force-spray the last of some peach-scented air freshener. I raked my nails through my uncombed hair and wished I had my makeup kit so I could apply some mascara and eyeliner. It wasn't until I found myself searching through the medicine cabinet that I shuddered.

What the hell was I doing? How had things gotten to this point? It had to be the fact that Lauren was there, walking around in the same spots that Aaron and I had graced nearly twelve hours before. Yep, that had to be it. Her presence was my reminder, my nudger, and I wasn't exactly thrilled at how that felt.

I took a deep breath and unlocked the door.

Aaron was leaning against the wall when I came out. His calm look didn't match my frenzied one.

"Hey, uh, I wouldn't go in there just yet if I were you." I half-smiled.

"That's all right. I know how to pinch my nose," he commented, and glided past me.

When I heard him sniff and then dramatically suck in his breath, I nearly hit the floor. I put some pep in my step and headed for my bedroom.

Stayed there a good ten minutes until I remembered my clothes were still sitting inside three washing machines. Because a pair of my jammies and some body towels had been stolen from the washateria in the past, I knew I'd better get my butt downstairs before it happened again.

When I came out, Aaron was sitting on the couch. He stood up and rushed to my side. I kept walking toward the kitchen and squatted to grab the box of fabric-softener sheets from the cabinet underneath the sink.

"What up with you, Miss Lady?" he said, his eyes finding mine.

I shook my head in an abrupt way.

I saw the pain in his eyes, and it touched the weakness of my heart. "Where's Lauren?" I inquired gently.

"Taking a shower. She wants me to drive her to Walmart, then she wants to get some dessert."

"Dessert? From where?" I asked, mildly curious.

"I dunno." He hesitated. "You wanna join us?"

"Aaron, what is your problem?"

"I don't have a problem. But maybe you do."

"Look," I said, not so nicely, "last night is the past. Don't ask me to join you on a date with my daughter."

"Tracey, are you asking me to choose between you and her?"

"I'm not asking you to do anything except use your common sense."

"Don't think with my little head?" he said with a slight edge.

I headed past him out the apartment and ran steps two at a time until I reached the washateria. I unloaded the three washers and tossed the damp clothes in several dryers. I almost went into cardiac arrest when I looked up and saw Aaron standing in the doorway.

"Aaron, what—what are you *doing*? Where's Lauren?"

"Would you calm down? You act like it's illegal for me to talk to you. Just came to tell you that we're leaving now. Lauren's waiting in the car."

Just looking at him standing there, so near yet seeming so far, my heart was touched.

"Well, how long have you been standing there?" I asked, my voice and legs trembling.

"Calm down . . . *Tracey Lorraine.*"

I didn't like how he said my name, but I couldn't chastise him because he left. The sound of burning rubber did not go unnoticed.

I knew he was angry, and I knew exactly why.

II

Aaron

"Aaron, I know you like driving fast, but you can't be in that damn big a hurry," was the first stream of badgering that flowed from Lauren's mouth. Then it was, "Hey, correct me if I'm wrong, but I think we just ran a red light; not really sure, though, 'cause it was like 'whoosh,' you know what I'm saying?" she squealed looking behind us like HPD was on my jock. Her feet were set rigidly against the floor of the car, both her hands braced against the console.

I didn't answer. Instead I gripped the steering wheel tighter, as if it were the source of my frustration. If Lauren was looking for me to slow down, she'd better keep looking. My nerves clashed against her wails of "What's wrong with you?" As soon as we pulled into a parking space at Walmart, Lauren hopped out of the car without waiting for me to open her door. She stomped toward the store entrance and failed to confirm whether I was following or not, so I remained in the car. I reached for my cell phone and punched some buttons.

"Hello."

"Tracey, it's me again," I said, feeling soothed by her raspy voice. Even though she had frustrated me only moments before, I still felt compelled to connect with her.

"Aaron? Wh—?"

"Hey, don't mean to bugaboo ya, but have you thought about when we're going to have that little chat?" I pressed, asking her the first thing I could think of.

"I can't say I have, Aaron. Where's Lauren?"

Lauren this. Lauren that.

"I'm in the car, she's in the store," I said, unenthused, like I was announcing the price of salt.

"Aaron, this is too dangerous. I don't like this at all. I'm about to hang up." Her words were crisp and filled with panic.

Panicky was the last thing I wanted Tracey to be.

"Hold up a sec. L-let's hook up Wednesday night."

"Why Wednesday?"

"Lauren has clarinet rehearsals. It would be a great time for us to get away."

"Gosh, Aaron. I feel like we're sneaking around behind her back, and we haven't even done anything."

The future had never looked so bright.

I paused. "It's all very innocent, Tracey. We just need to talk. I want to tell you a few things."

"Oh yeah?" She hesitated for a moment, then replied, "Well, o-okay. We—we can get together."

I exhaled and responded with a quick "Where?"

"You tell me."

"Meet me at the Golden Corral on the Northwest Freeway."

"Why so far?"

I didn't say anything.

"Okay," she told me. "Wednesday at Golden Corral. Six o'clock?"

"I'll be there, Tracey. Hope you will, too." I disconnected the call, but kept on the power. Not that I thought she'd call me back. At least I didn't expect her to that night.

Lauren begged me to take her to the House of Pies, a restaurant and pie shop that sells fruit pies, cream pies, cheesecake, and other delights. Since I have a bit of a sweet tooth, I agreed. The moment we left Wal-mart's parking lot, Lauren rambled on and on about the slumber party.

"Aaron, you should have been there. Oops, well, you know what I'm trying to say. That Regis Collier is a trip. I don't see how her momma takes it."

"Oh yeah?" I murmured.

"Th-they were talking about sex a lot. A *whole* lot."

"And you're saying that to say what?" I asked, flashing a hardened look.

"I—I don't know. Just making conversation."

"No you're not, Lauren."

"Well, how do you know that, Aaron? Gosh, you're salty tonight. What happened yesterday? Ever since you came over, it's like you're acting too weird." She kneaded her forehead over and over again. Mumbled so low I couldn't hear. Didn't matter.

After a while we pulled into the half-empty parking lot and entered the restaurant. The interior had a homey feel with its large, open space, mirrored walls, and wooden tabletops.

We were shown to a booth and wasted no time ordering two thick slices of key lime pie and coffee. Well, actually she got iced tea. I chose decaf.

Instead of chilling out, Lauren decided to poke out—her mouth, that is. This was a view I hadn't seen or noticed in a long time. Even though I saw her and knew why she was acting that way, at first I refused to make eye contact. I felt like I was behaving like a jerk, but the realization didn't compel me to change.

"So, what's going on, Aaron?"

I stirred a half-pack of sugar substitute in my coffee and clanked the spoon real hard against the cup.

"Hey, have I done anything wrong? You are so moody. I *hate* when you're like that," she said, and pitched her back against her seat.

"Save it, Lauren. There's nothing going on. Just tired," was what I said.

Of you, was what she didn't hear.

I guess my answer appeased her, because I noticed her eyes softening. A look of remorse flashed across her sweet face. In a way I felt remorseful myself. Was it wrong to begin closing my heart against someone who didn't deserve it? Especially when she couldn't even figure out, didn't have a single clue, what was going on inside of me?

It took great effort to sit in that booth pretending I wanted to be with Lauren when my mind was on someone else.

"I'm sorry, honey. Did you work yesterday or something?"

I cringed at "honey." She was starting to sound like an insecure wife, and the way she was acting gave me the heebie-jeebies.

"Now that's a stupid question, Lauren. You know I don't work weekends."

"Oh well, I don't know. Whatever. I just hope you feel better. Wish I could do something to help you out of your funky attitude."

"Don't need help. Nothing's wrong. Told you that."

"Okay, okay, okay."

She scowled like her stomach hurt, but lit up when the waitress brought over the plates of pie.

"Mmmm, yummy, this is so good. I need to be ashamed after all that food I pigged out on at Regis's. Gotta watch my weight 'cause I sure don't wanna be fat like my momma."

"She's *not* fat."

"Geesh, why are you yelling at me?"

She blinked back tears and wrinkled her nose. Confusion combined with hurt. I felt like an idiotic super-duper maximum asshole.

"What do you care if my mom is fat or not, or anybody else, for that matter? It's like you don't want me to have my own opinions about things. Well, I do have an opinion. Just because I'm younger than you doesn't mean I can't have a legitimate opinion."

I swallowed hard and tried to control my heavy breathing. I had a sudden urge to leave the House of Pies. Problem was I still had half a plate of pie to eat; I loved pie too much not to finish it.

"Yep, I'm about sick and tired of people trying to tell me what to do and how to be," she continued, her voice upgrading to a higher volume and pitch.

"Where's all this coming from, Lauren?"

"*You*, you acting like I can't call nobody fat."

"I didn't say you can't—"

"*Mom*, and her telling me not to have sex when she had it herself. She told me how she started screwing when she was younger. Why was it good enough for her but not for me?"

I leaned forward.

"What she tell you?" I asked, hoping my great interest didn't bust me.

"Oh, some slutty little story about when she and her old boyfriend Poncho had sex on a hotel roof; then she told me about the time she had sex with my dad in his apartment when his roommate Elester was there. Then she was like 'Oops, I shouldn't be telling you all this.' It was too late, though. Now don't you think it's unfair for her to tell me all that stuff? Wouldn't you think that would make me want to find out what it's like on my own?"

I leaned back, amused. "So, what you plan to do, Lauren?"

"Don't you mean what do *we* plan to do?" She gave a sexy kind of grin.

Decaf flew out my mouth and rained on the table-top. I grabbed a napkin and tried to wipe the surface calmly, like spewing coffee was nothing unusual.

"Hmmm," she said with a shameless glow in her eyes. "Maybe I can figure something out before the end of the year. Maybe I can spend some time over my dad's and just have you meet me over there."

"Oh," I replied in a monotone.

"And if that doesn't work out, we can always get a room," she said as a brilliant afterthought.

I shot her a rank look.

"Would you *really* take me to a hotel, Aaron? I've never been to the Doubletree or the Four Seasons."

"Hell, I haven't either. Not just to get a piece of—"

"Excuse me?" she replied.

I ducked my head and started scratching behind my ear.

"What were you about to say?" she pressed.

"Nothing."

"I don't buy that."

"Wasn't selling that."

Her laugh sounded like two-year-old giggles.

"Oh, Aaron, I don't know what's going to happen. Just running my mouth for now."

"Uh-huh."

She cocked her sweet head. "Aaron, what's up? You seem like you're not game for us doing it anymore."

"What you talking about, Lauren?"

"I mean, I mention us possibly getting a room and you acting like I was talking about going to the store and buying a loaf of bread. Whoopee, huh?"

"It's not . . . it's not that. Just don't wanna get my hopes up," were the shocking words that barreled from my head and out my mouth.

"Oh, poor baby," she said looking at me and stroking my cheek. "I guess it's been so long you don't want to get all built up just to be let down. Don't worry. I'm going to make the rain check up to you. I know you can't wait on me forever."

Oh, great, I thought, and slumped in my seat.

12
Tracey

Has there ever been a day where everything works the way it's supposed to?

It was Wednesday morning. I knew things would probably go strange when I decided not to go to work. I took a too-trifling-to-come-to-work day, but dubbed it a sick day for the record. After calling in, I really did hug my pillows for a few hours. But around ten o'clock I hopped out of the bed, splashed some lukewarm water on my face, and threw on the first clothes my hands touched: stonewashed jeans and a Powerpuff Girls T-shirt. Ten minutes later I found myself behind the wheel of my car. I was heading north on Gessner.

Destination?

Memorial City Mall.

Even as I entered the virtually empty shopping center, I felt like the walls were staring at me and they could read my pathetic thoughts. Even though our last few disappointing encounters made Steve seem insensitive, if he saw me today, what if he took one good look and realized he owed me some respect? Besides, being around Aaron felt good, yet I knew he was trouble. Maybe getting back with Steve on a friendly basis was the escape I needed to stop what probably shouldn't have been started. Maybe Steve was my only way out.

The aroma of every perfume you could name crashed against my nose as soon as I entered Foley's. I shook my head at the employee who brandished a perfume sample at me, and rushed through the cosmetics department like a woman on a mission.

I saw him from a distance.

He was helping a roly-poly, fortyish-looking Hispanic woman try on some shoes. Once I reached his department, I paused and stared at him like he was standing on a stage. Scream-Machine still looked the same. Except the glasses. This time he wore a pair of wire-framed designer glasses.

He didn't notice me until I stood quietly before him. Crouching to assist his customer, he looked up and the color drained from his face when he saw me. I couldn't tell if his reaction was "it's been so long since I've seen you," or a *Fatal Attraction* heads-up.

I clasped my purse close to my hip and waited quietly for Steve to ring up his customer. Kept looking around, but no other shoppers seemed to be in the area.

Once the lady departed, I thought Steve would at least ask, "May I help you?" but I didn't even get that. Instead of acknowledging me, he disappeared into the stockroom without one word. What? Did Steve think I was coming to Foley's to stab him with a butcher knife? He didn't have to worry. If necessary, my way of cutting ties would draw no blood.

I waited and waited. Abandoned like a customer who looked like she had no money.

Spewing "Forget this," I walked right into the stockroom and got a side view of Steve standing there like he wished he could do that abracadabra stuff, as if that would help. He was muttering quietly and facing a floor-to-ceiling shelf that was crammed with inventory.

"Can somebody help me, please?" I asked.

He jerked and whirled around. Instead of giving me a "Hey, Tracey," all I got from Steve was a monstrous look.

"What are *you* doing here, Tracey?"

"Looking at shoes," I said, looking at him.

"If you really want to look at shoes, you can drive to the Foley's at Sharpstown. Don't have to come all the way out here."

My ears bristled and I stepped farther into the room.

"I didn't want to go to Sharpstown, Steve. You're not at Sharpstown," was my soft yet forced reply. Steve groaned so loud I felt his voice penetrate my belly. And just that quick I went from thinking how much I missed his unworthy ass to not believing he was behaving this way. He acted as if we'd never had a relationship, like I was Ms. Who-the-Hell-Are-You? Or maybe the brother was pissed because I never offered to replace his eyeglasses. Yep, that had to be it.

"By the way, how much do I owe you?" I asked, grabbing my checkbook.

"Owe me for what?"

"I was wondering if you wanted me to offer to pay to replace those glasses," I said, connecting the dots.

"Oh no. I don't want you to do anything except leave, Tracey. This is my job and you don't belong here," he said, shaking his ponytail wildly and pushing his new glasses against his prominent nose.

"Steve, what the heck is wrong with you? You mean to tell me that I'm not even welcome in the shoe department at Foley's?" When my heart made the connection to those words, I shuddered at how much it hurt even to get that out, like hearing truth is something that's nothing but a lie.

"Do you understand Black English, Tracey? We're through."

"No, we're *not*," I said looking at him and hoping he was joking.

"Yes, we *are*," he said with quiet and calm finality.

Steve isn't playing. The man who used to want me doesn't want me anymore. And he's not going to give me the closure I wish I could have.

While the tension mounted between us, I glanced at Steve's chest and noticed this solid gold rope I'd given him as a gift a few months ago. I stared at the jewelry and realized that at one time the chain had represented my feelings for him. But now it didn't look right anymore. In a quick move, I reached out and yanked it, grunted, pulling hard and swift, until the thing snapped off his neck and rested in my burning hands.

"See, that's what I'm talking about," he said, scowling and rubbing his neck. "You don't have it all. I'm calling security."

I got right under his nose.

"Call security and I'll make you wish you'd never met me."

"I already wish that."

I spat at him, a poisonous liquid that streaked his cheek and spotted the surface of his lenses.

His eyes widened and he clutched a corner of his shirt in his hand and dabbed it across his cheek.

"Dammit, Tracey. You think you're acting like an insaniac is going to make me fall in love with you again? No man on earth would want your crazy ass."

As much as I don't like quitting, there are times when there's no other choice.

I laid his lifeless chain on a table next to the stockroom's cash register.

"Look, you don't have to call security. I'll leave."

He looked like he wanted to say something, but changed his mind and simply placed down the receiver.

"Steve, whether you know it or not, it was a good thing that I came out here. I had to see for myself, know in my heart, that I can finally put whatever we had behind us and go on with my life," I said.

His eyes were red and grimy-looking, and I could see his chest rising up and down.

"Look, Steve. I really didn't mean to—oh, forget it. I'm gone."

I ran, not walked, out of that room. Blinded. Scorned. Unaware of what my next move would be. Whereas before the shoe department was empty, it seemed now everybody and their momma had come. I had to rush past a sea of probing faces. I felt so heartbroken, so ashamed. Couldn't believe my desire for this person had brought me this low. Wasn't sure I deserved the love of a man anymore. Once I got inside my car, I let out weeks of pent-up tears. Warm, salty, flowing, and long overdue, the tears at last came.

That evening, Aaron and I met at the Golden Corral, as agreed. It's an all-you-can-eat joint featuring fried and baked meats, all kinds of steaming hot vegetables, breads, garden and pasta salads, and desserts. On any given night the restaurant is packed with seniors, families, and single men and women who want to get their grub on.

Aaron arrived before I did. He lingered in front of the restaurant as I pulled up. After greeting me with a warm smile, he escorted me into the restaurant, paid for our meals, and asked me what I wanted to eat. He made the rounds and returned handing me a plate filled with one large piece of baked chicken, a butterless roll, and a ton of vegetables.

As soon as he got back with his food, I had a revelation for him. "Men are such assholes."

"Hey, *some* men—"

"No, *all* men are assholes. How'd you think the word 'asshole' was created in the first place? I'm telling you, whoever made it up was referring to a man."

"Tracey, I'm a man," he replied gently.

"No, you're not."

He gave me a come-again look.

"Well, yes, you are . . . oh, you know what I'm trying to say."

"Yep, I know, but just because things didn't work out with Steve Monroe doesn't make all men assholes."

"Okay, then how about ninety-nine percent?"

"You're just hurt. You can't mean that."

"Who are you to tell me what I mean? Have *you* ever slept with a man?"

"Hell nah," he said, and leaned back.

"Then you don't know what being mistreated by one feels like, do you? You don't know what it's like to be treated well as long as you're giving a man what he says he wants, and then when he finds out he can get it from another woman and doesn't need you anymore, you're kicked—no, make that buried—up under the freaking curb."

He sat up and raised his hand. "But, Tracey—"

"And another thing—the fact that that *punk* would try and call security on me, like he can't defend himself, like I'm some psycho off the street. What? He thinks I have nothing better to do than hang around Foley's shoe department?"

"Well, you did go off on the man in the past, and he probably didn't want to take any chances."

"If he didn't want to take any chances, the fool never should have gotten into a relationship with me in the first damn place. Shoot, you're taking chances just going out the house every damn day. You're taking chances every time you sit your naked booty on somebody's toilet."

Aaron reeled back and gave me an odd look, which quickly turned into a warm smile. "Okay, okay. I give up. Apparently, you feel you have a right to be hurt. And I'm sorry things didn't work out the way you hoped, but maybe it's time to move on with your life."

"What life?"

"*Your* life, Ms. Tracey Davenport. Think about it. You were there for Steve, but you didn't exist for him. Don't forget, you were breathing before you ever knew homeboy existed."

Hearing him analyze the situation made me feel uneasy. Maybe I shouldn't let Aaron see this side of me. I patted my forehead with a cloth napkin and then focused on the food before me. But before I could put the fork in my mouth, Aaron smiled and placed his hand over mine.

"May I tell you what I think? I think you're much more beautiful than you realize, Tracey. Feisty, sensual, strong yet vulnerable. And even though Steve wasn't the one, you're entitled to someone much better," he said gently. I believed he was sincere because he didn't customarily pour out the compliments, and it felt good to hear him say that.

Whereas one person's words can make you feel like dirt, another person's are like seeds of hope that's planted within the dirt. With every positive and affirming word that Aaron fed me, I felt my strength return and my worth rise within my soul. I held up my head and adjusted my posture, sitting straight in my seat, and looked in Aaron's eyes.

"Tracey, I don't care what Steve Monroe did to you or how he made you feel. Regardless, now's the time for you to believe you're a flower, a gem. You *are*. There's no other woman on earth like you."

"Please don't say that," I said, feeling my posture give way.

"Yes, I will say that. And I won't stop saying it until I have you believing that you're a special person. I know this."

"But I feel *so* stupid. I gave so much, and for what? And this thing with his ex-girlfriend, and how he didn't defend me. Well, that let me know that maybe things weren't as solid as I thought they were." I couldn't believe that my voice wavered, my emotions unearthing what I wished could stay buried.

"Hmmm! Okay, maybe your judgment was a bit off in that relationship. Everybody makes mistakes, Tracey. Hey, as my mom tells it, you really don't stop screwing up until you're in your mid-fifties. So you still have a long way to go, more lessons to learn. But I think you'll be all right. You're going to be better than you ever were before."

I laughed.

"Aaron, listen to the things you're telling me. Steve hardly ever said uplifting things to me. I wonder why I never noticed that."

"Probably because you looked at him through rose-colored glasses. The sex was the bomb, so you thought the man was, too."

I leaned toward Aaron and moved my hands toward his. He shook his head and held me at bay. After a while he began feeding me my vegetables. He scooped them up with a fork and placed them inside my mouth. I ate slowly, making sure I could taste every little fiber.

I made a face, though, when he tried to feed me some of his spinach.

"I don't do spinach."

"There's a first time for everything," he smiled, and held the fork in midair. I wanted to know what he was implying, yet I didn't.

"So, Mr. Oliver," I said, scraping up a forkful of broccoli, rice, and cheese. "What makes you so knowledgeable about women?"

"Hey, I've been there and done that."

"Meaning?"

"I've had my share of relationships."

"How many?"

"I'm sorry, Tracey, but I don't have a counter on my—"

"Spare me," I smiled, giving him a stop sign with my left hand.

"What I mean is," he explained, "I've been involved with enough women to know what they want to hear, how they want to be treated."

"And what do we—" I blushed. "What do *they* want to hear?"

"Anything that validates a woman, that's pretty much what she wants to hear. She doesn't want to hear how fat she is even if she weighs four hundred pounds. She doesn't want to hear that her hair is through, even if it feels like a Brillo pad."

My heart lifted and I giggled. "And what does a man like to hear?"

"That he's the best lover in the world, the greatest man you've ever known, the only man you want to be with," he said with a huge grin.

"All lies."

"Hey, it works both ways. But then again, if you find the right person, the things you say won't be a bunch of lies. It'll be the truth . . . because you have found the right person."

"So, with all the young ladies that you've dated . . ." I twisted in my seat. "Well . . ."

"Well, what?"

"I just wonder why you're . . ."

"Why I date your daughter?"

"Bingo."

He squirmed and looked down at the table. "She's sweet, attentive, tries hard."

"And those few things would allow you to be with a girl who's a virgin?"

"Who *was* a virgin," he said without smiling.

"Aaron, don't play," I said, and popped him on the hand.

"Hey, it's not often that I cross paths with a virgin. Hell, I don't know, maybe I'm curious."

"Don't be too curious. She's so young. She has plenty of time to, well, you know what I'm trying to say. I'd rather for Lauren to concentrate on school, her activities. She needs to be well rounded, not just putting all her efforts on how to please a man."

"I hear ya," he said, and spread a little bit of that fake-looking margarine on his roll.

"I've been where Lauren's trying to go. Hey, I know what it's like to be a mom. Not a babysitter, mind you, but somebody's seventeen-year-old mother, you know what I'm saying? Wasn't easy. Mom and I clashed many days. There were tons of screaming, tears, and slamming doors between us. One minute my mother was acting like she wanted to throw me and Lauren out the house, the next minute she was acting like my baby was hers."

"Your mom's here in Houston?"

I wrinkled my nose. "Yep."

"Y'all get along these days?" he asked.

I shifted my eyes. "I'll go out of my way to see my mother when it's absolutely necessary. Birthday. Mother's Day. I got my life and she's got hers."

"Dang, most daughters love hanging around their mothers."

"That's true only in the movies. Mom and I had a tolerable relationship years ago, but I started feeling uncomfortable. Even though I was young, I had responsibilities and was grown as far as I was concerned. But Mom still saw me as this kid and would voice strong opinions about the decisions I'd make concerning Lauren, how to spend money, who she hung around, how to dress my child. I felt suffocated and drifted away. It's too much of a hassle, and once in a while I go see her, but she usually has to initiate the call and promise me that she'll lay off."

"That's too bad," Aaron commented with enlarged eyes. "And your father?"

"What father?" I asked.

"Everybody has a father."

"Well, if you're referring to the man who impregnated, married, but abandoned my mother after five years of marriage, then I guess you're right. I guess I do have a father," I told him with a heartfelt sigh.

"So I presume you're not in touch with your dad, either?"

"I could be if I knew where the bastard was, but that's another story. Details at ten."

"Okay, okay. Don't talk about it if you're not feeling the parent thang."

He surveyed the crowd for a minute, and patted his tummy. "I don't know about you, but I can use some dessert. Want anything?"

"What do they have?" I asked, lifting my body up in my seat and looking toward the dessert area.

"Banana pudding, peach cobbler, cherry pie, brownies, some of everything."

"Mmmm. Sounds good, but I'll pass."

"Suit yourself. I'll be right back."

I watched Aaron walk away from me. The farther he went, the less complete I felt. Seemed like we'd been hanging around each other all our lives, and the more I was with him, the more I wanted to be with him. A friend, I thought, maybe he could be a good friend. But with friends who looked and acted like Aaron Oliver, who needed boyfriends?

He returned with a small bowl of banana pudding, creamy-looking with soft bananas and crushed vanilla wafers sprinkled on top. Our eyes locked when Aaron caught me staring at his food.

"Hey, want some?"

I shook my head and sipped some water. He scooped

some dessert onto a spoon and placed it against the center of my lips. I shook my head again. He nodded his. I opened my mouth and he thrust in the pudding.

"Mmmm, yummy."

He smiled at me and scooped up some more dessert and I opened my mouth again, and again, and again. Took me all of three minutes to clean out his bowl. I walked up to the dessert counter and selected a bowl of peach cobbler, the kind where the crust is thick and juicy and the peaches melt in your mouth.

"Now it's my turn to feed you, Aaron."

He blushed and let me spoon-feed him some pie. I discerned the glances, the outright stares, of the other diners. Knowing we had an audience irritated me but made me feel pleased at the same time.

"Hey, Tracey. I like when you feed me."

"And I like when you feed *me*."

"This is nuts."

"But it's fun, isn't it?" I smiled.

"*You're* fun," he said, and caressed my hand. I grabbed his and we held on to each other for the longest; no words, no nothing. I enjoyed how good it felt to be with him, how soothing his presence felt to my soul. Didn't really want it to end, either.

Maybe that's why I began to entertain thoughts that our becoming emotionally attached was all right. If fate was in charge, maybe it was telling me there was nothing wrong with my getting to know Aaron, a man who didn't put me down but built me up. I had been put down so much in life that it felt good to see how the other side felt.

Likewise, right then Aaron was someone who proved to me that Steve was wrong when he said that no man on earth would want me. Not that Aaron wanted me, but at least he treated me with respect, something my soul craved at that point.

So, as the evening ended, I released a few more of my fears and set my feet at the base of a hill called Temptation. A long, steep hill, too steep for me to know what I'd find once I reached the top.

13
Tracey

A few days later I had just gotten home after browsing at both Office Depot and Academy. Set down my purse and checked my voice mail. Nada. Good. I was a little tired and looked forward to spending a quiet evening at home. When I went to the kitchen to attack the last can of soda, I noticed that Lauren had left me a note attached to the front of the fridge underneath a Pizza Hut magnet. It read:

Mom, Came home from school but had to leave.
Daddy called and is picking me up.
I packed a light bag & should be back tomorrow night.
Love you.

I smiled, felt lighthearted, and popped open my drink; the cool, zippy grape flavor seemed to taste even better. I massaged the upper part of my back with three fingers. I imagined myself taking a nice, long, hot bath. Turning on some mood music and grabbing an engaging book.

I headed for my bathroom and turned on the water. Poured a generous portion of some tropical peach bath foam in the bottom of the tub. At the unexpected ringing of the telephone, I had to balance my hands against the wall to keep from falling in. At first I started not to answer, but I turned off the water and rushed to catch it on the third ring.

"Hello."

"May I speak to Lauren?"

"Hi, Aaron. Lauren's not here. She's—"

"Over her father's for the night?" he said in a rushed tone.

"I assume she called and told you?"

"Yep, she did."

"Oh."

He didn't say anything for the longest. Was he waiting for me to give him an invitation? Make a suggestion? I didn't know what to say, so I just listened to him listening to me listen to him.

"So, what were you doing?" Aaron asked.

"Running my bath. Thought I'd relax and . . . read."

"Hmmm! Sounds good." He paused. "Well, I was just checking on you to see how you were doing. Was worried about you."

"Awww, that's very kind, Aaron. But I'm doing good." I felt the tenseness of my shoulders ease, and I allowed myself to stretch out on the couch. "Because of you, I feel much stronger. More positive."

"Good, I'm glad to hear that," he said softly.

"And thanks. I don't remember if I ever said that, but I'm saying it now. Your support meant a lot."

"No problem." We talked another ten minutes, then Aaron said, "Hey, I don't mean to rush you off the phone, but I do have plans tonight. Gotta break. You take care, all right?"

I blinked and stared at the ceiling.

"Hello?" he said with an edge.

"Yeah, okay. Well . . . thanks for calling. 'Bye," I said, and hung up the phone before he could respond. I stomped back toward the bathroom and made a tiny circle in the bathwater with my finger.

Cold. Bubbleless.

Damn him.

Wasted time, water, and foam.

I drained the water and began refilling the tub. Went to my bedroom to get a book from my nightstand, the novel *Preconceived Notions* by Robyn Williams. Seems like an odd choice, since I was about to take a bath. The author's sex scenes were *sooo* hot, so tender, more like lovemaking than simply sex. I wished I were the main character, Imagany, who had love made to her the way it was supposed to be done, the way *I* used to be done.

Boy, that bath felt good. I allowed the tubful of steaming, silky water to cover my body and take away most of the tension and soreness. The water felt so wonderful and soothing. Like it was giving me another chance. When I got out of the tub, I slipped on a long-sleeved nightgown. I sat on the couch, curled my legs underneath me, and read for about a half hour. As good as the story was, I kept listening for the phone.

After reading the same paragraph eight times, I laid aside the novel and reached for the phone. I pressed *69 and hoped I wasn't about to make a fool of myself. The phone rang and rang and eventually went into voice mail. Damn! I hung up. What message could I leave? I hoped that if Aaron had caller ID, he would think Lauren had called. But then again, he knew she was at her dad's tonight. What if he realized I was the one who'd tried to reach out and touch?

Feeling like an idiot, I went and slumped on the couch, pulled my legs against my chest, and wrapped my arms around my knees. Two minutes later I found myself dusting. Dusting! And right after that I headed toward the sliding glass door and slipped out onto the balcony. By then it was eight o'clock. The night was pitch-black, cool, and inviting. With a lump in my throat I watched people coming and going, laughing. All of them with things to do, places to go, people to see.

I honestly didn't see the Legend drive up. Didn't hear a thing. Then I heard my phone ring. I raced to pick it up. Out of breath. Hopeful.

"Hello."

"Tracey."

"Hi, Aaron." My voice was an infant's feeble cry.

"Are you okay?"

"Yes, why?"

"Well, I've been trying to get your attention to-night, and you act like you're out of it."

"What do you mean, trying to get my attention?"

"Go open your front door," he said.

"What?"

"*Open* your front door, Tracey."

With phone still in hand, I opened the door. My jaw dropped when I saw Aaron standing outside, his cell phone stuck against his ear.

"You sure know how to waste a college student's money," he laughed into the phone. Aaron stepped inside the doorway, turned off his phone, and pressed his cheek against the retractable antenna, causing it to disappear.

"Oh, Lord. How long have you been standing out there?" I asked.

"About thirteen hours," he deadpanned.

"Oh, Aaron. I'm sorry. I—I didn't know," I blushed.

"It's okay. I'm here now."

I smiled at him for the first time. Felt titillated. It seemed dangerous yet exciting to have him in the apartment with me that night.

First I deleted all his incoming calls from caller ID. Then I took a seat on the couch. Aaron plopped next to me, his thigh touching mine, and immediately put his arm around me. The heat that developed inside me created enough warmth to make the sun seem frozen. He hugged me, yanking at my shoulders like he was trying to shake some sense into my head. I frown-laughed but looked away from him.

"I'm glad to see you," he replied in a gentle voice.

My cheeks flushed. I patted him friendly-like on his leg.

"Are you glad to see me, Tracey?"

I looked at him. Melting, melting, melting. A nod was the only thing I could offer.

"That makes me feel good," he whispered.

I said nothing. Just stared at the fireplace.

"Look at me," he commanded.

I turned my head and met his intense gaze. He swallowed me up. Tasted my face with his eyes. I swallowed so hard I wasn't positive I still had a tongue.

His eyes snaked across every inch of my face: cheeks, eyebrows, chin, and mouth. He stared at my mouth a long, long time. I felt excited, yet afraid. I closed my eyes and soon felt his lips covering mine.

"Mmmm," I murmured in shock. He kissed me, long, deep, hot, and sensually. His juices intermingled with mine, his tongue traveling the scope of my mouth.

Within seconds I knew the texture of his tongue: strong, long, wet, and warm. I started wiggling my hips, shaking my legs as he grabbed the back of my head and pulled it even closer to him. I heard the smacks from our kisses, loud, inviting.

My eyes were closed, but the tears still formed.

"Mmmm," I moaned again, wanting to pull away, yet not knowing if I was strong enough to do it. So I let him kiss me. Felt like hours, but I'm sure it was ten, fifteen minutes tops. When he finally released me, my eyes fluttered, my head wobbly, intoxicated. I licked and smacked my lips.

He stared at me still. Not yet ready to give me up.

"You all right?" he asked, and ran his hand through my hair, sweeping it to the side of my face.

I nodded. Fiddled with my hands. Felt weird. Here I was on the couch, necking like a hormone-driven teenager.

I caught Aaron gaping at my erect nipples. We locked eyes.

I hopped up.

"Thirsty, Aaron?" I asked in a raspy voice. I grabbed my throat, rubbing it as if it had betrayed me. When I swung open the refrigerator, the only beverages in stock were a liter of bottled water and a jar of kiwi-strawberry juice. I removed two glasses from the kitchen cabinet and noticed a pack of stress tabs that were hiding between two coffee mugs.

"Stress tabs?" Aaron asked.

I closed my eyes. His chest and midsection were now molded against my back and my booty. His head extended over my shoulder, his right cheek pressing against my left cheek.

"Y-yep," I admitted.

"Stressed?"

"Maybe."

"Oh, I see." He backed away. I turned around and handed him a glass. He turned it upside down and smacked the bottom.

"Kiwi juice? This the best you can do?"

"Gotta buy groceries. Probably will go tomorrow morning."

"Let's go tonight."

"Grocery shopping now? Why, Aaron?"

"Why not? You got anything better to do?"

I smiled. Looked at myself. Dressed in a frilly gown that covered my body. A body that, even without the gown, felt much too hot to even be wearing a small Band-Aid.

"I—I'm not dressed to go shopping."

"Tracey, that sounds like an excuse."

"It *is* an excuse."

"Well, okay, what else do you suggest?"

"Why suggest anything, Aaron? Why can't we just stay here and . . . talk?"

"Okay, I'm all right with talking."

Aaron smiled and set his glass on the counter. I poured kiwi juice till his glass was full. He took a huge gulp, throwing back his head and wiping his top lip when he was done.

He grabbed my hand and led me back to the couch. I felt like a kid. He had me sit on the floor while he sat behind me on the couch. He grabbed my shoulders between his hands. His silken fingers, long and strong, began to knead the tension in my neck. I felt the tender heat generated by his fingers.

"Ouch."

"Hey, it may start out hurting, but in a minute it's going to start feeling like 'please, baby, baby, please.' "

"Oh, really?" I smiled. "You have magical hands, huh?"

"That's what I've been told."

I felt Aaron grab my head and gently push it to the side, exposing my sensitive neck.

"What are you—"

"Shhhh, be quiet, woman."

I laughed.

His warm, wet, and sensuous lips began to nibble across my neck. Kissing, licking it. I shuddered. Trembled.

"Ooooh, Aaron."

My eyes rolled. I threw back my head and rocked it back and forth.

Kiss, nibble, smack.

Sensations rippled everywhere.

"Why are you—"

His hands cupped my breasts.

"Sssss, awww, Aaron, please."

"I'm trying to . . ."

Have you ever known the feeling of a man kissing your neck and massaging your breasts at the same time?

I like to died.

Suddenly he let go.

Breasts untouched. Neck again exposed.

I opened my eyes. The room seemed so bright. I blinked. Wondered where he'd gone.

"Tracey, get up."

I obeyed. He made room for me on the couch by scooting to the side. I shocked myself by placing one of my legs on top of his. He smiled. Just a little. Just enough.

"Look at me," he ordered.

We stared at each other. I noticed that Aaron's eyes were glazed like he was under the influence.

"Tracey?"

"What?"

"You want me to make love to you?"

"No!"

I said that quick, like it was a fact, when in fact it was nothing but a quick lie.

He stared at me, then stood up.

"Let's go," he commanded.

"Go where?"

"We're getting a room. Pack a bag."

"*What?*"

"Tracey, stop trying to fight this. Let's get a room. Doesn't mean anything is gonna happen. But we should get away from here. Maybe it's the fact that you're here that you can't relax. Come with me and I'll make you so relaxed you'll think you were born with me laying inside of you."

I fled to my bedroom and packed a toothbrush, toothpaste, a couple pairs of underwear, and some more junk I don't recall. While cramming things in my overnight bag, I felt excited, yet burdened. Liberated, yet selfish.

Lauren hadn't called all night.

Good thing she didn't.

I would have been hard-pressed to find a lie that would satisfy her.

14

Aaron

I led the way in my ride. Tracey followed in her own. Nighttime had settled, and the darkness robbed my ability to see clearly, but I could still imagine the expression on her face. Maybe it matched the way I felt inside. I was about to be with Tracey, yet the contour of her daughter's face popped in my head no less than five times. I turned up the music, selecting various preset FM radio stations. The latest Will Smith song, one of Lauren's favorite jams, invaded the radio. I didn't even give Big Willie a chance to make my head bob before I pink-slipped the sounds.

After driving thirty minutes, we stopped at a motel near Hobby Airport.

Tracey waited in her car while I got the room. I fingered the key in my hand, took a deep breath, and drove around to room 180. When Tracey entered the suite, she went straight inside the bathroom, opened the door to the walk-in closet, and inspected windows and locks.

"You are too paranoid, Miss Lady," I told her.

"I can't afford not to be, don't you think?"

"Don't tell me you're having second thoughts."

"Okay, I won't tell you." She sat on the bed hard enough to make it squeak. Her protruding mouth was filled with trepidation. I could tell she was her daughter's mother. This wasn't going to be as easy as I thought.

"Tell you what, Tracey. Let's get undressed, turn off all the lights, and cuddle. I know you can use that. Ain't no harm in me holding you, is there?"

Her face brightened like lightning, but darkened just as fast.

"I—I don't know," she uttered, gnawing on a fingernail and looking at the floor.

"Hey, this room is paid for. We're not leaving until the morning, so let's—let's just relax, Tracey."

She went to lie down on the bed and closed her eyes.

It wasn't my birthday, but I still put on my favorite birthday suit.

Then I slid in bed next to Tracey and started rubbing her from the top of her warm shoulders to her cool fingertips.

I know one thing for sure—I've walked on concrete that felt softer than Tracey.

"Hey, what can I do to make you relax?" I asked, and squeezed one of her hands.

She opened her eyes. "How do you feel about Lauren?"

"Huh?" I asked with a where-did-that-come-from look.

"What are your feelings toward her?" she asked with a you-knowexactly-where-that-came-from glance.

"I—I like her," I said, gently releasing her hand and hoping she wouldn't notice.

"Like her?"

"Yep."

"Nothing more?"

I hate when women dig, because they usually regret discovering what they find, which lets me know they probably shouldn't be digging in the first place.

"Uh, she's cool. Young. Impressionable. But—"

"But you're not exactly in love with her?"

"Noooo, nothing like that," I answered, shaking my head like an accused little boy.

"I see, mmmmm," she nodded, and then made a noise that was a combination moan/airplane-about-to-crash/I-feel-sick sound.

"Why do you ask?" I said.

"Just wondering."

"What'd you expect me to say?"

"Didn't know. I guess I need to do something to assuage this—this *nagging* feeling I have inside. I can't even believe I'm here with you right now."

"Believe it, because you are."

"Hmmm," she said, and bit and then spit out fragments of a fingernail.

That looked so nasty I wanted to gag, but instead I got refocused and asked, "Tracey, may I flip the script?"

"Flip it," she mumbled like she had nothing else to lose.

"What . . . how do you feel about me?"

She laughed. "I've never met a guy who wanted to know how I felt about him. Most of them never seemed to care."

"I'm not most guys."

"Oh, really now. Well, what makes you different, Aaron?"

"Everything."

"Sounds like a good answer, but I'm not sure it's the correct answer," she said.

"Look, I don't mean to sound rude, but I didn't spend sixty bucks on this room just to chit-chat."

Even though I wasn't touching her, I could feel her stiffen.

Muttering, "What the hell?" I lay on top of her. With my body hovering over hers, I was careful not to place my entire weight on her. She was too fragile, perhaps more delicate than she appeared. So I lay over her, looking down at her closed eyes and her long eyelashes. She smiled like she could see what I was doing. I was adoring her, taking in her physical beauty like she was the finest woman on earth. I began to tantalize her with a slow grind. Her legs opened automatically, like they were electronic doors inviting me to come inside her super-store. At least that's what I thought.

"Ooohh, please. Hold up," she said struggling underneath me.

"No. No hold up."

"Yes, wait. Wait," she pleaded. Tracey scooted away from me and then stood up. "Let me get undressed. My clothes feel like a nuisance."

"Don't take your time."

I leaned against the headboard. Her attempt at modesty made me laugh. Miss Tracey hid behind the bathroom door for a few minutes and came out wearing some peach panties and a black bra. Curvy, thick thighs, a nice deep valley between her breasts. Hair tousled and sticking out. My eyes glazed once again.

"Come to me, beautiful."

She gave me a pouty smile and blew me a gentle kiss. Crawled next to me and laid her head on the crook of my arm. I rubbed her other arm, nice, slow, smooth.

"May I turn off the light, or at least dim it?" she asked.

"Go right ahead."

The low hum of the air conditioner and our expectant breathing offered the only sounds. After a measured deep breath, I positioned Tracey on her side. Using one hand, I rubbed the top of her shoulder, my hands traveled along her curves and felt like I was riding over hills. She shivered like she was cold, but I knew for a fact that she wasn't.

"Mmmm, that feels good, Aaron," she said while I caressed her thigh.

"I know it does."

"So when do I get to touch you?"

"When you slap a 'Touch Here' tag on my butt."

"Well, let me run to the store and buy some real quick."

"You ain't running nowhere, woman."

She laughed inside her mouth.

She ran her fingers across my chest; then squeezed my coarse nipples between her fingers.

Woo, that felt good. I wanted to bite my own hands and my feet too, if my mouth could reach 'em.

"Damn, baby," I moaned.

"Whassa matter?" She snatched back her hands.

"No, keep going. You're taking me there."

"Mmmm, good." She continued stroking me, rubbing my chest using every finger that she was born with. Then she placed her entire mouth on my right nipple. Biting, nipping, sucking. Sending shock waves throughout my entire body.

She mounted me. Got on top. I could smell her perfume, gardenias; the sweet fragrance filled my eyes and my nose. She started kissing me with such assertiveness it made me think her fears had run away. I was glad. Maybe the darkness and being far from home would make her forget what we were doing.

I let her dominate. She blew hot air against my neck, making me shiver. Then her warm tongue darted briefly inside my mouth. Using her hands, she turned my head toward her mouth and stuck her tongue in the center of my ear. I jerked.

"Awwww, hell, Tracey."

"You like?" she asked.

"Mmmm, yes."

Tracey licked me and put her warm mouth around my entire ear. It felt like she was tickling me and hurting me at the same time.

We simultaneously stroked each other. A tangle of legs and hands. I traced my fingers along the curve of her hips. Groped my way across the contour of her luscious body. I could feel the ridges of a few stretch marks. At first I stiffened, but then I remembered this woman was a thirty-four-year-old mother and not a young coed.

She abandoned my ear and made a move for my navel. I'm an outie, in more ways than one. She kissed my navel, squeezed and patted it. Her kisses then went below my invisible belt, between my legs. She took the most sensitive part of me inside her mouth, licking my growing desire and sucking me hard, like a thirsty baby just awakening to its mother's breast.

"Mmmm, mmmm." That was Tracey groaning, not me. I was floating in and out of consciousness with half-closed eyes. When I couldn't contain the pressure any longer, I flipped Tracey on her back like she was an African-American pancake.

I started to remove her panties, but she pushed my hand away and flung 'em off herself. Moistened peach fabric hurled unmercifully against the wall. She positioned herself in the center of the bed, and right before I was about to enter her, something clicked.

"Tie up that horse," she said.

"Oh yeah. Almost forgot." I fumbled around till I found the lamp switch. Grabbed a Trojan from my wallet and did some expert horse-mounting.

Lights off.

No cameras.

Lots of action.

Her vagina felt like a bed of tangled roses after a light rain: furry, yet soft, slippery, and wet. And even though she begged and pleaded with me to go down on her, my nose and mouth weren't about to go nowhere near that Petrified Forest.

"Mow your lawn and I might think about it," I told her.

She groaned but, truth be told, the best thing I could do to make up for that was to pump her like she was my future wife. I rammed her slow but hard. It took a good fifteen minutes for me to find her G-spot. I knew I stumbled upon it because—well, one moment was normal breathing, and the next was this: "Oooohhhh, awwww, awwww, ughhhhh." It was almost one in the morning, and Tracey was yelling and grunting like she was auditioning for a major role in a *Scream* movie. On top of that, the woman started scratching me with the remainder of her long fingernails, digging deep in my back, marking her territory.

Both major no-nos. I clamped my hand over her mouth. Felt her sharp teeth tear into the flesh of my finger. Then Tracey started the next round of "Oh, Aaron, aww, awww, awwww." Her screams reminded me of that girl in the movie *Jurassic Park* after T. rex appeared.

"Would you *not* say my name?" I asked, and popped out of her so some sense could rush back inside her head. My back hurt like hell, feeling like flames nipping and burning without concern or mercy.

I turned on the lights so that they were low and not too bright. Heard folks knocking on the wall from the room next door.

"Don't worry, we're done," I murmured to myself.

She cupped both her bouncy breasts, lifted her illuminated face toward the ceiling, and burst out laughing. "Ha, ha, aaaahhhh."

But wasn't anything funny.

I watched this incredible woman settle into a sensual sleep; she twisting next to me in bed, me staring at her voluptuous frame. I was pissed off yet amazed at what transpired. Ever since I was fourteen, I wondered if I could get with an experienced, mature woman. And Tracey didn't even care about age. I must be the man; I *have* to be. Capturing her affection is no small thing.

Even though I didn't climax, I still could have shouted until the walls vibrated. I sexually knocked her out just the way I imagined. And because I made her happy, I knew I did my job. But she also left me hanging, my job not quite finished. Our first encounter wouldn't be enough. It would be like having the left shoe, but not the right. And since my crush on Tracey seemed to be escalating, I wondered if I could complete what I'd started.

And if that time came, I could only hope she'd feel the same.

Tracey hardly slept like a baby. She tossed and turned all Saturday night, banging and bumping her knees against my leg. By the time I woke up—if you can call it that—my back and legs were sore like I'd been running and throwing myself against a sharp-pointed object.

The only reason I got up was because I could smell her breath. I thought I'd heard her in there brushing her teeth, but still. Damn.

"You up yet, sleepyhead?" she asked with a light-sounding voice.

I opened one eye. She looked blurry, but I could still see her smiling and arranging her hair into a ponytail. I shut my eye and rolled over, pulling the covers over my head and my toes.

"Get up, you," she sang.

What was she so damned happy about? That she almost killed me last night? That she had a colossal orgasm?

I'm glad she got hers.

"Aaron, it's time to get up. I need to eat. Want some breakfast buffet?"

I opened my eyes under the covers like she could see me. This woman had to be out of her mind. *She* needed to *eat*. Hell, I needed to call 911 so the EMS could haul my mauled ass into a private room.

She nudged me on my leg.

"Stop it, Tracey."

"Aaron!"

She snatched the covers off me.

"I didn't know you liked to sleep late. What's up?" she asked.

"It's not that I like to sleep late. I like to sleep, *period*. Didn't get any sleep. I guess you didn't notice, you were so busy snoring."

"I don't snore." She looked at me like I was a lying fool.

"Yep, you do."

"No, I don't," she insisted.

"Look, I'm the one who heard you. You were sleeping. You don't know."

"Oh, well—if I disturbed you, I apologize. Didn't do it on purpose."

"That's okay. I *love* hearing women snore," I murmured, and pulled the sheet up to my chest.

She paused a second and her mouth flopped open. "At any rate, I don't want to spend all morning arguing about whether or not I snore. Okay, if it makes you feel better, I snore, but right now I want to eat."

"I heard you once already, Trace."

"Let's go. I'll pay," she said.

I already have, I thought, as I dragged myself out the bed.

We breakfasted at the motel's restaurant. It was packed with people rushing to get some eats before they had to be at Hobby Airport so they could fly the hell out of Houston. Wished I were going with them.

"Hey, this buffet is great. I love these fresh strawberries and bananas and these sausage patties," Tracey said.

The strawberries were slimy-looking, and if you stuck a fork in the sausage, you'd better make sure both your eyes were closed. I fiddled with my eggs, grits, and French toast, but enjoyed generous cups of coffee.

"So, you got any plans today?" she asked.

"Not that I know of. Why?"

"Just wondering."

"I'm wondering something myself," I added.

"What?" she asked, fork-severing a piece of link sausage.

"I take it you enjoyed yourself last night."

"Most definitely. You took me there."

"I noticed."

"What?" She stopped chewing and started playing with her ear. "Oh, the screaming?" she blushed.

"Why didn't you warn me? I could've rented a cabin out in the woods somewhere. *Inglewood.*"

"Oh, Aaron, I wasn't *that* loud."

"Not to a deaf person."

"No, sweetheart, believe me, it is an honor for me to scream like that. Not every man can make me scream."

I shifted in my seat.

"Who is every man?" I asked.

She blinked. "Well, there's only you, really. Nobody else. I was really talking about in the past."

"Oh . . . and what about the future?" I said in a barely audible voice.

"What about it?" she said nonchalantly.

"You plan on us hooking up again?" I said, choking out the words.

"Nope," she said and scooped up some grits.

I set down my fork and stared at her. "Nope?"

"Nope."

"Why not?"

"To be honest, Aaron, I haven't really thought about it. Hell, I can't predict the future. Being with you was good, wonderful. But hey, you never know, you know?"

"Yeah. I thought it would be something like that," I told her, and was shocked at how much I allowed myself to get attached. Glad to finally spend time with her, but not so glad if it meant I'd be too vulnerable.

"What are you getting at, Aaron?"

I just stared straight at her, lost in thought.

"Okay, Aaron, let me ask you something." She blushed. "How . . . was it okay for you?"

I grunted. "That's the point. I took *you* there, but I got stranded somewhere on the north side."

"Oh, is that why you have this cute little attitude?" She blushed. "I'm sorry."

Yeah, I can really tell, I thought. I watched Tracey cram her mouth with a biscuit.

We sat in silence for a couple of minutes, me staring either at her or at my food, not wanting to look anywhere else, not wanting to acknowledge outside interference.

"So, in other words, you want us to hook up again so you can get yours?" she asked.

I raised my eyebrows and simply looked at her.

She finished eating her biscuit and thought for a second. "Well, I'll have to come up with something. The only reason we could—" She looked around the restaurant and whispered, "The only reason we could do this is because Miss L was away with her F-A-T-H-E-R."

I scratched the side of my neck. Cleared my throat.

"About Miss L . . . you're not going to—"

"Aaron, hell no, and neither are you. I know you know better than to kiss and tell, right?"

"It's cool. Trust me. Your daughter will never know a thing," I promised.

*   *   *

Tracey and I broke from each other about one hour later. She decided to go grocery shopping at a nearby Kroger. I headed on home, and was driving north toward downtown. It was around eleven-fifteen by then. I had just made the transition from I-45 to the Southwest Freeway when my phone rang.

"What you want now?" I said, frowning into the phone.

"You expecting somebody?" she said with an edge.

"L-Lauren?"

"Yes, Lauren, who else?"

"N-nobody, bunny."

"Humph. Where are you at?"

"I'm, uh, on the free—the freeway." I swerved and almost collided with an SUV that was flying past me.

"Where you coming from, Aaron?"

"Huh?"

"I called my house and there was no answer. Mom's cell phone is off. My dad is taking me to church, twelve-o'clock service, and I'll be home later this afternoon."

"Oh," I said, glancing at my watch.

"Have you seen or heard from Mommy?"

I turned up the CD player. Montell Jordan blasted from my speakers.

"What? Can't hear you. Hey, I'll call you back," I yelled.

I hung up the phone and cut off the damn power. Cut off the damn thing that would connect Lauren to me. Couldn't be connected. Not right then.

I decided to ride out to my parents' at the last minute. They live forty-five miles north of Houston, in

Conroe. I didn't think they'd be home, but I have an extra key to their house. Pulled into the driveway and let myself in.

The house was empty of my parents, but still exhibited their warmth. I could smell my mother's habit of spraying disinfectant throughout the house. A fresh floral arrangement of roses, tulips, lilies, and baby's breath sat in the center of the dining-room table.

And Pudgie, my dad's rottweiler, started barking at me as soon as I hit the door.

"Hey, fat boy. What they been feeding you these days?" He started sniffing around my feet and following me down the hall. My parents own a twenty-year-old, single-story frame house with black shutters and a metal roof. I don't get to visit as often as I should, but when I do, I always leave with a warm and connected feeling.

In the living room, I glanced at the hearth. Spread across the mantel were dozens of silver-framed photos that captured me in poses from the time I was two months old until I was twenty. I looked at my images for a while, but turned away. Too many smiles for me to handle; didn't seem to match how I was feeling on the inside.

The thing I'd imagined for weeks had finally happened. I got to be with this sensuous woman, all night long, my body inside her body, soaking up her feminine warmth. Oh yeah, it was cool, but the morning after, when I had a chance to think about what I didn't want to think about, when I allowed my conscience to overrule my libido, something else was going down. I enjoyed being with her, but I felt a wee bit dirty. Yet, in my short lifetime, I was used to the battle within, and figured that those prickly nudgings would pass.

They always do, somehow.

"Dang, where are my folks at, Pudgie? Did they tell you where they were going?"

Pudge looked at me as if to say, "I'm not my master's keeper."

"Okay, it's like that, huh? It'll be a long time before I bring *your* secretive butt another doggie bag."

After waiting another fifteen minutes, I wrote my dad a brief note and locked the door behind me. May as well get home. Can't always delay the inevitable.

When I walked through the door, Brad was raising a spoon to his mouth and sampling the grub he'd prepared. The aroma of pork chops smothered with gravy, cabbage, broccoli, rice and cheese, and a pot of boiling white potatoes held our kitchen hostage.

"Hey, brother," he yelled while standing in front of the electric burner. "I ain't seen you in a month of Sundays. Where your ever-loving behind been?"

I kicked off my gym shoes and picked them up. As I walked through the apartment, Brad's eyes bored into my back. I closed my bedroom door behind me and locked it. Took a long soap shower and was patting my legs with the towel when the phone rang.

"*Aaarrron.* Phone."

I unlocked the bathroom door and stuck my head out.

"Who is it?"

"They wouldn't say," he called.

"Male or female?"

"Female, dawg."

"Uh, be right out."

Twisting the bath towel around my waist, I snatched the phone from Brad's outstretched hand. He grinned at me and shook his raggedy-looking Afro.

"Hello?" I said.

"I hope I wasn't disturbing you."

"No, uh, I had to take a shower," I murmured into the mouthpiece.

"Wonder why?" I heard Brad say out loud and laugh. With the phone in my hand, I walked past Brad and into the living room.

"Getting rid of the evidence, huh?" she joked.

"What evi— No, I'm just tired, I guess," I said, and kicked back on the sofa.

"Well, uh, looks like Lauren has called here at least two times. Has she called you?"

"Yep."

"She did? What she say?"

Brad made his presence known, and was lurking in the living room, messing with the CD player and going back and forth listening to some Kenny G songs that I knew he couldn't stand. I stood up. "Uh, it's not a good time right now. I'll call you back from my portable. You gonna be there?"

"Yes, I'll be here. Hurry and call back."

"Yeah," I said, and casually hung up the phone.

I locked eyes with Brad.

"Tracey Davenport, huh?"

Shock erupted in my belly and I jerked my head, but continued staring at him.

"If my memory serves me correctly, Tracey is the woman you're seeing, right?" he said.

I didn't say anything.

"Aw, man, I ain't gone tell nobody. We boys." He

slammed his fist against his chest. I don't know who invented that little gesture, but it meant nothing to me.

"So, where'd you meet this woman, man? Come on, tell me." Brad had the nerve to sit on the arm of the couch, as if I owed him some type of explanation about the women I was sexing. He never told me about the girls he was sexing.

"Brad, hey, we may be boys, but this has to be kept on the down low. It's not even serious, okay? Nothing to even be concerned about."

"Hey, it's got to be more than serious if you're trying to hide it. What? You love her?"

"Brad, you're stupid."

"Aw, man, that must be it." He broke into the type of grin where you weren't sure if it was genuine or not. "You sprung, A.?"

"Man, is the food ready?"

"What, you giving your loving to someone else and want me to cook for you? Let your pigeon break out her pots and pans," he said with that stupid grin on his face.

He thought he was funny, but my jaw tightened. I went in my room and got dressed.

Eating out looked better and better every day.

After I got back home from dinner at Luby's, Brad had left, so I went straight for the telephone. My mind warned, *No, do not call her,* but if my heart didn't agree with my mind, what else was I supposed to do?

So I ordered my mind, *Stay outta my business,* and I dialed those digits.

"Tracey, I miss you. Can we get together tonight?"

"Aaron, we just saw each other this morning, and why on earth are you calling me on my cell phone?"

"Would you rather me take the chance of calling you at the house so Lauren can pick up?"

"No, nooo. It's just that . . . I mean, you never know if I'm going to leave my phone unattended. What if Lauren happens to be nearby and picks up that line? What excuse would you give for calling me on my cell?"

"Hell, I don't know."

"See what I'm saying?"

"So, how are we going to work this, then? You know I'm going to want to call you."

I smiled and imagined my face cushioned between her soft yet shapely breasts. Rubbed myself and groaned.

"Ohhh, Tracey, let's hook up tonight. Please?"

"Oh, wow, he's begging."

"I'm not begging," I said, fronting.

"And he's lying, too."

"Okay, I *am* begging, pleading," I said in an unintentionally husky voice.

"You miss me already, huh?"

"Not answering that."

"Why not?"

"Because you already know the answer. Women play dumb, but they know if a man is sweet on 'em or not."

"Mommy, I'm home."

"Yo, Tracey, is that Lauren? You gotta go?" I said, prepared to push the disconnect button.

"Uh, no. I'm in my room with the door locked. It's cool." I heard her clamp her hand over the phone and yell, "Hey, baby, I'm in here. Food is on the stove."

"Okay," Lauren yelled back.

"So everything's cool, right, Tracey?" I asked, holding the phone with my finger still in the just-in-case position.

"Yes, that girl will probably get something to eat, look at TV, and pass out in her bed."

"I heard that," I said. "So, we hooking up tonight or not?"

"I—I don't think so, Mister Man. It's getting late and, ahhhhh, I'm a bit wore out." I heard her yawn.

"Wonder why?" I asked.

"What's that noise?" Tracey wanted to know.

"My other line is ringing. Hold on," I told her, and clicked over.

"Hello."

"Hey, honey."

My hands shook and I almost dropped the phone.

"Heeeyyyy!" I said in that fake, high-pitched voice reserved for scoundrels.

"Why didn't you ever call me back? Or did you? I went over to a friend's house after I got home this afternoon, so I would've missed you anyway," Lauren explained.

"Uh, yeah."

"So, Aaron, what are you doing?"

"N-nothing."

"You want to come get me?"

"Hey, Bunny, let me call you back. I'm talking to Mom on the other line."

"Tell your mom I said hi."

"O-okay," I told her.

"And call me back, Aaron. I'll be here."

After she hung up, I waited a full minute before clicking back over. And once I did click back to Tracey, I clicked the line two more times just to make sure.

"Hey, you still there?"

"Mmm-hmmm. You okay? You sound funny."

"Guess who that was?" I whispered.

"Who?"

"Lauren."

"Omigod. I'm outta here. Call me sometime this week. Tomorrow at work." She told me the phone number and hung up quick.

15
Tracey

As I look back, I see that once I hit my thirties, every-thing changed: my body, my philosophy, and my goals. I was tired of being expected to do the right thing, even if it was something I didn't want to do. Yet I wanted to be able to try to find what would make me feel good. So, once I turned thirty-four, which hap-pened last summer on the seventh of August, doing things that made Tracey happy became the theme of the second half of my life. And if being happy meant taking more chances, to try to be less afraid, then I was willing to do that. Yet I was scared. I knew in my heart that all I had to do was say the word and Aaron would've swapped sides so fast it would've made Michael Johnson seem like a crawling six-month-old. But I wasn't sure I was ready to do that. Wasn't sure it was morally acceptable for me to be with Aaron. But as unnerving as it all was, that didn't stop me from want-ing him.

Hey, people break up all the time, and I was the queen of being dumped. Lauren wasn't anything special when it came to getting hurt. And I didn't want to be one of those involved in having her get hurt. Yet before I really thought things through, I dove headfirst into "the world revolves around me." I came to the conclusion that I liked Aaron, enjoyed being with him, loved making love to him, and he was the remedy I needed to get over Mr. Monroe. As pathetic as Steve was, the emotional and physical ties couldn't be ignored, and I still needed major help getting over him.

So Aaron and I continued to hang out together. And like the military, we adopted a "don't ask, don't tell" policy. If Lauren saw me rushing out of the apartment without notice, I'd just yell "Be right back," over my shoulder and would do eighty miles an hour down the freeway toward a magnet called Aaron. He wanted to be with me as much as I wanted to be with him. But it was hard for Aaron. Take, for example, a recent Friday night. He really wanted to see me, but Lauren wanted him to take her out, too. What could the brother do? Double-date? I don't think so. Lauren won out that time.

I even helped her get ready.

We were in the main bathroom. I rubbed perfumed lotion on her arms while she tended to her makeup.

"So, are you and your *friend* going out tonight?" I asked, and squirted some lotion in the palm of my hand.

"Yeah," Lauren told me. She raised her left elbow. "He's been kind of out of it lately, but it looks like he's returning to his old self, finally," she smiled.

"Oh yeah?" My mouth felt like it was full of cotton balls. "How? What has he been doing—exactly?"

"I don't know. Sometimes I can't catch him," she said, and swiped her lips with strawberry gloss. "And he leaves his cell phone either at home or with the power off. He never used to do that before. Anyway, tonight I may talk to him and get inside his head. Maybe something's bothering him. I know his dad has been sick, so maybe his moods have something to do with that."

"You know, you're probably right. Kids are very concerned about their parents' health. Sometimes they're in denial, though; so maybe Aaron exhibits his hurt through other means."

"Huh? Mom, what are you talking about?" She was done with her makeup and peered at me while scratching her scalp with her house key.

You don't want to know, I thought.

"Oh, never mind. Here, Lauren, let me straighten your hair a little bit. God, you need a touch-up."

"Mom, you were just sounding like Aaron's psychologist. I know y'all talk on the phone sometimes. Has he been confiding in you?"

Define confiding.

"Me? Why would he confide in me?" I said, and ran a brush through her hair several times. It felt good to be standing behind Lauren instead of in front of her.

"I don't know. I'm just playing. Dang, can't you take a joke? You're not as silly as you used to be. I want my old mom back."

I'll bet you do, I thought.

"Well, you're looking good tonight, Lauren," I said and followed her to the living room. "Don't stay out late, though."

"Hey, I'll be glad when Christmas break comes," she said glancing at her watch. "Come next Thursday, we're out of school for almost three whole weeks."

"Yeah, that's going to be nice," I said.

Real nice.

"Now remember, you said I can go visit my daddy's

folks in Georgia. You haven't changed your mind, have you?"

Are you kidding? I can't wait till that plane leaves the ground.

Lauren watched me as my eyes glazed. A few months before, she'd asked me if it would be okay for her to visit Derrick's parents in College Park, Georgia, for the Christmas holidays. Back then I was like "Hell, naw." Just being difficult. But now, hey, things were different.

"Oh no, baby. I gave you my word; you're going for sure. Didn't Derrick already get your plane ticket?"

"Yeah, he got it, but we're just checking. Making sure you're okay with this and all."

"They're still your grandparents, Lauren. Just because your father and I aren't together doesn't mean you can't know his side of the family. You look just like 'em."

"Thanks, Mom." She beamed at me and actually came and hugged me, something she hadn't done in a while. My throat tightened like someone had placed their hands around my neck and squeezed, but I managed to grab her too.

Aaron honked for Lauren from the parking lot. She waved good-bye and hightailed it through the door. I turned off the lamp switch before I eased my way to the living room window and looked out. She got in the Legend, slid next to him, and they kissed. I saw it. But wasn't a damned thing I could do about it.

Around four o'clock the next day, I dropped Lauren off at Foley's for her hair appointment. Because Lauren was getting a relaxer, a wrap, and a cut, I knew that the hair salon would kidnap her for a good three to four hours.

The moment after I waved to Lauren, I dialed Aaron's cell number.

"Hello, this is the Legend," he answered.

"Hi, and this is the Malibu."

"What's going on, sexy?"

"Well, I'm free right now. Can we meet?"

"When? Where? What time?"

I laughed. "Meet me at Best Western in Stafford."

"Hey, that's close to both you and me."

"Yep. I feel like a thirty-something freakazoid to-night."

"A what? Mmmm, I gotcha," he said, with sexiness oozing from his voice.

"So, you gonna meet me?"

"Tracey, are you positive you want to meet so close to your home?"

"Hey, by the time we fight traffic trying to drive to the other side of town, an hour will have passed. That's an extra hour of moaning that's lost."

"Be there in ten minutes," he said.

"I'll be there in five."

We had just entered the room. I felt tingly, naughty, and hot all at the same time.

"Why so rushed?" Aaron asked when I came up be-hind him and squeezed him on his behind.

"Hey, it's been a while."

"Only a week, Tracey," he replied.

"Hey, it feels like two years, Aaron."

"You're just spoiled. You gots to have it, huh?" he said in a voice that massaged my ears as well as my heart.

"Yep, Aaron," I said, squeezing him around his waist and kissing him on his neck. "I do."

Even though I wanted to get right to it, Aaron insisted that we wait until it got dark outside. Guess he felt like the dark would cover our sins.

Wasn't enough darkness in the world.

As soon as nighttime crossed the border, we broke rules for four hours straight.

I attacked him the second he dimmed the lights. I clasped my hands around his head and pressed my lips against his. Then I cocked my head and said in a kittenish voice, "I may be an adult, but sometimes I forget how to undress myself."

"No problem. I'll help you get undressed, baby."

I was wearing a leopard-print camise shirt and some black stirrup pants. I looked up at Aaron and slowly raised my hands like a child waiting to get assistance from an adult. He pulled my shirt over my head, and I could feel him biting my nipples through the fabric.

"Oooh, will you hurry the hell up?" I fussed through clenched teeth.

Then he stood and observed me in my red panties; stared at me so long I wanted to cover my belly with my hands, and I did. But he snatched back my hands and took his fingers and hooked the sides of my panties, pulling them down slow, slower, and more slowly as he peeked at every inch of my nakedness until his eyes were full and glazing.

"You like what you see, or you see what you like?" I said, and placed my hands on my bare hips.

He only had enough strength to nod his reply.

Once we were both nude, I pulled him on top of me, stroking his back and his smooth yet firm behind. I rubbed my hands along the back of his legs and I wanted him inside me so bad I finagled his butt around until he found me.

The impact was immediate. I was so hot for him. My

inner passage pulsated around his thick, hard, and wet manhood, and I swear if anybody would've called me Whoopi Goldberg, I would've answered. We rolled around on that bed, sweating like we were wearing fur coats in a steam bath. My breasts were smashed against his chest, and he kept thrusting himself inside me so hard I cussed him out at least seven times.

"Damn, Aaron, what in the hell you doing to me? You know you doing something freaky to me. You know you making me hate your butt, don't you? Why you so damn rough and I can't stand for someone to do me like you're doing and you better not stop doing it either or I'll kick your ass."

Aaron was grinning, sweat streaming down his face like his skin was crying.

"Da-hamn you're crazy, baby. This is great, though. Just slap me one time, one time. Ooohhh, mine's is coming. Woo, Tracey, I'm there, I'm there, dayumm-mmmm."

We rattled against each other, sounding like wood-peckers for a full ten minutes. Aaron wore me out so bad I felt like I'd just given birth to quintuplets and got pregnant again two minutes later.

But finally, when words found themselves inside my mouth, I nudged Aaron, who was slumped on top of me like a dead body.

"Hey, Aaron. That was great! The ultimate. I can't ever let you go. No, no, never."

He didn't answer.

I shook him again.

"Aaron, hey, Aaron."

And I smiled when I saw that Aaron's silence was because he'd fallen asleep.

And that's when I knew that, even though he didn't say it, he *did* get his.

* * *

I was in the middle of taking a nice, long, hot shower when I heard the sound of Lauren's knuckle-rap on my bathroom door. I wanted to ignore her so bad; the heated water felt like massaging hands, the shower gel smelled like fresh strawberries, and I just wasn't ready to be set free from this erotic moment, but she pounded harder and I turned off the shower and yelled, "What is it, Lauren?"

"Mommmm, telephone," she sang, but it was an angry kind of singing.

"I'm taking a shower. Who is it?"

"Mr. Steve."

Her words barely hit the air as I snatched the first towel my hands could reach. My drippy, soapy fingers fumbled to unlock the bathroom door. Lauren looked at me like I was stark naked and riding a camel down Westheimer Road. I ignored her and seized the portable from her tight grip. She just stood there staring at me, so I raced into my bedroom and locked the door and even retreated further into my big walk-in closet and shut that door behind me, too.

I waited until I could catch my breath. I didn't even care that water was dripping off my body onto my suede Bandolinos.

"Hello!"

"Hey, baby," answered Steve. He was speaking so low I thought he was sitting somewhere in the freaking library.

"Baby?"

"You know you love me, Tracey."

"Oh God," I said. "Steve, wh-what the heck is your problem?"

"Ahhh, Tracey. I know it's been a while since we've talked—"

"Right, and the last time we talked, you said we were through."

"Uh, yeah, I remember," he said, sounding like he'd rather forget.

"So why are you calling me, then?"

"You know what? If it weren't for Lelani, none of this would be happening. She trips out so much I can barely stay in my right mind."

So Lelani was the only reason he would try to creep back? Had nothing to do with how he possibly felt about *me?*

"Lani is nothing but a cock-blocker," he said in this really casual and nonchalant way that quite frankly irritated the hell out of me. It was just like Steve to blame that drama all on Lani—like he had no part in it whatsoever—and I know no woman has *that* much control over a man.

Please!

"Looks like she succeeded," I murmured.

"Ah, she ain't done nothing," he continued in that low voice.

"Are you at home?"

"Yep," he whispered.

"Alone?"

He started coughing hard, like he had bronchitis or something, and I thought how very convenient it was for him to start hacking at that moment.

"So what's up, Steve? What's the real reason you're calling me?"

"I'm calling you because I was thinking about you . . . and wanted to see you, if possible."

"*You* want to see *me?*"

"Yes, Tracey," he replied, sounding insulted because I needed confirmation.

"But why?"

He paused. "Because I—I miss you."

I stood there in shock, and wondered if an already big-ass nose could grow any bigger.

"I don't believe that."

"You don't have to. I know what I feel in my heart."

"What heart?"

"Very funny, Tracey."

I sighed. Rubbed my temples hard and long. Him calling me definitely made things more confusing. Weeks ago, if he'd called, I would've jumped up and rushed to his side even if it was three o'clock in the morning and the Malibu's gas needle was on *E*. But now?

"Hello?" he asked, after my long silence.

"I'm here," I said, amused. I wondered if my silence made him feel insecure. Wouldn't *that* be awesome?

"Well," he hesitated, then asked, "when you gonna come see me?"

"I have no . . . I don't know what to say, Steve. I just—woo, this is so shocking."

"You don't know what to say?"

"No, I don't."

"What, you got somebody else already?" he laughed, like he knew my hooking up with another man was unlikely. Maybe that's because while he and I were dating, his confidence tripled once he recognized how dedicated I was to him.

"And what if I did have someone else?"

"That would be cool," he claimed in an unnatural-sounding, high-pitched tone. "No rain on my convertible."

"Don't worry, Steve. You'll never see any love residue on my lips."

"What did you say?"

"Never mind."

"Hmmm. Well, anyway, I just wanted to hear the sound of your voice, Tracey. I didn't want you to be over there still pissed off and crying over me."

"Don't worry," I murmured. "I'm not."

"What are you not? Pissed off or crying over me?"

"Yeah, right."

The return of silence made things awkward. What else was I supposed to say? Do? Stroke his gigantic ego because he was praise deficient? Given a choice, I'd rather hold my tongue until the Klan sliced it off. Besides, I knew silence was an effective weapon, that the one who remains silent the longest is the one who wins.

"Well, Tracey"—he cleared his throat—"when you do want to hook up, I'm here. I'll let you go now. Bye."

He didn't wait to hear my good-bye.

That's because he probably didn't think I had the heart to say good-bye. But Steve Monroe had better think again. For the first time in a long time when it came to Steve and me, I had the motivation to think. And in my mind and heart, I sensed and accepted that he wasn't the one. That no matter how hard I tried, if something wasn't meant to be and left me in continuous despair, feeling like a mental case, and questioning my own self-worth, then it was time to name things exactly what they were, instead of how I hoped they could be.

16
Tracey

Early the next Sunday morning, Indira invited my daughter and me to her home for an after-church dinner. I twisted the phone cord around my waist and told Indira, "Well, I don't have anything to bring."

"Bring yourself."

"Hmmm. You know I really am tired."

"From what? You don't go to church anymore. What you tired from?"

"You wouldn't understand, Indira."

"Girl, the only thing tired is all your excuses. I don't care what's going on, ain't no reason why you and Lauren can't come visit. Free home-cooked meal? Don't have to wait in line? Don't have to search for a parking space? Bring your tail over here, girl. Dinner will be ready by one-thirty."

"Yes, ma'am."

The weather that Sunday afternoon was cool and breezy, clouds resembling an ocean dotted by clusters of orchids. I wore my favorite tan jogging suit and a brand-new pair of running shoes. Lauren, who'd ducked out of going to church with her dad, was pensive, refusing to initiate conversation all morning. We were on our way to the Colliers' when I cast Lauren a piercing look.

"Girl, I don't know what your problem is, but you better hope you're not speaking because you don't feel well. I will not have you disrespecting me."

She gave me a look that made her resemble the devil's niece, and turned around in her seat so that her back was facing me. I was so upset I wanted to shove her out of the car and onto the freeway. Lucky for Lauren I wasn't adept at reaching across her seat, opening the door, and keeping myself from crashing all at the same time.

"What's the matter with you, anyhow?" I asked her.

Silence.

"Oh, forget it. So moody."

More silence.

I started singing along with the radio and purposely screwed up the words to a Mariah Carey song, but Lauren still wouldn't act like she had a pulse. Had a feeling I should have turned around and went back home, but it seemed like it was too late to change my mind.

"Okay, Lauren, we're here. Tuck in your lip and act civilized before we go inside that house."

"Whatever," she muttered.

"Hold up, what did you say, girl? Don't you know I'll slap the—"

"What, Mom, what will you slap?" she asked with a piercing, wide-eyed look.

"M-mind, mind your manners and you won't have to find out what I'll slap."

I let Lauren get out of the car first, and I waited a few minutes before I felt I could handle getting out.

Even though I was frowning when I knocked on the door, I smiled like I was Miss America accepting her crown as soon as Indira answered. She wiped her runny nose with the back of her hand. I took one look, turned around, and headed straight for my car.

"Woman, get your paranoid behind back here. It's not like I've put the back of my hand in the food."

My hands found my hips. "Prove it."

"Tracey, get on up in here and give me a hug."

I returned. Smiled. We hugged. Held each other.

Once we entered the dining room, I took a look at the spread arranged by Indira: a platter of southern fried chicken, a bowl of steaming hot mashed potatoes with a tub of real butter on the side, collard greens with some of those yummy ham hocks, a pan of hot-water corn bread, candied yams, pistachio salad, peach cobbler, and a cooler filled with diet sodas.

After washing our hands and saying our hellos and how-you-doings, Indira blessed the food and we began pigging out.

"So, what's been up, Miss Thang? What you know good?" Indira said, once we were seated at the ivory dining room table.

"Oh, nothing much. I've just been working and . . . working."

"Hmmm! How's the job?" said Indira.

"It's coming."

"How long you been at the University of Houston now?" she asked.

"Let's see. Almost eight years."

"That long? You like it?"

"Well, a job's a job. If it weren't for the benefits, I'd be like *hasta la vista*. You know, we usually get a week to two weeks off at Christmas, depending on what day Christmas falls on. I mean, I could complain, but what good would it do?"

"Y'all get pretty good raises?" asked Indira.

"What's pretty good?"

"Anything at all?"

"Oh, uh, I guess we get pretty good raises."

"Well, praise the Lord, then," she smiled. "And what's up with, uh, you-know-who?" Indira asked, casting a glance at Lauren, who was busy letting Regis fill her ears with whatever cockamamy stuff she could think of.

"Well, you-know-who is still no more. But he did call me this week."

"Oooh, Tracey, did you cuss him out?"

"Mmmmm, no," I laughed. "I was nice."

"So, with him gone, that means you have a lot of free time on your hands, huh?"

Lauren looked up at us.

I squirmed.

"Penn State," I said looking at Indira.

"Penn State" was the code Indira and I used whenever we needed to let the other know we couldn't talk freely.

"Oh," she nodded.

We ate and talked for another twenty minutes. Then my cell phone, which was on the table in front of Lauren, started singing "The Entertainer." She picked up before I could intercept.

"Hello?" she answered, looking bored. Her brows creased; she stared at the phone, then disconnected the call.

"W-who was that?" I asked, putting down my fork laden with yams.

"Don't know. They hung up."

Indira eyed me, and I stared at my plate. "Must not have been important," I said.

"The Entertainer" started playing again.

"Pass me my phone, Lauren."

She scowled and pushed it across with table with her hand.

I grabbed the phone and left the dining room with everybody staring at me like I'd just kidnapped Elian Gonzalez.

"Hello?" I said.

"Hey, there, it's me. I just called—"

"I know," I snapped, and walked toward Indira's front door.

"Didn't sound like—"

"That wasn't me, it was Lauren."

"Ooh, damn."

"Yeah, damn," I said.

"Hey, how am I supposed to know where you are and if the phone is near you or not?"

"My point exactly."

"Well, where are you, Miss Lady?"

I was now outside Indira's house, heading for my Malibu.

"I'm actually at a friend's."

Silence.

"A *girlfriend*. I'm over Indira's house; she's Regis's mom."

"Oh, okay."

Pause.

"So, are you having any fun?" he asked.

"Nope. Miss Lauren is acting like an authenticated I've-got-my-certificate-to-prove-it asshole. Have y'all been fighting or something?"

"No, not really. Last night she wanted me to come get her," he explained. "But I wouldn't."

"Why not?"

" 'Cause."

"Excuse me?"

"I just wasn't feeling Lauren last night, and so I gave her the slip. I guess she's pissed about that. She kept questioning me why I do this and why I do that. Sheesh, I don't know what to tell her."

"Hmmm! Thanks for the heads-up. Now I know why Lauren's in a salty mood. She's coming very close to getting slapped. But I'll lighten up. Seems like a little boyfriend-girlfriend stuff."

"Uh-huh," was all Aaron said.

"You still there?" I asked after a while.

"I'm here."

"Barely, you're there. What's wrong with you now?"

"Can we hook up today?" he pleaded.

"Mmmm, I want to, I really do. But I need a plan . . . Have you talked to Lauren at all today?"

"Nope."

"Expect to?"

"Noooo."

"Well, maybe I'll leave her here and act like I gotta make a run. We can pick a place once I leave. I'll call you on your portable. Have the power turned on."

"Don't worry," he told me. "The power's already turned on."

" 'Bye, Aaron."

I sat in the car another three minutes, moving my mouth like I was still talking on the phone. I imagined that everybody in the house was stealing a look at me from the windows. Things felt very strange, surreal. I wondered what I had gotten myself into, but didn't give myself enough time to really think about it.

Being caught up. Enduring the pressures of doing what felt good to me but wasn't exactly good for me.

And some days I wished I could just die, just disappear, or at least make things different from how they were. I wanted to pretend being with Aaron wasn't so bad. Two consenting adults, right? Two people who didn't get tired of being around each other.

"It'll be okay," I told myself. "If there was anything wrong with this, it would be far more difficult than it is," I said before getting out of the car.

"Well, took you long enough," Indira teased, giving me a wink once I returned to the dining room.

Lauren was in the midst of a conversation with Regis, but as soon as she saw me, she squinted until I sat down at the table and looked back at her.

"What?" I asked.

She looked me up and down real slow, and then leapt from the table.

"Come on, Regis."

Regis grinned at us and trailed behind Lauren, running upstairs and laughing.

"What's up with them?" Indira asked.

"Don't know and don't want to know," I commented, annoyed at Lauren's behavior and anxious to get out from under her moodiness. "Hey, I realize this is sudden, but something's come up and I want to leave Lauren here. I'll come get her in a few hours. That okay?"

"Go on, girl," Indira said, "Take care of your business. She's safe here. Hey, as a matter of fact, she can even spend the night with us, since the kids are on Christmas break now. Don't worry. Just give me a holler in the morning, all right, sweetie?"

I fought hard to hide the smile that tried to spread across my face, coughing and hacking like something was caught in my throat. And it was.

Relief.

* * *

I raced home like a billion pieces of cheesecake were waiting on me.

On the way, though, I did take the time to call Aaron.

"Yeah," he answered.

"Well, just wanted to let you know that . . . I'm on my way home to pack a bag and . . . we're going to spend the night together. My treat."

"Damn. What brought all this on?"

"Lauren is staying over with Regis. She doesn't have to be back at school until January, and I'm calling in tomorrow and taking a too-damn-lazy-to-work day. Since you're out of school, too, I'm hoping you can cancel everything else you may have planned and be with me."

"Hey, now. I'm game. What you need me to do?"

"Well, pack yourself a small overnight bag and I'll call and make a reservation at . . . meet me at . . . hmmm, what about the Marriott on Eldridge Parkway in Katy?"

"Cool. I'm on my way."

I laughed and hung up the phone. Fifteen minutes later I was home, trying to find something sexy to wear. I changed from my jogging suit to a skort set and slipped on a pair of small black slingbacks. I brought along two different expensive bottles of perfume, a new pair of leopard print panties, and several bottles of scented lotions.

When I arrived at the hotel, Aaron had just pulled up. We waved and strapped our overnight bags on our shoulders. Kissed in the parking lot. Started walking toward the hotel's entrance, but stopped and kissed again.

"Damn, woman, can't you wait?"

"Aaron, I feel like a kid out on prom night."

"You are a kid."

"No, I'm not."

He smiled and grabbed my free hand, kissing my fingertips and making me blush.

By that time it was almost five o'clock, and the lobby was crowded with people coming to register for some kind of convention. Aaron hung back while I got the room. We got our keycard and waited until there was an empty elevator before getting on. Our suite had a mini fridge, two queen-size beds, a hair dryer, a coffeemaker, two telephones, and a big color television.

"Man, baby, you got us a cool room with a view," he said, looking out the window as the twilight gave way to evening. "Isn't it the bomb?"

The sky had a reddish orange glow to it, peaceful, illuminating, mysterious. Once we snapped out of our scenic view zone, we made ourselves at home by unpacking the few personal items we'd managed to toss in our bags. Aaron removed his shirt and only wore some black sweatpants with a white border, some leather house slippers, and a gold chain. His chest rippled, called out to me, but I averted my eyes and concentrated on combing my hair.

"Woman, what is your problem? Why are you combing your hair now? By the time I get through with you, your hair's going to be all over your head."

"I don't know about all that," I said moving away from him as he came up behind me.

"Well, I do. Last time was *sooo* good. Let's sneak some real quick."

"No, no, Aaron, not now."

He stopped following me, and his playful mood slowed its roll real fast.

"Whassup with you, Tracey?"

"Nothing," I told him, and shrugged. "Nothing."

"Don't lie."

"I—I'm not lying. I just don't think . . . hey, we have plenty of time. It's only, what"—I glanced at my watch—"it's not even six yet."

"So?" he said, giving me one of those "and your point is?" looks.

"So we have time. Let's talk."

"Aw hell," he said, and flopped on one of the beds so hard the springs squeaked.

"Aaron, come on. Don't be mad. Everything doesn't have to center around S-E-X."

"Damn, you're spelling the word now? I feel like I'm with some middle-school kid or something."

"No, no, it's not that. I don't know . . ."

"You do know, you're just not telling me." He got up and snatched the comb from my hand. Squeezed my chin between his fingers like it was a soft rubber ball.

"Look at me and tell me what's on your mind," he commanded.

I looked at Aaron from his brown eyes to his thick lips. Opened my mouth and licked my bottom lip real slow. He moved his lips near mine, getting closer and closer.

I jerked my head.

"Oh, hell no. *Hell* no."

"Aaron." I winced. "Please."

"Please nothing, Tracey. What kind of game you trying to pull?" he asked, getting all up in my face.

I clenched my teeth, then blew a shot of breath. "No game. No game. Just need to talk."

"Ahhh," he moaned, and slapped his hand against

his thigh. "Here it comes. The eternal need of woman to let stuff off her chest."

Aaron crashed back on the bed, laid his head on the pillow, and placed one fist on his forehead.

"Okay, let me have it. No, on second thought, I'll do the honors. 'Do you only want me for sex?' " he asked in this whiny, soft voice. "Or 'I think we're rushing and should slow down.' "

He said all this with his eyes closed, moving his head back and forth, snapping his little neck around.

I sat next to him, smiling but wanting to wring his fine-ass neck.

"Aw, baby," I said in a gruff voice. "You know I don't want you just for your body. But your tight booty and luscious tits are a big part of it."

His eyes sprang open. He sat up and grabbed me around the waist, pulling me down next to him. "Oh, honey, I'm so glad we had this little talk. Now I *feeeeelllll* so much better (sniff, sniff). Finally, a man who has a heart, a man who understands my *feeeliinnngss*."

"Awwww, Aaron. You're a mess."

"You're the mess. Playing those teenaged games. I thought you were a real woman."

I didn't answer that. Didn't know the answer.

He sighed and sat up. "Seriously, Tracey. What's on your mind? If you want to talk, we can talk. The least I can do is hear you out."

"Okay," I told him. "To be honest, I . . . Let's get to know each other even better. There's still a whole lot I don't really know about you."

He scratched the inside of his ear. "Whatcha wanna know?"

"What was your childhood like?" I said in a soft voice.

"Get the fug outta here."

"I'm serious, Aaron. I want you to answer whatever questions I ask."

"This is some fool-ass—"

"Just answer."

He groaned real loud but managed to say, "Okay, one score and one year ago, Aaron Khristian Oliver was born to one Lendan and Nethora Oliver . . ."

My eyes twinkled. He looked so cute sitting up there, trying his best to do what I asked.

"I don't know what you want me to say. My folks waited a while before having me. They were in their forties. Dad was busy hoofing it up making money with his business, an auto-repair shop, and Mom was an educator."

"You're an only child right?" I asked him.

"That's what they tell me."

"So you're studying . . . ?"

"Yeah, this semester I'm attending UH in Fort Bend and—"

"As what? Are you a junior?"

"Nope, a sophomore. Got started late."

"And you work at the main campus?"

"Yeah, part-time job as a CAD intern."

"Oh," I said, and picked at my cuticles, which were really looking yucky, and hurt whenever I . . .

"See what I'm saying, Tracey? We're talking, but you still don't look very satisfied. Why do women insist on talking like it's going to make some kind of difference as far as where a relationship goes?"

I averted my eyes.

"I thought so."

"No, Aaron, see, you're contradicting yourself. Way back when, you told me you had a lot of experience with women and that you know what they want to hear and all that. Now you're acting like what I'm doing is so foreign."

"Look, it's not like I don't know what you're doing. But there's a big difference between knowing what you're doing and me being in the mood to put up with it."

"What?"

"Ooooh, wait a sec, this is all wrong. We came here to be together. I feel you're trying to play some kind of game, some emotional tug-of-war, and I'm destined to lose. I want to hold you in my arms, Tracey, and I thought you wanted me to. Surely we don't have to fork over cash to the Marriott just to talk, do we?"

I stared into space, feeling like a telemarketer trying to sell funeral plots. It was like I wanted to be with him, yet I tried to do what I could to justify what I thought we had. Talk, bond, do *anything* as long as the emphasis didn't focus on the lovemaking. Don't get me wrong, the sex was more than adequate, but I guess I wanted to balance our relationship even if I didn't have firm plans to make him a serious boyfriend. Wasn't sure that I could maintain Aaron as a serious boyfriend.

"Hey, y-you got a problem being with me, Tracey?"

He had such a serious, concerned look on his face. My heart softened and I held him and closed my eyes. He grabbed me around my waist and pressed his face against my hair, caressing and rubbing it, stroking the top of my head.

"God, I wish you didn't act so crazy," he told me in a husky voice.

"If I didn't, I wouldn't be me, now would I?"

"True, but your moods can take a toll on a brother. Why you so damn moody?"

We sat on the floor, me between his legs, him holding me around my waist. I opened my eyes, leaned against his chest, pulled his hands in front of me, and played with his fingers.

"I don't know. I guess I'm afraid."

"Of?"

"I like what we have, and I want it to last for a long, long time."

"Do you?" he asked, and I heard the smile in his voice. I turned my head so that my lips met his, and gave him a clumsy yet warm kiss.

"Yes, I do. Being with you feels so good, yet so bizarre. But sometimes I wonder if I'm better off yearning for Steve . . . he called me a little while ago. You knew that, didn't you?"

"How would I know that, through osmosis?"

"Well, I'm telling you now."

He let go of my fingers and pressed his cheek against my cheek.

"What he say?"

I moved my head away. "It was so odd. He told me . . . never mind."

"Uh-uh. Nope, tell me," he insisted, sticking his neck out until I had a side view of his face.

"I'm sorry, Aaron. I never should have brought that man's name up in the first place. I know you probably don't want to hear about Steve, and I don't blame you. There shouldn't be any competition between you and another man. There *is* no competition."

"Hey, when it comes to men, there's always competition, even when there isn't any competition."

"That right?"

"Hell, yeah."

Still nestled between his legs, I grabbed his fingers and grazed them across my cheek, staring into space.

"Aaron? You feel the same about me as I feel about you?"

"I'll let you decide."

"No." I shook my head. "Would you please tell me so I'll *know* that I know."

"Well," he said, and moved his hands from my face to my nipples, "you know I love being with you, love touching you, love making love to you, if you'd only let me."

I laughed and struggled to close my eyes. His magical hands squeezing and rubbing my breasts made me one breath away from a faint.

"Mmmm, I love doing it to you, too," I told him. His hands felt so good on my nipples, I had no doubt that my body's milk factory was in production. I squirmed and pressed my legs together.

"I wish I could see you all the time. And I think I might have to do something about that," he said.

"Something like what?"

"I don't think I should date Lauren anymore," is what it sounded like he said.

I opened my eyes. "Oh yeah?"

He was silent.

"What are you going to do, Aaron?"

"I may have a talk with her and break things off."

"When?"

"That's the problem. Christmas is this Saturday. For some reason people always break up right before Christmas. I'd hate to do that to her, though. Already got her a present," he said, and I felt him release my breasts.

I sighed and said tersely. "You never told me what you got her."

"Does it matter at this point?"

"If you still plan on giving it to her, it does," I said,

staring straight ahead, knowing that he was near, yet he seemed so far.

He came and slid next to me on the floor, studying my expression for a moment. "D-do you mind if I give Lauren a present?"

"Hell," I said, and jerked to the side, "I don't know. It's too close to Christmas to take back the gift . . . so maybe you should give it to her. That would only be right."

"Okay, cool."

"What did you get her, Aaron?" I said, and bumped my shoulder against his.

"I-I got her a quartz watch with a black leather band."

"Oh, really? That sounds good," I said, and looked at my wrist.

"You mad?"

"Why would I be mad, Aaron?" I replied, and forced a smile.

"Just checking."

"Well, you don't need to check. I know that at the time you got her a present, you two were on different terms."

"But things have changed since then, right?" he said, and raised his eyebrows.

"Most definitely." I swallowed a lump in my throat.

"Well, I think it's very considerate of you to let me give her the gift. I think we'll do the Christmas thing and I'll tell her that we gotta break things off. Think that would be okay?"

"I don't want to be in on the decision of when and how you break up with my daughter. Already feels strange as it is."

"Yeah, you're right. You are okay with this, aren't you?" he said, and grabbed my hand.

"Aaron, it doesn't matter how I feel, it's your relationship. Do what you think is best," I said, hoping my words would convince him in a way my heart couldn't.

"I think being with the one I'd rather be with is best," he said, squeezing my hand with a finality I couldn't ignore.

I turned my head, my lips, toward him. We kissed hungrily, tongues raking across one another, exchanging sensual juices and reckless love.

"Mmmmm," I groaned after grabbing his head between my hands, sucking his tongue for a few minutes, and feeling instantly overheated. "I have a suggestion."

"What's that?" he asked, wiping his mouth.

"Whatever you plan to do with Lauren, however you plan to break it off, it's better that you don't tell me."

"Why?" he asked, kissing me once more.

"Mmmm, yummy, thanks. If you don't tell me, I'll be genuinely surprised when she lets me in on what's going on," I told him, and raked my hands through my hair. "She's probably going to come to me, and I have to be able to play things off, so it's better if I don't know anything, even if I know something."

"Gotcha."

"Hey," I said, patting his leg and rising to my feet. "Let's go downstairs and find something to get into."

"Sure. I'm with you."

We went to the first level, walked around in the hallway for a while, and then made a stop in the quaint gift shop. Dozens of souvenirs were arranged on various shelves: coffee mugs, shot glasses, oversized Texas T-shirts, and postcards were marked up at such high prices that the average shopper probably wouldn't want the merchandise even if he could afford it. Walking through the store, I noticed quite a few hotel guests who wore badges that said RETAILING IN THE YEAR 2000. At first I didn't think too much about it. But minutes later the hairs on the back of my neck stood up when I saw Derrick's unmistakable side view. He was standing in the hallway, holding a conversation with one of his supposed colleagues.

"Damn," I muttered when I saw him turn and walk toward me.

"Tracey Lorraine Davenport, what are you doing here?" he asked.

"Hi, Derrick. I'm—I'm just, uh, looking at the gift shop items. They are so ni—"

"You're here at a conference?" Derrick glancing at his watch made me glance at mine. It was six-thirty-five.

"Uh, not really."

"Hmmm! Why else would you be hanging out at the Marriott on a Sunday night?" He raised his eyebrows and had the nerve to grin. Our eyes connected, and I was afraid to try to look anywhere else. The palms of my hands felt hot and sweaty, yet the tips of my fingers were cold.

I was cheesing so hard it felt like my face was about to explode. "Well, you know, I'm just—"

"She's with me, Mr. Hayes. How are you doing?" Aaron extended his hand, but Derrick simply stared distastefully, as if Aaron had just handed him a glass of fresh urine.

"Hey, Aaron?" He looked from me to Aaron with narrowed eyes. "What—what the hell is going on here?"

"Nothing," I blurted.

Derrick placed both hands on his hips and looked at Aaron and me like we were hoodlums who'd just run over his favorite dog with an eighteen-wheeler.

"Well, sir," Aaron told him, "I needed to talk to Tracey about something, and that's why we're here."

Derrick spread out his arms and looked around the gift shop. "Couldn't you have talked somewhere else besides a hotel? This doesn't look too favorable," he said, his big nostrils flaring big-time.

"You know, being that we bumped into you, I can only guess that your mind is taking you places that it shouldn't go. But let me assure you—things are cool. We won't be here long."

"You don't have to explain anything to me . . . son," he said, and stabbed me with his eyes before he walked away.

My legs felt like tires wedged in thick mud after a torrential rain, and I stayed in that position until Aaron tapped me on the arm a few minutes later. We walked without talking. He had self-assurance in his step. His head was upright, but my head felt like it was cemented to my chest, like it was weighed down as low as the surface of the earth.

We returned to our room and I threw myself on the chair. I kicked off my shoes and kneaded the corners of my head as if that alone would make sense of what just happened.

"Uggghhhh, stupid, stupid, stupid. Dumb, dumb, dumb," I said, and slapped both sides of my face in rapid succession.

"Hey, whoa, Tracey," Aaron said, and knelt next to me. He grabbed both of my hands and placed them in my lap, holding them in place until I relented. "Please, don't start tripping. Everything was cool."

"That's what you say, but what if Derrick opens his mouth to Lauren before you get a chance to tell her anything?"

"He wouldn't do that," he said, and poked my leg with one strong fingertip.

"You don't know him. He'll do anything to make me look bad." My mind was going, going, and spinning a web of the worst images possible.

"Hey, you guys haven't been together in how many years?"

"Seventeen."

"Ain't no way somebody would hold a grudge that long."

"Like I said, you don't know Derrick. Damn, I hate that we saw him."

"You're really scared he's going to say something to Lauren?"

"It's just that it's none of his business. He doesn't have the right—"

"Tracey, Tracey, don't worry about something that you have no control over. So what if he tells? Let me do the talking. I don't want you to have to say anything to Lauren."

"Aaron, that's going to be pretty hard to manage, don't you think, being that we do live in the same apartment."

I slapped my legs together. "Aw, shoot, this is impossible. We can't do this," I said, and leaped from the couch, nearly twisting my ankle in the process.

"Yes, we can, Tracey. You're just upset over Derrick, but nothing is going to change. We can still get together. It's all up to you, because my plans haven't changed," he said, following behind me.

"Hmmm!" I was hearing him, yet I wasn't.

"Tracey, talk to me."

I thought a minute before I gave Aaron my answer.

"Well, to me this kind of messes everything up, because you hadn't planned on saying anything for another two weeks or so." I glanced at Aaron. "You still going to wait?"

"That I don't know. I know you're worried, but I don't think he's going to say anything. What can he say? That he saw us at a gift shop? It's not like we were making love in the middle of the floor."

"Doesn't matter. Anybody's mind would go there if they saw two people together at a hotel. Shoot, even if I was seen with a woman, someone would think something trashy."

"Well, we can't worry about what other people think. If you want us to be together, not worrying about other people will be one of the first things you're going to have to get over. That includes your daughter, your friends, your mother, whoever. Once you start making what they think a priority, our relationship will be on a countdown to nothing. If anything happens to make us not be together, I want it to come from us alone, not from any outside sources."

Aaron, twenty-one? I couldn't see it.

An hour later I tapped Aaron on his shoulder. He was sitting on the edge of the bed watching network news, and looked up.

"Let's go," I told him.

He didn't ask a single question, just immediately turned off the television and followed me. Just like that.

I almost did a cartwheel.

For the first time since we'd been hanging out, we drove in the same vehicle. He sat next to me in the Malibu, both cell phones turned off, and we stole away to a bustling and noisy Red Lobster on Highway 6 near Westheimer Road.

I ordered snow crabs; he ordered steak and lobster. Both of us had virgin daiquiris. Two apiece.

"Hey, a long time ago, I know the name 'Tracey' was the bomb. If you were a girl and that was your name, you were automatically popular," he said looking intently at me.

"Tell me about it. Even when I was coming up, the girls in my class couldn't stand my guts. Just because my name was Tracey, like that alone guaranteed me a great life or something," I said perplexed.

"I'll bet you looked like a Tracey. A cutie pie with nice clothes and hair."

"Yep, and I acted like one, too."

"What would you do?" he grinned and sat up in his seat.

"Shoot, I really wouldn't do anything, but the boys would still be all over me. Following me. Begging for my number. Wanting to buy me stuff. I ate it up, too. Loved that attention."

"And what would the girls do?"

"Talk about me like a dog, or refuse to talk to me at all. Then they'd set me up. Do rude things to me just to try and start a fight. And I never went out of my way to bother them. I wasn't thinking about them," I told him, and sipped on my daiquiri.

"But they were thinking about you, huh?" he asked.

"I guess so," I told him.

"It's like that when you're young." He shrugged.

"Aaron, that sounds funny coming from you."

"You're not so old, though," he said.

I cracked the legs of one of my snow crabs. Snow crabs taste great but the looks of them always remind me of the monster in the *Aliens* movie.

"Hey, I'll be thirty-five in August. My body's ever changing and I hate that. I'm sure you've noticed all the c-lite and birthmarks on my legs."

"Not really, Tracey. You look better than you think. Besides, no one has a perfect body."

"How would you know that?"

"Well, I've been around plenty of so-called tens. And I don't care how long their hair was, how great a complexion they had, or how small their waist, every single one of them still had physical flaws. And these women would be fine as hell, but they'd feel so unattractive because of one zit or the fact that one breast was bigger than the other. Or they'd be depressed because of skin discolorations on their hands. I didn't understand that."

"Aaron . . ." I lowered my head and gave him an intense stare. "Do you think you look good? Be honest."

"I'm *all right*." He blushed. "I think I'm healthy, got great skin, nice hair."

"How much do you weigh?"

"Uh, around one-ninety," he told me, and dipped a piece of lobster in the butter sauce.

"Are you into fitness?"

"Yep. I try to run three or four days a week, treadmill, and aerobics sometimes. I was trying to get Lauren to—"

I ducked my head and began toying with my baked potato.

"How about you? You work out?" He stared while I sprinkled salt and pepper on my food.

"Does Jennifer Lopez need a booty inflator?"

"I see. So what's the problem?" he asked with sternness.

"Working out is *sooo* boring."

"And being fat is exciting? Not that you're fat, but if you don't watch out, you could be."

I raised an eyebrow, but he was too busy trying to scrape out a piece of lobster to notice me.

"Say, Tracey, what size do you wear?"

"Excuse me?"

"Oops, sorry." He meditated for a moment. "Okay, if you wanted to buy yourself a new dress, what store would you go to?"

I set down my fork and stared at him. He snapped his neck and gave me a 'what's up with that?' kind of look. I gave him a 'no, you did not go there' glance. He shuddered and rolled his eyes.

"Rrrrrr, okay, let's change the subject. What are your plans during Christmas? Traveling anywhere?"

I shoved my carb-filled baked potato to the edge of the table.

"Nah, I'll be home. You know that Lauren is going to Georgia. I think she leaves the day before Christmas Eve."

"So you'll be alone on New Year's Eve?"

"Indira will probably bring in the New Year at Solomon's Temple. I know I'm not going, so I guess I'll be home alone. Why?"

"I could come be with you if you want some company."

"You're making me blush, Aaron. You know, I really enjoy being with you. And see, all this talking isn't so bad, is it?"

"It sucks. I hate it," he said, and wrinkled his nose.

"Liar," I laughed. "You are a real trip."

We clicked glasses.

"Here's to a happy future together. Are you in agreement with me, Tracey?"

I paused. Tried to mentally fast-forward to even happier days.

"Put it this way, Aaron. If you believe we can have a happy future together, I'm in agreement with you."

We clicked glasses again.

Later that night we were in bed, wearing our pajamas. The TV was turned to The Movie Channel, but we weren't watching.

"Aaron, tell me something."

"Shoot," he said, setting aside a hotel brochure.

"Why didn't you run from the gift shop when you saw Derrick approach me?"

"Tracey, only punks run from gift shops."

I giggled. "Again, I ask, why didn't you—"

He smacked me playfully on the cheek with the back of his hand.

"Seriously, Aaron. I just think it's possible to be a man and still not want to face what could have been an uncomfortable situation."

He nodded. "Well, first of all, I knew you were probably tripping. Humiliated. I couldn't leave you, Tracey. How could I have left you?"

My eyes glistened, and for a moment I meditated on what he just said.

"Thanks, Aaron," I said in a soft voice. "You're so good to me."

"Hey, a true friend will always be a friend. *Always.*"

"I'm so glad you said that."

"Said what?" he asked.

"That you're my friend. It's important that we be friends and not just lovers, you know what I mean?" My eyes began tearing again just at the thought; he was saying all the things I wanted to hear, and then some.

"You think that by tagging on 'friend,' you're making what we've developed more legitimate, don't you?" he asked.

Instead of immediately answering, I rubbed my ice-cold toes against his ankle. He didn't even flinch.

"Well, I guess in a way you're right, but I just appreciate that you think of me in that way," I replied.

"Oh, here you go again. Thinking I want you just for your fine-azz body."

I laughed without opening my mouth; stared at him like he was a treasure of love. He took my hand and raised it to his lips. Kissed my fingers like they belonged to an infant, and kept looking in my eyes while he was doing it.

I snuggled closer to Aaron, licked my lips, and gave him sweet and gentle kisses. He closed his eyes and stuck his tongue inside my starving mouth.

Tongue-Wrestle Mania was on.

And if I had a spare eight hundred bucks, we would've been holed up at the Marriott another six nights.

17
Aaron

Monday morning. Different time. Same place.

After making love three times last night, our exhaustion surrendered to much-needed sleep. Usually my body jars me out of my unconscious state right around 6:00 A.M., but this morning I had a little outside assistance. The brilliance of the sun penetrated the curtains and the window, causing me to stretch and yawn.

I looked at the clock. It was seven-thirty.

I glanced over at the shapely, precious lump that was sitting next to me reading a book.

"Tracey, what up with your hair, woman?"

"What do you mean? You don't like it?" she asked, setting aside a mass-market copy of *Summer Sisters*.

"You just woke up and your hair is smashed up and sticking all over your head; you look like *Planet of the Apes Meets the Creature from the Black Lagoon*."

"And so?" she said, lifting the book and reading again.

"Uh, you need to be putting a comb to that. Or find you one of those bad-hair-day hats. Something."

"Well, I think you shouldn't be too concerned about how my hair is looking," she told me, still having the nerve to read. "Think about what we were doing all night. It's not like I can break out my wig."

"That's no excuse, ma'am. You've probably been up long enough to get yourself fixed up. That's what I love about my mom. No matter what's going on, she never lets Daddy see her looking like Aunt Esther on *Sanford and Son*."

She dropped the book on the bed without even inserting her bookmark. "I'm glad to see you're an expert on all your old TV shows, but Aaron, nobody can look like a 'ten,' three hundred sixty-five days a year."

"Janet Jackson does."

"No, she doesn't. I know someone who saw her at an airport one time, and unless she was purposely trying to disguise herself, Miss Jackson looked like any other broad on the street."

"Aw, why you hatin' on Janet?"

"I don't even know the woman. I'm just saying hey, if you care about me, you'll like me if my hair is wrapped or not. Plus just last night you told me I look good and that no one has a perfect body."

"You may not have a perfect body, but you can still do something to that hair," I told her, and reached out to smooth her flyaway strands.

"Oh, you're just a chauvinist."

"No, I'm not."

"So you say. Be for real, Aaron. Do *you* look good all the time?" she challenged.

"Yep!"

"I see you're very humble, too," she said, not smiling one bit.

"I *know* I'm humble."

She groaned. "Aaron, if a person has to call himself humble, he's really not humble."

"But I *am* humble," I said, winking and reaching out for her.

"No, no, no, move," she said, shoving me and nearly pushing me out of the bed. "Shoot, Aaron, I need to get my lazy butt up and do something resourceful. I'm so tired, though." She yawned and rotated her shoulder. "Excuse me, but I feel like I could stay in bed for a week."

"Let's do it," I said reaching toward her again, but she moved away.

"No, you need to go and live your life. You can't be under me all the time."

"But what if I like it and I want to be with you?"

"Well, I like being with you, too," she said in a soothing voice, "but we just can't keep doing this." She shook her head. "It's insane."

"But why not? If we like being around each other, why can't we?" I asked.

"Aaron, if I'm around you all the time, I won't be of any use to you. No one appreciates things that are too accessible. They'll take it for granted."

"Oh yeah?"

"Yes, believe me when I tell you. We need a break from each other—"

"Oh, hell no."

"Now, I know you might not want to hear it, but we need to try, Aaron. I mean, can't we just try?"

"Well, what if I don't want to?"

She snorted and laughed. "What you want doesn't matter. All couples need a break sometime, and it's going to happen either purposely or by a force of nature."

I stiffened. "Meaning?"

"Meaning if we don't give ourselves some space, even if we don't want to, something else or another will cause it to happen."

I cleared my throat and stared at her. Sighed and started getting dressed.

"Daddy, what was it about mom that made you wanna be with her for the rest of your life?"

It was later on that night, and I was hanging at my folks' place for a change. We were in Dad's cozy study. My father, Lendan Oliver, was a man of average height but big-framed. Tonight he was dressed in a maroon and green rugby shirt and dark slacks, sitting at his desk stroking his beard while reading a day-old copy of the *Houston Chronicle*. Patience was having its perfect work tonight. I let him take his usual time in saying what he had to say.

After ten full minutes, Dad placed the newspaper on his lap and asked, "What's a five-letter word for 'Ex of "The Donald" '?"

" 'Ex of "The Donald" '? Hmmm. Marla?"

"Heh, heh," he laughed. "You sure about that?"

"Yep, Daddy, I'm sure. Marla Trump is Donald Trump's ex."

"Well, what about Ivana? That's a five-letter word, too."

"Who?"

"Ah, never mind; maybe Marla is more of your type," he joked.

I laughed in my throat and patted my dad on his back.

Using a pen, he jotted down a few letters, then raised his chin and smiled.

"So when's the wedding?"

"Huh?"

"You must be thinking about hooking up with some fine young lady, since you need all these answers, Khristian."

I winced. From time to time, Dad got a kick out of calling me by my middle name. Maybe it's because he chose Khristian for my birth name, but Mom insisted on Aaron. I didn't really like him calling me that, but I wasn't about to dispute him.

"Oh no, Daddy. Don't put that on me. I'm still in school, barely got a job. I'm in no position to get married."

"How do you know that?"

"Because . . . I just know."

"Ah, you don't know, son. When you're in love with a woman, it doesn't matter if you have one grand or if you're in debt by ten grand. You'll do whatever it takes to be with her, shield her . . . love her."

"Are you saying you were in debt when you married Mom?"

"Son, unless you're a Kennedy or a third-generation Jackson, you're in debt the day you're born."

He chuckled and turned his swivel chair back to the crossword puzzle. Although I asked him two more questions, he ignored me for the longest. Then finally he turned and asked, "Okay, here's a good one. What's a five letter word for 'the future wife of Aaron'?"

"That's not in there, Daddy."

He chuckled again, leaned back in his chair, and closed his eyes.

18
Lauren

That Sunday night, after Mom left, Regis and I had a heart-to-heart. A heart-to-heart is when you let go of all the doubts and fears that have been cowering inside your mouth and head. You say whatever needs to be said. The rule is to be kind, but to say what's on your mind.

In Regis's room, the radio was playing very low and we listened to song after song by Ginuwine, Mya, and Destiny's Child. Regis and I were lying on our bellies, on her bed, squinting and looking down at *Vibe, Glamour,* and *Word Up!,* strewn before us on the floor.

"Damn, what up with you and your moms today?" Regis frowned.

"She's getting on my last little nerve."

"I figured that much," she said, kicking her legs in the air and crossing them at the ankles.

"Do you always get along with your mother, Regis?"

"Hell no. She don't listen half the time, and when she not listening, she trying to run my life."

"What life, Regis? You're only fifteen."

"Like I don't know that?" she sputtered. "Still . . . I mean just because you a teen don't mean you don't know what you want out of life. Or what you *don't* want."

"Such as?"

"I don't want my momma breathing down my neck every time the phone ring. Seem like she ain't thinking about no phone till I get a call. Then, boom, it's like, 'I gotta call Ma Dear' or some other creative excuse."

"I thought you were going to get your own line."

"Yeah, I heard her telling my auntie something like that, so maybe I can get my own line by the end of the year or something." She swiveled her neck back and forth like an Egyptian dancer.

"Does she listen to your phone conversations?"

Her neck-dance halted and she stared at me. "Is the Pope on crack? Moms ain't that crazy. The most she can do is rush me off my calls. How 'bout yours?"

"No, I don't think she really cares enough to try and peep into my phone calls. But it seems like whenever Aaron dials me up, she can't just hand over the phone. She always has to chat with him at least ten to fifteen minutes before she lets me talk to him."

Regis uncrossed her legs and stared at me. "Say what? She talking to Aaron 'fore you do? What's up with that?"

I knew Regis was the type to go for the jugular, and once I started making these confessions, there was no way to go in reverse.

"I don't know. Maybe she's asking him personal questions about what we do or something. You know she's scared that I'm messing around and stuff—like

I'll get pregnant like she did. She ain't got nothing to worry about, though, 'cause Aaron and I aren't doing a doggoned thang." I humped my butt up and down with a sigh.

"Hey, girl, if he ain't doing it with you, you can bet he rubbing up against some other hoochie," Regis said, and started humping her booty, too, like she was a guy and her bed was the girl.

"I—I doubt it," I said, even though I wasn't sure.

Regis sat up. "Then you stupid, Lauren. That man ain't no nun."

"Nun?"

"Or whatever you wanna call it. He getting some. Girl, I'm telling you," she said in a tone that made me feel uncomfortable.

"Rege, you know something I don't know?"

"No, no, fool," she told me. "I ain't saying that, but you hafta use common sense. He hardly a virgin, he look like something that stepped out a doggoned magazine, and he a man. There you go," she said, looking at me like I was dumb as a piece of soap.

"All guys don't cheat," I told her, disturbed by her unsettling theory. "Besides, Aaron specifically said he'd take a rain check. I don't think he'd lie."

"You don't think he'd lie. Girl, you bugging *big time*. Aaron'll tell you anything to keep your conscience off his ass. What, y'all been dating for almost six months? Now do you really believe that a man who loves sweets can keep his hand out the cookie jar for six months, Lauren?"

Her voice volume was climbing higher and higher like she didn't need a microphone to reach dozens of people; all she had to do was have passion about what she was saying.

I sighed and clenched my teeth.

"Wh-when would Aaron have time to eat cookies?" I asked her. "He works and goes to school."

"Are you with the brother twenty-four-seven, Lauren? Huh?" she asked, waving her hand in a large circle.

"No, but—"

"And ain't there times when you can't get in touch with him, and he MIA for hours and hours?"

"Yeah, but—"

"So where you think Aaron is during those times, catechism class?"

I covered my ears with my hands. I could see Regis moving her mouth and waving her hands, and because I didn't want her to be screaming all my business, I removed my hands from my ears.

"—you better quit hiding your head under a rock and open up those big ole eyes, chile. I ain't saying he's screwing around on you for sho', but it's possible. Like, where your man right now? He called you? Have you even called him?"

I opened my mouth, then clamped it shut. Scratched the side of my neck and coughed.

"Lauren," she said, her jaw sagging, "you *haven't* called him, have you?"

"No, Regis, no. I'm giving Aaron some space. He pissed me off yesterday because he wouldn't come get me, so I'm giving him a *lot* of space."

She looked at me like that was the sorriest lie she'd ever heard.

"Awww, how clever, Lauren. Like that's gone make him want you more. You giving Aaron space all right— to hook up with some other heifer besides you. That's all you doing. Better wake up."

Right then I could see that heart-to-hearts weren't

as great as they sounded. Telling the truth is one thing, but feeling bad about expressing the truth is another. And hearing the truth, especially when it came from Regis Collier, was an altogether different thing.

"Oh, Regis, save it. I don't see you having a solid grip on Sporty. He does whatever the hell he wants to do and there's nothing you can do about it. So don't preach to me . . . need to keep tabs on your own man."

She raised her head and announced with pride, "Me and Sporty have an understanding."

"Oh, really now?" I told her, unimpressed.

"Yeah, really now. I understand that he sees other girls and he understand he gotta hand over the cash."

"Ha! That's a great substitute, Regis. A walking ATM is better than having a man that's holding you? I don't think so," I said, starting to feel better about my own situation now that I knew about hers.

"Well, it ain't for you to think. It's for me to think, because Sporty and me have it like that," she claimed, like it didn't matter whether I believed her or not.

"Yeah, right," I told her. "You can say—"

"Plus," she said her voice drowning me out, "on top of that, at least I can get some loving from him. You ain't getting money *or* loving."

"Aaron gives me things." My voice quivered.

"But nothing that really count."

"Sex isn't everything, Regis," I said, wishing I even knew what it was like to have sex. *Any* sex.

"*Bad* sex ain't everything, but *great* sex? Hey now," she stood up, twisted her butt, and lifted her palms several times toward the ceiling.

I shrugged and watched her plop back down on her bed.

"Lauren, chile, don't play that role with me. You

know sex is important, or else you wouldn't have brought it up with Aaron. You don't wanna lose him, am I right?"

I nodded.

"And didn't you tell me how you mentioned that promise about y'all getting together?"

"Yeah."

"So you did that to keep him *interested,* to hold him. If *sex* is what you promised Aaron in order to *hold* him, then I'm sorry, but it screams 'I'm important,' " she said, with her neck swiveling to emphasize every word that she thought was important.

"Rege, you know, it's pointless to argue with you. You have an answer for everything."

"I tells it like it is." She grinned.

"Well, whatever. All I know is, if and when I do get with Aaron, it's gonna be for the right reason and at the right time. I know it sounds corny, but I'd rather look corny than regretful."

I hushed up after saying that. Wondered where that firm determination came from. Even though its release was a surprise, somehow, some way, those words felt right, and a peace settled over me that made me feel more confident, and I didn't care what Regis thought anymore.

Instead of her usual snappy comeback, Regis gave me an odd look, her eyes partly covered by her wayward braids. She remained quiet for several minutes and chewed on her bottom lip.

"Okay," she told me, "I ain't all that cool with what Sporty and me have. I think he spoiled and like to have his way all the time, but I try to get my way, too. That's the way it oughta be in relationships. That's how you know the guy care about you—'cause he give in to what you want sometimes, too."

I sighed at the fact that she didn't seem to be listening to anything I said. "But what if he gets his way more than you do?"

"Then he the one in control. He got the power," she said, like all this was a clinically tested and proven fact.

"Hmmm! Regis, how can you know all this and I'm two years older than you?"

"Chile, ain't you heard that age ain't nothing but a number?"

"Yeah, I've heard that song."

"Well, it ain't just no song, Lauren, it's a fact of life," she said in a tone that made me feel like I was an airhead.

"Thank you for explaining that. I had no idea. Now I feel more informed," I said, clapping my hands at her.

"You'll be all right, chile. You just need to keep on top of your man— in more ways than one, keep on top of that Aaron Oliver," she said, and jumped up and ran toward the mirror.

19
Tracey

It was Monday, twelve-fifteen in the afternoon.

I was approximately ten minutes away from home and was in the process of making a side trip to Randall's to pick up four cans of tuna, relish, potato chips, mayonnaise, a loaf of wheat bread, and a case of ginger ale. I stood behind two customers in the express lane. One person, a platinum blond who looked like Macaulay Culkin in a dress, stood elbow to elbow with another man who could've passed for Fat Albert with dreadlocks. Someone's cell phone started ringing, and the feminine-looking man opened his purse. I saw him withdrawing his phone, so I didn't bother to reach for mine. But the ringer kept ringing and I fished my Nokia from my purse and muttered, "Hello?"

"Tracey, this is Derrick. How are you doing?"

"I'm—I'm fine." I started to ask how he was doing, but I knew I really didn't care, so I didn't say anything.

"That's good. I was just calling because I tried you at home and there was no answer. Lauren with you?"

"No, she's uh, she's probably still at Regis's. She—she's probably over there."

"Oh yeah? How long has she been there?"

"Why you want to know?"

"I've been trying to get y'all at home since yesterday. I guess your cell was turned off all night 'cause I tried that number too."

"Oh." I was hoping Derrick's asshole-itis wouldn't take over.

His pause choked the air, suspended with suspense.

"I see you're not answering my question."

"What question, Derrick?" I asked him. "Yes, I found everything," I told the cashier.

"What did you say, Tracey? You talking to me?"

"I'm in the checkout line at Randall's, Derrick, buying groceries. What did you want? I'm about to get off the phone and go home."

"Well, are you going to be busy later on tonight?"

"I don't know if I'll be busy or not. Who wants to know?"

"When will Lauren be home?" he asked.

"You know, I'm really not sure. She may be spending the night with her friend again."

"Again?"

Damn!

"Yes, Derrick. Lauren stayed with Regis last night."

"So what did you do after I saw you?"

"I don't know what you mean by all these nosy questions." I had popped open the trunk of my car and was trying to load plastic bags in the back and talk to Derrick at the same time.

"Tracey, just answer the question."

"What are you getting at, Derrick?"

"Tracey, I need to ask you something, and I know it might be a big stretch, but I'd like for you to be honest."

I gritted my teeth and plopped my butt in the front seat of the car.

Derrick asked, "Are you doing inappropriate things with Aaron?"

"What you mean? Inappropriate like what?"

"Sexing."

I sat up and pressed my lips against the phone, wanting to spit through the mouthpiece but knowing it wouldn't do any good. "Excuse me? Derrick, who the hell you think you are to judge me?"

"Hey, I thought it looked very scandalous—"

"I don't give a damn how you think something looks, you just can't sit up and judge me and assume that I'd do something . . . I mean Aaron . . . th-that's Lauren's boyfriend, Derrick . . . you know that."

"Tracey, I'm not stupid, of course I know that, I was just—"

"You were just smoking crack, reefer, or whatever the hell the druggies use these days. Derrick, I suggest you break out your HMO card or start dialing 1-800-MANIACS and make an appointment ASAP."

Click.

It's rare that I throw up. That's why, when I opened the car door and puked on the ground, I didn't think it would harm anything. After all, it was so rare that I did that.

As soon as I got home I yelled, "Lauren."

No answer. Good. I checked caller ID. Aaron had just called. Shoot. I really wished he wouldn't call me at home. I mean I was glad he was calling, but I still wished he wouldn't do that.

The apartment seemed so dead and lifeless. Or maybe it wasn't so much the apartment as my optimism. All the thoughts of what happened with Derrick came crashing against my mind. My head was hurting so bad I ran to the medicine cabinet and jammed three Advils down my throat. My aching body pleaded with me to get some sleep but every time I tried to lie on the bed, I'd hop right up and go look out the window. Lauren still hadn't pulled up. So I fell across my bed and jumped up three minutes later to get a sip of apple juice. Then I picked up an *Essence* magazine, one from June 1998, and by the time I read Susan Taylor's column, it might as well have been written in Arabic.

My mind skipped to my daughter.

Maybe I'll call her. Maybe she's waiting for me to come get her.

I picked up the telephone and started punching buttons.

"Hello? Hello?" Sounded like someone was talking inside the phone.

I put the phone against my ear and sat on the couch. "Hello?"

"Tracey, I'm trying to call you and it sounds like you're trying to call out. You trying to call me?"

"Hi, Aaron. Nope, I was trying to call Lauren. Have you heard from her today?"

"No, I haven't."

"Oh, well, her father called me a little while ago and he asked me the foulest question."

"Which was?"

I held on to my answer for a bit. "He asked if you and I were sleeping together."

"Oh yeah? What you tell him?"

"Told him to go get some therapy."

"Tracey. Why'd you say that?"

"What did you expect me to say? 'Oh yes, Aaron and I have been screwing for a few weeks and he sure knows how to make me moan'?"

"No, noooo."

"Then what? Huh?"

"It's just that you need to know how to give an answer that doesn't put things back on Derrick."

"Wait a second, Aaron. I hope you don't think I'm going to go around and willingly tell people I sleep with you, even if it is true. Haven't you heard of discretion?"

"Yeah, but—"

"Look, if you're going to be with me, if we're going to do this, do not blab and give people the juicy details. You cannot kiss and tell, you hear me?"

"Okay, okay."

"I'm very serious, Aaron. I'm not trying to threaten you, but nothing, absolutely nothing's going to happen if you act all happily juvenile and tell people whatever they think they want to hear. I don't want to lie, but this is nobody's business."

"Yeah, but—"

"And please don't be so insecure as to think that just because I haven't gone on Jerry Springer to tell America I sleep with you, that I'm trying to deny you. Hey, I have a job, a kid, I can't just go out and behave like I don't have a bit of sense. They're already going to think I'm nuts."

"See, there you go. You're too concerned about what other people think. I told you this relationship won't work if you care too much—"

"It's not that I care—"

"But see, Tracey, you *do* care. You do care what

other people think, or else you wouldn't be going off like you are. You're afraid of Derrick Hayes. You let him scare you just by his insinuations. Just by his questioning. Have you thought about what you're going to say when the truth really comes out? Then he'll know you've lied to him."

"Huh! Like I care."

"But Tracey, you *do* care, or else you wouldn't have played it off, am I right?"

"Oh, I don't know, I don't know."

"Okay, okay. Let's slow this down."

He paused.

"You need me to come over? You want me to call Lauren and get this over with right now?"

"No!"

"No, to both questions?"

"Yes. Don't come over, Aaron. I'll be okay and please don't tell Lauren anything just yet."

"You changed your mind, Tracey?"

I was silent.

"Tracey? Tell me—"

I hung up.

Lauren was home.

It was too late for me to delete Aaron's incoming calls from caller ID. So instead of me hurrying to erase any fiber-optic evidence, I grabbed a damp dishrag and started wiping down the kitchen counter. Rub, rub, rub I went, rubbing dirt that didn't even exist—at least not on the counter.

"Hey, Lauren. Indira drop you off?"

She looked me up and down, then answered, "Yeah." Her face was so sour-looking you'd have thought all the malls in America had been foreclosed. Her gloomy mood made me put that rag down real quick. I went into my bedroom and locked the door. I rubbed both my arms and rocked on the edge of the bed.

A few minutes later I heard knocking.

"Mommy? Did Aaron call me?"

"Uh, yeah. You gonna call him back?" I yelled, my mind distracted.

"Oh, I don't know. We're having problems right now."

Aw, damn.

"You—you want to talk about it?" I mumbled.

Just say no, please just say no.

"Yes."

I sighed and took a deep breath before opening the door. Lauren walked in, and the first thing she looked at was my unmade bed. Then she looked at me, but I went and got in bed and pulled the covers up to my chin.

"What's going on with you two?" I asked through clenched teeth.

"Mom, Aaron's not acting like himself. He treats me like he doesn't have time like he used to, like he doesn't want to be with me. Not sure why, though."

"Hmmm, have you asked him?"

"No, not really. I keep thinking he's going to go back to his old self. But so far he's still like a stranger. Like I never knew him."

She tapped me on the leg.

"Mom? Do you have any idea what I'm talking about?"

I yawned, produced a few crocodile tears, and rubbed my moistened eyes.

"No, I don't know what you're talking—"

"I mean, do you have any idea of what it's like to be involved with someone who suddenly seems like a stranger? Like you thought you knew them, but you find out you didn't know them at all?"

I turned over in bed, facing the wall and wishing other walls would suddenly spring up and surround me; helping me to disappear. Maybe that way Lauren couldn't see me, the flawed parts of me that I wasn't ready for her to see.

"I, um, that too bad," I said and slurred my speech.

"Mom, are you listening? You going to sleep on me?"

"Lauren, I'm just tired right now."

"Well, I won't bug you anymore. Daddy called and said he's going to pick me up."

The hairs on my neck rose.

I sat up.

"He is? Wh-when he say that?"

"He called me while I was at Regis's house," she said, and lifted her eyes toward the ceiling like I should have been able to know all that without having to ask.

"Did he? I didn't know he even knew that number," I murmured, and hoped my enlarged eyes wouldn't betray me.

"Daddy has all my friends' numbers. You know Daddy," Lauren said with a wide wave of her hand.

"*All* your friends?"

"Yes, Mommm," she sang. "He always wants to know who I'm involved with, where I'm going. Anyway, he said he'll pick me up and later we're going to get some burgers."

"Hmmm. Interesting." I pulled at my hair, yanking the strands and twisting them between my angry hands.

"You going to spend the night with him, or will you be back?"

"Oh, I'll be back. I'm tired of being everywhere else

except at my own home. Anyway, go on back to sleep, Mom. I'll see you later." She brushed my cheek with a dry kiss.

I stared into a blurry and unfocused space and stroked my cheek once I was sure she had left.

Later that night I called Indira. I was sitting on the edge of my unmade bed, with pillows surrounding me like I was in a cave, and bedcovers sprawling partially on the floor.

"Indira, it's me," I sniffed, and dabbed underneath my nose with some facial tissue.

"Oh, hey."

"Uh, thanks, girl, for letting my daughter stay over there."

"No problem. Were you able to handle your emergency?"

"Y-yeah. Somewhat."

"Hmmm. You wanna talk about it?"

"God, Indira," I said, reaching down and pulling the misplaced covers over my shoulders, "I feel *sooo* stupid," I whispered.

"What, what?" she whispered back conspiratorially.

"It's *sooo crazy,*" I exclaimed with one big astonished shake of the head.

"What, Tracey," she laughed, "are you talking about?"

Even though I was at home by myself, I sprung up, closed and locked my bedroom door, walked all the way to the back of my walk-in closet, and sat in the dark, Indian-style.

"First, Indy, promise me you won't judge me," I commanded, "because what I'm about to tell you is very sensitive and all I want you to do is listen, that's all."

"Okay."

"The quickest way for me to go from being your friend to your enemy is for you to judge me. So please listen and maybe you can help me to make sense of this."

"Gosh, girl," she said, "you're scaring me."

My voice softened. "I don't mean to scare you, I just need an ear that hears. You got it?" I pressed, knowing I was being anal, but making sure Indy was with me nonetheless.

"Got it."

"Well, Indy," I told her, my voice rising, "Lauren's boyfriend and I are . . . are *talking*."

"Okay. You and uh . . . what's his name again?" she said, sounding a bit embarrassed for not remembering.

"Aaron," I told her. His name rolled off my tongue like melted butter, and I couldn't help but smile.

"Okay, you and Aaron are talking. Uh-huh," she said, sounding like it was the most boring so-what-ish news flash of the week. "What y'all talking about?"

"Nooo, Indira." I laughed like I was releasing something and glad that there seemed to be something to laugh about. I don't know, maybe Indira would be happy for me. Maybe this thing wasn't as bad as I thought it to be. Maybe.

"It's more like a we-like-each-other kind of talking."

"Uh-huh, hmmm."

"Indira—"

"Okay, let me process this. And Lauren—she doesn't know, right?"

The air thickened and so did my throat, and so did my guilt, and so did my conscience.

"Right," I muttered. "She does not even know."

"Good," she said, and sucked in her breath. "Well, has it gotten . . . uh, has it become intim—"

"Yes!" I told her. Because she was my friend, I didn't want to lie to her; I wanted to let out all that was inside, that is, if I could afford to be transparent without suffering too much. At this point, what difference would it make? The cat was all the way out of the bag and looking me smack in my face.

"We've gone there, Indira."

"Okay . . . okay," she said, sounding like she was trying to be supportive but finding it challenging. And at that moment it seemed that the thing I hoped was so beautiful might not have been as rosy as I yearned for it to be. Why couldn't the thing that I wanted run smoothly, have no ramifications, and at the same time be something that couldn't be judged as right or wrong?

"Indira, I'm doing things with my daughter's boyfriend that I didn't even want my own daughter to do."

"Jesus, Tracey, my God," she exclaimed, sounding like she hoped I'd say no and was wounded to hear me say yes.

Then silence. Whether it was the silence of judgment or the silence of comfort, I couldn't tell. I sat in the dark and picked at my fingers, surrounded by thick air, tall ceilings, and thin walls, walls that I wished I could walk right into and then mercifully become a part of, because if that disappearing act happened, I'd be unknown, unaccountable, and free from having to make confessions.

"How are you feeling, girl?"

The sound of her soothing voice made me wrap both my arms around myself and rock back and forth, back and forth, so very desperate for understanding, so full of need. "Happy, terrible, desired, afraid."

"Wow, Tracey. I hardly know what to say. I'm not judging, I'm just—"

"Repulsed?" Ewww, it hurt to say that, to think that.

Indy made a quick gurgling sound inside her throat. "No, sweetheart, liking a younger man ain't nothing new . . ." Her voice drifted away slowly, the sound of a distant thunder.

"But why do I have to like *this* particular younger man?"

"Tracey, what exactly do you like about Aaron?"

I smiled through my scattered emotions.

"Our conversations, his kindness and attentiveness to me. He's very affectionate, and I know it sounds strange, but I like what he's giving to me."

"And—so, how does *he* feel?"

I raised my chin, thankful there was something solid to tell her. "He lets me know how he feels by the way he treats me. It's strange, Aaron may be younger than me, but sometimes it seems like he's on the same level. Sometimes."

"So, it sounds like you like all this, yet you're . . . hesitant?"

"Absolutely. My child—she doesn't know a thing. I think that we— that *Aaron*—is going to break things off with her. Soon."

"So y'all can be free to get together?" she said matter-of-factly.

"Indira, you're judging me?" *Can I please find someone else to blame beside myself?*

"Nooo, I'm not."

"I can tell by your voice. You're talking in that she-can-believe-that-junk-if-she-wants-to type of voice."

"Wait a sec, Tracey. What you tell me doesn't extend beyond me. Shoot, who the hell am I to judge you? All I can do is listen and be supportive. For all I know, my own day may come when I'm telling you some tripped-out stuff about my own life. I'm doing this now because should I ever be in your position, I'd want you to do the same for me, girl."

I closed my eyes and a gush of tears flowed and swirled across my cheeks, but at that moment all I wanted to know was if my tears would eventually stop falling or were my eyes just beginning to well.

A half hour later, Indira was in my living room, perched on her knees, with her bare feet exposed. She removed a large red brush from her purse and started raking it through the back of my hair, sweeping its thickness over and over again. With every stroke of her brush, I moaned. I felt so blessed to have her there with me, especially because I hadn't asked her to come.

"Why didn't you tell me this before now, Tracey?" she gently fussed.

"Huh! Ain't like anyone is going to rush out and spread news like that. Gotta think long and hard before you go telling people stuff like that."

"I hear ya."

"So, Indy?" I said, turning my head toward her. "What would you do if you were in my shoes?"

"I'd take 'em off," she said, rocking back and forth on her knees.

"Funny," I said, ducking and covering my head with my hands, which she promptly removed and resumed brushing my hair.

"Hey, babe, it's easy for me to say what I'd do, but I'm not in your shoes. I—I guess anything is possible, though. We usually end up with a guy we never thought we'd be with, am I right?"

"Yours truly is living proof of that. I mean, I never would have guessed that I'd be digging Aaron . . . hanging out with Aaron . . . and *liking* it."

She set down her brush and began massaging my shoulders, making several swirls on my tingling and aching flesh with the tips of her fingers.

"So, Indira, even though you haven't been in my shoes, just pretend like you are. Think about how it would be if you met someone younger. And that isn't even the main issue. The fact that he's dating your kid or hangs out with your kid, that's the clincher. What would you do?"

"Girl, I can't believe you're asking me, but okay. I'll try and imagine myself in something like that."

Indy removed her hands from my back and sighed. I turned around and faced her to get a good listen. She raised her eyes to the ceiling, her right hand holding her chin, the other hand supporting the bottom of her right elbow.

"Okay, I'm forty and Regis is hanging out with that Spotty, Spooty, or whatever his name is, and I look up one day and old Spotty looking kind of cute to me. It's been two years and counting on the celibacy thing. My birth control pills have disintegrated into dust, death, and hell, and I got needs. So me and the young man maybe look at each other one day and it's the kind of look that a man gives a woman when he wants her, when he likes what he sees and maybe, just maybe, I'm kinda digging him and blushing over the fact that he's scoping me and maybe at first I tell myself, 'Self, uh-oh, no way, nooooo,' but then again, maybe my ego is saying 'Why the hell not?' and perhaps my body is saying yes to how the guy is making me feel. I mean, he's paying attention to me, telling me I look good with my forty-something self, and you know at that age we need every compliment we can get. So one day I get weak and the next thing I know we're in bed and he's proving to me that he knows how to work it."

She stopped looking at the ceiling and stuck out her neck to gawk at me. "Dang, Tracey, now I kinda know what you might be going through."

"You do?" I squealed. "You get what I'm talking about now?"

Indy nodded, not repeating her affirmation, but a nod made perfect sense.

"So, Indy, does it seem so absurd now that you've thought about how something like that can happen to you, to anybody?"

"Well," she said carefully, "by thinking about it I've come as close to it as I can get. And I can imagine that possibly happening, but baby, the reality is these were just my thoughts—but you're the one who's in deep in the midst of this thing. Ain't like it's something you can turn off once you've finished enjoying your fantasy," she said, and twisted her hand like she was turning a knob. "Baby, you're *living* that fantasy. Plus a fantasy can be controlled, and I'll bet anything that you're going through some things right now that you just cannot control."

"Indira, you've never lied. Take the other night, for example. You will not believe who saw me and Aaron at a hotel."

"Who, girl? Was it Pastor Solomon?"

I burst out laughing.

"I wish. All Pastor would have done is prayed for

me, and hey, that would've been cool compared to what I really went through."

She just stared at me, motionless for a change.

"Derrick," I told her.

"Aw, boo, so what did you do?"

"I could have really freaked, but Aaron handled things."

"My God. Mmmmm. You think he's a threat?"

"Girl, I don't put anything past Derrick. Think about it. Why would Derrick cover for me? He loves Lauren more than he loves me."

"Well, if that's the case, then he might cover for you. Why would a father go out of his way to hurt his daughter?" she said sympathetically, covering her heart with both her hands.

"And why would a mother go out of her way to hurt her daughter?" I blurted. "Oh, Indira, I *can't* do this."

"Oh no, Tracey," she said, shaking her head furiously. "I wasn't trying to imply that you—"

I jumped up.

"I know, but it's very odd how that came out, isn't it? You think you thought of something like that arbitrarily? Maybe it's the Lord talking to me through you."

Indira's eyes fluttered like she was about to hit the floor headfirst.

"No, baby. God can talk to you directly. He doesn't have to speak through me. You know that."

"God doesn't have to, but he will. Since I don't go to church anymore, he may be trying to get a message to me the best way he can."

"Tracey, you're paranoid. Just because you feel you don't measure up in comparison to all the other church members doesn't mean the Lord won't speak to you anymore, or has forgotten about you. That was a poor excuse to stop going to church anyway."

"Well," I coughed, feeling self-conscious. "I still think you're a better spiritual vessel than me."

"Look, Tracey, I believe in God, but trust me, I am not him," she said, raising her eyes to the ceiling and bringing her hands together as if she were not worthy.

"Yeah, but . . . getting back to what you said about me and Lauren . . . it means something, Indira."

"So what's really going on with you and Aaron? It's not like you two are discussing a commitment or anything . . . right?"

"Not at all. I think we just want to be free to be together. If we're up front with Lauren, we won't have to sneak around and lie and hide. We're hoping she can deal with this and somehow give us the space to have a relationship."

"Tracey, I'm your friend, but I think you have your work cut out for you big-time," she said, wiggling two fingers like she was using a pair of scissors.

"I know," I sighed, smiling to myself about how Indira was so animated just about every time words came out of her mouth.

"You really like him that much?"

"I know it seems like 'why I gotta be with him?' Out of all the fine-ass chocolate brothers in Houston, why him?"

"Right!"

"Well, problem is, I don't know all the fine brothers in Houston. They aren't all running after me and trying to get with me. Only one fine brother is doing that."

"I tell you, your life is a lot more interesting than mine, Tracey. You believe in drama, huh?"

I couldn't believe she said that. To me she was the dramatic one. But I dramatically waved one finger back and forth and told her, "No, I don't believe in drama. I believe in going after what I want, and if drama is a part of it, then I'll just have to go through it."

20
Lauren

Daddy came and got me just like he said, ten minutes earlier than what he said. That was odd, since I know him to run late some days. He smiled at me in a distant kind of way, like his body was there but his mind was still stuck in traffic somewhere. I didn't pay him a lot of attention. Was just glad we were on our way to grab a burger.

He was taking me to Fuddruckers, which claims it makes the world's greatest hamburgers. I love those big, juicy burgers, mounted with sliced onions, pickles, lettuce, ketchup, and diced tomatoes, all quietly sitting on a soft bun. Yummy, I could taste those onions already and almost choked on disbelief when Daddy pulled his car into the lot of a Shell station.

"Daddy, what are you doing here? We have a full tank of gas."

"I know that. Need to use the pay phone."

He opened the door and got out of the car so quick I thought he'd seen hundred-dollar bills falling from the sky or something. I noticed the outline of Daddy's hands while he fumbled in his pockets and pulled out change. And even though I could see him, I couldn't hear him, but he turned his back toward me just the same. I turned away from him, too. Why would he think I'd want to hear whatever he had to say to whomever he was saying it? I just wanted my gigantic cheeseburger with French fries and a large root beer.

Daddy took so long I had to stop my neck from snapping. More tired than I ever thought I could be at seven in the evening. I wondered what Aaron was doing. We really hadn't talked like we usually did, thought he should've called me first, and maybe he thought I should have called him. So even with all that thinking going on, nobody was calling anybody. I couldn't believe how stubborn Aaron was. If I meant anything at all to him, couldn't he lay aside whatever it was that stopped him from dialing my number?

Then what Regis said the other day really tortured me: that if Aaron and me weren't doing it, then Aaron had to be rubbing up against some other babe. I couldn't see it. Or didn't want to. There's no way I could believe Aaron would betray me like that. Regis just didn't know what the hell she was talking about.

Daddy finally finished his long phone conversation with the mystery person and got in the car without even saying "I'm sorry." He didn't say much to me at all, and even when I said something to him, he mumbled back at me—saying things that didn't make sense. I figured he was mad at something, or as hungry as I was and maybe that's why he didn't feel like talking right then.

When we arrived at Fuddruckers, it was crowded just like always. I scanned the restaurant and the first thing I saw was the ever-present Elvis Presley replica, and a long line of teens, young adults, and families eager to place their orders. When Stevie Wonder's *For Once in My Life* thumped from several mounted speakers, I found myself twisting my butt and bobbing my head.

We placed our order, were issued an electronic pager with the number 79, and found our seats. As soon as I sat down, I got back up to get us some straws, a plastic knife, and, most important, a dozen napkins. That's how big and sloppy my burger would be.

We hadn't been there a good ten minutes when Daddy casually pointed toward the entrance. "There's Aaron."

"Who?" I asked, like I forgot who my boyfriend was. Sure enough, Aaron Oliver had stepped inside the restaurant. It must have just started raining, because he was shaking water from a long black umbrella. He craned his neck like he was looking for somebody. I ducked in my seat, hoping to see nothing, yet anxious to see something. I wished I were invisible, but I'd learned early on that wishes hardly ever come true.

Daddy had the gumption to stand up and wave. I like to died. He was messing everything up. Nobody will cheat if they know somebody is looking. Apparently, Dad wasn't hip on how to play the game.

Aaron walked toward our table in a confident stride, but the second he noticed me, it looked as if his legs were walking against tall, invisible ocean waves. He slowed his pace and looked directly at me, blinking rapidly, but not able to make my image go away.

You know when people are glad to see you, and you can damn sure tell when they're not. I noticed this rotten, punkish, awful smirk that only a man who's full of embarrassing regret can give. We hadn't seen, talked, or kissed each other in I don't know when, and that's the best he could offer?

Once Aaron reached our table, he acted like Daddy was the only one in the whole room.

Aaron smiled and looked disgusted at the same time. "Mr. Hayes."

Daddy stood up like a meeting of some kind was about to start. I felt uncomfortable; nobody acknowledged me. Felt like I was intruding, and I hadn't done anything except be there.

I looked at Aaron and forced a smile of greeting, but it was wasted effort. He never looked at me once. Just stared at Daddy something strange. Looked at him like he was the only thing he wished he could see.

I rose to my feet.

"Did they beep our number yet? I'm starving."

"Go and see what's taking so long. I know we got here before those people, and they're eatin' already. Go on, Lauren," Daddy said rushing me off with his hands.

My droopy eyes suddenly popped open like a trunk, acutely awakened by the smell of raw onions. I waved my electronic pager in the cashier's face. She yelled to the back, and soon a uniformed employee handed me a plastic tray with our food.

I returned to the table, wanting to rush, yet taking my time. Aaron was bent over the table, leaning toward Daddy. The lines that appeared in Aaron's face told me he didn't like what he was hearing. I started to go sit at an empty table, but Daddy turned and saw me and waved me over with his hands.

"Girl, I paid for that food, you better bring me my dinner," he complained reaching toward his burger. I snatched back the tray. His hands flailed the air and he couldn't help but laugh.

One bite into my thick, juicy, delicious smelling burger, and I was ready to forgive the network for yanking *The Wayans Brothers* off the air.

"Aaron, what made you come here tonight?" I asked after sipping some soda.

He looked at my dad but didn't say anything.

"Why you looking at Daddy? What's up with—"

"I asked him to come," Daddy said with lifeless eyes.

As juicy as my burger was, right then it tasted like a jar of flour.

"For what?" I wanted to know.

Daddy lifted his sandwich and talked to it like I was inside the bun.

"He needs to tell you something, Lauren."

"Hey, can't this wait? Let her eat first," Aaron pleaded.

Aaron looked sick. But then again, "peculiar" may be an even better description. Eyes were red, face ashy, his fingers drumming the tabletop, really getting on my nerves.

"Okay, as you wish," Daddy replied, and shook his head like a hundred-year-old regret.

I averted my eyes, trying to keep Aaron from chasing me with his odd-looking stares. I felt resentful, worried even. Why here? Why now? Whatever happened to Southwestern Bell? My number hadn't changed.

He watched me eat, tapping his foot on the floor. Whether the rhythm was to the beat of the music or to his own anxiety, I really couldn't tell.

With my burger being three-fourths gone and root beer now sipped down to ice water, I wiped my mouth with a napkin and asked, "What's wrong, Aaron?"

My dad rose from the table and shuffled about to

linger a couple of tables over. Once he was out of listening range, Aaron cleared his throat and reached across the table to grab my rigid hands.

"Lauren?"

He sighed and his eyes dropped downward.

"Spit it out, Aaron."

"Lauren, uh, I don't know how to say this other than to say it. We're going to have to stop seeing each other."

"Oooohhhh, nooooo. Nooooo," I shook my head, wanting to snatch back my hands, but Aaron held them in a tight grip.

"Yes, Lauren, yes," he said to me and managing to still look at me without dropping his gaze. "I know you won't understand right now, but we gotta break it . . . off."

"No, no, we don't."

"Yes, we do."

"Mmmmm, no," I wailed.

"Lauren, you're not listening, but you'd better, because I'm serious about what I've said. Not a joke, it's for real."

"But . . . what do you mean, 'gotta,' like you have no choice?"

The music was still thumping, folks still yapping, and I wished I could be swallowed up deep inside the noise, becoming a forgotten melody.

I recognized Daddy across the way and wanted to make some type of visual contact, but tonight his eyes were hidden and unavailable, blinded by the pain of a daughter's heart.

"Well, if I had all the time in the world to try and explain things to you, you still probably wouldn't understand. Just trust me that this is real, it's happening, it's right now, and there's not anything that can be done about it."

"But why so extreme? I mean, is this like temporary or permanent? You never, ever want to get back with me?"

"Lauren, don't even try to figure it out because I don't think you can. I just need you to accept this. Please don't question it. Please?"

"Well, how did Daddy know about this? I mean, I don't get it."

"And you won't get it," he said.

I felt like I was suffocating, like his mouth was a vacuum that consumed my sensibilities. Didn't seem possible that Aaron would say those things to me, yet I couldn't deny what I knew I heard.

"So what does this mean?"

"Lauren, we'll still be friends."

"How can you tell me we'll still be friends? Like that means something?"

"Hey, I'm just trying to help—"

"Your help feels like hurt."

My freaking lips started trembling like I gave them permission or something. Didn't mean to, but hurt has a mind of its own. I started sputtering and choking away tears right there in the restaurant. By then Daddy had returned to my side, and he asked Aaron to leave. My brand-new ex-boyfriend shrugged his shoulders, jammed his umbrella under his arm, and walked away without even saying "Thanks for the memories."

For the longest I couldn't even look at my dad. Wished he had gone away too, and left me there to suffer alone. But he refused to leave. Daddy sat next to me and stroked my arm and shoulder. I sat rigid, thinking and rethinking everything I could have done wrong that had brought on Aaron's decision. I felt so humiliated. How could I tell Regis? My mom? Who else would understand such pain? Pain that didn't make sense.

Daddy may not have been a woman, but that night I felt he somehow understood.

21
Tracey

It was Thursday, the day before Christmas Eve, and a few days since Aaron gave Lauren her walking papers. It was a little past twilight, and I had just gotten back from a day at the mall. Found some to-die-for Liz Claiborne pumps for myself, and bought a new juicer for Indira.

Lauren was home. She hadn't slept well all that week. Stayed up till three in the morning listening to music, weeping, and hugging her pillow. I wanted to come to her, but didn't know what to say. All Lauren told me was "we broke up." Never said anything else. I didn't ask either. So we stayed out of each other's way. But on Thursday, I called Aaron on his cell phone. I was in my walk-in closet on the far side of the apartment.

"Where are you, Aaron?"

"In the neighborhood."

"Are you really?"

"Yep, I'm at Best Buy on South Gessner, checking out CDs."

"You and those CDs."

"Hey, I just bought some Master P. May I swing by and kick it with you, maybe listen to some sounds?"

"No, better not."

"Why not? Lauren there?"

"You got it. She basically stayed up all night and most of the morning. Right now she's knocked out and dead to the world."

"Good. I'm coming over," he said firmly.

"No," I told him with a firmness of my own.

"Yes, I just paid for my CD and I'm walking to my car right now. I can be there in two, three minutes."

"Oh, you."

He laughed. "Y-you miss me?"

"Mmmm, don't ask stupid questions."

"Hey, won't be long now. Look out the window and I'll be over sooner than you think."

I rushed to Lauren's room, careful to open her door without making any noise. A couple of pillows were positioned on her head. I heard her inhaling deep, uneven breaths. My heart melted and I stepped back out of the room. I knew Aaron's coming by was risky, yet I wanted to see him. I hoped the visit would be brief; maybe sneak a kiss or two, and then send him on his way.

When Aaron arrived, I didn't let him ring the bell. I saw him coming and opened the door before he got upstairs. He walked through the entrance wearing one gold stud in his left ear, a gold silk shirt, and a tan pair of slacks, the kind where the belt falls below the waist.

He smiled at me, I at him. The moment our finger-tips touched, Aaron drew me into his arms. Standing in the living room, I let him hold me around my waist for a second, but I shook my head wildly and nodded toward my daughter's room. He grimaced, but wrapped his arms around my shoulders, his strong hands forcing me snug against his chest.

Aaron was so near, I pressed my nose against his shirt. He smelled *sooo* good, like a man with excellent grooming should. He smiled at me with encouragement. Kissed me twice right beneath my ear. His lips were wet. My knees buckled. I thought for a second, drew one finger to my lips, then grabbed his right hand and squeezed.

He shuddered, nodded. Obeyed, followed me. Once we were inside my bedroom, I locked the door. Aaron pushed his hands against me. I fell on my bed. While I lay there staring, I noticed Aaron's manhood grow rock-hard against his slacks. The bulge looked as thick as a dill pickle sitting in a jar full of juice.

He climbed in bed with me. At first he crawled on top, but I entwined my legs between his like a human octopus and threw him on his back. We started kissing, sucking each other's tongues and lips, and running our hands over each other's body parts. I went for his chest and legs, he caressed my breasts and behind.

Kissing everything, lips, noses, cheeks, and eyelids.

"Mmmm, I missed you, A," I whispered.

"Same here," he whispered and then put his hands inside my panties, and rubbed between my legs. Patting softly, rubbing gently.

"Mmm," I moaned and bit my bottom lip.

He stopped rubbing and stared at me, his mouth open.

"What?" I whispered, alarmed. I placed his hand back between my legs.

"Can I have some?" he asked in a voice so drenched with desire, no way I could say no.

First I listened for any sounds outside the door. Hearing nothing, I sighed real deep. My panties were saturated and felt uncomfortable. I removed my sheer stockings and panties, but kept on my coat dress. He unzipped his pants, pulled down his tan Joe Boxers. I stood up and went to lean against the far wall of my bedroom. Aaron planted wet kisses on my neck, then sucked on me like I was the last lollipop in a five-and-dime. When I stopped panting long enough to unbutton and open my dress, his lips abandoned my neck and started doing a number on my tingling breasts. After sucking my sensitive nipples right through the fabric, he had mercy on me and unlatched my bra, and resumed his oral dance on my bosom. Aching with extreme desire, I thrust my breasts against his eyes, nose, and mouth.

I felt irrational, but my desire urged me to keep going. Convincing myself this could be over in minutes and then Aaron could leave, I blocked all distractions from my mind.

I was so hot for Aaron. I felt an urging building inside my loins, my desire pulsating with great intensity. Hot became scorching. Our hands were fire. I caressed his firm muscles, tracing my fingers over his skin, rubbing him like he was my baby, but wanting him to be my man.

Once he rolled on a condom, he pulled up my dress and exposed all my desire. Then he entered me and kept thrusting and thrusting and jabbing me so hard that tears formed in the corners of my eyes. But I decided not to stop his flow, let him do his thing, and I got weaker and weaker, wanting to slide down the wall onto the floor. But Aaron held me up, lifting one of my legs and getting positioned just right, dead center inside of me. I could tell by all those horrid, ago-

nizing faces he was making that he wanted to come
and so did I, but our bodies remained latched together so tight you'd have to call in the love police to
pull us off each other.

"Aaron?" I whispered.

"What?"

"Do me, go down on me *right now*. I've mowed my
lawn."

"Okay," he whimpered.

I sprawled on the floor and parted my legs for
Aaron like he was standing in front of the Red Sea. He
bent over me, first placing sweet kisses on my stomach.
Then he dove between my thighs and moved his way
downtown. I could feel the heat of his breath on my
pubic hairs, and even though I was already lying down,
I still could have fainted at the thought of what he was
about to do to me.

I was already wet, but once his tongue nuzzled me,
licked, kissed, and sucked me like he knew the true value
of a tongue, even more of my body's juice squirted out.

"Ahhhh, oh my Lord," I squealed, like I was in
shock. He maintained a slow but firm pace, taking
twenty minutes to build me up. I kept thinking, *Where
is Lauren?* but then whimpered, "Ahhh, ooohhhhh,
mmmmm." I clutched both his ears like they were
motorcycle handles and I was going for a wild and
dangerous ride.

"Shhh," he said, but I could feel my orgasm mount-
ing.

Aaron's tongue was like a precise paintbrush. His
tongue probed deeper between my legs, slicking me,
and flicking my most sensitive parts. Each stroke sent a
wave of tremors through my body that felt so good I almost scraped the color off his skin. One final lick and
I lost it.

"Ahhhhhhh, ahhhhhhh, ahhhhhhh." My scream-ing jumped five octaves. I *was* Mariah Carey, dammit. He cupped his hand over my mouth and widened his eyes like Gator in the movie *Jungle Fever.* When he heard the doorknob rattle, he jerked his head toward the sound. I was thinking, *What the door got to do with this? Don't look at the door, look at* me, *dammit.* That thang ripped through me so hard I started screaming inside his hand, wanting to sink my teeth into it. I twisted and turned and hunched my butt up and down as the orgasm tortured my body like flammable electricity. My legs thrashed and knocked against the floor, and I couldn't believe I was actually crying, cry-ing like someone had died, weeping like I was releas-ing a burden.

"Mom, are you okay?" we heard her voice slice through the door.

"Oh, hell." Aaron sprung to his feet, sucking mas-sive pockets of air, the color draining from his face while his eyes darted from wall to wall like he didn't know where he was. He folded his penis inside his drawers. I wanted to get up but couldn't. I was limp and damn near motionless, legs stretched east and west, mind woozy, my body still going through after-shocks as I fought to recover from what Aaron had just done to me.

"Mom?" she yelled louder.

"I'm okay," I sniffed. I could only lift my head a cou-ple inches before letting it drop against the floor.

Aaron sat next to me, looking like he needed writ-ten instructions. I wanted to laugh. Don't know why I was so calm. Maybe it's because I felt confident that a closed door would shield me.

She rattled the doorknob again. "Mom, I'm about to come in there." Aaron dove headfirst under the bed. I struggled to stand, but flopped down on my butt with a pitiful "Ugh."

Lauren opened the door, smiling and waving a butter knife.

"Aaron taught me how to break into locks like these," she said.

There I was, sitting on the floor next to my bed, dress unbuttoned, titties flopping, wearing no panties, sex milk dripping out of my body, my daughter's ex-boyfriend inches away with both of his feet poking from underneath the bed, and I'm speechless while she's smiling at me and wielding a butter knife.

Once Ms. Lockbuster stopped grinning long enough to see what she was looking at, time felt like it took a smoke break. She narrowed her eyes at me, and I don't know if it was because she saw my private parts or because they saw her, but it sure didn't matter at that point. Her eyes darkened, then she turned and faced the door.

"Mom, what's that smell?" she called over her shoulder. "What are you *doing*?"

"Lauren, get out."

"You don't have to worry about that. I just want to know what's going on. Do you have company up in here?"

"I—I need you to leave, not just the room, but the apartment. Give me fifteen minutes and then you can come back. No more questions, just go."

"Nasty thang," I heard her mumble, and she left the room, slamming the door.

After Aaron crawled from underneath the bed, neither he nor I said anything for a good ten and a half minutes. I stared at the door, trying to regain normal thoughts and breathing.

I felt so ashamed, so out of control. I wondered if my lust was worth all the risk of trying to hide my ways.

Aaron zipped his slacks. Tucked in his shirt. I knew he wanted to get the hell out of there. His pacing and swearing told me that much. But he stooped next to me and caressed my shoulder.

"You all right, Trace?"

"Mmmm-hmmm."

"You want me to leave?"

"Mmmm-hmmm. No, well, yeah, you need to—to go. I'll catch up with you later."

"You think it's safe?" he asked.

"I don't have the foggiest idea. I asked her to leave, but she may be nearby trying to see what's up. Ain't no telling. If she knows you're in here, I can't even imagine what's going to happen. Damn!"

Aaron moaned. I felt like I'd wounded the two people I should have cared about the most. Blamed myself. I should learn when to say no and what to say no to. But I hadn't thought long enough about what might happen. My heart felt heavy, swollen with regret. I didn't want to lose Lauren, but I didn't want to lose Aaron, either. Why did I have to choose between the two?

"Well, I don't know where she is right now, but regardless, I'm about to break outta here. Going home. Need to think," he told me, and made a move toward the door.

He didn't wait for me to say my parting words. Just left. Hearing the door close, I froze, anticipating the sounds of despair, accusations or discovery of betrayal. But I heard nothing except the constant hammer of guilt inside my own heart.

*   *   *

I clung to my room for a whole lot longer than fifteen minutes. When I was finally courageous enough to poke my neck out the bedroom door, Lauren still hadn't returned. I was relieved more than anything else. Still couldn't find words to explain what had happened, and was becoming more confused by the minute. So I got dressed. Forget taking a shower. I hauled my funky and humiliated butt into the car and called Indira from my cell phone.

"Hello," she answered.

"What are you doing?" I mumbled, grimacing at how slimy my fresh underwear felt.

"Looking at BET movies."

"Anything good on?" I asked.

"This movie called *Kappaccino* is airing."

"Oh yeah? What's the movie about?"

"It's a movie about this fraternity guy who writes a movie—"

"Indira, I hate to cut you short, but girl, can we meet right now?"

"Dang, don't even give me a chance to . . . oh, I guess so. What's up?"

I felt so selfish, but when you feel selfish, apathy is not far behind. I decided to give her my pitiful-sounding voice.

"I—I just need to talk to somebody *really bad*. I'll even pick you up. No, no, could you meet me somewhere? What about, oh Jesus, how about that all-you-can-eat Chinese food joint right across from me? Southwest Freeway and Bissonnet?"

"Dang, Tracey, that's quite a little drive from here." Her voice was laced with agitation.

"Okay, well, never mind. Forget I ever asked."

"All right, all right, Tracey, dang. I'll be there, but I know you'll beat me."

"I don't care if you're late, as long as you show up. I *really, really, really* need to talk to somebody."

She softened. "And you got somebody. I'll be there as soon as I can."

I sighed and rubbed my neck. It was almost eight-thirty.

Where was Lauren?

King Bo restaurant was hopping with activity, probably filled with folks who'd been out shopping that day and who were too lazy to cook. The host smiled a greeting and led me to a table near the buffet. For a while I sat in my seat in a daze, not even bothering to swipe a peek at the grimy-looking menu.

Indira didn't take as long as I thought she would. I had been sitting at our table approximately twenty minutes before she showed up.

"You must have broke the speed limit to get here, girl," I said, watching her limp toward our table.

"That's not the only thing I broke," she said pointing at her toe and wincing.

"I'm sorry. You know how things can be."

"Don't I, though?" she grunted. She set her purse on top of the table and lifted her foot.

"Ouch," she winced. "It's not broke, just twisted my ankle running in here from the parking lot."

I felt real bad then; not too many people would come and see somebody when they didn't feel like it, and especially if they had to get injured in the process. My heart softened, and I smiled at her.

"So, girl," she said, surveying the restaurant. "You didn't start eating yet?"

"Not really. Waiting for you. I just ordered two sweet teas with lemon."

"Cool. Let's go check out the buffet, then we can talk."

We loaded our plates with the typical fried rice, pepper steak, veggie foo yung, and some other stuff that looked safe but I couldn't pronounce.

"Girl," I told her, "I'm so hungry I could bring down a rhinoceros with my bare teeth."

Indira grinned at me and picked at her entrées. I'd forgotten she wasn't too crazy about Chinese cuisine, but would indulge if there was nothing better to eat.

"Okay, Miss Tracey Davenport. Why you have me meet you all the way out here?"

"Girl, Aaron and I had a close call today."

She set down her fork and leaned in. "Oh yeah?"

"I don't know what my problem was, but he called and told me he was in the area and wanted to come by. I was like 'Okay.' Well, girl, when he walked through the door, it was like Brian McKnight was saying, 'Here's your one and only chance.' Not to tell all our business, but one thing led to another and—"

"Lauren busted y'all?"

"No, at least I don't think so. She walked in the bedroom and she saw something, but I don't think she saw everything. But I told her to leave and I haven't seen her since."

Indira leaned back in her chair, looking at me like she was trying to sort out everything I'd told her.

"Anyway, after that close call, I'm having some serious thoughts about what I'm getting myself into. I mean, I've never done anything like this before. It's not like I'm cheating with my next-door neighbor."

"Yeah," she agreed, still musing over my confession.

"But the good thing about it, if you want to put it that way, is that Aaron broke things off with her, so it doesn't seem as bad, but still, you know, she's not hip to the real reason why they're not together anymore."

She peered at me. "How's Lauren taking it?"

I paused before I spoke.

"She's holding it in, and I haven't been an ounce of help to her. If it had been any other guy that disappointed her, I'd be right there, soothing her pain and talking to her about things, but I've been withdrawn and feeling really uncomfortable about the whole thing. I know it sounds strange, but this is some weird stuff. I don't know how to handle this."

"And you think I do?"

"Okay, Indira. I know you've never done a single thing wrong in your life, but for the regular folks who don't do everything perfect, this is a true dilemma."

"Well, Tracey, only thing I can see is that you can't be around Aaron anymore," she said, and picked up her glass of tea and swirled it around.

I frowned my disapproval. How could I have expected Indira to understand? Sometimes I felt having a friend in whom to confide was great, but if the sharing had something to do with a complex situation that they'd never before experienced, there was a risk. You'd either find out that the friend would support you no matter what you did, or you'd discover your differences, see how your values might clash, and sometimes friends have to withdraw their support, or lessen it.

"I guess by that little look, you're telling me you still want to be with this here chile," she asked in a loud voice.

I looked around the restaurant and leaned in.

"Could you Penn State your broadcaster voice, please?"

She turned red and gave me an "Oops."

"Indira, I guess you don't understand. I didn't think anybody would, but I was hoping—"

"Look, Tracey, it's not like I hear about things like this every day. I'm not Oprah, so don't expect me to have some miracle solution in twenty minutes' time," she said, snapping her fingers. "I don't know. I guess I'm trying to figure out—"

"Don't, Indy. You will not be able to figure this one out. I'm in it and *I* can't even figure it out."

"May I ask a personal question?" she whispered, her face turning a darker shade of red.

I nodded my approval.

"Okay, so you and he have been . . . intimate, but have he and, uh, uh . . ." she said, twirling her finger around so I could say the thing she didn't want to say.

"Lauren?"

"Yeah, have they done . . . anything?"

I shook my head for a short while, thought for a long while, and shook my head again. "I doubt it. I can't see it. I can't even see Aaron trying to sleep with both of us at the same time."

"But how do you know?" she asked.

"Look, Indira, believe me, you don't have to throw that in the pot as a way to get me to get away from Aaron. I don't know it for sure, but I don't think he's gone beyond kissing her, let alone screwing her."

"And what if he was . . . screwing her?" she said, rocking back and forth in her seat in a frenzy.

"What the hell could I do about it? Ain't nothing I could do about something like that. Except set it on fire. Castrate him. Toss that smoked sausage in the Gulf of Mexico."

Indira frowned. "Like that would solve things."

"Hey, Aaron's a grown man. I don't keep tabs on him. Although there are some times when I can't reach him, but that's pretty typical when it comes to dealing with some men."

"Oh yeah. What's been happening with that?"

"Well, sometimes he says he's going to call, but doesn't, or he promises to stop by, but I wait for him until I can't wait anymore."

"Uh-huh. You've never asked him why he does that?"

"What good would it do? It's not like I know if he's telling the truth or not. You know how some guys lie so much that it sounds like the truth even to themselves."

"So now what are you going to do?"

"I'm playing it by ear, Indira."

She ate a forkful of food and chased it with a long sip of tea. "What do you want from him exactly? That's the part I don't get."

"I knew you wouldn't get it, but thank you for not going completely off on me."

"Answer the question."

"Well, I want a chance to pursue this relationship. Maybe it's total selfishness, probably lust thrown in, too. Call it whatever you want. I want to just see this through till the end. Give myself a real chance to be with him, as friends, lovers, and wherever else it may lead. Just try it and see where it takes us."

"Hmmmm. Now if this Steve guy were still in the picture," she said, and wiggled one hand like she was holding a camera, "would you even give Aaron a second thought?"

"That's a non-question. If it weren't for Steve, I wouldn't be with Aaron in the first place, remember?"

"Huh?"

"This whole damned incident got started because Steve broke up with me."

"So you're getting Steve back by tagging Aaron on the rebound?"

"No, noooo, Indira. That sounds so tacky. I mean, I did not go out of my way to be with Aaron just to get back at Steve." I shrugged. "Just happened. Wasn't planned."

"And that's your excuse?"

"That's the truth." I didn't like the way Indira was looking at me, and I hopped up from my seat to fill my plate with seconds. I could feel her eyes boring into my back. Maybe I shouldn't have asked Indira to come meet me after all. Maybe I should have kept my secrets to myself. I knew she was my friend, but I also believed friendship only went so far. I wondered how far this one would go.

That night, When I lay my head on my pillow, insecurity was my bed buddy, and I hardly liked how that felt. The lights were out, the room as dark as blindness, and I still felt like a nation of people could see me. What would happen if Lauren had seen Aaron exiting our apartment? Would her female intuition clue her in on what's been going on? Maybe she'd seen him, but just hadn't said anything yet.

In denial.

I didn't know; didn't want to know.

22
Aaron

It was around nine o'clock in the evening and quite dark, but I knew Lauren's profile like it was daytime. She was standing in front of the Exxon station at the corner of Bissonnet and the Southwest Freeway. Even though I hadn't planned on getting any gas, I drove into the station and stopped right next to a pump. She still didn't see me. I grabbed my wallet from my back pocket and fished out a twenty-dollar bill. She was talking to the sales attendant through the station's window.

"How much will it cost for one jumbo Snickers, a big bag of Cheetos, the thick ones, not those undernourished ones, and a liter of root beer?"

The Iranian attendant rolled his eyes and started mumbling to himself.

I stepped up to the window. "Whatever she wants, ring it up. I got it."

She turned around and gave me an indignant sistergirl look, like who the hell did I think I was? Any other time I would have smiled and teased her. But I was

tired and still didn't know what she knew. So I gave
her a firm look and paid for both my gas and her stuff.

"What the hell you doing up here, Aaron?"

"Milking my cow, what it look like I'm doing?"

"Oh, why are you even talking to me? I'm history,
remember?"

"Lauren, just because we're not going together anymore doesn't mean I have to act ignorant."

She swiveled her neck and put her hand on her hip.
"How could you tell the difference?"

"Look, Lauren," I said in an even tone, "I'm trying
to be nice. Nobody owes you anything."

"Oh, I don't know if I agree with that," she replied,
and crossed her arms in front of her chest.

I held the bag of junk food toward her, but instead
of grabbing it, she stepped back and the bag went
crashing to the ground.

I sighed. "You lucky this soda isn't in a glass bottle.
Your ass would be cut by now."

"Oh, I don't think so," she laughed.

I started pumping fifteen bucks' worth of gasoline
in the Legend while she stood there looking at me all
crazy, like she just got back from a buy-one-get-one-free
crack sale. Her hair, which usually looked neat and so-
phisticated, appeared matted and soiled. Dozens of
strands were sticking out from underneath a bad-hair-
day cap. And even though she had on one of those
five-dollar Tweety Bird T-shirts that you get from the
flea market, her little shape still looked good. She had
nice hips, long legs, and ample breasts. Since I'd been
hanging with her mother, for some reason I'd forgotten what I'd ever seen in Lauren.

I swallowed the mild regret that filled my mouth.

"So, what are you doing out here?" I asked, as cool
as possible.

"Don't have a man anymore. What else am I supposed to be doing?"

"Acting pitiful doesn't impress me, Lauren. Be a strong woman, count your losses, and go on with your life."

"Count my losses? Count my— Well, what am I supposed to do after I get through counting them? Put 'em in alphabetical order?"

I gave her a blank look like, *Yep, she's a goner,* shook my head a couple times, then replied, "Look, this is nothing, Lauren. I don't know why you're out here tripping."

"Ugh! Aaron, how you can stand here and act like it's no big deal? I *do not* appreciate what you *did*. I mean, you come and tell me we can't be together anymore. No explanation, no freaking reason, like I'm supposed to sit up and just accept what you say, just like that. Just because you prefaced your request with a 'please'? *Pu-lease!*"

She started pacing around the car, waving her hands and walking around like everything would make sense if she heard it out loud. By then I'd finished pumping the gas. Just leaned against my car, arms crossed, watching her cut up like she was on camera.

"And another thing that was *really* messed up—I don't like that you *never* explained the reason for the breakup. In case you forgot, we dated for months, Aaron. I thought we were close, at least close enough for you to respect my feelings and to realize that shoving everything under a rug just won't do. I don't understand guys, but this silence crap, this I'm-dumping-you-take-it-or-leave-it attitude, ain't cutting it. I *demand* closure, or else this mess will be locked up inside me till Jesus comes back."

She started crying real hard after she said that. I

stepped up to Lauren and put my arms around her. She stiffened, but I grabbed her even more forcefully and pulled her against my chest. She hiccuped and sniffed and boo-hoo'd all over my favorite silk shirt.

"Lauren, Lauren, let's talk, okay?" She was covering her face by then, crying inside her hands. And I was getting flat-out sick of the onlookers who were peeping at us like we were actors on stage at a gospel play.

"Hey, Cool. Everything all right?" this boy stepped up to me and asked. Little man couldn't have been any older than twelve. I just gaped at him like "don't even go there." He backed off with his hands thrown up and went about his business.

Once Lauren's tears turned to sniffles, I got her to sit in my car. I fastened her seat belt because she was too involved with looking straight ahead like a mannequin, her attitude as cold as a corpse. My first mind told me to leave her ass in the parking lot, but I decided to drive her over to my place. On the way home I was hoping that Brad wouldn't be there. It would be difficult enough for me to try and explain things to Lauren without being forced to give him an account, too. When I pulled up in front of my place, the apartment looked midnight black. No lights on, no Brad.

Lauren trailed me inside the apartment. For some reason her stride and spirits picked up when she realized we were at my place. She came in smiling and began looking all around the living room, her eyes darting here and there like camera lenses. However, after giving the living room the once-over, her face returned to its gloomy look.

"Have a seat. You still want these Cheetos and soda?"

She sat at the bar. Signaled yes with her head.

I sat next to her. Folded my arms across my chest.

"Okay, Lauren. You're right. I—I should've given you a better explanation—"

"You didn't give me *any* explanation."

"Okay, I should give you some explanation because if I don't, you won't accept the fact that what happened *did* happen. Downsizing is a fact of life."

She was crunching on Cheetos and her face flinched at my words, but she kept chewing and wouldn't look at me.

After a momentary silence, she asked, "So, Mr. Boss Man, what else do you have to say for yourself?"

"What you want to know?"

"Why'd you do it?"

"Had to," was my speedy answer.

"But why, Aaron? Would you please answer the damn question and quit skirting the issue?"

"There's really not much to—"

"Aaron, cut the bull!"

"Okay, okay. The reason why . . . we broke up is because . . . I needed—I needed space."

"Space?"

"Space."

"That is *soooo* stupid. Where'd you get that one from?"

"I didn't get it—"

"Aaron, Aaron. Whether you admit it or not, you fired me for a reason, and I *will* know what it is before I leave tonight. As a matter of fact, why don't I help you out? Would you like for me to do that, huh? Need some help?"

She jumped up, grabbed two tumblers, and hurled them against the floor, a thousand splinters sounding like wind chimes scattering and decorating the linoleum. She better be glad I still had on my shoes.

"Damn, bitch."

"Hold up, you don't have to go there. Just tell the truth, and leave your bitches in your mouth."

I bent down and started picking up the largest pieces of glass, but I felt her hand brush aggressively against my back.

"That glass ain't going anywhere. Now stand up, be the man that you say you are, and tell me right now, what is your problem?" she ordered.

I jerked my shoulder and felt her hand drop. "Nooo, nooo, uh-uh, Lauren. You will not come up in my house tripping and breaking stuff. Who do you think you are?"

"Well, who do you think *you* are? Obviously you don't know *who the hell I am*, or else you wouldn't have *played me* like you did. Since you're too full of hell to tell me yourself why you did you what you did, I'll help you out. I know it has to do with another woman."

I just looked at her.

"Ummm-hummm. Didn't think I knew about it, did you?" she said.

I didn't say a word.

"Aaron, like I said before, I'm young, but I'm nowhere near as dumb as you think I am."

I lowered my eyes to the floor. Who was going to clean up all that broken glass?

"How come you aren't saying anything?" she asked. "Admit it, Aaron. Isn't that the reason? You aren't denying it, so it must be true," she said.

I caught that.

Must be.

She still didn't know jack.

She shut her eyes and screamed, "Answer me, Aaron."

All I had to do was whack her one good time and Lauren's head would've landed on Mars in record time. So she got dumped. What made her think she was so special? And that she had a right to reveal her Sheneneh side by taking her anger out on my kitchen floor?

I guess all Lauren's shouting was giving her some much-needed confidence, but I knew one thing, she'd better stop all that yelling like she was playing the slot machine at the damned casino.

"Lauren, chill. If you lower your voice, we'll talk. Please."

"I'm tired, Aaron. Tired of you stalling, tired of your lies. Why won't you just answer the question?"

"Okay, the hell with being nice. I'll answer. I wanted space so I could be with somebody else. Happy now?"

She growled and grabbed another glass. Raising it high in the air, she looked at me and smirked. I stepped up to her before she could start breaking stuff again.

"Lauren, I'm sorry, I'm really sorry about all this. But you know how things were going between us. I think, I don't know, I needed a more—someone who could meet my needs."

"I knew it. Regis told me you'd be out screwing someone else if you weren't screwing me," she said, lowering her hand.

"Why you listening to her? She doesn't know anything about me. She's never even met me."

"Then what's your excuse?"

"It wasn't just the sex part, Lauren. It was some other things, too. And for the record, I haven't screwed anybody else. I was just talking to this person on the phone. I didn't want to be with you and her at the same time knowing you wouldn't be down with that."

Her chest sank. And just like I thought it would happen, the thing she begged me to tell her was the thing she couldn't stand hearing. Women do that all the time. Beg you to tell them something, and when you do, they wish you'd never opened up your big mouth in the first place.

She covered up her ears and shook her head. "I don't believe this. I am not hearing this."

"Lauren, what's wrong now?"

"Don't piss on me and tell me it's raining."

"Tracey, I'm—"

"*Tracey?* As in my *mother*, Tracey?" she asked.

I threw up my hands and started walking toward the bedroom door.

"Aaron, get your narrow ass back here right now. I'm not done with you."

I swung around.

"Well, you know what? I'm tired of this back-and-forth shit and I'm done with *you*."

"No, you're *not*," she said.

Before I knew it, Lauren ran up to me and clasped her skinny little fingers around my throat.

"Ugh, uggh, what is your *problem?*" I tried my best to step back and loosen her fanatical grip. With tears popping in my eyes, I grabbed her hands and pried her fingers from around my throat, coughing and sputtering like I'd been trying to keep from drowning in an ocean. She looked at me, delirious, eyes blazing, face all bunched up like an escaped demonette.

Wished I had my dad's pistol. With gun in hand, I would've become the most meticulous troubleshooter she'd ever seen.

"Lauren, you've got to chill out. Get your ass up off me," I said, backing away from her. But the more I backed away, the more she stepped up to me, stabbing me in the chest with one pointed finger and increasing her frenzied tone.

"No, Aaron, you need to chill out because if you think you can come up here and tell me you ain't bumpin' some other girl, you're lying. And why'd you call me by my mom's name, huh? Y'all that tight now? She making you moan these days?"

"Shhhh! Could you lower your voice? I got neighbors," I pleaded.

"You *what?*"

I groaned and averted my eyes. Turned my back against Lauren and rubbed my sore and aching neck.

"Prick. Can't even face me. Acting like a little— ugh! I can't stand you. I hope you die and go to hell in a gas-filled eighteen-wheeler."

"Lauren, you don't have to go there. We can talk about this—"

"What's there to talk about? *You* screwing somebody, my *momma* screwing somebody. *Everybody* screwing and enjoying themselves, but all I'm getting is *screwed.*"

"Lauren, you're tripping. If you would just take a seat and calm down—"

"Look, I don't ever want to see you again, in this life or the next. And I know I won't have to worry about bumping into you in heaven, 'cause ain't no way they letting your lying ass up in there."

Damn! I felt like mucho mega shit!

I couldn't believe this was the day before Christmas Eve. Supposed to be chilling out, being happy, and looking forward to peace on earth, goodwill toward men. Here I was sitting up at eleven-something at night, wondering how to get this lunatic teenager under control so I could have peace in my apartment, let alone on earth.

I was sitting on one end of the couch, she was sitting on the other, defiant legs crossed, mouth rigid, back pressed against the cushions like she was some kind of security guard.

My eyes fluttered and I yawned. "Lauren, it's getting late. Let me take you home."

"I'm not *going* home."

"Well, you don't have to go home, but you got to get the hell up out of here."

"Nope, not going."

"Look, get gone, bit—"

She uncrossed her legs. "I *told* you not to *call* me *that*."

"Stop *acting* like that."

"Stop *doing* things that *make* me *act* like *that*." She moved her head with every word she emphasized, like her feelings were attached to her neck or something, and if she didn't do the head-motion thingy, then I might not understand.

"Look, don't blame me for your insaniac ass. Nobody's making you do anything, Lauren."

"Aaron, why'd you have to go and do something stupid and mess everything up just so you can talk to some other girl? Who is this girl, huh?" she whined. "What's her name?"

"Even if I knew, I wouldn't tell you."

"What do you mean, even if you knew? See, that's what I'm talking about. Why are you lying? If you wouldn't lie, I wouldn't be acting like this, Aaron."

"I didn't mean that. I meant it's just someone—"

"How can you cover for some girl that you just met?"

I averted my eyes.

"We were tight all that time, and it's like it counted for nothing. That's bull, Aaron."

"Okay, what do you want? What do you want me to say? I'm trying to be patient with you. You've come in here yelling and breaking stuff. I don't understand what your problem is," I said.

"If you don't understand, then you don't need to understand. This stuff is elementary, Aaron. Hell, it's *pre-K*. One, I cared about you. Two, you promised me that you'd take that rain check. And three, Christmas is two days from now, but our so-called relationship is almost nonexistent. It's all messed up. Can't you understand that?"

"Okay, yes, the timing sucks, but—"

"Oh, I get it, you'd rather be with her than me on Christmas," she said.

"Lauren, you weren't going to be in Houston anyway, remember?"

"Oh, how convenient, Aaron. How freaking convenient," she said, and started clapping her hands.

I could tell we weren't getting past "Go" with our conversation. Treading the same old ground and stuck in the same old place. Damn, if I had some TNT I would've blasted her butt clear across the Southwest Freeway. I needed to think of a way to get her to leave.

Twenty minutes later, and after a few more insults courtesy of Lauren, I noticed that it had started raining. I could hear the noisy pelting of raindrops on the roof. I tried to catch Lauren's attention, but she was making yawny-sleepy faces and stretching her arms.

"You ready to go home yet, Lauren? I know your mom's probably worried about you."

"Who cares?"

"You want me to call your dad and ask him to pick you up?"

"Nope, I don't," she said with drowsy eyes and a couple of neck-snaps.

"So when do you plan to make your way back home, huh?" I asked in a polite voice.

"When I get good and ready, that good enough for you?" came her toxic reply.

"Okay, I know what's up, Lauren." I stood up. "If you want me to say I screwed up, okay, I'll say it. I screwed up. Happy now?"

A small grin tugged at the corner of her mouth. She was still yawning her butt off, knew she was about to pass out from sleep, but kept trying to fight it like it was twelve noon.

"That's better. Aaron, may I ask you a question?"

My legs froze.

"What?"

"May I have a kiss for old times' sake?"

"Wh—"

"Pretty please. Let me have a kiss and then you can drive me home."

I tugged at my ear and went and stood in front of her.

She grabbed me around my waist, hugging real tight. I waited to see if I could feel a knife piercing me in the side. I couldn't, so I hugged her back. Not tightly, but enough for her to know I still had a heart.

Then she looked up at me, all Bambi-eyed, her mole looking sexy as ever, and she brushed her lips against mine. I didn't respond much, just a smidgen. Enough so that she wouldn't cop an attitude and get mad again.

I felt her resolve melt under my mere response. Lauren blushed, looking at me like I was her best friend. Even giggled. She probably was very sleepy, or hallucinating that a kiss meant I was going to get back with her. At any rate, I was relieved when she released her claws from my neck and grabbed her purse. She started walking toward the door and stopped to tell me, "Hey, Aaron, I didn't mean to break all your glasses, but you gotta understand how I was feeling at the time. This isn't easy for me to handle; I never really saw our breakup coming."

I just nodded and scooped up my car keys, which were lying on the breakfast bar. I heard the splattering of rain outside my window. The night had an eerie quietness that hovered over the building.

Lauren went to open the front door. She was still talking as she stepped outside. "I wish we could have talked out our problems before you decided—"

As soon as she walked out the door, I slammed it, and secured all three locks. I slid my back against the door, sitting down on the floor, listening to her on the other side.

"Aaron, Aaron? What the hell you doing?"

I heard the sound of her fists pounding against the door.

"Open the door. Did you know it's raining out here?" she yelled.

I closed my eyes, lowered my head, and prayed real hard, asking God to forgive me for this one. In my book, Lauren had shown her true self tonight, and as far as I was concerned, I never wanted to see it again.

23
Tracey

Christmas Eve.

I basically slept the night away, warding off torturous dreams. Kept seeing buckets of rain in my dream, hard rain that kept coming and coming. Thunder and lightning invaded my mind, too. When I awoke, it was almost 7:00 A.M. The rain had stopped in my dream, but not in real life. Water was streaming down the window. I shivered. Felt a little bit cold, so I got up and turned up the thermostat.

When I went to check on Lauren, I saw her knocked out, spread across her bed facedown with her clothes still on. She looked like death, so I walked toward her and knelt close to her mouth. The moment I heard the faint sound of her breathing, I raised my face to the heavens. I knew that she'd be leaving for College Park tonight. Her plane would take off at eight-thirty and she'd land at Hartsfield International two hours later.

It had been a horrendous week, and I was very eager for Lauren to get out of town. Seemed like when she was there, when she was close by, I couldn't think straight. If she went away, maybe that would give me a chance to step back and evaluate everything that was going on. Nothing could happen as long as she was there.

I tinkered around the house, feeling like I was just going through the motions. I made a cup of hot apple cider and tried to look at the morning news, but all the television anchors started getting on my last nerve with their I-get-paid-mucho-money-to-grin-like-this smiles, so I chopped off the news right when the weather segment began to air.

I knew that Aaron told me he'd come and spend time with me, and I started wishing tomorrow would get here already. I knew we were going to exchange gifts, too. He'd told me he'd changed his mind about giving Lauren her present, and I didn't know what to say about that one, so I kept my mouth shut. Felt like an airhead in a way, still unable to completely reconcile everything that was happening. But that's one reason why both Aaron and I were glad Lauren was going out of town. We craved the privacy, time and space to talk everything through.

The ringing of the phone pierced the air.

"Hello!" I answered without enthusiasm.

"Hello there."

Derrick.

I didn't say anything.

"Well, I thought you'd be up. That's why I'm calling so early." He sounded apologetic.

"Ummm-hmmm. Is there an emergency of some sort?" I asked.

He laughed like I was way off base.

"No, Tracey. Just wanted to touch base regarding Lauren. Is she up yet?"

"Uh, no. Still asleep. You need to talk to her? I'll wake her up." I yawned and started walking toward Lauren's bedroom.

"No, no, don't do that. I guess I can get with her later. You know, with it being her first time flying alone, she might be nervous."

"Oh, she'll be all right. People fly solo all the time," I replied, and stared down the clock on the stove.

"I know that, Tracey, but still . . . maybe you could encourage her and help her to feel comfortable about flying."

"Uh, well, okay, whatever. So you want to call her later on this morning? Say around eleven?"

"Sounds good. And how are you doing today, Tracey? Glad to be off?"

He always did remember that I have a week off at Christmas.

"Yeah, I ain't complaining. Some people's jobs only let them off today, and then they'll be back at work on Monday."

"I know that's right. Like me, I'll be working like a slave today. So, uh, are we both on the same page as far as you taking Lauren to the airport?"

"Yes, Derrick. I'm still the designated driver." I sighed. I hate telling people things they already know. Why bother?

"And I'll pick her up on January third, ten-fifteen, at Hobby?"

"Yes, Derrick."

"Okay, uh, I'll let you go back to whatever you were doing. And I guess I'll talk to you later, with your fine self."

"Fine? Yeah, right," I said in a bored tone.

"Tracey, why the sarcasm? I really meant that. You need to learn how to accept a compliment."

"Derrick, I'll accept your compliment for the trap that it is."

"Aw heck, being nice to you is as pointless as shaving a bald head. Can't say I didn't try."

"You could say it if you really tried hard enough," I laughed. "Hmmm, anyway, I'll let you go," he said, with hurt woven in his voice.

"Yeah, let me go." I hung up.

Whatever.

I stuck around the house for as long as I could stand, but at around 10:00 A.M., my daughter was still asleep. I grabbed the phone, hid myself inside the walk-in closet, and called Aaron. "Hello? Lauren?"

Aw, hell. It was that roommate of Aaron's. What's-his-face.

"Oh no, it's not Lauren. You must have caller ID." Damn, caller identifi-fucking-cation.

"You got it," the smiling voice said.

"Well, is Aaron available?" my fake-happy voice responded.

"Nope, he's out and about right now."

"Oh, hmmm!" I murmured, lost in thought.

"Hey, is Lauren okay?"

"Yeah, as far as I know," I said, with no certainty in my voice.

"Good. I was sort of worried about her. She was shaken up last night."

"And how would you know that?"

"Oh, that's right, you must've been asleep when I dropped her off. Well, she was—uh, she was over here last night, and I—I gave her a ride home."

"Lauren? Over there?"

"Uh, yeah," I heard him force out his answer.

"What was she doing over there?" I asked, gripping the phone.

"Hey, that's not for me to say, but I'll let Aaron know you called, all right, Miss Tracey?" He hung up in my face before I could reply. I stood clutching the phone in my hand, wondering if I should even believe a word that what's-his-face said. Started to try and reach Aaron on his portable, but instead disconnected the line and got dressed.

The mall was congested as soon as I turned into the parking lot. I had to drive from row to row, waiting for a space to open up. When one finally did, I zipped into my spot and rushed in the mall, making my way through the throng of last-minute shoppers, mostly middle-aged men, looking haggard and stroking their beards or their foreheads.

"Y'all shouldn't have waited till the last minute," I said to no one in particular, trying to rush past a few men who were lingering outside Zales jewelry store.

Foley's looked as dazzling as ever. Red and white decorations brimming with holiday cheer hung from the ceiling, spreading tantalizing sights, alluring smells, and mellow but festive sounds throughout the store.

"I don't have the foggiest idea why I'm here," I murmured to myself. I was now in the shoe department. As usual, many female shoppers were located strategically throughout the area. Most stood dangling one or two shoes in one hand; the other hand rested on their hip, their faces wearing the look of forced patience.

I searched throughout the department, but didn't see him. Wasn't surprised. Thought he might have been there, but for all I knew he'd be on vacation that day.

Spotting another employee who was busy ringing up a sale, I walked up to her.

"Excuse me," I said.

"Be with you in a minute," she replied, her eyes never leaving the cash register.

"This'll only take a minute," I insisted.

She looked up.

"Oh, really? Well, tending to my *customer* will take *five* minutes. First *come,* first *served.*"

She said "served" real loud, like I was either mentally retarded or spoke English as a second language. The woman who was being waited on fake-smiled at me and patted her four boxes of shoes. I shook my head and backed away, my rear making contact with another customer.

"Oh, sorry," I mumbled in embarrassment, then looked up at my victim.

Lelani.

She made an I-can't-stand-you face, lips twisting as if she'd tasted poison.

"I *know* you aren't up here in Foley's," she told me.

"How could you know that I'm not here when you're standing here looking right at me?"

"Oh, bitch, you know exactly what I'm talking about."

I flinched. "Listen, Lani. If you call me anything, call me by my name."

"Oops," she laughed. "I thought I did . . . *bitch.*"

My purse hit the floor. "Look, I'm about as sick of you—"

"And I'm sick of *you.* A long time ago, I told you to get a life. Why you keep chasing the man?" she said in a loud, irritated voice.

"I'm not chasing the man."

"Then what're you doing up here at Steve's job? Passing out gospel tracts?"

I looked at her dumbfounded.

"Steve told me you've been harassing him, and that

he's warned you at least two times to leave him alone. I guess you don't believe fat meat's greasy."

The fact that Steve acted like he was still interested in me, but could diss me to someone like Lani, infuriated me. It was as if he'd invited Lani in our bed, pulled back the covers, and patted a space for her to occupy. As far as I was concerned, it was a space that didn't hold enough room for both her and me.

"I don't care what Steve said, I know for a fact he'd still want to talk to me."

"Look, I don't have to convince you that Steve is not even *thinking* about your crusty ass. Leave him alone, 'cause he ain't got time for you. Take a hint: *he don't want ya.*"

She opened up her coat and gave me a hardened look.

"He wants us," she announced with an I-know-you-can-see-it-and-you'd-better-believe-it expression on her face.

I looked inside her coat.

Lelani's belly was shaped like she'd swallowed a watermelon.

Steve's watermelon.

In many people's lives, there's a time when a defining moment arrives. It sneaks up on you most of the time because you're not expecting it, not really wanting it to appear. But this time around, the definition was too loud for me not to hear, too big for me not to see. And looking at Lelani, really *looking* at her and what her protruding belly represented, made me face yet one more sad reality. Why had I even come to Foley's? Why had I convinced myself I was over him, but was still trying to hold on, as if I had anything solid to hold on to? I needed to get this Steve situation settled and be done. Call it for what it was, so that both Steve and me knew.

Since looking at Lelani, any parts of her, hurt like hell, I veered my eyes to a nearby shoe display and asked in a crisp voice, "Is he here?"

"What you want with him?" she asked with a smile that sounded as if she were enjoying herself.

I casually picked up a taupe-colored three-inch-heeled pump and turned it to its bottom, like Lani standing before me didn't affect me. "It's personal."

"He's probably out in the mall, at a jewelry store . . . buying a ring . . . for the mother of his child."

I cringed and threw the shoe on the table. I faced the one woman who somehow always seemed to play a role in a movie that I didn't care to be part of.

"You can save that one," I told her. "Steve's not the type to get married, even if you were stupid enough to get pregnant."

"Look, I don't need you to advise me about my life with Steve. I don't know what he ever saw in you in the first place. You're not all that. No class, desperate acting, can't-get-your-own-man-always-gotta-go-after-somebody-else's-man type of bitch."

If Lani didn't have on all those gold chains, my hands could have easily fit around her neck. But instead of going postal, I exhaled deeply and thought about what she said. Her words, specifically the part about me always having to go after someone else's man, made me feel like I had no place to lay my head. Like I didn't have an advocate. And as much as I wanted to prove that woman wrong, to act the fool with her, word for word, I turned and walked away.

I got in my car and drove toward Katy, a suburb on the west end of Houston. I was just driving, not wanting to stop anywhere. Wishing I was anywhere except where I was. The rain was still coming down from the sky, a menagerie of gray smoke. I drove until I was so far out that the surroundings seemed foreign. I thought that if I were somewhere unfamiliar, the break from my reality would give me comfort. But it didn't take long for me to surmise that comfort doesn't come from being in a place that seems to shield me from my problems. No matter how far I could have driven, even if I reached Ontario, my situation still existed, and would not soon go away. So I said a prayer, wiped away a few loose tears, and contemplated deep thoughts all the way home.

Lauren was up.

Several bright blue nylon travel bags were spread across the living room floor. One was jammed with underwear, slacks, pajamas, shirts, and socks. Another one seemed to be packed with toiletries. Then there was the bag she'd carry on board, her ever-present duffel that held a couple of books, her camera, boxes of raisins, dried fruit mixed with nuts, and a purse-sized New Testament.

"Hi, Mom."

I raised my eyelids. So much had happened, I couldn't recall if we were still on speaking terms or not.

"Hey there," I replied softly. She looked calmer than I thought she would. I knew that flying rattled Lauren's nerves even if she had a travel companion. I thought about Derrick's earlier call, and rubbed her on the arm.

"You okay, Lauren?"

She nodded but wouldn't look at me. Too busy sitting on the floor perched on her knees and folding a few pair of blue jeans and another shirt or two.

"You hungry?" I asked.

"I ate a little bit of grits and a boiled egg. Not really hungry."

"Well, are you excited about seeing your grandparents? It's been, what, about three years since you last saw them."

She smiled but didn't exactly light up.

"I'm just glad to get away, more than anything." My heart tore. Here I was glad she was leaving, and I didn't think she'd be glad to get away, too. I fought the inner voice that said it was because of me that she wanted to go. I knew that trip had been planned long before I ever started screwing up her life.

"Oh yeah?" I paused. "What time you get in last night?"

"Oh, it was so late I don't even remember. I was so tired I just crashed."

"Uh-huh. Did you see, uh, Aaron?"

She looked at me. Pain flashed across her face. "Yeah, he—he finally admitted . . ." She winced and continued in a barely audible voice, "He told me the reason why he broke up with me is because of another girl."

I almost bit off my tongue. "A girl?"

"Yep. He didn't say who she is. I guess it doesn't matter, though."

I sat on the couch and crossed my legs. Then I uncrossed them and started fiddling with my fingers, tearing off the dead cuticles and flicking them onto the floor like it didn't even matter.

"Yep. Sometimes I don't understand. I knew our relationship wasn't perfect, but it was decent, you know what I mean?" she said, and set a pair of jeans on her legs. "Only thing, the *only* thing we didn't have was a—a sex life. That's it. And I think that's a foul reason to break up with somebody."

"Hmmm. Well, it happens." I shifted in my seat. "Hey, when I was about your age, well, actually, I was fourteen, I met this guy named Yuri. I liked him a lot and he seemed to like me. He was probably two years older than I was. Well, he kept pressuring me for sex and I wanted to do it, but not with Yuri. So, when I kept stalling, he dumped me. Sure did. Funny thing is I never forgot Yuri and I'd bet he never forgot me, either."

"Really?" she asked.

"Yes. Lauren, guys will remember you if you told them no, just like they remember the girls who said yes."

"But will saying no make Aaron want me again?"

I wanted her to feel better, but hey, let's not overdo things here. And even though what she said shook me, I managed to smile with sympathy. "He may want you in his mind, but I can't promise you he'll try and get back. Usually, once a guy is done with you, it's over. No repeats. But you never know. Why do you ask?"

"Mom, I just can't shake the feeling that what we had isn't over. Even though Aaron gave me a little bit of closure by telling me something as opposed to nothing—I still think there's some unfinished business. You know what I mean?"

I nodded but in reality, I did not know what Lauren meant.

"Okay, time to go," I said with finality.

It was 7:00 P.M. Bags were packed, tickets were in

hand. I had to drive Lauren to Hobby Airport, which was a good thirty-minute ride. I liked flying, but every time I had to drive to the airport, my stomach would tighten and I'd get this gutted, fluttery feeling, like I was on the slow, upward crawl of a steep roller coaster. I guess my daughter inherited the same reaction. When we were finally settled in the car and began backing out of our parking space, Lauren kept looking at the apartment building like she'd never see it again. Even after I'd driven fifteen yards, she turned her head like she was trying to create a mental picture of our building. Maybe she'd miss being home more than she expected.

The airport bustled with the usual activity surrounding holiday travel. I spotted numerous vans from Channel 2 and Channel 13 with reporters interviewing people about their impending flights. We checked Lauren's luggage and I escorted her to the Delta terminal. Sat next to her for a few minutes and grabbed her hand.

"Why so gloomy, girl? You're about to have a ball. Your pockets are padded, you're on break. Hey, you may meet new friends."

She smiled weakly. "Yeah, I guess I should look on the bright side of things, huh? I do want to see my grandparents and stuff."

"All they're going to do is spoil you, take you shopping at Lennox Mall. Better enjoy it while you can."

She smiled. "Yeah, you're right. Well, Mom, I know you don't like sitting around in airports, so go on and leave. I'll be okay."

"Sure?" I asked.

"Yep."

I stood up and gestured at her. She stood with me. I

pulled her body into my chest, closing my eyes and hugging her tight. She hugged me tight, too. Rubbing me on the back.

"Okay, 'bye, Mom. Have a good Christmas. I'll call you when I get in. Try not to get too lonely," she said with a teasing gleam in her eye.

"I'll try," I said without returning her smile.

We waved at each other and I headed toward the parking garage.

I drove ten minutes before picking up the Nokia.

"Hey, Aaron, it's me," I said solemnly. "Lauren's gone with the wind."

24
Aaron

As soon as I intercepted Tracey's call, the only thing left to do was to scoop up my prepacked overnight bag, a bag I'd actually prepared and stored right inside my bedroom door the night that Lauren came over.

Earlier that morning, after a grueling night's sleep, of course, the first person I ran into was Brad. Both he and I were yawning like we hadn't slept since 1975. I grabbed my favorite chipped cereal bowl and rummaged through the cupboard for some Cap'n Crunch.

"Morning to you," Brad said, coming into the kitchen with a pick stuck to the back of his lopsided Afro. He had on a violet muscle tee and black karate pants, and was barefoot.

"What up?" I answered and took a seat at the breakfast bar. My bones popped as I stretched, and then I starting pouring the last of the gallon of milk over my cereal.

Brad hovered in the kitchen, staring me into my uncomfort zone. When I looked back at him like *What the hell is up?* he averted his eyes and started fumbling around the dish rack, clanking dishes and bowls. After five minutes of this nonsense, he finally blurted, "Yo, Aaron. Why'd you play Lauren so tough last night?"

I was enjoying the sweet crunchiness of my cereal, but paused and asked, "Excuse me?"

"I came home last night and she's standing outside crying and looking like someone set her puppy on fire."

"Oh," I said and returned to my breakfast.

"Damn, it's like that, A? I thought you didn't want to hurt her."

"I didn't want to hurt her," I insisted in a loud voice.

I wondered if Brad believed me.

Then I wondered if *I* believed me.

"Yeah, Aaron, I could really tell you were going out of your way not to hurt her. She told me how you kicked her out of the apartment and didn't even have the decency to escort her home."

"Damn, man, she's only telling you her side of the story. There are always two sides to every story."

"Sounds like to me there are two sides to every man."

What he say? This was getting ridiculous. "Look, why would you even care, Brad? What happened between Lauren and me is between me and Lauren."

"I don't think so, Aaron. Not when I return to our home and your woman, or whatever the hell she is, is out there crying and bitching about you, and filling my ear up with all her pain. And on top of *that*, what's with all the glass that I found scattered across the kitchen floor? For a minute I thought I was in Kmart's parking lot."

"Aw, man, she was flipping out on me," I said, dismissing his comment with a wave of my hand.

But instead of responding to my excuses, Brad remained steadfast both in his observation of me and in him staying put. I began humming a tune that nobody on earth had ever heard before, but when he still didn't leave, I looked at him and asked, "What exactly did Lauren tell you?"

"That you got another woman—and you dumped Lauren for her," he said, raising his chin and looking back at me with intense eyes.

I shrugged and tipped the bowl, finished off the remaining drops of milk.

"Hey, A, I don't mean to dip, but would this other woman be Lauren's mother?"

I froze and gripped the bowl between my hands. "Is that what Lauren told you?"

Brad just looked at me, but didn't say anything.

I walked to the kitchen sink and started seasoning it with some disinfectant cleanser. Turned on the hot water faucet.

"Hey, by the way, Ms. Tracey Davenport called you this morning," Brad said casually.

I faced Brad and raised an eyebrow.

"And?"

"And nothing . . . just thought I'd let you know."

"That's cool," I replied, and gave my attention back to cleaning the sink.

"Hey, man. Is it *that* good to you?" he asked.

I paused, then answered without looking at him. "I'll let you decide."

The encounter in the kitchen was the only time I was around Brad that day. He hit the shower and was gone before I even thought about how much I wished I were by myself. I liked having a roommate but sometimes I preferred privacy; I didn't want to have to answer to anybody and didn't feel like I should have to just because we shared a few expenses. So with him gone, I felt free, less scrutinized, which made me feel better, and that was key.

After a few minutes of contemplation, I hopped in my ride. Drove around the corner and several miles away to the nearest YMCA. Worked out and did some treadmill for a little over an hour, an hour that forced me to think about the events that had recently unfolded. In some ways I was relieved. For Lauren's sake it was better for her to know something, even if she didn't know everything about why I dumped her. I'd been around enough women to know that most demand closure. Some women act like being dumped is no biggie; they'll put on a hard façade like it's business as usual. But then some ladies tend to be borderline suicidal. Not that I thought that Lauren would take that route. As much as she and I dug each other in the past, I doubted she was that strung out over me. I knew Lauren would come to terms with what had happened, and let the past stay put.

Once I returned home from working out, I spent the rest of the afternoon concentrating on getting rid of anything that reminded me of Lauren. For every room I entered, I'd notice tiny slips of paper where I'd written her name. It sounds kind of juvenile, but yep, back in the good old days, whenever I'd think of Lauren, I used to scribble her name. Would write it down, then look at it and get a warm and fuzzy hit just from realizing I had a woman as sweet as Lauren in my life. Even though I never told her, in my heart I felt that Lauren was one of the sweetest young ladies I'd ever met. She was the type to call me first if I didn't call her, and cared absolutely nothing about boy-girl protocol.

And who else would think enough of me to call my answering machine and serenade me with the song "Angel of Mine"? I'd come home from work or class and hear Lauren's nasal voice singing the chorus, a smile in her voice, a longing that extended from her heart to mine. When I'd ask her why she left a message like that on my answering machine, she'd say, "That song reminds me of you." I'd smile to myself and shake my head, realizing the things that Lauren did were what made her who she was.

After venturing into the kitchen, I found myself removing a yellowed sticky note that was lodged behind a coffeepot-shaped refrigerator magnet. Lauren's flowery handwriting was scribbled on the paper along with her dad's phone number. I looked at it with a lump in my throat, but crumpled the tiny sheet of paper and dumped it in the trash.

Walking through the apartment, I stepped on a couple of her bobby pins that I promptly picked up and tossed in the garbage. I dug out Lauren's copy of a Sandra Kitt romance novel that had slipped between the couch cushions. And when I went into my room, I remembered to look in the closet and get that Magic 102 T-shirt that was given to her on the day we went to the Phenomenal Women's Empowerment Expo.

Once I gathered a few more Lauren-related items, I dropped her belongings into an HEB Pantry grocery store bag, tied the top into a firm knot, and stuffed it inside a garbage container.

After Tracey called and told me that Lauren was gone with the wind, I scooped up my belongings and headed east toward Williamstown Apartments. It was approximately seven o'clock when I pulled up in front of Tracey's unit. A few minutes later Tracey pulled up in her Malibu and cut off the ignition. She moved slowly like she was tired but sacrificed a smile anyway. I waved and rushed to open her door. She got out and leaned against the car for a moment. God, how I wanted to comfort her, take her in my arms and reassure her that everything would be all right.

"So, she's on her way to GA, huh?" I said walking alongside Tracey up the stairs.

"Yep, plane leaves in fifteen minutes."

"So, what are we going to do tonight?"

She smiled. "Not what you think we're going to do. Got plenty of time for all that."

I followed Tracey through the doorway, and instead of letting me dump my stuff on the couch, she held out her hand. I pretended like I was going to give her my overnight bag, but put my hand in hers instead. She shivered. "Ooh, that's just what I needed." I wriggled my finger in the center of her hand, and she blushed and rolled her eyes.

"Let me get your bag for you, Aaron. Make yourself at home."

She looked longingly in my eyes, but gathered enough composure to stow away my things.

She returned from the bedroom and had changed clothes. I loved how she looked wearing a Capri blue jean skirt and a red drawstring shirt. Then she smiled at me while she wrapped a large yellow apron around my waist that said, DANGER: MEN COOKING.

"Okay, Mister Man, you're going to help me prepare the meal tonight," she announced.

"Oh yeah?" I said.

"Yes. I've already done a little cooking earlier this afternoon. Tonight we're just going to make the stuffing. Tomorrow we'll do the birds. No big deal."

"Yes, ma'am," I told her, and went to wash my hands.

And for an hour and fifteen minutes, cook we did. I sliced onions, celery, turkey necks, and gizzards for the stuffing. She made a few pans of homemade corn bread. Had the house hot and smelling as good as a spice factory.

I tore away from Tracey for several moments to call my mom. Knowing Nethora Oliver, she was long past sleep; seven o'clock was usually her bedtime, so I knew I'd be chancing it. Mom and I said our hellos and good-byes, then I was back at Tracey's side.

"Now that the food is taken care of, when are you going to take care of me?" I asked. I had removed my shoes and loosened my shirt.

"Let's do it now, before you have a fit." She pouted and rolled her eyes. She made a quick move toward the couch, sat down, and patted the spot next to her. We touched thighs, and she let me place my arm around her.

Soft music played on her stereo, strains of the Boyz II Men *Christmas Interpretations* followed by Donald Lawrence's *Hello Christmas* CD.

I started rubbing her hair, massaging her scalp. Ain't nothing like being around a woman whose hair is soft, clean, and smells like fresh flowers. My older lady smiled deeply in my eyes and caressed the left side of my chin with the back of her hand.

Tracey looked tired but beautiful, as beautiful as a woman who's lived long enough to know the true essence of beauty, and wasn't too insecure to forget. When I reached underneath her skirt to caress her thighs, her hand popped my hands real quick.

"Just hold me, okay? That's all I want you to do."

So hold her I did. I placed my arms around her curves, felt her breasts brush against my chest. She was soft, authentic, a precious woman in my sight. Smelled of a touch of perfume, her skin as ripe as peaches. Again I started to trace the upper part of her thigh, but she blocked me when my middle finger neared her more sensitive part. She shook her head. I sighed and sank my face in the crevice of her neck. The rain and thunder intruded upon our holiday concert, but once we started kissing, it was like nothing else mattered. I would have loved to do more than attack her lips with a smooth kiss, but she wouldn't let me. And since kissing Tracey was the only thing I was allowed to do, I began to enjoy the taste of her lips like it was the last sweetness left in the world.

"See, this is exactly what I'm talking about," she moaned softly. Her tender voice was breathy and raspy, pockets of air stealing her normal volume.

"What, babe?" My eyes misted and I felt like putty, melting, moldable in her hands.

"I love this too much to let anything take it away," she sighed in satisfaction.

"I know, I know."

"Do you?"

"Yep, I do, Tracey," I moaned, hoping so desperately that she could hear my heart.

"You promise me we're going to be together no matter what?" she asked mildly teasing.

"No matter what."

She giggled. "Ahhh, you know just what to say, but I'm not sure you realize what you're saying."

"Try me. All you can do is try."

"Hmmm. So, we're going to spend all night making love, right, Aaron?"

"Hey, you look kinda pooped, but if you got the strength, I got the desire," I said.

"Mmmmm," she yawned. Large tears swirled in her

brown eyes. "Well, to be honest, I'm feeling a wee bit touched. Seems my energy's been sapped the last couple days."

"I can dig it." I looked at my watch. It was nine-forty. "Well, babe, we can cuddle all night long if you want. I don't mind."

"Okay, you're so good to me, Aaron. Just too good." Within fifteen minutes she was knocked out. Once I heard her even, steady breathing, I hoisted her in my arms and struggled to carry her into the bedroom. Then I laid her on the bed, turned off the light, and slid in beside her.

Not intending to go to sleep myself, but wanting to watch her dark frame in the stillness of the night, glad that I was there and spending time with her.

I had just dozed off when—

"Mom, I'm—*Aaron?*"

I jerked and sat up, blinking my eyes and trying to adjust to the lights, which were now on. Lauren hovered over us, and the expression on her face was hardly a Kodak moment. She scowled, and then her hand covered her open mouth. Tracey was stirring in her sleep, mumbling and yawning.

"So, is this what happens when Lauren goes out of state?" Her eyes flashed fire and she rushed at me, tugging my arm.

"Get your scandalous ass out of my mother's bed."

"What?" Tracey woke up, squinting and rubbing her eyes.

Lauren's hands swiped at my face, but I blocked her before she could get at me. I sat up and held her by her wrists, looking in her eyes for the first time in a long time.

"Lauren? Oh God." Tracey scattered from the bed like a frightened animal. Her shirt and blue jean skirt

were crushed and wrinkled. She rushed to her offspring and grabbed Lauren's left arm; I secured her
right arm, but Lauren grunted and snatched her arms
from the both of us.

"No, Mom, no. I'm not leaving this time. This is
messed up. I know this is not what I think it is."

Tracey's lip quivered, her face was sunken like ancient treasure. I didn't know what to do, so I remained
seated on the bed, grateful I was still fully dressed.

"Okay, Lauren, we need to talk."

"Start talking. I *gotta* hear this," she half-laughed,
half-cried.

"Okay, I need a few minutes. Go wait in the living
room. Go on."

"I'm not going anywhere. I'm not going out there
so you two can collaborate on some story. I want to
know the truth, Mom. Why is he here? With you? I'm
not gone two hours and he's here with you? What?
Was this in the plans all along? See, this is not making
any sense, and I'm not leaving this room till I get some
answers."

"Okay, okay," Tracey snapped. She flung her arms
around her body, squeezing and rubbing her arms
and moaning. I jumped up and ran to her side, but before I could get there, Lauren stood directly in my
path.

Suddenly Lauren resembled a hastily constructed
wall, one that had not been there before. I wanted to
shove my hands against her, against the wall, but she
stood with both feet firmly planted on the floor.

"Now hold up, Lauren. I know you're mad, but hey,
this is how things are."

"Oh, really now? Aaron, what do you call yourself
doing? Oh, let me stop playing dumb," she said, and

looked me in the eyes. "My *mom* is the other woman, isn't she?" She screamed with her whole face. "Isn't she?"

"Yes," I replied.

"No," Tracey said at the same time.

"Well, maybe I'd better leave so y'all can get your stories straight. God knows you need to do better than what you're doing."

She bolted from the room, leaving the sound of a slamming door in her wake. It was ten-forty, but for some reason it felt much later than that.

By then Tracey was weeping, sputtering, chest heaving in and out, tears streaming down her face. She perched on her knees at the side of the bed, rocking back and forth.

"This is too much. I knew it was too good to be true. How can God bless this kind of mess?"

I sighed internally. Let Tracey get all cried out. Let her find some words.

Fifteen minutes later.

We had assembled in the dining room. Tracey was waiting for the water to boil. Had placed several hot apple cider packets on the counter. Lauren sat perched on a dining room chair, her eyes dark, without a flicker of vitality. I sat across from her, moving my legs back and forth while my hands slapped my thighs.

Tracey stood before us, barely able to look at her daughter, eyes drained, and giving the impression that she'd rather be anywhere else but there.

"Lauren, I'm so embarrassed. That's all I can say. It's—it's not, I don't know," she said.

"Let me tell her, Tracey."

"Okay." She nodded and returned to prepare the cider.

I blew out a short breath and tried to maintain a calm voice. "Lauren, for a long time I was attracted to you and only you. I felt we had a good thing, but somehow, some way . . . I began liking your mom."

Lauren winced and hung her head.

"Hey, what happened wasn't intentional. It just happened."

She stared at me. "Aaron, nothing just happens. And if we had such a good thing, why wasn't it good enough to hold you? Couldn't have been that good, huh?"

She came and stood next to me. I could feel her breath on my cheek.

"You know, Aaron, I always wondered what it would feel like to be fucked by you."

I froze.

"Now I know." Her voice broke, face crumbling into despair.

My moistened shirt clung to my skin and I wished I were spiritual enough to know how to pray in tongues.

"I guess you were too horny to remember what you told me last month. That you'd wait for me, Aaron. And I believed you, but what has that gotten me?"

"Lauren, it's not like what it sounds," I lowered my voice and looked toward the kitchen. "At the time, I did mean it when I said I'd take you up on that rain check. It's just that I couldn't predict the future. And I didn't want to stay stuck in the past, either."

"And what's that supposed to mean?"

"I guess your being a virgin was always on my mind. And if that's something that you wanted to hold on to, I wasn't going to stop you."

"Oohhh, that is *sooo* foul. And it's so homemade, Aaron. How can you stand up here and expect me to believe lies from the pit of hell?"

I closed my eyes and did something I rarely do.

I prayed. The words were in English and stayed inside my mind, but I still prayed that the good Lord, who already had enough on his plate, could fit one more thing on his schedule. I hoped he would listen to my plea for help, 'cause at the rate we were going, seems like only God could get me out of this one.

25
Tracey

I told Aaron he could leave, but he hung around like an accused person waiting on a verdict. He holed up in my bedroom. Knowing that he was behind that door comforted me, but made me nervous as hell at the same time. I didn't know what Lauren was capable of doing. But although I sensed she was hurt, I still was the authority figure. Right or wrong, I knew I had the authority to take control of the situation.

She remained in the dining room, staring into space and drumming her thumbs on the tabletop. Tap, tap, tap. Tap, tap, tap. I almost lost my damn mind listening to her repetitive thumping. Her hands sounded like they were trying to tell me something.

I sighed and thrust a simmering mug toward my daughter.

"Here, Lauren, drink this."

"Why?" she said, lifting her voice. "Apple cider ain't going to change nothing. Shoot, by the looks of everything, you and Aaron have hooked up and I'm forced to watch it. What kind of mother are you?"

I sat down across from Lauren and tried my best to look her in her face.

"Okay, Lauren. Let's talk and get this out in the open."

"Talk!" she snapped, looking intensely at me like I'd been taken in for questioning.

"You might as well know that Aaron and I have a—a special relationship. Now you must realize, you gotta believe, this was not planned, it just happened. I'm sorry. I can say I'm sorry a thousand times and I know it won't make you feel any better, but—"

"You're sorry?" she asked.

"Yeah, I am," I told her, but was unsure that I was.

"Sorry about what, Mom? That you got caught? People are always sorry after the fact. Did you feel sorry when you were going to bed with my man?"

I grimaced and raked my fingers through my hair.

"That part I refuse . . . to discuss."

"Oh, I don't believe you. What other part is there, Mom? If you can't discuss that, what's the whole damn point of getting things out in the so-called open?"

"Don't curse."

"You curse."

"You're not me, Lauren."

"Wouldn't want to be."

I didn't say anything.

"Mom, after hearing this kind of news flash, what do you expect me to do? Break out the bubbly? Give y'all a standing ovation? I mean, I can't even stand to think about all the things you two were doing behind my back. I'm your daughter, Mom, not some unknown girl off the street. We live in the same apartment. You're my mom, but I thought we were friends. And you know better than anybody how I felt about Aaron.

He was *my* guy, Mom. *Mine.* At least I thought he was mine."

Her voice caught, and she groaned and went to lie on the couch. She lay on her back and raised her head toward the ceiling, rubbing her hand against her throat.

I didn't know what to do with my hands, so I covered my mouth and prayed for some magical words to be released that would appease this situation. My legs felt like sticks stuck in miry clay but I forced myself to come and kneel next to Lauren. I hated seeing her in such pain, hated knowing it was almost Christmas and we were going through such drama.

"Lauren, oh God. This is so hard."

"Oh no, you didn't say that it's hard." She narrowed her eyes and looked up at me. "Why would this be hard for you? I'm the one who got . . . ugh, that sounds so fake," she laughed like she was hiccuping, abruptly stopped, then laughed again.

I swallowed deeply and wiped my forehead. It seemed so hot in the apartment, and I went to turn up the air conditioner.

There's a mirror that covers the entire wall of our dining room, a mirror that follows your every expression, your every move. I averted my eyes all the time that I was in there. Left the room just as quickly as I came.

Air filled my cheeks and I blew out a loud breath.

"Lauren, believe me, it's not easy when you're in my shoes. I feel really bad—"

"Why couldn't you feel bad *before* you realized that what you were doing sucks?"

"I *did* feel bad."

"How bad? A teensy bit, until you counted up the

cost and felt you'd be missing out on a lot if you gave up Aaron?"

"I never—"

"Why couldn't you forget about yourself for once and think about how it would affect me?"

"I did think—"

"And if you really were concerned, didn't you even think for one second that one day you'd get caught?"

"Lauren, I don't—*I just don't know.*"

My voice bounced off the walls and I jumped away before my words could come back and hit me. Boomerang. Knock me to my knees. Feeling afraid, I started making a trail back and forth across the living room. Moving my legs toward air, life, something that would make me make sense.

"Lauren, nobody really thinks about the things they're doing until they've blown up in their face."

She looked at me like I hung out with smelly zoo animals.

I averted my eyes. "But the main thing is that I don't want you to think I'm a bad mother who doesn't care about you—".

"But, Mom, listen to yourself. Your actions prove you don't give a damn about me. No wonder you never came to comfort me and try and get Aaron and me reconciled. Did you want Aaron for yourself?"

"No."

"Yes, Mom, yes. Admit it." Lauren stood up and was in my face, yelling to the point that my eardrums vibrated, hurt from the sting of her words and from the volume of her voice. I covered my ears and watched her mouth moving and arms flailing.

I saw Aaron emerge from the bedroom. He started yelling something at Lauren and she raised her hand

and swung her open hand across his face and sent him crashing against the wall.

"Okay, now that is enough, Lauren. You will not be hitting anybody up in here. You do that one more time and you can go stay with your daddy." My eyes blazed and I stood in her face with my hand raised. She was breathing real hard and staring at the red mark she'd made on Aaron's cheek. He just stood there, back propped against the wall, opening and closing his eyes like a bright light was making things hard to see.

She cut her eyes at both Aaron and me and sat back down on the couch.

"I swear," he croaked, "if she puts her hands on me one more time—"

"No, Aaron, please, don't react, that's all she needs is for you to act like her."

He groaned and shuffled back to my bedroom.

For some reason I just then noticed that the Christmas music was still playing—soft, subtle, like it was trying to remind us of what the season was all about. I shivered and rubbed my shoulders, neck, and back.

Lauren turned over on her side and kept shaking her head. She gave me this pensive look and said sadly, "Mom, all I know is, if this was something legitimate, you wouldn't be trying so hard to deny it."

After she said that, there really wasn't a thing I could say. At least nothing I could say that I thought she'd believe.

"Mom, it's not so much that you became attracted to Aaron and vice versa. Believe it or not, I'm not so blind that I don't know Aaron is someone that women want to be with. And then I knew that you and Mr. Steve weren't together anymore. I knew you were unhappy about that. And I'd noticed that you would hold little conversations with Aaron whenever he'd call over here to speak to me. I wondered what was up with that, but I didn't linger too much about it in my mind. Hey, Aaron is friendly like that. But the worst thing is, well, I—I *trusted* you. I felt I could come to you and talk about anything. I listened, or I tried to listen, to the things you'd say. You told me not to become intimate with Aaron, and I guess"—her voice broke—"I can only guess you've gone and done the very things with him you told me not to do." She was sobbing by then. It sounded ugly, tortured, like a cry that had been hidden and buried for three thousand years. She tried to muffle the sound by covering her face with both her hands; she didn't muffle anything, and actually sounded worse than before.

My first instinct was to cover my ears, but as much as I was aching to do so, I forced myself to let my hands remain as they were, resting underneath my chin while I lay on my side looking down at my daughter. Looking at her, facing the reality of what I'd done, and trying to get over the mountain of the pain that I'd caused.

I let her cry. No fake condolences, no more excuses. Let her get it all out.

Let her go.

It was now eleven-thirty. All cried out, Lauren had gotten a can of Sprite from the fridge and was swallowing, gulping it down, burping at the same time. She wiped her mouth and sat back down in the front of the couch.

"Lauren?"

"Yes, ma'am?"

I flinched. She wasn't speaking respectfully; I could hear the sarcasm.

"Lauren, why aren't you in Georgia?"

She laughed weakly and rolled her eyes.

"Too scared to board the plane."

"Oh yeah?" I said.

"About a half hour before the flight was to leave, they started asking the first-class passengers to board and stuff. I was sitting up there thinking about getting on that plane and how dark and eerie it looked outside. Of course, the constant raining didn't help. And so I left the boarding area and walked a little ways down to another empty terminal. And the more I imagined myself stepping on that plane, being strapped inside that metal tube, flying twenty-five thousand feet above the earth, the more I knew I couldn't go. Then I heard my name being announced on the loudspeaker and I returned to the Delta terminal. Everybody had boarded the plane and the Delta employee asked me if I was Lauren Hayes. I told her that I was but I wasn't going. She looked a little pissed because I'd delayed the flight by ten minutes, but she was understanding and told me another flight was going to leave in the morning, around seven, and the lady told me to get re-ticketed, and so I did."

"Humph. So if you had boarded that plane . . ."

"What did you say?"

"Never mind." I paused. "So how did you get home?"

"Well, Mom, I tried to call home, but the phone just rang and rang. I thought that was weird, so I called Daddy and he came and got me, brought me on home."

I gulped and shook my head. "Good ole Derrick Hayes. Always there in the clutch."

She didn't say anything.

"So, are you still going to go to Georgia?"

She looked at me hard.

"I'm not trying to get rid of you, I was just wondering. It's getting late. You need to get some sleep so we can get up in the morning. I assume I'm taking you to the airport."

"And I'll bet you're going to make sure I get on that plane this time, huh?" She yawned and rubbed the bags under her eyes.

I gave a weak smile.

"Well, put it this way, Lauren. I'll be there when the plane leaves this time. I'll make sure to watch it burst through the clouds."

"Yeah, Mom. I'm going. What else am I supposed to do? With all this junk that's going on here, I know it's better for me to go."

"Okay, okay," I said and looked at her. I extended my hand toward her. She looked at it for the longest, examining it like it was an unusual sight, but soon she reached out and grabbed my hand. She held on to my hand until inevitable sleep consumed both our bodies.

26
Aaron

I slept through the night with one eye open, one ear closed. It was hard to sleep like that, a waste if there ever was one. When I decided to get up for the day, I immediately noticed the dead atmosphere. Empty. Lifeless.

When it occurred to me that Lauren and her mom weren't there, I felt like the world had disappeared without me knowing about it. I wanted nothing more than to leave, but something urged me to stay. When I went to take a leak in Tracey's bathroom, I saw a sheet of lavender stationery taped to the mirror. It said:

Aaron,
Be back soon
Lauren is catching early flight to GA
Taking her to airport
Don't leave
Yours,
Tracey

I hesitated for a second before deciding to step into Tracey's shower. Once the water was running nice and good, I let myself be soothed by the liquid heat longer than I normally would. After I re-dressed in the same clothes I'd worn the day before, I drifted around the apartment touching things I probably shouldn't have been touching. Being alone in the apartment felt strange. Felt odd to be there, in a place where the two women that I'd been fond of resided. Sometimes you never know how to take stuff, and I didn't want to dwell too much on what had happened. I just knew that the word was now out. Lauren knew, but somehow, some way, I was still determined to remain peacefully in both of their lives.

I wandered into the kitchen and saw a holiday basket sitting on the kitchen shelf. It was filled with goodies such as oranges, apples, nuts, crackers, and cheese. I'd grabbed an apple when I heard my cell phone ring. I rushed to pick up the line.

"Hello?" I said, my ears burning.

"Well, merry Christmas, son."

I blew out a happy breath. "Hey, Mom, merry Christmas to you, too."

"I know we talked just last night, but I wanted to hear your voice, make sure you're okay."

"Yep, Mom, I'm fine. You and Daddy up pretty early this morning."

"Oh, your dad's been up puttering around the house. He's out walking Pudgie right now. I'm drinking my coffee and watching those retarded talk shows."

I laughed.

"Oh, and he told me to tell Khristian *Feliz Navidad.*"

I gave a weak laugh and curled my upper lip.

"So I tried to call you at home, son, but Brad said

you was gone. I assume you'll be seeing Miss Lauren today?"

"Uh-huh."

"Well, I know you gonna bring her by so we can get a quick look at her."

"Uh, Mom, I don't know any other way to put this, but I think you should know—Lauren and I broke up."

"Broke up? Well, this must've been recently, because you just showed me the present you got her a couple weeks ago. Hmmm, I'm sorry to hear that, son."

"Yeah, well, I—all I can say is we're not together and, well, she's going to be out of town for Christmas anyway."

"Is that right? Things happen so fast these days I can't keep up."

"Mom, it's nothing to worry about. No big deal."

"Well, are you still coming by the house today? Your dad and I still want to see you. You know he hasn't been feeling all that good. His eyesight is failing and now he's wearing these thick ole glasses, the ones like that security guard on *Martin* used to wear. Thick, thick, thick."

"Yuck!"

"What you talking about? Lendan Oliver still looking good to me."

"Yes, ma'am."

"Anyway, I've been getting on him about watching his diet and . . . maybe you can come on by here and spend time with him. You know he's the only father you got, and can't too many people say that these days."

I cleared my throat. "Uh, hmmm, I'll see what I can do."

"Aw, son, you going to have to do better than that. It's not like we live all the way in Austin. Now I expect you to come by here sometime today."

"Yes, ma'am." I hoped that "sometime today" could be left to my own interpretation. After chatting for a few minutes more, we ended the call and I finished off my apple and threw the core in the trash.

Christmas dinner was brief. Neither Tracey nor I had much of an appetite. I think it had to do something with Tracey's way of shooting the breeze. Fortunately, she looked stunning in a rose-colored knit turtleneck and some tapered black trousers. She was letting the back of her hair grow out, and it was combed in a straight style that was lightly flipped on the ends.

"Aaron," she scolded, rushing past me to the stove, "why'd you leave the pot uncovered? The vegetables may dry up."

"Oh, sorry 'bout dat," I replied.

Then later on it was "Why can't you help me do some of these dishes? I don't appreciate you slouching on the couch while I'm busting suds in the kitchen. So inconsiderate."

I gave her a what-in-the-heck-is-wrong-with-you look, but swiped a dish towel and started drying silverware, plates, and bowls.

"The meal was great, Tracey," I said to her profile. She never responded, even refused to look at me when she handed me dishes she'd rinsed. I sighed inwardly and was dying to get this over with.

Once we finished up the dishes I leaned against the kitchen counter and folded my arms across my chest. Miss Tracey poked out her bottom lip. Ordinarily this would be my cue that she was trying to look sexy and playing hard to get, but tonight Tracey was just playing hard.

"Hey," I asked, spreading my arms, "can a brother at least get a little Christmas hug?"

"No," she said, throwing the dishrag in the sink and rushing past me to the bedroom. The door whacked shut and then a lock clicked in place. I held up my finger and said, "Hey, aren't you forgetting someone? Women!" I spread out on the couch and proceeded to watch any and every corny little Christmas movie that was airing that afternoon.

I was just about to settle in and check out Sinbad in *Jingle All the Way* when the phone rang. It didn't seem like Tracey was going to pick it up, so I sprang out of my seat.

"Hello?" I said.

A long pause.

"Hello?" I repeated.

"Hi. Uh, is this 555-2030?" he asked.

"Probably is. Who did you want to talk to?"

"Is this Aaron?"

"You're on a roll. Who is this?" I told him.

"It's . . . it's Derrick. Mr. Hayes."

"Ohhh, uh, happy holidays to you."

"Same to . . . where's Tracey?"

"Uh, she's not available right now."

"I'll bet she's not." Much attitude.

"I'd be glad to let Trace know you called . . . that is, if you need her to call you back."

"Yes, I need *Trace* to call me back ASAP."

"You got it," I promised, and hung up.

I rubbed the flabbiest part of my throat for a few minutes.

Tracey walked out of the bedroom clutching the wrapped gift I'd brought over last night.

"I heard you talking on the phone. Who was that?" she asked.

"Your ex."

"Which ex?"

"How many exes you got that still have your current number?"

"All of them. Now which one, Aaron?"

"Derrick X."

"Ha, ha, ha. What did he want?"

"Not me."

"Aaron."

"Hell, I don't know. I tried to get him to share his feelings, but he wouldn't open up."

"Yeah, right. Hmmm. I might call him back later . . . and I might not. Let's go."

"Go wh—" I asked.

"Just come on. You're driving."

"Okay, Miss Daisy," I said, stepping up to her. "May I have a kiss first?"

"No, you may not, Hoke."

I tried to swat her booty, but she skipped ahead of me and disappeared through the front door. I forced a laugh I didn't feel. Grabbed my car keys and closed the door behind me.

Houston's Tranquility Park is near the Transco Tower. Joggers, walkers, and families gather there to relax on any one of Houston's notoriously hot and muggy days. There's a lavish fountain, and dozens of white, black, and Hispanic kids, shoes still on their feet, dart about the cascading water or get their photograph taken while they pose inside the steady stream.

I didn't say anything when Tracey barked the directions to the park. While I was driving, I'd glance at her but she'd turn her head away, preoccupied more with what was outside the car than in.

"You want to get out?" I asked after we sat in the car for the first few minutes with no words between us.

"All right."

I opened her door. Felt my heart warm when, at my shy invitation, she placed her hand in mine. She still wouldn't look at me, though. I didn't mind too much, and was content just feeling the heat generated from our touch.

There were more people at the park than I'd imagined there'd be on a day like Christmas. We noticed a wedding party traipsing across the grass to stand in front of a tree. Smile-for-the-camera time. Dressed in a floor-length white silk and lace gown, the bride glistened. She clasped hands with her new spouse, holding on to his arm and brushing her lips against his bearded cheek.

Even Tracey allowed a smile at that one.

"What you thinking about?" I asked walking beside her.

"How I always thought I would have made that move by now," she said, nodding at the bride and groom.

"Uh-huh."

"Not that I think it's too late. There are women much older than me who've yet to find a suitable mate. I think if getting married is something you dwell on all the time, if you allow it to become a fixation, it seems harder to attain."

"You want to sit down on this bench?" I asked.

She nodded and sat down, stretching her legs before her.

"People always want what they don't have. Always chasing after things they haven't yet touched," she continued.

"And what do you want?"

"Simple stuff. A man that I respect who will give me attention and affection and make me feel valuable."

She paused. "Is that asking for too much?"

"Depends."

"Why you say that?"

"If the things you want require the cooperation of another, they may be difficult to get."

"Hmmm. Well, I—"

"For example, I don't mean to go back in time, but take yourself and Steve Monroe. Based on the things you told me, it sounded like you wanted things from him that he couldn't give, would you agree?"

"Well, yes, in a way—"

"And even though it seemed simple to you, it turned into something difficult because your ability to get it hinged on someone else's actions and desires."

"I get what you're saying, but by the same token, isn't that true for everything that a person could want? I think that just about anything we want requires somebody else doing something to help us get it, whether it be a man who gives me attention and affection, or otherwise."

"That's what I'm talking about."

"Okay, I hear what you're saying, but what's your point?" she said.

"My point is, when you allow the things that you want to be controlled by someone else, you might always be frustrated. You expected Steve to give you things, and when he didn't, it left you feeling unsatisfied."

"Hmmm. I don't like this; it sounds like my life is controlled by others or something."

"Not necessarily. When you really think about it, your life is controlled by you, Miss Tracey. It's up to you to decide what you want and make sure it's something that you have the authority to do something about."

"And what does this have to do with me and Steve Monroe?"

"Everything. If you were ready to solidify or advance your relationship with him, but he wasn't ready, then it wasn't going to happen. All the elements have to be there and working for things to happen as you wished."

"But that's what I'm talking about. That goes back to my believing someone else is in control of what you want."

"Nope, *you* were in control of what you wanted; you just weren't with the right man to make that happen for you."

She sighed and swallowed hard, looking like she wanted to say something but not really sure how.

"*You* can control and have those things you want. You just have to make sure that you surround yourself with the people who can make that happen. Steve wasn't the one. He and you wanted two different things."

"You're making it sound like I was used."

"But you used him too, Tracey. Y'all used each other . . . and to me it sounds like you *did* get want you wanted, even if it wasn't for as long as you'd hoped it would be."

"I don't know about all that. I really thought Steve

and I had more than that. But the way things ended made me realize we didn't have what I thought we had. I still can't get over what he did. And for him to call me later on—"

"He called you? Why?"

She reddened.

"Well, yes, he tried to get in touch—"

"Tried to or did?"

"Okay, he *did* get in touch with me, but I never understood what he wanted. Didn't really care enough to know. By then it was too late."

"What if Steve Monroe told you he wanted to get back with you?"

She started slapping her legs together.

"I doubt that, Aaron. Besides, I didn't allow it to go there."

"So was that the last time you talked to him? When was this? A few weeks ago?"

Tracey fanned her face with her hands. "Something like that. Hey, you ready to open presents now? I brought them with us so we could be under the heat of the sun and enjoy each other somewhere else besides Williamstown Apartments, you know what I mean?"

I knew what she meant, all right.

"Okay, Miss Avoiding-the-Issue, let's do the present stuff. You first."

Tracey blushed and retrieved the large box from a Foley's shopping bag. Smiling, she slid her fingers across the wrapping paper, a rich-looking silver and gold metallic design with matching bow and ribbon. She picked up the box and shook it and then brought her nose close and inhaled.

"Whatever it is, it smells good."

She tore the paper, removed the lid, and laughed.

"Ohhh, thanks, Aaron. This is so awesome," she replied, and took out a gift box filled with lavender everything: bath crystals, body mist, shower gel, two containers of lotion, candles, incense sticks, and cologne spray. She held the soap to her nose like she could taste it with her nostrils.

I leaned back and grinned.

"I *love* things like this. Makes me feel so feminine and pure. Thanks again."

"My pleasure."

"Okay, now your turn." She handed me a teeny-weeny, itsy-bitsy box.

I cocked my head and gave her a teasing look.

"Look, don't act all funny and stuff. I—I special-ordered this for you a couple weeks ago. It's not much, something different. Hope you like it."

"I'm sure I will." I let my eyes linger over the Afro-centric wrapping paper, a brown, black, and gold decoration.

Within the box was a black watch ring with a white face, something I'd seen before, but never really thought I'd own one day.

I placed the ring on my finger and looked at Tracey and reached over to graze her cheek with a kiss.

"I like it," I told her.

"You're sure? Positive?"

I laid down the box, grabbed Tracey in my arms, and kissed her on the lips, kissed her like she was the woman in the long white gown and I was the proud man who stood by her side.

27
Aaron

The day after Christmas started out looking like a normal day. Sun rising like always, birds singing the morning's arrival.

My loins were moved by the tons of soda I drank the day before, so I hopped out of bed and headed for Tracey's bathroom. The phone rang.

"Hello?" Tracey answered, looking at me with the phone pinned tight to her ear like it was a lover's mouth.

Her eyes rolled.

"Hey," she said. "How's GA? How was your trip?"

I hobbled off to use the toilet and closed the bathroom door.

Ten minutes later, when I returned to the room, Tracey was off the phone and dressed in some navy blue sweats with matching pants. She bent down to lace her running shoes.

"Going somewhere?" I asked.

"No, silly, I always cook breakfast in this outfit. Hey, let's hop in the car and park at that lot near Brays

Bayou. We need to get out and walk, get away from the apartment."

"I'm right behind you."

Brays Bayou is a man-made river that extends for miles in southwest Houston. People jog, walk, ride their bicycles, and do exercises along the adjacent pathway. Several fitness-conscious folks were already out this morning, mostly toned-looking white guys who wore shorts with no shirts. No matter what day of the year it is, there's always someone who's going to be wearing shorts in Houston.

Tracey and I began our excursion walking against the brisk winds of the morning.

"So how did the conversation go with your daughter?" I asked.

"To be honest, she wasn't too happy, Aaron. Of course, the topic of the day was you and me. She fussed and rattled on and I listened for about as long as I could take, then I let her go."

"You think she'll tell her grandparents?"

"For what? They can't do anything about it. I don't talk to them anymore, and I know they won't be calling me, getting into my business."

"Well, you know when women are going through something, they always feel they have to tell somebody—a friend, a cyber pal, a talk-show host."

"Well, if you ever see Lauren on *The Ricki Lake Show*, I don't want to know."

"Nah, she's not that crazy. She'll be all right."

"Aaron, let me ask you something. Why do you seem so calm through all this? It seems like you're taking things way too casually."

I cleared my throat. "It's not that I don't care. I do. About you."

"So, just that quick you've lost feelings for Lauren? Like she never meant anything?"

"It's not that I've lost feelings for her. My main thing is that the decision has been made not to be with her anymore. That's a done deal. What am I supposed to do, try and be buddies with her while I'm spending time with you? That's not going to work."

"I know, I know, I know what you're saying; it's just that you seem kind of emotionally unattached."

"Hey, just because I don't show it doesn't mean it's not there. I'm just fast-forwarding my mind to a future with you. Why stay stuck in the past? Because like it or not, things will never be the same between me and Lauren."

The intensity of Tracey's eyes mellowed, as did her voice. "I think you're right."

She continued walking without saying anything to me for a long while. I let her nurse her thoughts, find some peace. After we'd walked about another half mile, she turned to me.

"Well, what about karma?"

"I don't know her."

"No, silly. Karma. Reaping what you sow. This thing that we're doing, it may come back to haunt us."

My eyes flickered into an unfocused view of Tracey's face.

"Aaron, if you want to know the truth, although I enjoy being with you, every night when I go to sleep, I pray that children's prayer:

> *Now I lay me down to sleep*
> *I pray the Lord my soul to keep*
> *If I should die before I wake*
> *I pray the Lord my soul to take*

"What's your point?" I asked.

"I haven't prayed that prayer in years. Or I'll only pray it when I think something bad might happen. At the end of the day, I can't shake the feeling that I'll go to sleep and never wake up again. So I speak it over me to make sure everything is squared away between the Lord above and me. You know what I'm saying?"

I nodded.

"Aaron, I haven't been to church in so long they're going to come after me for back tithes in a minute, but I still remember certain things. When it comes to God, knowing right and wrong, some things you never forget."

I sighed and stopped walking. She kept going.

"Trace, hold up."

She stopped and returned to my side.

"Yeah?"

"Look, I want to be with you, but if our being together has you to the point that you think God is going to pull a fast one on you in your sleep, then maybe we should just end this right now. I mean, I think you overanalyze everything, you say one thing with your mouth, and do something else with your actions. So what, you pray that prayer every night? If you wake up in the morning and find you still have a pulse, but go right back out and do the things you feel guilty about, doesn't that cancel out the prayer? You think the God who knows everything is stupid all of a sudden and that He can't see through all that?" My voice trembled and so did my hand when I tried to place it on her shoulder, forcing her to look me in the eyes.

She blinked and said softly, "Aaron, I'll let you in on something else. I just don't pray the children's prayer at night. I find myself praying every time I get in my car to go somewhere, anywhere. Any strange movement of another vehicle driving near scares me, especially eighteen-wheelers. I wonder if they're going to accidentally crash into me and send me to an early grave. Oh, Aaron, you just don't know how hard all this is." Her fear snatched her breath, like she was hyperventilating, and she rubbed her forehead.

"Tracey." I grabbed her. "Your being scared scares *me*."

"Well, there's no need in both of us being scared," she told me, loosing herself from my grasp.

"So, what do you want to do?" I wanted to know.

She grabbed her hair and yanked on a couple of strands but didn't say anything.

Felt like my heart skipped a few beats. My hands felt sweaty, like they were crying and advertising my fears.

"Well . . ." She winced. "If we stop this, if we . . . okay, let's say we stop the sex part. You think it would be okay for us to just know each other as good friends, but leave out the sex?"

I bared my teeth, but closed my mouth real quick.

"Sure, yeah, whatever, Tracey. If you think that our not physically being involved would clear your conscience, then go ahead. Go ahead and leave me alone, because I can't promise you I'd want to know you as just a friend. Men and women who've been lovers can't go back to being just good friends. You just can't do it."

"But what if we—"

"Steve Monroe! You guys were involved big-time. Are you still friends now?"

"No, but—"

"That's my point! If you really think I'd let you go to the place where I can't touch you but can only talk to you and be happy with that, think again. When I want a woman, I want all of her. And I've come to the conclusion that it's not enough for me to have just some of you."

She looked at me and a small grin escaped through her frustrated mouth. Her brown eyes, large and engaging, lassoed me inside her mind. I could almost hear her brain clicking, calculating what I'd just told her. She grabbed my face between her hands and kissed me warmly on my lips.

I let her kiss me, but I didn't grab her. Just stood there, and she broke the kiss shortly thereafter.

"What up with that, Tracey?"

"You just don't know what your words did to me. It's like you're validating or confirming what it is you want from me. In my mind, that's just what I needed to hear, because if that's how you feel, maybe all this is worth the risk. Maybe there's more to this than what I thought. I'm glad you want me for more than sex, because that's what it's going to take for us to make it. I mean, I don't know what the future holds, but if we're going to have a fighting chance, then we're going to have to have more than just surface feelings, you know what I mean?"

I smiled at her. Hesitated before I spoke again.

"Yep, I do. So, Tracey, how do you feel about me?"

"I'm crazy about your jailbait behind," she laughed. "I don't know what it is, but I do enjoy you. We don't fight all the time; there are very few hassles, and the few that we have come from outside sources. So I think we get along pretty well, and I like that. With Steve—hate to keep bringing him up—"

"I'm secure enough for you to talk about him, baby."

"—but we didn't always see eye-to-eye. I don't know. The sex was the bomb, like you said, but there was a price to pay. I never understood how Steve could want his ex and me at the same time. It always made me feel like something was wrong with me, like I didn't have everything he needed in a woman. And let me tell you something, I gave a whole lot to that relationship. I lived the air that he breathed, I mean, it was deep."

"You make him sound so bad, why'd you want the dude in the first place?"

She sputtered out a laugh, then got serious. "Rose-colored glasses make you see all kinds of things that end up not being there. It's like any other relationship. In the beginning you accentuate all your good sides, just to entice someone. But once you feel you have the person in your grip, boom, all the skeletons come flying out the closet and you gotta run for cover."

"Dig that," I told her. "But on the other hand, if it weren't for him, maybe you and I wouldn't have gotten together, huh?"

"Oh Lord, there you go. So I should be thankful Steve is an asshole? Is that what you're saying?"

"I'm not saying that. I'm trying to keep you focused and help you feel better about things. About how all this is really just life when you think about it. Put it like this: if it hadn't been me who'd just broken up with Lauren, it would have been somebody else. She'd still be mad, hurt, and angry. She'd still have to work through her feelings, and in my eyes, this is the same."

"Oh, I don't know about all that. Come on, let's start heading back."

We started walking west toward my car.

"Why don't you agree with me, Tracey?"

"For the simple fact that it would be different if Lauren and a guy had broken up but they didn't have to be in each other's faces all the time. But because

you'll still be coming to see me, well, she's forced to
see it. She can't really heal if what we're doing is still
going on right in her face."

"I have a solution for that."

She looked doubtful. "Which is?"

"I won't come visit you at your place anymore.
Once she returns from Christmas break, you can start
coming to mine. How's that sound?"

"Hmmm! Uh, I don't know. I've never been to your
place. What would your roommate say? What's his
name?"

"Brad. What could he say? You're my company, my
lady friend, and plus he's not there all the time anyway."

"Oh. Well, your parents. Do they know? About us?"

I cleared my throat.

"Uh, not really. They know Lauren and I aren't together anymore, but I haven't told them about you."

She stopped walking and grabbed my hand till I
stopped, too. "Why not?" Her voice was sharp, cutting.

"Tracey, be for real," I said in a calm, logical voice.
"This just happened."

"No, it hasn't—"

"What? You think just because I tell my parents
about you, that alone will solidify or validate us? Hey,
just by the very nature of our age differences and Lauren's relation to you, we're going to have to jump
through hoops to please everybody. Some folks aren't
going to like it, but we're not living for them."

She waved one finger at me, and I walked alongside
her once more. "Okay, that being said, maybe a future
meeting with your parents is a must."

"Yeah, okay, Tracey. Very future, though. I don't
think it'll prove anything."

"It's not to prove anything. It's just so they'll know what their son is up to."

"You talking all that noise," I said, stepping over a trashed paper bag, "but are you really ready to have a face-to-face with my parents?"

"No."

"I thought so. Scared?"

"Ahh, not really. Just not ready. Maybe one day. Definitely later than sooner, though."

28
Tracey

Once the after-Christmas sales hit, I made a trip out to West Oaks mall. I found a pair of Anne Kleins and a pair of Sporto shoes; then I went straight to Foley's and charged some sixty-dollar Liz Taylor perfume, a cute black-and-white backpack, three pairs of jeans, and two holiday sweater vests. I waited in line to purchase a few gift boxes, took every item to the gift wrapping cart located in the middle of the mall, and had everything wrapped separately at five bucks a pop.

Lugging all my packages, I smiled and thought, *Lauren will really enjoy these things; she loves getting gifts and I just know she'll like them.*

New Year's Eve started out quiet. Aaron wanted us to hang out downtown for a change, but because of the Y2K uncertainties, I insisted we stay close to home.

"Scared. Chicken. Quack, quack," he said.

"Excuse me. Ducks quack, not chickens!"

Instead of answering, he shoved me onto the living

room couch and crawled on top of me. I squirmed underneath his body, and got a little heated up when I felt his hardness pressing against me. We hadn't done anything in a while; I guess we were subconsciously trying to prove that our relationship was built on something more than sexual intimacy. With our holding back going beyond six days and counting. I felt there was nothing left to prove.

"Get naked," I commanded, and started pulling Aaron's shirttail from his pants.

"I'm yours tonight, baby. Do whatever you want to do to me."

"Oh, goodie," I squealed. I had Aaron get totally naked and I stripped down to my socks.

"Woman, take those damn socks off your feet. I can't suck your toes if you have socks on."

"Yes, you can and you will. You'll do whatever I tell you to do."

"Yes, ma'am," he replied and leaned back on the couch with his hands clasped behind his head.

I waved bye-bye at Aaron and began walking backward toward the kitchen.

"Where you going?" he asked.

"Don't ask questions. Just listen for my commands and do what I say."

I went to the refrigerator and poured a tall glass of pink lemonade. Aaron watched me carry the glass, and I knelt by his side. I gulped a few swallows of the cold beverage until remnants were spilling from my mouth. He was still watching me, bobbing his head, grinning and laughing at the same time.

His manhood looked mega-solid and I thought, *Great!* When I took him inside my mouth, he jerked and moaned. But after a while he relaxed, started pumping and gyrating his hips while I sucked him, swallowing the sugary drink and then loving him with all my mouth.

"Tracey, I *knew* I liked you. Damn, baby, why you been holding back on a brother?" He moaned and twisted and I smiled within from seeing how much he enjoyed himself. Once I was done with that, I started doing an oral dance that extended from his forehead to the nape of his neck; I made my way to his ears, his shoulders, his waist, in between his thighs, and all the way down his legs until I kissed, licked, and sucked on his smooth toes. They curled in my mouth, fighting me with all their little might. I laughed and turned Aaron on his stomach, kissing and biting him on his butt, which was thick and solid, but still as smooth as a baby's bottom.

"Damn, Tracey, okay, I can't take this anymore," he yelled, wriggling his body.

"Where's a condom?"

"Hell if I know. Call Target and ask a salesclerk. Tracey, baby, would you *please* turn me over right now?"

"No." I was holding him down with my left hand.

"I'm about to stick my foot up your—"

"No!"

"Don't you care that I'm about to explode? Now stop playing, woman."

"I'm not playing."

He jerked his torso like a sickly fish on Galveston Beach.

"Please, baby, *please* let me come inside you. Please, please," he asked, struggling to turn over and look at me.

Giggling, I felt my heart race with dangerous excitement. I spread out on the floor, opened my legs, and caught my breath as Aaron wiggled and forced his way inside. He pushed himself into me, inch by inch, deeper and deeper, until he filled me as tight as a hand fills a latex glove. I grabbed his head, squeezing him every time he thrust inside me. And I cried, jerked, and talked about things that didn't make any sense.

"Ooohhhhh, baby, you give good love, Aaron, you know that, ouch, ohhh, hurts so good. Oh, I love how you feel inside me, don't ever leave me, ouch, ouch, ouch, that felt good."

My orgasm rewound itself at least four times. And for the first time I didn't let out a bloodcurdling scream. I melted while he held me, felt like two separate bodies merged into one, a singular unit, with nothing more to come between us.

As we collapsed in each other's arms, I could say with assurance that the New Year definitely started out with a bang.

The rest of January flowed like a river. Lauren returned from Georgia. I gave her the gifts and her attitude was distant, but at least she was still speaking to me. Like we'd previously agreed, Aaron no longer came by the apartment. He'd taken to calling me at my job, and I'd have to rush and close my office door so we could get our love jones on. We'd talk on the phone a couple times a day, and I'd see him twice a week. Sometimes at his place, other times at a restaurant or a scaled-down Marriott, when I had the time and the funds.

I tried not to mention Aaron when in Lauren's presence. She just threw herself into her schoolwork, still going to band rehearsals, photography workshop, hanging out with Regis, and keeping to herself. Some nights she wouldn't come home at all, but I'd call Regis and that's where she'd be, which was fine with me. I enjoyed the solitude, felt more relaxed, and was free to talk to Aaron on the phone without being forced to steal away to my walk-in closet.

One night my stomach lurched with violence. I clutched it and squeezed a few times, hoping that would ease my discomfort. And even after it seemed my health was on the upswing, moments later I'd rush to sit on the toilet, flush, and return to my room, just to have to jump out of the bed and race back to the bathroom. When it seemed it was safe to go out, I decided to make a quick trip to the twenty-four-hour Walgreen's. It was around ten-thirty and I was sleepy, but I threw on some jogging pants, slapped a golf cap on my head, and jumped in the Malibu.

If you were to base your judgment on all the cars that were in the parking lot, you could assume that Walgreen's was having a late-night dollar sale. As I walked toward the entrance, I heard a man loudly singing, "Float, float on. Float on. Float on." I looked up and saw a short, three-hundred-pound Chinese dude singing the Floaters' biggest hit. He was snapping his fingers and saw me looking at him. The dude winked and I gave him the black-power sign and rushed into the store.

Once I'd selected some diarrhea medicine, I decided to search for a greeting card for a coworker whose birthday was coming up. On the way there, I passed by the aisle where all the baby food, diapers, and infant products are stocked. I saw just one shopper in the aisle, but the profile of the person made me do a double-take.

I was surprised yet not surprised to see him there. At first I started to keep on going and act like I didn't see him, but changed my mind. When I walked up to him, he didn't notice me. His knees were bent and his shoulders inclined forward while he examined the shelves.

I asked, just to see what he'd say. "What are you doing in the baby aisle, Steve?"

He looked from the baby food to me, to his basket, and back at me again. "I—uh—uh—I—"

"I—uh—uh nothing. I heard you were going to be a father."

He looked confused like he was trying to figure out who spread his business.

"Lelani told me."

"Oh," he replied, and shifted his eyes.

"You know, I really can't picture you being a daddy, Steve, but I guess it happens to most men at some point in their lives."

"Uh, yeah."

"Why didn't you tell me you were going to be a father the last time we spoke on the phone?"

He straightened his posture and forced out a stingy little grin. "Hey, I—I—I *was* going to tell you, but *you* didn't want to see me, remember?"

"Save it, Steve."

He gave me an "oh, well" shrug and continued reading baby-food labels.

"So, do you know if the baby's going to be a boy asshole or a girl asshole?"

He glared at me like he wished I would just go away. But I looked straight at him and didn't blink.

"Okay, Steve, sorry." I laughed. "That was a low blow. But seriously, boy or girl?" I asked, offering him a sweet smile.

He sputtered, "I have no idea. Lani probably knows, though."

"Hmmm, I guess that would make sense, being she's the mother."

Instead of responding, he deposited a half-dozen jars of baby food and a small pack of diapers into a shopping basket. Then Steve walked down the aisle and disappeared without saying good-bye.

I rolled my eyes and wondered why I'd ever wasted my time trying to hold on to him. Then I decided to go search for a decent but inexpensive birthday card. While trying to pick out something, I also spotted various greeting card lines and thought about how I used to buy Steve sentimental products just to be doing something, trying to show him how special he was to me. I had it so bad for him, spending four bucks on cards that he probably rushed to open just to see if there was some money inside. I'm sure he pretended to read the words, and then threw the card up on a shelf somewhere so it could collect dust. *No more,* I thought. *I'm glad I'm not the woman I used to be and I don't have to try and prove something to someone who doesn't really deserve me.*

Soon after finding something suitable, I entered the checkout line. I saw Steve one aisle over, standing next to a woman who was holding a four-month-old baby. The woman looked like she was a size sixteen, had on a multicolored smock, and her hair was bundled in a red bandanna. The woman was smiling and cooing at the baby. "See Daddy. Peaches, can you see Daddy? Poor thing, too bad she's allergic to tapioca, but this applesauce should do just fine." Instead of acting like he didn't know what the hell the woman was talking about, he got all friendly and grazed his nose against the baby's cheek. "Give Daddy a smile, Peaches."

My box of medicine crashed to the floor. I bent over to get it and looked up.

The woman appeared content, secure. How did she manage to do that, I wondered.

"Baby, hey, baby, put the *National Enquirer* in the basket, okay?" she said, gesturing at Steve.

Ain't this nothing?

"Hey, baby, Peaches is a little bit fussy. I'm going to wait for you in the car, all right?" She kissed the big baby on his cheek, then bundled their daughter and departed from the store.

Steve placed his items on the counter and paid for them. He turned around and noticed me standing a couple of customers behind him.

"Hey, you still here?" he asked.

I brushed past two old ladies and looked up at Steve. He didn't have on glasses tonight. Maybe he got smart and bought some bitch-proof contact lenses.

He started walking away with his packages, and extended his thumb and index finger next to his ear as if to say, "Call me."

"Who's the baby food for, Steve, you and Lani's baby? The one that's still in her womb? Or is this for some other fool's baby?" I said, wanting to yell but being wise enough not to do so.

He lowered his head, rolled his eyes, and scurried out of the store like a little Fifth Ward rat.

Just looking at Steve Monroe made me raise my head to the ceiling and exclaim, "Thank God for answering this prayer. The camel's back is now broken."

Feeling happy yet anxious, I paid for my items, fled to the Malibu, and listened to my tires violently kiss the asphalt while I raced from the parking lot.

"What up?" he asked, barely opening the door as I stood before him.

"I know I should have called first, but I had something on my mind and wanted to see you."

He looked at me, perplexed, not budging.

"Aaron, is this a bad time?" My voice cracked.

He sighed and motioned for me to follow him outside. We walked through the parking lot until we were standing underneath a flickering streetlight that winked at us every few seconds.

"What's—what's going on, Aaron?" My hands found the comforting place of my hips and I stared at him.

"Uh, bad timing. My dad is over right now. He's not doing too well. He just stopped by without calling, too. Hasn't been here too long himself. Hey, maybe I can call you in the morning at work. Would that be all right?"

I huffed and rotated my neck.

"What's wrong with your father?"

Aaron glanced up at his apartment then looked at me and frowned. "He was just diagnosed with multiple myeloma."

"With who?"

"Bone-marrow cancer. Gonna have to start getting chemotherapy. Apparently when he was given the news, he jumped in his ride and started driving. He caught himself trying to drive all the way out to Victoria, but realized he was too tired to drive a hundred miles one way. That's when Dad decided he needed to come see me. Hey, why all the questions, Tracey? You don't believe me?"

I flinched and felt like an asshole of the worst kind. I tried to reach out and touch his arm, but he backed away a bit and it didn't bother me. "Hey, I'm sorry, Aaron. I didn't know. Go ahead and be with your dad, I'll get with you tomorrow." I turned and headed back to my car, feeling Aaron's eyes on me all the way.

* * *

That weekend Lauren initiated a conversation with me, something she hadn't done in weeks. I was holed away in my bedroom, reshelving my hundreds of books: my Sidney Sheldon collection, the E. Lynn Harris trilogy, and the others were giving the impression that they'd been all shook up, and I was sick of looking at the disorder. Lauren's knuckles made light tapping sounds on my half-open door. I turned away from my work, swallowed the shock that was lodged deep in my throat, and asked her, "What's going on?"

She stood in the doorway, twisting and digging her big toe in the carpet until I gaped at her so hard that either bravery or fear lifted her feet and she entered the room and stood next to me.

"Well, um, I forgot to tell you that the band is, uh, going to Dallas next month. S-s-statewide competition at Reunion Center." She stood there staring at my piles of books and yanking on her beaded necklace, which made a clinking sound.

"And you're saying that to say what?"

She hesitated. "I need you to fill out the permission slip."

I waved my hand. "That's all? Well, give it here. I'll fill it out right now."

She remained immobile, like I hadn't even said anything.

"Lauren, why are you acting so weird? Just go and get—"

"Well, uh, Daddy's already paid for my airplane ticket, but we need, uh, since you have all this, this, this," she said rattling the necklace more rapidly, "extra money to use for hotel rooms, what about . . . spending some of it . . . on me?"

A couple of Nelson George novels fell from my hands. I turned and faced her.

"What did you say?"

She took a few steps back, but continued to look at me.

"Mom, I don't think it's fair you have all this money to be throwing away . . . and I have a little cash in my savings account, but not enough to buy it."

"Buy it? Buy what? Lauren, what are you talking about?"

"Uniform," she snapped, like I ought to be able to know what she was thinking automatically. "They want us to wear these new uniforms, but they cost a lot of money. Daddy can't buy the plane ticket *and* the hotel room *and* the uniform, so since you . . . could you pay for it?" She stopped to pick the Nelson George books up off the floor.

"Well, if you just need some money, that's all you gotta say. I don't appreciate your bringing up how I spend my money. My cash is my business. I'm grown, I work, and I can do whatever the hell I want to do, and if you don't like it, you can always go live with your father."

I rose up and started to stomp over to my night-stand, but instead snapped, "Bring me my purse."

She trudged with her head hung low, dragging her long legs like a female Charlie Brown. I turned my back. My hands jerked and convulsed when I began throwing Whitfield's, Briscoe's, and Mosley's books on the shelves, forgetting to put them in alphabetical order.

She returned with my purse, but the way she was holding it, I would need arms the length of King Kong's to reach it.

I folded my arms. "Lauren, either hand me the

purse or you can figure out a way to pay for your uniform yourself."

She turned up her nose and mouth, her eyes thin slits, and pressed the purse hard in my hand, but it dropped to the floor.

One, two, three, I whispered, aiming for a count of ten, but what good would it have done?

"Look, Lauren, I may be your mother, but I don't have to do jack for you. I gave birth to you, but I won't have you treating me like vomit just because you don't understand how things operate in a grown-up world. But if you live long enough, you'll see, and if you don't watch it, I'll let you see it sooner than you think."

"Okay, okay," she said, and placed her hands over her ears.

I dumped the contents of my purse on the bureau. Tore off a blank check.

"How much is it again?" I asked.

She mumbled something.

"Lauren, please speak up. I don't interpret mumbling."

"Uniform is a hundred and fifty bucks, but could I get two-fifty? I could use a little spending money."

I really didn't want to come up with that much cash, and started to say "hell, no," but thought how that might make things worse, so I hastily scribbled out the check.

"When is this trip again?" I asked.

She snatched the check and examined it closely and looked back at me.

"The second week in February. On a Thursday."

"That's two weeks from now," I told her, realizing how soon that day would get here.

"Yeah, and I'll need you to take me to Hobby Airport that morning and pick me up on Saturday," she said, folding the check and sliding it in her pants pocket.

"Gee, thanks for letting me know all this. Dang, Lauren."

She shrugged and looked at the floor. Maybe relieved that she got some money out of me, but still failing to look the part. But considering everything, maybe I owed her that; maybe a monetary blessing would be one of my sacrifices.

"So, Lauren, you have to spend the night, huh? Where are you staying?"

"At the Days Inn. Daddy's paying for my meals and lodging."

I reeled back, irritated. "You already told me."

"And my airfare."

"I'm not deaf."

"Umph."

"Well, Lauren," I said, "seems like you told Derrick about this trip before you told me."

She just looked at me like I didn't have brains for brains.

"Why was I the last to know?" I asked. I knew I sounded insecure, but it was certainly a blow to my ego when I realized how hurt I felt (yes, hurt) about being left out. Sure, I knew she was upset about what had transpired between Aaron and me, but shouldn't the fact that I gave birth to her count for something? Was it too much to expect my daughter to still honor my position? And wouldn't all the other things I did right as a mom make up for the things I flunked at?

Lauren squinted at me for a moment. "Truthfully, you're hardly ever here anymore, and by the time I see you, I just forget to tell you some things. But that's not important. The deal is I'm going now and I can't wait to leave. I doubt that you'll miss me," she said, and stormed from the room.

It was hard to get in touch with Aaron all the next week. I'd call his cell every two minutes just to get one of those "the customer you're trying to reach, blah-blah-blah" messages. He didn't call me, and I wasn't about to go by his place again unannounced.

"Hmmm, I wonder what's going on with him," I said to Indira one weekend while we were malling at First Colony. We'd already combed the anchor stores like Dillard's, Mervyn's, and Foley's. Now we were browsing in Walden Books. I was hovering in the magazine section; she was raking her hands over books at the nearby bargain book display.

"Girl, who you asking? If he hasn't called you in a week, something must be wrong. Doesn't sound like him at all."

"What you think could be wrong, Indy?"

"Girl, if you could see the look on your face," she said, flipping to the back cover of a Michael Jordan book. "Say, Tracey, I don't know the degree of your feelings for Aaron and vice versa, but if you have a bond that's strong, then you will hear from him, that I'm sure of. You can't have a thick and solid relationship with someone and it just breaks up without warning."

"Lauren and Aaron did." Gosh, that rushed out of my mouth fast.

"But did they really? Maybe Lauren was disillusioned over what she thought she had with Aaron. Maybe he wasn't as into her as she thought, or else— well, you know what I'm trying to say."

"Hmm! I guess," I said, picking up and staring at a ton of plain-looking yet pricey journals.

Right then my cell started ringing. I dropped the journals on the floor and fumbled for the phone.

"Hello? Aaron?"

He laughed in my ear, his voice thick and hoarse, yet sounding like a sweet melody.

"Aaron, what's wrong? Where are you?"

"Memorial Hermann Southwest."

"At the hospital? What's wrong?"

"Daddy. That damned cancer again. Has to take a liver test. I've been back and forth to the hospital the past few days. Sorry for not calling. Lots going on."

"What's going on, Aaron? Is he all right?"

"Yeah, looks like he's going to pull through. We almost lost him, though."

"Aaron." My voice softened. "You should have called me. I wish you would have called me, let me do something."

"No, no, baby girl."

That brought on a smile, the baby calling his baby a baby.

"Nothing you could do. Hey, I can't talk long. Just wanted to get with you about what's up. I'll be back home tonight. I want to see you, too. Can you swing by, say around eight?"

"Sure," I said softly. "You take care of yourself and I'll see you tonight."

Indira cocked her head and smiled.

"See, I told you so."

I pulled up outside Aaron's building at seven-fifty. His car was there, but instead of rushing to him, I forced myself to remain outside for another few minutes. I'd wondered what I'd see when I next saw his face. Six days is a long time not to see someone you want to be around.

When I finally did go up, he answered the door with a damp body towel hanging around his glistening neck.

"Excuse me, babe, just got out of the shower. Make yourself at home. I'll be back."

My eyes followed him until he disappeared from my sight.

When he returned, I pointed to the breakfast bar stool. He slumped in the chair and I walked over to him and started massaging his shoulders, rubbing little circles on his back.

"Uh, uh, lower, lower, right there. Ssssss, thanks, Tracey."

"My pleasure. Anything I can do for you? Your dad?"

"Pay the hospital bill."

I playfully smacked him on his head with the nearby cable TV guide.

"No, being here with me is enough. God, how I wanted to see you, but it was . . . there wasn't much I could do. Some of my relatives, aunts and uncles, drove in from Alexandria, Louisiana. People I hadn't seen in years. I knew it was serious then."

"Oh Lord. That must've been hard to deal with."

"Hey, we had our moments. Grown men crying over my dad. But he's pulling through. They have him on an IV, and he's responding and eating pretty well. Hopefully, he'll be home within a few days."

"That's great."

"But," Aaron said, holding up one finger, "he's not out of the woods yet. He needs someone around to help him, give him his medicine and baths and stuff. Mom can only do so much, so I expect to spend more time over in Conroe than I'd usually spend."

"Uh-huh." I squinted.

"And what I need you to understand, Tracey, is that with my father getting sick and all, I can't promise you I'll be able to give you all the attention you might want. You know, those three simple things you said you want in a relationship? Attention, affection, and uh, I forget—"

"Being made to feel valuable," I mumbled, and frowned.

"Yeah, that's it."

"Well," I said wistfully, "I can understand how you need to be there for your dad, your mom. When it boils down to it, family is all you got."

"Yeah, my parents have come through for me many times, mostly financially, but other times, too. Like when I was a kid, Daddy would come out to all my Little League games. Even though he was working and trying to keep his business afloat, he'd sacrifice and be there. He'd be late—" Aaron's face flushed, his voice cracked. "He'd be late . . . but he'd always make it in time to see me at bat, hitting those doubles and stuff. He'd be the loudest one in the stands. You know, I'd be so embarrassed when my pops would yell and shout, raising the roof before there was even such a thing as raising the roof, but on the inside I was proud, glad he was doing that, all on account of me."

I touched Aaron's hand, ran my fingers alongside his knuckles, picked up his hand and pressed it against my lips.

"Babe, you're so good to me," he said.

"What did you say?" I asked.

His eyes widened. "I said something wrong?"

"No, usually I'm the one who says 'you're so good to me.' I'm surprised to hear you say that. Never thought I'd hear you say that."

"Well, it's true. I know I should have called you sooner than what I did. But I was so exhausted and Daddy's health was key. I was just hoping you weren't getting pissed at me and feeling like I was out doing something behind your back. Because I wouldn't do that to you, and even if I were to do it, it would be in front of your face."

"Oooh, you make me sick," I told him and fell against Aaron's head, pressing upon him like my bones had melted and I was fainting.

"Hey, I'll help you get better too . . . baaabbbyyy."

My insides warmed over like a sudden wave of heat showing up on a frosty winter day. I kissed the sides of his face and his moist nose, and blew my warm and sweetened breath on his eyelids. Even though I could tell he sucked in his breath so as not to smell mine, I didn't hate on him, didn't pop him upside the head. I held Aaron close in my arms, feeling like I was his mother in a way, yet loving him like his lover.

29
Lauren

The first Saturday in February, I worked the 10:30-to 2:30 shift. Once I punched out, instead of asking Mom to pick me up, I caught Metro. First thing I did when I got home was dial up Regis. Earlier in the week she'd mentioned something about hanging out.

"Rege, what's up this weekend?"

"Hey, heifer. Uh, me and some of the crew going joy-riding tonight. Wanna roll?"

"Sure, I ain't got nothing better to do. Who is 'some of the crew'?"

"Well, Justine's sister gave her a car last Christmas, and she's our chauffeur. My cousin Hope is over, so she game. Then Zoe and Lia coming, too."

"What about Charisse?"

Regis laughed. "What about her?"

"Oh, it's like that, huh? Well, anyway, shoot, how many of us are going? One, two, three . . . six people. We can all fit in Justy's car?"

"Yeah, we'll fit. Don't even sweat it."

After that conversation, it felt good to know I had

the place to myself. I mostly poked around the house, opening and closing the refrigerator every ten minutes until the girls came and scooped me up. That was around seven. Since my mother never showed up that afternoon or even bothered to call home, I decided not to leave her a note on the fridge.

Let her worry.

If only I were that fortunate.

"Hey, y'all, what's happening?" I said, sitting down and fastening my seat belt.

"Whassup? Your hair looking cute, girl," Zoe said. I turned my head around so she could see the back, too.

"Thanks. I know I'm blazing," yelled Regis, who was sitting up front. Regis's hairstyle, a display of tiny ringlets bunched up on top of her head, was so crisp it crackled. I could smell the holding spray before I even got in the car. She started patting the top of her hair and smiling.

Zoe stared at Regis. Then she turned back toward me and laughed. "I like those knots in your hair, Lauren."

"Thanks, Zoe." Ever since the beginning of the year, I'd been sporting Nubian knots on the crown of my head; the edges were resting at my shoulders in a light flip. Guys would usually look at me longer than a little bit, and I'd look back at them, but so far no phone numbers had been exchanged, no love connections made.

"Hey, boo, we ain't seen you in a while. This is going to be fun, y'all. Just like at the slumber party." That was Lia.

"Yeah, I could use a girls' night out. Hey, can someone turn up the radio?" I asked.

I was squeezed behind the driver's seat, next to the window. The seating arrangements were myself, Zoe, and Lia in the back. Up front Justine had the wheel, Hope was in the middle, and Regis had the window seat.

"Happy now?" asked Hope turning up the radio and bouncing and waving her hands. "The Thong Song" by Sisqo was on.

"Aw, heck. Every time I turn on the radio, that song is either coming on or going off," complained Justine. She was heading north on Beltway Eight.

"What, you got something against Sisqo? Shoot, he sexy," yelled Regis.

"Define sexy."

"Uh, Justy, what planet are you from? The boy got the moves, the money, and the mike. What else he need? What else *you* need, Justy?" asked Regis.

"I like intelligence," Justine said firmly.

"Duh, this is Houston." Regis laughed. "Ain't too many intelligent guys here. You gotta go to Austin to get that."

"Oh, I don't think so," said Justine. "There's some intelligent guys here. You might have to go to a college campus to find them, but they're here, right, Lauren?"

"What you say?" I yelled, and leaned toward the front.

"Lauren's not the one to ask. She and her college guy bit the dust," shouted Regis, who was rocking in her seat and singing.

"Ooohh. What happened? I thought y'all were tight," Lia asked, and leaned across Zoe to peer at me.

"Aaron dumped Lauren like a pot of burned rice."

I reached across Zoe and squeezed the flab on Miss Bigmouth's neck.

"Ouch. Lauren, stop. You know I'm telling the truth," Regis moaned, rubbing her pinched skin.

"Well, no one asked you to do that, Regis. I know how to talk for myself."

"Well, talk, sister, talk."

"Regis, you need to quit," I told her, almost wishing that I hadn't agreed to hang out with the crew.

"No, I don't. Now go ahead and tell us, Lauren. I wanna hear this one myself, 'cause you never told me the whole story."

"Thank the Lord I didn't. It'd be on Headline News by now."

"Seriously, Lauren," urged Justine. "Please tell us what happened."

"Okay," I told Justine. "But first, could Hope turn down that music? I can't even hear myself talk."

"Well, make up your mind," said Hope. "First you want it up, then you want it down. What I look like? Kunta Kinte cloth?" she said jokingly.

With Sisqo's voice now a faint cry, I leaned toward the front and looked around at all the crew. "Well, my boyfriend, rather ex-boyfriend, dumped me because . . . I wouldn't give him none."

"That bastard," said Hope.

"Ole scrub," added Lia.

"Ah, that sucks, Lauren," said Zoe. "I mean, how did it happen? He just came right out and told you the reason why?"

"Well, he didn't say it directly, but he did in so many words. I still can't believe it, and it's been about six weeks now."

"If he dumped you over that, you didn't need him anyway. You'll find someone more deserving of you, girl."

"Thanks, Justy."

"So, when's the last time you talked to the foul Negro?" asked Lia.

I squirmed in my seat. "You know, I don't know. I— I try not to think about it."

"I know that's right. Huh, I'll bet he was screwing someone else, tipping out on you while you trying to be faithful to his cheatin' ass," said Regis.

I smiled. I hoped that wherever Aaron was, he knew we were talking about him.

"So tell me something, Lauren. Did you have any idea that he was cheating on you, assuming that he was?" asked Justine.

"I didn't have a clue." I said this with bitterness. "Aaron was as slick as Clinton, and Clinton ain't that slick."

"Huh, I don't see how you missed that one, Lauren. Ray Charles could have seen that," claimed Regis.

"Well, Ray better be glad he wasn't dating Aaron," I said softly, and looked out the window.

As soon as I let those words out of my mouth, Justine made a right turn, heading east on Westheimer. Westheimer is Houston's primary street for joy-riding and hanging out, kind of like a scaled-down version of Hollywood's Sunset Boulevard.

Soon after making our turn, Lia yelled, "Hey, any of y'all's wallets flowing tonight?"

"Sounds like yours ain't," murmured Regis. She pulled out a bill. "I got a five. Why?"

"How 'bout the rest of y'all?" Lia said looking around at us.

"I'm broke," snapped Hope.

"I got a ten," chimed in Justine.

"I got three bucks and fiddy-two cents," said Zoe.

"And I have about seven or eight dollars, I think," I said.

"Hey, y'all, let's go and get two twenty-piece McNuggets," Lia suggested.

"Oh no. In case you forgot, I work at Mickey D's," I reminded Lia.

"So what? It still tastes good, and I want some nuggets." She laughed like what I thought didn't mean a damn thing.

"Justy, there will be a McDonald's on the left-hand side, right before you get to, uh, South Voss, I think," said Zoe.

I rolled my eyes and slumped in my seat.

Seems like a few minutes later we pulled up to the McDonald's.

With Regis leading the way, us girls filed into the restaurant.

Soon as we neared the service counter, I noticed them: my mom and my ex pulling up to the pickup window. Aaron was in the driver's seat. Mom sat next to him, smiling. I got this awful feeling in the pit of my stomach, like I'd just got the news that someone died, and I didn't want to believe it even if it was true.

But as close as they seemed, I was relieved that they were outside, that we didn't suffer the drama of them actually coming inside the restaurant.

Thank God for small blessings, I thought, when I saw the car lurch away.

We went ahead and placed our order and were glad to find empty seats.

"So, Lauren," Justy was saying to me while we waited on our nuggets, "do you regret not giving Aaron any loving?"

Fortunately she was sitting right next to me and talked in a low voice so that Regis and the others couldn't hear. When I heard her question, it seemed like an opening that I'd been waiting for. Although I'd hardly admitted it to myself, I realized that, yes, I was very torn up over what had happened between me and Aaron, especially since I'd decided to wait to have sex based on Mom's recommendation. The fact that she could advise me, yet didn't know how to keep her own self in line, just made me wish I hadn't listened to her in the first place. She got to know what I was missing out on, and somehow that just didn't seem fair. Somehow it seems when you're committed to doing the right thing, the wrong things happen.

"Well, Justy, I'd be lying if I said I don't have some regrets. I mean, I didn't want to be with Aaron because every other girl seems like she's already been with her boyfriend," I said, and swallowed deeply. "More than anything, I wondered if he was the right one, and the fact that he couldn't wait for me, well, that made me wonder . . ."

I couldn't go on, unable to imagine that the guy I strongly believed was the best real boyfriend—the *only* real boyfriend—I ever had, turned out to be someone who I wasn't really sure cared about me. I felt major dumb, used in a way, even though I never even gave Aaron a significant part of my body. It was the principle. The fact that he could promise me one thing and do another, and then to get with . . .

I decided to hop up right then and fill my cup with Sprite and lots of ice.

By that time Regis, Lia, and Zoe were coming toward our table, carrying a couple of trays. Just as I was passing them, Regis stopped walking and pointed. "Hey, y'all, look over there."

I saw what she saw, and wished for the first time in my life that I didn't have the gift of sight.

"What?" Hope asked.

"Lauren, what's your momma doing here with Aaron?"

"It's not what you think it is," I blurted, and looked at the floor.

"Uh-uh, I don't even believe them," Regis said. "They got some nerve. Your momma's acting like she in high school or something. Hanging out on West-heimer. Girl, you need to get that shit straight."

Her voice was loud and booming; the rest of the crew was torn between staring at Aaron and my mother, and trying to not steal peeks at me. I felt someone grab my elbow and I began walking back-ward. The vision of the two people in the world who had hurt me the most became smaller and smaller.

As loud as Regis was, I felt relieved that it appeared neither my mother nor Aaron saw us. They were standing at a register holding a white paper McDon-ald's bag and looking like they were talking to the store manager. Justine ushered us together and waved at us girls to grab our food the best way we could, and we then ducked out of the restaurant. I looked at Jus-tine and thanked her with my eyes. Eyes that were too shocked to produce moisture.

30
Lauren

"Take me to Aaron's," I ordered Justine, as soon as we drove about a mile away from the restaurant.

"Why you wanna go there, girl? He still back there with—"

"Will you just shut the hell up, Regis?"

"Excuse me!" she said, like she really didn't care one way or the other, and increased the volume to the radio.

Zoe patted me on the thigh. I didn't look at her. Looked out the window, into the blackness of the night. Knowing that something had to give.

We pulled up in front of Aaron's place.

"Thanks for the ride. I'm getting out here."

Regis shot me a look. "I know you not going to see that scrub."

"You have no idea what I'm going to do, so don't even try it."

I stepped away from the car and waved at the crew.

Justine's Buick crawled away; she kept looking at me with cautious eyes. One final look from Justy, and I found myself alone in the parking lot. I sighed and walked up to Aaron's front door. Tapped lightly two times, then harder four times until my knock was answered.

"Oh, hey, how you doing?"

"Fine," I mumbled.

He stared at me. My face and body felt the warmth of humiliation, like I'd just spilled a pitcher of grape juice on brand-new clothes.

"You all right, Lauren?"

"Yeah, I—I'm—no, I'm not all right. May I come in, please?"

Brad swung open the door and I slid past him into the living room. Set my purse on the couch and looked around. Sniffed the air. It smelled like nothing. Just like I felt.

"Whassup, Lauren? What's going on?"

I opened my mouth, but it was like English was no longer my first or second language. I wished that he could read my mind, that he could say the words that were omitted from my mouth. Instead of reading my mind, he examined my empty hands, clasped one of them in his, and motioned at me to sit on the couch. I crossed my arms and began rocking back and forth like an eighty-year-old woman sitting on earth without a thing to do. He said nothing for the longest. But his silence didn't make me feel bad at all. Felt like he understood. Or like he wanted to.

After a while he said softly, "You know, don't you?"

I stopped rocking. "How could you tell?"

"Easy."

"How?" I pleaded.

"Your face says it all, your body."

"I just don't under . . . I just don't get it."

He said nothing.

"Am I ugly?"

"Hell, nah, Lauren. Nothing ugly about you."

"You're just saying that."

"No, nooo. Wouldn't do that. You're fine and you know it. Maybe your boy doesn't know it."

"Hmmm. My—my mom looks better than me, though, right?"

He shook his head. "Look, I don't think it's about how you look compared to your mother. Y'all two different women. Two different generations. No comparison."

"But why didn't he stick it out with me, Brad? Did he . . . did he ever tell you?"

He shifted in his seat.

"Never mind," I told him, and rocked even more vigorously.

"Nooo, Lauren. I don't have anything to tell you as far as all that. All I know is, stuff happens. Aaron, well, maybe he just felt he had to move on, you know what I mean?"

"No, I don't know. I feel it's messed up to dump me because I'm trying to keep myself . . . and not because I wanted to, either, but just to please a woman who . . . I should've gone and done something anyway. Shouldn't have listened to her. Hypocrite!" I yelled, releasing a lot of my pain.

The color in Brad's face changed from brown to strawberry. His eyes grew as round as saucers. I wanted to laugh at his reaction, but I kept pulling my fingernails and twisting all my rings.

I thought about my mother. "I'm the one who tries to do the right thing, and I end up getting done wrong."

Silence.

I jumped up and looked in the kitchen.

"Ugh, I could just—"

Brad leaped to his feet.

"You're not going to start breaking things are you?"

"Ahh, ha-ha. That's all you're worried about, Brad?"

"No, that's not all. Worried about you, too, Lauren."

I looked at him. What he said sounded suspicious, but good. He walked to me and was so close I could detect the faint scent of his deodorant. He put his arms around me. Patted me on the back real softlike. Barely felt it, but I knew his hands were on me. I stiffened at first. His hands on my body felt strange. Like they didn't belong. But it was like his body couldn't hear what my mind was saying. And he pulled me closer to him, against the warmth of his chest.

Comfort.

Acceptance.

"Am I ugly?"

"Nooo. Now stop asking me that before I lie and say yes."

I smiled. Shoulders relaxed. My hands moved up his side, around his strong waist. Moved my head in closer to his shoulder.

Resting. Releasing. Feeling good. Feeling not so good. Wondering what I'd do if Aaron walked in. Wondering why I'd even care what he thought. Wondering what he and my mom were doing.

I looked up at Brad. One eye bigger than the other, yet they were still taking in all of me. Eyes talking to me. Telling me I'm okay. Nothing's wrong with me.

I tilted my head. My lips advancing toward his. Been so long. Just this once. Couldn't hurt. Already hurt.

Mmmmm.

Sweet connection.

His lips were sweeter than what I *ever* thought (not that I ever thought).

Brad's tongue licked and folded my lips inside his wet mouth. I felt that familiar stirring. A stirring I thought belonged to Aaron alone.

My panties had no mouth but still spoke volumes, whispering in my ear, *You're wet and getting wetter.* Maybe this is how it's supposed to go. Maybe Aaron wasn't the one. Maybe that's why things happened the way they did. Maybe I'm losing my mind.

Brad's hand inching down my back. Warm. Caressing. Sliding toward my starving behind.

Damn, that feels sooo good.

My legs shake, rattling like an impatient child's. My butt automatically sticks farther out.

Touch me all over. I deserve this. Need this. Shoulda been *had* this.

Brad's eyes were closed, his mouth open.

I could feel the heat of his breath stroking my cheek. Wanted his breath on more than just my cheek.

"You all right?" he asked huskily.

"I'm fi—I'm fine," I croaked.

My knees were weak and as undependable as the rickety legs of an old wooden table.

"You want to go to my room?"

His voice sounded crackly and uneven. Like I couldn't hear straight.

"Think you can carry me?" I heard myself say.

"Well, we're about to find out," he whispered.

I closed my eyes.

Felt him wrap his arms about me. One hand across my back, the other under the backs of my knees. Hoisting me up. I cradled my face in his neck. Eyes shut tight. Blacker than black is what I can see. He fumbled with the doorknob.

I heard a door squeaking and turning.

I smelled gym shoes, Lagerfeld cologne, and chlorine, like someone had been swimming.

Plop, I was on his bed. Don't want to think about it. Don't think about it. I heard the door being locked. My eyes were still closed. I saw nothing but blackness. Nothing but total darkness. And Aaron's Chris Webber–like smile shines bright within my darkness.

Why is *he* smiling? He glad for me? Glad someone else can pay a rain check besides him?

I swallowed hard when I felt Brad lay next to me in bed.

"Lauren," he whispered, but it was more of a statement than a question.

"I wanna see your body," he said.

His words caused my knees and legs to shake. I had on black slacks and a black T-shirt, black knee-highs, and black Mary Janes. Felt his hands on my feet, on my shoes. Unbuckling them. Sliding off my knee-highs. I was as stiff as a corpse.

Hurry up, please hurry.

I listened for sounds, laughter, and additional voices. Hearing nothing, my body moaned within my soul. The coolness of the night caressed my breasts as soon as my T-shirt fell to the floor.

Is my Mom to blame for my shirt being on Brad's floor?

If she hadn't shown up at Mickey D's with Aaron, would I be giving up my body? With Brad McMillan of all people?

Is this how I want to go out?

My feet were now bare. My soul exposed.

Zzzzzzzzz.

Brad's hands unzipped my slacks. Warm hands. No, actually they were scorching. Didn't know hands could feel like this, especially ones that didn't belong to Aaron Oliver.

My eyes were closed, and I felt Brad looking at me. All that was left were my panties and a bra. I could feel his eyes walking up and down my body like it was an open field. His hands were shaking, and I was opening and closing my fists. He slid next to me. I opened my eyes. All he had on was his BVDs. He poked his finger under the fabric of my brassiere. My legs wobbled.

"Ahhhh, Lauren," he moaned, and pressed himself into my thigh. His penis was hard, like it was made of mortar. I shuddered at the thought of mortar penetrating my body. Making itself at home inside the deepest part of me.

Brad ground himself against me, my thigh, my leg. I grimaced, wanted to roll out of the bed. His breathing was heavy, like he'd been running an all-day marathon. I guess I was the finish line.

I *am* finished if I let Brad McMillan be the first man to infiltrate my body.

Is this how I want to go out?

I wanted to cry.

Cry.

Anguish bursting within me like a dam, I let my insides out.

"You okay, Lauren? Why you crying? You worried it's going to hurt?"

I sat up.

"No," I said wiping my eyes. "I'm not worried it's going to hurt. I *know* it's going to hurt."

"It's always like that the first time," he assured me.

I finally looked at him. The serious expression on

his face suggested he was concerned, so caring. But was his expression sincere, or did he have the I'm-about-to-get-some look down pat?

"Don't worry," he said. "I promise not to hurt you."

"Don't say that."

"What?"

"Don't promise me you won't hurt me. How do you know what will or will not hurt me?"

He raised his eyebrows, looking baffled, and shifted his eyes to the side.

"Okay, I can't promise you that it won't hurt, but if it does, I won't be doing it on purpose."

I laughed.

"Gee, thanks for being honest, Brad."

He looked at me without smiling, began sliding his moist hand against my bare shoulder.

I felt so weak. So close, yet so far. Brad embraced me tight, pulling me against his chest, squeezing me so hard I thought I'd done something wrong. He kissed my neck, lightly, sweetly. His body was a magnet. So hard to pull away. He grabbed my hand and we plopped on the bed, our arms and legs a mass of amorous entanglement.

The ringing phone made us stop what we'd started.

We locked eyes.

It rang again.

He hopped out of bed and opened the door. The answering machine did its thing.

"Hey, thanks for calling, but no one is home, so it's entirely impossible for us to pick up this phone. Please leave us a message after the t-t-tone."

"Hi, Brad, it's A. Pick up if you're there."

Brad looked at me and then disappeared like a vapor. My hands fumbled for my shirt and slacks. Had one shoe on and was inserting my foot inside the other when Brad reappeared. He wore a hopeful smile and his eyes danced and sparkled.

"You leaving already? Don't go. He ain't coming home tonight."

Instead of looking at Brad, I raised my eyes to the ceiling and mumbled, "Do you take rain checks?"

31
Tracey

The following Sunday morning, Lauren's dad picked her up for church. I just sat on the couch, forced myself to sit still for one hour straight. No getting up every ten minutes to open the refrigerator. No tinkering with the stereo.

I wanted to think, to have one clear thought after another, to get in touch with my inner spirit and hear what, if anything, was being said. Even though I didn't want them to, my thoughts kept going back to my mother. I'd shut my eyes and shake my head, but I could still see her face. Her looking at me, face all miserable looking, and frowning. Showing me nothing more than what I'd been looking at most of my life.

It's the spring of '82. I'm sixteen. For the past few weeks I've been waking up feeling so dizzy that as soon as I stand I feel like slumping to the floor. I've been urinating seems like every half hour. The smell of anything greasy gives me migraines. And don't forget about the nausea. I hate throwing up. Hate when my throat narrows and then contracts as I spew out the most horrid taste imaginable. When I ate the catfish last night, it looked and tasted so good that I devoured it, letting it go down my throat, hot, spicy, and flavorful. But twelve hours later, as I looked inside the toilet, I saw pink remnants of my meal floating in the water, and I cursed this thing that was causing me to lose my peace of mind.

I had just flushed the toilet and was rinsing my mouth with tap water when my mother burst into the bathroom. I stood upright and felt my legs shaking.

"Tracey, I heard you in here puking. Girl, what's wrong with you?"

"N-nothing."

Her stern eyes penetrated my face and crisscrossed down to my stomach, which I began rubbing.

Her jaw tightened and her fingers beckoned me to follow her.

I began praying really hard, hoping for a miracle to turn my life around.

"Have a seat," she said, and pointed to the kitchen table. I sat and looked at my hands.

"Tracey, I'm going to ask you something, and I want you to tell me the truth."

I nodded.

"Are you pregnant?"

"I—no," I told her cuttingly. My mother grunted and narrowed her eyes. My lips trembled as I felt my heart hiccup inside my chest.

My mother grunted again and said, "Let me rephrase that. Have you gotten a test to see if you're pregnant or not?"

First my shoulders started shaking, then my legs followed. I tried to hide my hands underneath the table, but they were trembling so hard they wouldn't fit.

"I asked you a question."

"Mom, I don't know, I think I'm just sick, think I'm just stressed."

"Stressed from what? 'Cause you're worried if you're pregnant or not?"

"Mmmm, mmmmm," that was me, weeping, wanting to be anywhere but in my mother's presence. Her tongue clucked, and the ridges in her jaw were enough to make any grown person want to run for his life.

"We're going to the doctor, Tracey. If you're pregnant, there's something we can do about it." She started thumbing through the Yellow Pages as if I weren't even there.

"What are you talking about?"

"You're not having it."

"Mom, what do you mean? What if I really am pregnant? I can't kill a baby."

"You should've thought about that before you lied down with Derrick. It is his, isn't it?"

I averted my eyes and swallowed deeply.

"Yes," I whispered.

Mom stormed from the kitchen and refused to speak to me until the day she dragged me over to Dr. Feinstein's office at Texas Medical Center. We sat in the waiting room, she on one side and me on the other. She waited stone-faced and clicking her heels together; I browsed through a couple of raggedy Seventeen magazines.

Once the urine test was complete, it only confirmed what I already knew inside. The strange feelings my body offered me throughout the day were my clue.

The baby was scheduled to be born in November, Dr. Feinstein informed my mom. Mom didn't even circle the date on her calendar. Didn't even accept the vitamins the doctor tried to give her. She immediately set an appointment for me to get an abortion. I'd hated her before, but once she tried to take control of my life and my unborn child's, hate was a mild description for how I felt about her from then on.

"Mom," I begged her. "I don't want to do this. I can't kill a baby."

"You ain't killing it. Doctor is. It ain't a baby anyway, just some gook at this stage."

"But, Mom, if the gook one day evolves into a baby, then it is a baby, an embryo that will one day be my offspring. Your grandchild, Mom."

"Ain't my grandchild. Just a mistake. You're too young. You haven't even gotten all your education. You got all the relatives talking about you and me behind our backs. Talking about you ain't nothing but a girl destined for welfare— government cheese and all the other ridiculous handouts. I may not make much money at my jobs, but at least I'm earning my own keep. I can't have you living off the welfare."

"Mom, why do you think I'm going to go get on welfare? And I really don't give a damn what they think, even if they are my relatives. They've never done anything for me anyway."

"Don't matter. We're blood, and blood can hurt you worse than anybody else."

"I can see that," I said, and rolled my eyes at her.

The night before I was supposed to get the "operation," I crawled into bed, tossing and turning, kicking the covers off while I imagined how it would feel to get that baby ripped from my insides. I screamed in the night, waking up with my clothes soaking wet and clinging to my chest. I shuddered and washed my face with cold water, crying and praying for a miracle.

The next morning, Mom was washing clothes and suffered a slight heart attack, unheard of for a thirty-eight-year-old woman. We missed our appointment, and a follow-up date was never set. Lauren Hayes was born the second week of November. On the day she made her entrance into the world, Mom handed Lauren to me, and when she did, I felt she was giving me my life back.

* * *

That afternoon, when I heard Lauren coming in from church, I thought she'd be alone. But the sole act of thinking something doesn't make it so, and I cringed when I looked up and saw Derrick walking through my doorway. His suit jacket was folded over his arm, and his jaw was rigid and his forehead taut.

"Hey, Tracey, I need to have a word with you."

I looked at him in distress, feeling numb and apathetic. I pointed at the couch, and Derrick took a seat. Lauren stalled, trying to take a peek at her dad, but he cleared his throat and she ducked inside her bedroom.

"Hey, how's everything been going?" he asked, looking around the apartment like his question really didn't require an answer. I obliged and stayed silent but eyed him like I wished he'd say whatever it is he came to say and be done with it.

"Uh, Tracey, I'm very concerned about Lauren. Her grades. They've been plummeting for the last few months. I doubt that you've noticed."

"Lauren hasn't shown me any report cards," I glowered.

"Have you even bothered to ask her for them? And aren't you provided a schedule that tells when report cards come out?"

"I—I uh, I don't know," I said, and shifted in my seat. "Well, Lauren's a smart girl, she couldn't be doing too bad," I mumbled.

"Two Bs, two Cs, and a D, Tracey. In my book, Cs and Ds are totally unacceptable. I know Lauren can do better than that. She's almost a senior and it's imperative for her to get all As and Bs if she wants to go to college via scholarship."

I scratched my arm and didn't say anything.

Derrick glared at me.

"You *do* still want her to go to college, right?"

"Of course, Derrick. What's that got to do—"

"Okay, okay, just checking."

He sighed and massaged the back of his neck.

"Tracey, you might as well know. It's not just her grades, either. I think that with everything that's been going on, Lauren's getting a little overwhelmed. And let me cut to the chase. You have everything to do with it."

I knew it was coming. Knew what was coming like I knew Whitney and Bobby would be in the headlines next month.

"What are you talking about, Derrick?"

"Aaron Oliver."

"Aaron?"

"Look, Tracey. Don't act stupid. Your daughter saw you and Aaron together the other night. She and her friends were out on Westheimer."

I jumped up.

"Why did she tell you that? I wasn't on Westheimer—"

"McDonald's. Did you and Aaron go to the McDonald's on Westheimer?" He said it real slow and precise, like he was talking to a freaking five-year-old.

"Oh . . . yeah. I forgot."

"You forgot. You're doing a lot more than forgetting, Tracey. Hey, I know you're attracted to this kid, but have you thought about how it humiliates Lauren to see her mom out in public with her ex-boy toy? You're thirty-four—"

"Well, I'll be damned. You know, I never ever knew that, Derrick."

"—and he's barely legal. I knew it was tight, but damn, Tracey. I hope you can do better than him."

"Wait a minute—"

"And furthermore whatever happened to your motherly commitments? When did you last spend any quality time with Lauren? If you weren't so busy acting like you're Stella trying to resurrect her groove, maybe you could develop some sensitivity and know what's going on in your only daughter's life."

At hearing Derrick's words, my cocked head turned into an order of four neck rolls.

"Hey, Derrick, it takes *two* to talk. And she's hardly *ever* here and when she is here, all I get is *attitude, moodiness, smart mouth—*"

"What makes you think Lauren should be Little Miss Nice and Cheery around you after what you did to her, Tracey? You're sleeping with her ex-boyfriend, for God's sake. And I know that has to be the only thing you and this kid can have in common. Boning," he spat.

I rushed at Derrick like a redneck charging toward anything black. He threw up his palm, then twisted my wrist until my skin felt like it was being severed. I'd never noticed before how Derrick's veins could pulsate from his thick neck like popping grease.

"Look, you're going to listen to me if it's the only thing you do. Both you and I are her parents. But lately, Tracey, I feel like I'm her only parent. *I* pay child support, *I* give her spending money, *I* take her out, buy her things, go to the school functions, I do it all."

"Derrick, you're a lying—"

"Shut up, Tracey, I'm not done yet. I'm the one who's there for Lauren whenever she needs anything. And church. I take her to church and she can't even

get you to commit to a mother-daughter event because you got intimidated by a few church folks and
decided you didn't want to deal with those kinds of
people anymore. Well, it's about time you woke up
and grew up, because you have a daughter in that
room who's hurting, in trouble, and she doesn't have
anybody to talk to because her mother's too busy trying to make sure she doesn't miss out on her next
high-pitched orgasm."

"You son of a bi—"

I lashed at his cheek, but he ducked before I could
make contact. After scowling for a couple minutes,
Derrick stepped square in my face and raised one eyebrow, never once averting his eyes.

"Unless you want to end up in the emergency
room, I advise you to keep your hands to yourself."

"Look, Derrick. I don't care what you say. I don't
care about your threats. How can you come into my
home, judging me over something you don't know
anything about? To listen to you, anyone would think
that I'm totally unsupportive of Lauren. But that isn't
even the case, it's not even what this is about. Quite
frankly, Derrick, I think the only reason you're saying
all this stuff is because you're jealous."

He scoffed. "About what?"

"Don't act shocked. None of this even begins with
Lauren and me. This has everything to do with how
we broke up a million years ago and the fact that you
never got over it. No one I've dated was ever good
enough for you, so it doesn't matter that Aaron is in
his twenties. Steve was thirty-eight and you gave me
hell over him, too. Well, let me tell it to you like this.
Even if you were the last man on earth, I would never
want your sorry, broke, uneducated, weak, and trifling
ass again."

"Look, Tracey. I'm going to say this and then I'm going to leave—"

"You don't have to say shit, you can get the hell out now."

"You are about the worst so-called mother I know, and I wish I'd never stuck my piece in your dried-up—"

"Ahhhhhh, get out, get out, get the *hell* out of my house right now." I grabbed Derrick by the arm, ripping his dress shirt at the sleeve, and trying to shove him into the door. He bumped the corner of his head and looked at me like I was insane.

"If you ever need help," his voice cracked, "don't call me."

"Don't worry. As a woman, I'm more of a man than you could *ever* be."

He spat at my cheek.

I ducked.

Spat back at him and gave him the finger sign.

And then he was gone, making the door slam hard behind him.

32
Lauren

I'm at home sitting on my own bed. I have decent clothes hanging in my closet, a part-time job that provides spending money, and reasonably good health, yet I can't shake this overwhelming feeling of abandonment, depression, and insecurity.

I couldn't help hearing my parents screaming all those horrible things at each other. Since I've never lived with both of them, hearing the sounds of hate, of clashing wills and viewpoints, was a rare occurrence. I wanted to cover my ears with my hands, but somehow my hands just weren't large enough. So I stretched out on my bed, face resting on my fist, and rocked back and forth, hoping no one would get hurt out there. Felt my hurt was enough for everybody.

I don't understand my mom. Seems like she's living in a dream world. She always has an excuse for every poor decision she makes. Blaming her actions on my dad. Holding him responsible for her falling into a relationship with Aaron. She has to have a few loose screws, and a couple of nails, too. But I've been told few people like to admit they've done wrong. There could be concrete evidence, actions recorded on camera, and the accused will still proclaim "not guilty."

Once I was certain my dad had left the apartment, I began going through all my piles of old magazines. I have subscriptions to *Teen People, Seventeen,* and *Teen.* I've saved every issue from the past few years, stockpiling them in a few legal-sized storage boxes. But that night I started ripping the magazines apart. I went through every advertisement, every article, every stupid claim of how the teenaged life was supposed to be so wonderful, and ripped the pages to shreds. Beyoncé's smiling face—tattered in a dozen pieces. Britney Spears's beautiful eyes—well, she couldn't see a thing after I got through with her. My hands and shoulders vibrated as if they were trying to warn me that my actions were going too far, that I'd regret what I was doing, but I kept ripping the pages into a heartfelt nothingness. Once I'd created a mountain of colored trash in the middle of my floor, I decided to go and get three plastic garbage bags from under the kitchen sink.

When I walked in the living room, Mom was crouched on her knees, crying and muttering to herself. I saw boxes and boxes of shoes, some of them looking unworn, and she was placing all those shoes in several black garbage bags that were spread next to her on the floor.

"Mom, what are you doing?"

She sniffled and wiped her nose but didn't look at me.

"Getting rid of poison. Shedding my life of things that don't belong." She continued to open up all these shoe boxes, taking out one shoe, then the other, and sniffing them, but returning each pair to the box, and then chunking them into a bag.

"Mom, those are brand-new shoes, some of them."

"Don't matter. They came from Steve and I'm tired of looking at them. He's not in my life anymore, and these shoes won't be, either. Storing them in my closet won't prove a doggoned thing. Goodwill can have 'em." Her tone was harsh, but I knew the harshness wasn't reserved for me. I heard the misery and regret in her voice, saw it in her hands, and grimaced at the signs of exorcism rampaging through her body.

Feeling eerie, I left my Mom alone and I went to get some garbage bags of my own.

Wednesday night the phone rang. Mom answered. It was Daddy calling to speak to me. He knew I'd be going out of town tomorrow, and I guess he wanted to touch base.

Right before we murmured our good-byes, Mom waved and motioned at me to give the phone back to her. I did, and went to the kitchen to finish rinsing off the chicken wings for our dinner. Her voice traveled around the corner and right into the center of my ear.

"Derrick, I'll be taking Lauren to the airport in the morning. Can you pick her up on Saturday? . . . Well, you don't have to get smart, I was just checking with you."

I heard a hush settle over the room where Mom was. "Look, don't start, Derrick. I have things to do just like you. Could you just promise to be at Hobby on Saturday at five? Southwest Airlines.

"Damn his trifling ass," she hissed, slamming the phone. I didn't know which hurt worse, the instrument or my ears. I tried not to think about it and resumed washing the chicken wings, turning over the pieces and making sure the water swam strongly across the wrinkled, smelly skin.

"Your father sure knows how to get me in a mood."

"Mmmm. Mom, I wish y'all could get along for just one day, one hour even," I said, and wiped my nose with my shirtsleeve.

"Shoot! Ain't easy to do, with a man like him. He's always pissed off about something. So negative."

I just stopped and looked at her.

Mom ignored my stares and started removing the salt, black pepper, and paprika from the cabinet.

"So, Lauren, you packed already? Got everything you need?" Her scratchy voice struggled to sound soothing.

"Uh, yeah, I just have a few more things to pack. It's only for a couple of nights, so I don't plan to take much."

"Your uniform?"

"You haven't seen it yet? It's on my bed. Go look at it. Maybe I'll try it on for you, once I season the chicken and put it in the oven."

"Okay, darling."

I shuddered when she said that. What an odd and strange thing to say to me. I cast the freaked-out feeling from my mind and continued preparing the meal.

Mom was gone for a long time. Too long. I had even started cutting up the white potatoes when I noticed her plodding into the kitchen. She held my nylon camera case in one hand and several photos in the other.

My face felt like it had been ripped open, and I dropped a potato on the floor. It rolled all the way across the linoleum, sounding like a steamroller, and landed near Mom's foot. I averted my eyes and knelt to pick up the potato, but she smashed my hand with her foot.

"Excuse me?" I said glaring up at her.

"Lauren, what you call yourself doing, girl?"

She lifted her foot and I stood up, holding the stray potato. She flashed some photographs in my face.

"Mom, why are you going in my stuff? That's *my* stuff."

"If it's your stuff, then what am *I* doing in it? Huh?"

"Y'all may have taken pictures together, but you did it using *my* camera, my film."

She shrieked and slapped my face with the photos. Didn't hurt, but that wasn't the point. I tried to snatch the pictures from her but, in a brief struggle, ended up tearing one photo. She held one half. It was a shot of Mom and Aaron hugged up together at a mall. I'm guessing they asked someone to take their picture. Aaron was standing close to my mom, cheek to cheek. I held the other half, the one that showed my mother smiling wide while Aaron gripped her right breast. I couldn't believe she'd pose like that using my camera.

She stood huffing, breathing hard like she was hyperventilating. I guess everyone develops breathing problems when all their sensibilities leave.

"Why'd you steal these pictures, Lauren?" she asked, flashing five others.

"Mom, when I got the film developed, I didn't know y'all were on the roll until I saw the pictures myself. Besides, what difference does it make? I already know about you and Aaron, so it's like who cares?"

"I care, Lauren. It doesn't matter if you didn't approve of us seeing each other, but you're moving into different territory when you do things like this. That roll of film was in my room, in my drawer."

"Mom, I'm aware that two wrongs don't make a right, but hey, you brought this on yourself."

"Right," she fumed, "go ahead and blame me. Everybody else does."

"Don't even bring my daddy into this. He doesn't have jack to do with this."

She opened up her mouth to speak, but it seemed like her conscience snatched her words before it could find her voice. I noticed her mouth moving, eyes flickering, her emotions unraveling like a water hose.

"Save the theatrics, Mom. You don't have to audition for the part you've already won."

She put her hand on her hip and laughed like I was the joke of the day.

"Listen, young lady, this is the final word. If you and Aaron had as great a relationship as you say you had, then he never ever would've looked my way."

"Mom, you're so full of it. If it weren't for *you*—"

"If it weren't for me what?"

I didn't say anything.

"No, no, Lauren. You can't blame that one on me. Even if you *didn't* have sex with him, haven't you figured out by now that if Aaron really gave a damn about you, the lack of sex wouldn't have made him dump you?"

My hands went for her neck—outstretched, heading straight for the part of her body that allowed such venom to pour from her mouth. I grabbed her flesh with one determined hand, squeezing and twisting until I heard her gurgle. Her eyes watered, then bulged, wider and wider, and she fell back against the counter.

"Ahhhhkkkkk, let g-go." Her screeching voice escaped from her throat, sounding like seven hundred screaming women trapped inside a well.

I let go.

Stared at her.

Looked at my hands, which were trembling like branches bracing against a strong wind.

As her voice scrambled toward the ceiling, I opened my mouth as wide as I could and my mangled emotions blasted through my soul. "Ahhhhh, ahhhhh, ahhhhh, I—can't—take—this—anymore."

One second I was in the apartment, the next second the menacing sky was my ceiling. Don't even remember opening the front door. Never knew I could run so fast. The sky was blacker than the nucleus of midnight. I felt afraid, but my legs didn't seem to care. They were moving like the wheels of a train, moving like they had no alternative.

And I felt like a child being introduced to the periphery of insanity.

"Mmmmm, mmmmm, please, please, God help me, please. Oh Lord, oooohhh. I can't take this anymore. Why am I going through this?"

My voice belonged to a screaming bat that was fleeing the dungeons of hell. My insides crawled with ugliness, and I felt like a witch. Didn't care how my hair looked, or about how wretched my face must've appeared.

All I knew, I was in the streets.

Near a Fiesta grocery store.

I had no money.

Had no sense.

But I knew a pay phone when I saw it.

I could barely distinguish the keypad as my fingers reached out and touched their way to my freedom.

"This is the operator. How may I assist you?" came the professional-sounding voice.

"I need to make a collect call to . . . oh, to uh . . . two-eight-one . . ."

"Yes?" she said, a little less professionally.

I gave her the number to call and my voice rose higher and higher.

I heard a concerned gasp.

"What's your name, sweetheart?"

"Lauren" (sniff) "just Lauren."

Pause.

"One moment, Lauren."

My fingers clutched the phone as if it were my lifeline. I shivered and shook in the chilliness of the night. Could feel pedestrians walking past me. Yelling, talking, laughing. Acting like all was well in the world.

"Hello."

Thank God he was home.

"This is the operator. Could you . . . would you *please* accept a collect call from Lauren?"

"Lauren? Uh, yeah, sure. I'll accept."

"Lauren?" he said.

"Hhhhhhh, hhhhhhhgggggg."

"You all right, girl? What's up? Where are you?"

"Will you" (sniff) "will you please come get meeee?"

"Okay . . . okay. Where are you, Lauren?"

"I'm so sorry about all . . . she said all this stuff and I just . . . it's just getting too . . . brrrrr . . ."

"Hey, I can barely understand you," he told me.

I swallowed an ounce of thick mucus that had made its home in my throat. Wiped my heated tears. Steadied my heaving chest.

"I'm at the . . . I'm at Fiesta on South Braeswood and Gessner."

"You sure? You don't sound so sure."

I shook my head so much it started hurting.

"I am sure. I know where I am. I do know."

"Okay, baby girl. I'm coming to get you right now. Be there in twenty minutes. Do not leave."

"Okay," I closed my eyes. "I won't. 'Bye. 'Bye."

I hung up the phone. Slammed my back against the willing brick wall of the grocery store. Even though the wall was sturdy, it still felt like it was about to give way, my head twirling like I'd been spinning around inside a clothes dryer. Wanted to throw up, but was too scared of what might emerge.

I looked at my watch. It was close to nine-fifteen. I knew I needed to be getting ready to take my shower. Needed to be getting my mind ready to travel to Dallas. But here I was in a place I didn't know I'd be visiting.

It was hard to digest everything that had happened. Never thought in a hundred years that I'd be going through some mess like this.

Brad came and picked me up and drove us to his place. He held me close, listened to my rambling, and wiped away my tears. Even though he wasn't Aaron, as far as I was concerned, he was the next best thing. And the more I talked to Brad, the stronger I felt. And maybe that's why being around him got me thinking about certain things and how something had to give.

When I realized how late it was, I stood up. "I need to get back home."

"Do you?"

His brow furrowed. He stepped up to me and challenged me with his eyes, refusing to blink.

I cleared my throat. "Yes, I do."

"What about—"

"Rain check?" My voice was crushed with softness.

He nodded, pressed his nose against my hair until I felt his heat.

"No." I shook my head with as much gentle honesty as possible.

Brad lifted his nose from my hair. His eyes crinkled with questions.

"Let's face it, Brad. If it weren't for this Aaron situation, I wouldn't be here right now. And us getting together would take zero effort. But I don't want to just go through the motions when it involves something so precious. Do you?"

I placed my hand on the front of his pants and squeezed.

Brad's stomach and legs pulsated with tiny jerks, but he whispered, "I'll get my car keys."

33
Tracey

After enduring sleep not even fit for a drunk, I got up grumpy and snapping at Lauren, who, not surprisingly, had overslept.

"Wake up, Lauren, I've been calling you three and four times," I yelled, looking at the flashing lights on my clock radio. We'd had a thunderstorm during the night, and our electricity must've been disrupted.

"Mom, I am about to get up. It's not my fault if my alarm didn't go off."

"Yeah, yeah, yeah, whatever. Just hurry up, we'll have to fight rush-hour traffic on both the Loop and I-45 to make it on time."

I hustled from the apartment, trying to lug baggage. We dodged huge raindrops and ducked inside the Malibu. I tossed Lauren's travel items in the backseat, then patted my face with tissue. Soon we were advancing toward the freeway.

"Damn, it's coming down hard this morning. Turn on the radio," I said.

Every station we heard was dominated by the weather: flash flood warnings, predictions of at least ten inches of rain within hours. "Don't go out if you don't have to," one reporter said.

Some roads out in West Houston were getting to be impassable; detours were being mapped as fast as Harris County could figure out what to do.

"Wonder if your flight will be delayed."

Lauren didn't answer. Instead she looked at me with closely knit eyebrows. "Mom, I'm kinda hungry. I hate airline food, and I got a taste for a big breakfast and a sausage sandwich."

"Uh-uh. No. Lauren, there's no way we'll have time to run by McDonald's and get you to Hobby by seven."

"But, Mom, yes we can. Since it's raining so hard, there might not be a lot of people waiting in line. And if there is, I'll just go inside and you can stand by. Only takes a few minutes."

"Standing in line never takes a few minutes."

"Please, Mom."

"Ugh, that is so . . . oh, whatever, if you miss your flight, don't blame me."

She sighed and settled back in her seat.

The intersection of South Gessner and Braeswood had a malfunctioning traffic light. So we had to do the first-come-first-served thingy before we could make any headway. This unforeseen inconvenience caused traffic to bottleneck. I sighed and kept thumping the steering wheel and listening to various newscasts.

Finally we made it a few miles down the road to the restaurant on Braeswood and Hillcroft. Lauren ran in and emerged fifteen and a half minutes later with her white bag of grub.

"Better hold on and try to eat at the same time.

Only a miracle will get us to the airport on time," I snapped as I accelerated out of McDonald's parking lot.

As I'd feared, there was a sea of red lights on 610. I gritted my teeth and gripped the steering wheel. The weather was in God's hands.

I asked Lauren questions about the trip, but she acted like she couldn't hear.

Instead, she nibbled at her food, eating a little bit of sausage and most of her hash-browns. The rest was left smiling and mocking her as it sat in the Styrofoam container.

"Hmmm, I don't want any more. Just some orange juice."

"I knew it, Lauren. Well, don't leave your trash in the car like you usually do. We had ants crawling all on the carpet last time you did that."

"Okay, okay, okay," she said turning away from me and leaning her head against the passenger-side window.

We finally rolled onto the airport grounds. All I could think about was the plans I had for my two days of vacation: relaxing, reading, maybe doing a little shopping, probably at West Oaks Mall or somewhere out on Westheimer. But I was in such a sour mood by then that nothing appealed to me more than just going home and crawling under the covers.

I pulled up to the Southwest Airlines passenger drop-off. Lauren jumped out of the car and removed her belongings from the backseat.

"Uh, see ya," I said halfheartedly, but Lauren didn't say a word, just made a mad sprint toward the building. I felt a tugging in my heart and exited the airport grounds. Since there was a combination of flooding and dozens of construction cones on Airport Boulevard, I decided to take another route. So I made a left turn and prayed I'd be home within an hour.

I was anxious to get somewhere safe. Bad weather made me miss home, even if it was a small apartment. I couldn't wait to get back to the familiar.

I had just turned down a road that looked free of cars.

"Cool," I said, smiling. "Maybe I can make some headway."

By the time I saw the water, it was too late. The road ahead was flooded, a foot or so, and there was no way I could turn around and go back. I looked out the window and estimated that the water level was probably at the bottom of my car door.

I winced, drove slowly, then put my foot on the accelerator and hoped I wouldn't start floating away.

The waters slapped against the car, rocking us both into fear.

I had driven midway through the flood when the engine died.

"Oh God, no, no, no, please." I pumped the accelerator a few times and waited a minute before trying the ignition.

I-i-i-i-i-i-i-i . . .

A horrible sound of automotive constipation, an utterly hopeless sound that told me I wasn't soon to go any place worth going.

I shivered and tried to wipe the condensation from the windshield and the driver's-side window. Hell, I didn't have the foggiest idea where I was. Just took a turn, not paying attention to street names.

It was so cloudy and dark I didn't even have the benefit of knowing where the sun was. It was hidden away, cowering behind some gray and evil clouds.

I rubbed my temples with my fingers. My skin was moist from the humidity.

Think, Tracey, think.

Think, think, think.

Cell phone.

"Thank the Lord for cell phones," I said aloud, and retrieved my precious little Nokia from my purse. I pulled out the retractable antenna. Pressed the one-touch speed-dial button that would get me to the one I missed.

Aaron.

At first I did a little bit of a dance while sitting in my seat, but frowned at the female voice that emerged from my phone. "The person you're trying to reach is unavailable."

Damn! Damn! Damn!

Where is that guy? Doesn't he know I need him? Doesn't he even care? I put the phone down on the seat next to me. That was when I noticed the bag of garbage, the irritating leftover food that Little Miss Lauren had neglected to trash.

"Ooooh, she gets on my nerves. The ants will be crawling all in my car. I'm the one who'll have to scratch my legs 'cause the stupid ants will be crawling all over me."

I got so tired of sitting, so weary of being stuck in a small place that made me feel like I was suffocating. My butt was starting to feel like I was sitting on a block of cement. I was dying to stretch my rubbery legs. And I was afraid that if I opened the door to stand up, all the water would pour inside my car, rushing over my feet, wetting the carpet, and causing my Malibu to smell like mildew forever.

"Oh, this is starting to get annoying," I complained to the window.

I looked at my Nokia, and it seemed to be talking to me.

Derrick.

Derrick? Call Derrick?

It was tempting. Derrick was always there for Lauren. Maybe he'd have mercy on me and at least call a tow truck if I asked. But I didn't even know where I was. And even if I did, how could I possibly grovel well enough to persuade this man to help me? Nah, it ain't gonna happen, I thought.

"Oh, forget it. Forget him," I said aloud, as if the car would care.

Steve Monroe.

I laughed.

"Yeah, right. I can just see myself calling Steve Monroe. His new woman, wife, mistress, or whatever the hell she is, will answer the phone and curse me out. And if that happened, I'd deserve getting told off this time. Nah, better leave Steve and his dysfunctional family alone."

I looked down at my clothes. In our rush to get to the airport, I'd thrown on the first clothes my hands could touch: a wrinkled denim shirt and some stained, stone-washed blue jeans; mismatched socks, one white, one tan; and my new running shoes. I'd slapped on Lauren's bad-hair-day cap and called it a day.

Usually when Houston was attacked by these crazy floods, I'd be the one at home, sitting in front of the television, shaking my head, looking at all the people who were trying to roll their cars out of the bayou, who were forced to abandon their precious little Ford pickups in the middle of the freeway-turned-parking lot. There'd be reporters all over town, sticking a microphone in some old grandma's face so she could tell how she was rescued from the top of a Metro bus, or some other dramatic story.

I shivered and noticed how my throat was starting to feel sore. Like I was coming down with the flu. I felt achy, itchy, cranky, and bad-weather blue. I wanted to get going. My fun-meter had died a half hour ago. Let's call it a day and get me home.

Another thirty minutes passed. I was getting hungry. Last night I'd only eaten one piece of chicken. Lauren didn't let the chicken stay in the oven long enough, and once I bit into the meat and saw the red and pink—well, chicken had never looked so bad. I ate some of the mashed potatoes she'd made, but basically I went to bed mad and hungry.

I thought about trying to call Aaron again. It had been a while since I last called him. I picked up the Nokia again, but when I tried to dial, I heard this horrid little beeping noise, the sound that lets you know you can't make a call on this phone 'cause this here phone is good and dead.

Shoot!

I started to plug the cell-phone charger into the cigarette lighter, but hell, what good would that do? I slapped the phone and jabbed the cigarette lighter. Felt like kicking the console and throwing back my head and screaming. I felt like someone was playing a trick on me.

God.

I started laughing and talking at the same time.

"Oh, okay, okay. I know what this is about. Church. You're mad at me because I haven't been to church in a while. Well, hey, what can I say? If it weren't for all the Christians, I'd have come to church. But you know how they are. Ha, they—oh, never mind."

I hovered in fear, looking through the window, up

at the sky. But it still looked dark, desolate, and eerie, like the Lord's day off.

Right about then I wished more than anything that I had a Bible. I used to keep one in the car. For months and months it lay underneath the seat, but probably a couple months ago I'd thrown it somewhere in my walk-in closet. Hadn't seen it or thought of it since. But now I just wished I could conjure up a word of hope, some scripture that would make me feel like I wasn't alone.

"The Lord is my shepherd I shall not want. He maketh me to lie down, he maketh me to lie, aw shoot."

If I'd been smart enough to leave King James where he should've been in the first place . . .

I picked up my Nokia again, rubbing it, pressing the little power button again and again. Ohh, how I wished my cell phone would miraculously come on. Then I could call, hmmm, oh, I could call . . .

Indira.

Indira was my buddy. Always there for me. She'd listen to me try to explain as best as I could where the hell I was. She'd try and come find me even if she didn't know where I was. Rushing out the door, almost breaking her leg trying to get to me. Now *that's* a friend.

Oh boy, my poor hands felt like they were about to go to sleep.

"Don't fall asleep on me now, hands," I said, shaking them to rid myself of that tingly feeling. I blew hot breath on them, hoping that would wake them up.

My hands woke up, but then my stomach growled.

"I know, I know. Mom knows the baby's hungry," I said, patting my tummy. My voice caught. It had been a couple of hours now. Felt like weeks, though. Things were getting monotonous. Surely I wasn't going to die out here on the road. I didn't even know if my daughter got to Dallas or not. What if she decided she couldn't go on the plane again and needed someone to come pick her up? What if she tried to call me but my phone was dead? Oh, I forgot. She wouldn't call me first; she'd call tight-butt Derrick. He was the one Lauren turned to when she was in trouble.

I wiped away the hot tears that make a surprising appearance on my face. My face, the sliding board for tears. Hot liquid that humiliated me: their very presence was proving to the world that, yes, I knew I was a low-down, unfit, uncaring, and selfish mother. I deserved just what I was getting. Death by starvation. Disintegrating into the nothingness that I was.

What good does it do to have a mom, if she acts like she doesn't love you? If she'd rather hang out with your boyfriend than with you? I hid my face in my hands and ducked my head. I knew that no one could see me, but it still felt like the entire solar system knew who I was.

"The clouds know my name," I told myself, and laughed. It was amazing to realize that such notoriety wasn't reserved just for the Creator.

I sat and stared at those clouds for the longest, praying that I could see over and above the clouds, believing that they could somehow reveal the secrets of what was happening in my life. Wasn't it logical to think that clouds were physically closer to God than I was, and that maybe, just maybe, the Almighty had whispered something to his creation about me, something that his heavenly haze was willing to share so I could receive some type of answer about the puzzling events of my life?

I think the fact that I found myself squinting, searching for those signs and wonders, showed how utterly desperate I'd become.

Say something, I screamed inside my head. *I'm listening,* I wanted them to understand. I was convinced that someone knew something, if I could only get them to admit it.

But when I got tired of the search, and took one final glance up in the crowded sky, I marveled at how the firmament displayed so much of God's glory. Beautiful colors, shapes, and images that perhaps the world hadn't before seen and might never see again. And by the time I decided the clouds weren't going to open their mouths, that they just wanted to show off how beautifully elegant they were, the only thing I could do was look and wonder. Wonder why, even when I felt desperate enough to unlock a mystery, the answers still refused to be revealed.

I wept inside my hands, shaking my head at all the things I'd been doing for the past few months. Secretly glad that Aaron liked me more than my daughter. Jealous of the time when he was still dating her until he could tell her that he'd chosen someone else. Elated that he'd changed his mind about giving her that Christmas present.

My heart felt mega-heavy. I was so afraid. So alone. I wanted to yell and scream, but what good would it do? Why have a voice, if there's no one who can listen? So I was quiet. My mouth was numb, tongue stuck inside it, feeling gluey, gummy, and tasteless.

"I'm so thirsty," I said, as my stomach growled pitifully again. It was a loud and vicious growl. An angry sound that blasted from the depths of my belly.

"Huh, that's a laugh. Even my stomach's pissed off at me," I thought.

I sighed and looked at the passenger seat. Saw the bag.

I tore open the bag and smiled when I saw the left-over food. Half a piece of sausage sandwich, a few eggs, and five swallows of orange juice.

"Oh, ohhhhh, thank you, Lauren."

I picked up the eggs with my hands; a few ants were crawling on them, but I flicked them off and filled my mouth with the food; the eggs were cold but I hardly cared. I was laughing and crying at the same time. I thought of my daughter, Lauren. Wished I could touch her and feel her kiss against my cheek. Wished I could hear her whine, "Oh, Mom." Wished I could hold her in my arms like I did when my mother first handed her to me on that eleventh day of November. My skinny self was bruised and sore, body shocked in a natural kind of way after just going through what nature called me to do. She was such a sweet baby and she smelled so good. Even when she was just three hours old, her eyes were big and luminous. She looked at me like I was the most wonderful thing she'd ever seen. And I looked back at her. "You're Lauren Hayes," I said. "And I'm your momma, I'm Tracey." I nuzzled her precious little cheek with my nose. "And—and I love you."

I told a person whom I hadn't even known a few hours that I loved her. She was breathing, she was healthy, and she was mine. I didn't abort her; I didn't sign her life away to an adoption agency. I wanted to keep her. Raise her. Have the privilege of leading her little life and seeing how she made out down through the years.

Lauren.

I opened my purse and fished out a wallet-size photo of her that was snapped when she was eight. She had a couple of missing teeth back then. Snaggle-toothed, cute, and smiling. Her head full of wavy red and blond strands. Kids would always tease her about her hair. Not because it was ugly but because it was different. She stood out even if she didn't want to.

Yep, that was my Lauren.

She was a pretty good kid, as kids go. She'd been making decent grades until recently. She abided by her curfew; she'd listen to me when I'd advise her. She might complain, but she'd always do as I asked. And she'd held off from having premarital sex.

She *listened* to me.

At one point, yes, she did.

"I'm so blessed," I thought.

A lot of other teens would have gone right out and gotten rebellious and had sex with ten different boys by now. Bringing home diseases, babies, and live-in boyfriends; sneaking boys in to live inside their rooms without their parents having a clue.

"But not my Lauren," I said aloud.

Stuck my chest out. Raised my head.

I wished I could hear her voice just more time, and that she could hear mine. If she were with me right then, I would've told her how proud I was of her. And that I did—I did love and care about her. I may not have told her often, but really I did.

After I digested the little bit of food, for some reason I started singing. It was a song they used to sing when I was a teenager in the Church of God in Christ.

Everything will be all right
Everything will be all right
After the storm comes passing over
Everything will be all right

I sang it softly to myself, the same old words, the only words I could remember. Sang it and didn't think of anything or anyone else. And once I'd completed my concert, I looked up and noticed the sun breaking through the clouds. The clouds looked like a horse galloping across the sky; a man was sitting on a giant horse and they were headed my way. I sat up in my seat, the sun brightening my face. The man was smiling and nodding at me. I waved, but he didn't wave back.

I looked around and noticed the water had receded.

When did that happen? I thought.

I opened the door, got out, and lifted the hood.

Jumped back inside the car and pressed my foot on the accelerator again.

I-i-i-i-i-i-i . . .

"Okay, okay, I recognize that sound," I said softly.

My bottom lip quivered, but I stopped it almost as soon as it started.

"No, no, no. Not gone cry, no more tears. I know I'm getting out of here, I just *know* it."

Another hour dragged by.

I sure wished I could use the bathroom. I could feel the tension, the hot liquid aching to be released.

One good laugh, and my car would've become a public restroom.

Lucky for me wasn't anything funny.

After a while I heard the sound of a car driving down the street. I looked up, barely having the strength to lift my head.

The car was taking its time, driving as slow as a hearse in a funeral procession.

I snapped my door locks. Looked around for something heavy to hold. My body was trembling and I didn't want anyone to know my true feelings. So I was sitting and shaking and I heard the car coming closer and closer. It stopped behind me. I kept looking straight ahead, acting like I was driving and I was going somewhere. The hood was lifted, but I was still driving. I'm getting the hell out of here, I think.

Moments later I sensed the presence of a person standing next to my window.

I averted my eyes. Had no time to play "eye tag." Got somewhere to go.

But their presence broke my concentration and I removed my hand from the steering wheel.

I heard a light tap on the window.

I froze. Took my foot off the accelerator.

They tapped again; one, two, three more times.

"Tracey? Tracey, it's me."

I looked up.

A man who looked just like Derrick Hayes was peering at me through the window. He was standing there wearing a Houston Astros hat, a black T-shirt, and some jeans.

What was he doing here?

"Open the door," he yelled.

I poked out my lips and shook my head.

This time the optical illusion surprised me by pounding on the window. I jumped and quivered in my seat.

"Tracey, open the damned door," he said.

Feeling like what-the-hell, I grabbed the door handle and counted.

Ten, twenty, thirty.

The door opened slightly; he swung the door open all the way and I gasped when he grabbed me.

He reached for me and lifted me out of the car, pressing my weakened body onto his.

I let him pull me against his chest; he was warm, strong, and determined enough to keep me from further trembling.

He stared into my eyes. Never flinched. Those penetrating eyes were quite gentle and warm, making me feel comforted. I stared at him like he was the knight on the horse.

Thing is, I didn't even know Derrick knew how to ride a horse. Didn't even know.

Derrick mercifully produced a pair of jumper cables and attached them to my battery. I was sipping on some lukewarm soda from a six-pack he had stored in his trunk.

"Tracey, when I say 'now,' I want you to pump the accelerator and start the car."

"Okay."

I sat in the car, waiting for Derrick to give me the word. My head erect and stiff, I mentally sifted through all the drama I'd recently endured. God knows, if you'd asked me what kind of hope I had a few hours before, I wouldn't have been able to give an answer. The outlook was too dark for me to be optimistic. But now that Derrick had arrived and things were being handled, the nightmare didn't seem as bad as it had when I was going through it. I shivered just thinking how, even though that experience was extremely trying and difficult, I had still gotten through it. I'd still won.

"Now!" Derrick yelled, interrupting my thoughts.

Vroom. Vroom. Vroom.

The roar of the Malibu's engine sounded like an elegant melody, like I could hear after being deaf all my life. I rested my head against the steering wheel.

"Thank you, God. Thank *you*."

Derrick called a towing company. Thought it would be safer.

We were bobbing along in his car.

"How'd you know I was here, Derrick?"

"I didn't know."

I looked at him.

"Seriously, Tracey. It was so bizarre. I was driving around in the area and something told me to turn left. I wanted to turn right and actually I did, but there was this ringing inside my ear, urging me to go back the way I came. I turned the car around and followed through until I came down this road, which looked like it had water receding from earlier flooding. When I kept driving and saw your Malibu, I then knew why I was led down that street."

I said nothing, just stared into space.

"How long were you out here?"

"I don't know. Had to be since . . . I dropped Lauren off around seven-fifteen. It was sometime after that. Seems like weeks, though."

"I'm sure it does."

I stared at Derrick's profile. It was so rare that we had been in the same car together, I didn't even have anything to compare it to.

Felt weird. Surreal.

"Have you heard from Lauren?" I asked softly.

"Yep, she made it. Flight was delayed, but believe it

or not, Lauren said the ride didn't feel any worse than normal. That was shocking."

"You're telling me."

"So, I told her I'd pick her up this weekend but she'd have to ice this flying stuff for a while."

I smiled. Rocked in my seat.

"Why aren't you at work today?"

"All the roads surrounding the store were closed down."

"You're kidding."

"And let me tell you, I've been working at that particular branch forever, and that has never happened before."

"I can't believe this," I said.

"Me either. Me not going to work is like—"

"No, I'm not talking about that. I'm talking about this. Us."

He looked at me.

"We're actually having a normal conversation."

"You're nuts, Tracey."

"No, I'm not. We never speak to each other like this. You know it's the truth."

"Well, if you ask me, we could have held decent conversations all along, but if it hadn't been for some stubborn, cocky—"

"Watch yourself, now."

"Just joking."

"And that's just fine with me," I said, and stared out the window like it was my first time seeing the world.

Derrick had overseen my car being dropped off at the local dealer. He drove me home, and waited on me as I took a shower and changed clothes. Thirty minutes later we were getting some lunch at the IHOP on Sam Houston Parkway near Westheimer. Every direction you turned, you could hear patrons relaying their flood story, or listening to someone else tell theirs.

"This is just a day of unprecedented occurrences, huh, Derrick?"

"Tracey, please, you're taking away all the fun."

"Okay, I'll shut up, but I can't help it."

"Yes, you can. Just chill out, relax, count your blessings, and keep breathing."

I ate my plate full of buttermilk pancakes; then I ordered a BLT sandwich and drank two large apple juices. I started to get a steak dinner, but Derrick shook his head.

"You already got rescued from death this morning, and now you about to come in IHOP and kill yourself from overeating?"

I laughed and nodded.

Felt good to be alive.

He stood in the doorway of my home. The cool afternoon air sent a thrust of wind through the apartment. I stood with my arms folded under my breasts. Felt kind of awkward. My rescuer was staring at me like he'd never seen me before.

"Tracey, I'm glad everything's turned out all right and that you're home safe. In the past I know I've swore up and down if you were ever in trouble, don't look my way, but I guess you didn't have to, because I looked yours. We always claim what we won't do if we're put in certain situations, but the true test of character comes when you're in the midst of that situation and you end up doing the thing you never thought you'd do. Don't look at me all crazy; I'm just as shocked as you are. Never thought I'd extend my hand out to you."

"I never thought I'd take your hand. Never knew I'd have to," I said solemnly.

"Well, today proves with everything we think we know, sometimes we just don't know *nada*."

"You're telling me . . . well, I don't know how I can ever repay you, Derrick. Hey, thanks for breakfast—"

"And lunch." He smiled.

I smiled, too.

Derrick turned and started hustling down the stairs. I waved at him, but he didn't wave back.

34
Aaron

"Daddy, we love you," I said aloud to his weakening body, because maybe he would hear me and respond. Maybe my dad would act like the one I always knew: vital, concerned, and supportive. Right now he looked like none of those things. He looked more like a kid than a dad. His face was parched and his cheeks sunken. His five-foot-ten body had shrunk to about half that size.

I was standing near his hospital bed. Tan walls, white sheets, and tiled floors. My dad looked like a little ball drowning in a sea of nothingness. And I felt guilty. Something I rarely feel.

"He hears you, baby. I know he does." That was Mom. Nethora Oliver looked a breath away from death herself. Her normally sparkly eyes were dim and darkened. She had new wrinkles, and her smile hadn't been seen in weeks. At least not the smile I was accustomed to seeing. I squeezed my mother's hand. She nodded, but refused to look at anything besides her husband.

"You really think Dad can hear us?" I asked.

He was in a coma. Had been that way for the past few days. I was so grieved I hadn't been able to sleep. Sleep would have been like a thief. I had to talk to my dad, or hear him talk to me, just one more time.

"I know he can. Sometimes I see his eyes twitch even though they're closed; and plus hearing is always the last sense to go . . . not that Lendan is going anywhere."

Her voice was strong, determined. She didn't have to put on for me. But I hoped she really believed what she was saying. It was going to take faith to believe something that didn't agree with your vision.

I laughed inside, feeling overwhelmed and incomplete, bewildered, with an unusual urge to weep.

"Why don't you go and get yourself something—"

I shook my head violently. Who could eat at a time like this? Dad wasting away, and I'm pigging out? I didn't think so. Fear had killed my appetite. It would take a miracle to resurrect it.

"Well, I don't know about you, but I'm getting a bit hungry," Mom declared. Her weary voice was left teasing the air, so I rose to my feet.

"What you want, Mom? I got it."

"Get me a veggie plate. No dessert, no dairy products either."

"I know, I know. Be right back," I said, and glanced at my dad's body. I was saying it for his benefit as much as hers.

I made my way down the hall, and just when I was about to get on the elevator, I looked up and noticed the pay phone. Smiled. Fished around my pocket for a quarter and two nickels. It had been a while since I'd used a pay phone, but my cellular was almost like an afterthought these days. I'd probably tossed it under-neath something at home.

I dialed her number. It had been so long.

Pick up, pick up, I thought when the phone rang three times.

Her recorded voice spoke from the answering ma-chine. I started to hang up, but instead cleared my throat.

"Hey, you. I'm here at the hosp—"

"Aaron?"

I closed my eyes and laughed.

"Why are you screening your calls, Tracey?"

"I'm not screening. Didn't get to the phone in time . . . how are you, baby?"

"You don't want to know."

"Oh, but I do. I wish I could be with you. I want to see you so bad. Hold you in my arms. How's your fa-ther?"

My chest heaved.

"Well, Tracey. He's uh . . . he's in a coma."

"Oh, no."

Silence.

"I'm so sorry."

"It's . . . uh, it's something that we kinda knew might happen, but didn't really want to face. I mean, no one knows if he'll pull out or if we'll be talking to his body for another week or another six months. We just don't know."

"Oh, Aaron."

"Yeah, it's like that . . . sometimes I wonder why, though. Like, is it my fault?"

"Aaron!"

"No, Tracey, remember what we discussed a while back? That karma stuff? Maybe this is my karma."

"Oh Jesus. Aaron, truly you cannot think that your dad is suffering . . . because of us."

"Well, why not? The good Lord might use the closest things to you, the most important things in your life, to get your attention. Well, I can tell you this much: he definitely has my attention these days," I said, and blotted a thin film of grease from my forehead.

"That's it! Aaron, I want to be with you. I have to. We gotta talk. We have to—"

"Well, I don't know if it's a good time, Trace."

"When is it ever a good time? I'm coming. I'm coming."

"But my mother—"

"What about her? You don't want your mother to know I exist?"

"I just don't think it's a good time to make these new introductions about my personal life right now."

"Aaron, weren't you the one who said a true friend is a friend always?"

I wet my bottom lip with my tongue.

"Well, I'm your friend and I want to be there. I don't care what your mother thinks. She has a lot more things to worry about than me. I have you to worry about."

I smiled. Felt a cry caught in my throat. It had been so long since I'd felt that way, I'd almost forgotten how a man's own tears can startle him. Yet the things that I was feeling seemed natural. Like even though they were rare, they were still acceptable.

I sat up in my seat.

"Okay, Tracey. We're on the seventh floor, but I'll meet you in the lobby."

"Thanks, Aaron."

* * *

I waited for her in the lobby of the hospital. The vast room was dotted with spaced-out looking visitors who were either pacing or slouched on the burgundy fabric seats. I was too hyped to be still. Kept jamming my hands in the pockets of my too-small jeans. The fashion police would have handcuffed me that day. It was like Hilfiger didn't matter anymore. I walked up and down the hallway like it was a treadmill until I saw the familiar shape of Tracey's head as she entered the lobby.

She looked to the right and to the left. Then our eyes met.

Her cheeks spread into a relieved grin. Her slow walk transformed into a sprint, and soon we were in each other's worlds again.

"Mmmmm, I've missed you so much. I have so much to tell you," she murmured, covering my cheeks with wet and wild kisses.

I knew I was blushing, and it didn't bother me as much as I might have thought. I grabbed her hand, gripping it tightly. She squeezed me back, searching my eyes for signs of life.

"Missed you too, love. You just don't know."

"I do, I do, believe me I do. I've been through *sooo* much."

I shot her a look.

"Oh, I'm so sorry, you have too. That's one reason why I'm glad you let me come. We need each other, Aaron. We really do."

Tracey and I then took a seat in some chairs near the grand piano. I was glad she was there with me, easing some of the pain, reducing some of the loneliness.

Her eyes traveled the scope of my attire. I waited for

her to ask, "What's wrong with your clothes?" but she simply smiled.

"You look good, Aaron."

"Uh-huh. Well, what been up with you?"

"Oh, it doesn't really matter. How are things with your dad? Your mom?"

"Same ole, same ole. I'm getting tired of this."

"Oh, Aaron, why you say that?" She looked stressed. Shocked, I guess.

"I'm sorta feeling a bit cynical these days. I can't get over what you said a while ago. That girl named Karma."

"Not funny, Aaron. I don't wanna hear anything like that. If anything, think positive. You gotta think the best, not the worst. You are not to blame for what's going on with your father, Aaron."

Her tone was sharp. Eyes ablaze. We were no longer holding each other's hands. I felt abandoned just that quick.

"What took you so long, son?"

I stood in the middle of the doorway to my father's room. Tracey was right behind me. I felt her firm breasts pressing against my back.

Took a deep breath.

"Mom, there's someone I want you to meet."

I stepped aside like a curtain unveiling a scene on a stage.

Tracey walked tentatively into the room. Mom's eyes bored into her with curiosity.

"Hi, I'm—"

"Mom, this is my . . . this is a close, close friend, Ms. Tracey Lorraine Davenport."

Nethora Oliver nodded her small head and inspected Tracey from the top of her hair to the tips of her leather boots. Managing a smile, my mother stepped forward. "Nice to meet you."

Then Mom looked at me like *Why didn't I know about this one before now?*

I tapped Tracey hard on the shoulder, and we stepped next to my father's weakened frame.

I smiled, but it held a hint of bitterness. "That's him, Tracey. That's my dad."

She reached out and stroked Dad's arm, rubbing it and rubbing it like she was a mechanical device.

"Hi, Mr. Oliver. I'm Tracey, Aaron's friend. I want you to know you have a wonderful son."

I punched her.

She jerked her shoulder.

"You have nothing to worry about, you've raised a fine young man." Her warmth embraced me as she smiled, her pupils a sea of water. I blinked like my vision was about to disappear. Never wanted things to be like this. Never thought that the first meeting between the lady in my life and the man in my life would be under these circumstances.

I glanced at Tracey again. This time her eyes were shut tight; I could see her mouth moving like she was mumbling. Her voice a faint whisper, but then, like the clanging of a church bell, her words began to rise:

> *The Lord is my shepherd*
> *I shall not want*
> *He maketh me to lie down in green pastures*
> *He leadeth me beside the still waters*
> *He restoreth my soul*

Then Mom's voice began to layer on top of Tracey's. Two women strong. The words of God filling

up the hospital room, filling my dad's soul, mind,
spirit, and body. I wanted to join in, but couldn't recall
all the words.

> *Surely goodness and mercy shall follow me*
> *All the days of my life*
> *And I will dwell in the house of the Lord*
> *Forever.*
> *Amen.*

I closed my eyes briefly and repeated, "Amen."
Mom teased me with a sad grin. "That's all you can say,
son? Amen?"

"Amen," I said, looking at my father with my head
held high.

Tracey I were standing outside my dad's room.
Mom was singing hymns over his body, talking to his
ear, rubbing his arms.

"Thanks for the spiritual backup, Tracey."

She blushed.

"I don't mean this the way it sounds, but . . . I didn't
know you knew stuff like that, Tracey."

"I didn't either. I mean, I know that passage, but
hadn't thought about it in a long time. As a matter of
fact, just recently I went through an experience where
I couldn't think of a biblical verse to save my life. The
words just wouldn't come, until now. It gives me chills
just thinking about it."

I nodded but didn't say anything.

"Well, with everything that's been going on, I
wanted to make sure and let you know I think everything between myself and Lauren is going to be okay."

"Oh yeah? What up?"

"Well, I had the strangest, scariest experience a couple days ago. I told you how I was stuck in the car and all and Derrick happened to come and . . . well, he rescued me."

A man's pride will crumble at times, and I blurted, "And now you've decided to be with him? Be a family?"

"No, no." Tracey shook her head. "I mean we held a civilized conversation. He's even called to check on me a couple of times since then, but we're not making plans to be together, or move in with each other. Not in the least."

"Oh."

"I was thinking more about Lauren. I was thinking how important she is to me, and how insensitive I've been toward her through this whole . . . experience."

My throat tightened like an invisible noose was being yanked hard around my neck. I wanted to say something, but couldn't. Couldn't do anything but listen. My voice disappeared as Tracey's voice took precedence.

"You know, sometimes it takes a crisis to pull a family together or to reestablish priorities," she said.

I lowered my head, slid my eyes to the floor.

"Aaron, I'm sure you can vouch for that. I know you've seen your mom more times in the past few weeks than you'd normally see her. Am I right?" Her voice projected, her volume was loud. And she talked as if she really didn't need me to answer. So I gave her the thing that was easiest to give, a nod.

"And right now I want nothing more than to hold my daughter in my arms, and try to lessen some of her pain." The pain of my own heart smashed my hope into a million pieces. And as much as it hurt to listen to her, I forced myself to look up.

Yep, things were just like I feared. Tracey had this

self-assured look on her face, a look of strength and
purpose. A look that swept me to a forgotten corner.
And I didn't like how that felt. As though who and
what I'd been to her no longer mattered. As though I
was disposable. How could she replace what we had?
Were the roots of our relationship that weak?

I paused. Didn't want to sound like a punk, but I
still needed her to know where I was coming from.

"That sounds all fine and good. But where does
that leave me?"

She blinked her eyes like she was returning from an
invisible place she'd been hiding.

"I can't leave you, Aaron. You are too important to
me, even more so right now. The way things have happened, the way they started, well, right now all I'm
doing is trying to learn from them. And, as odd as it
sounds, I think it's okay for me to care about my
daughter and you both at the same time. I'm determined to make this happen, Aaron. I know I want
both of you in my life. And that's the bottom line."

Again, I was silent. But this time the silence of fear
was replaced by the silence of astonishment.

After a one-hour conversation, Tracey and I walked
out to the concourse, me to buy a bottle of soda from
the vending machine, she to use her cell phone.

It was late Saturday evening, and she wanted to
know if Lauren had made it back from Dallas. Tracey
looked at me and smiled.

"She made it back safe," she whispered, moving her
mouth away from the phone.

I nodded, smiled. Hoped that what we'd talked
about that afternoon wouldn't have to be proven
again. That what we had was solid enough to get us
through potentially tough times.

"Well, Derrick, is she available? May I speak to her? I want to tell her something."

Tracey's facial expression went from relief to something indescribable.

"What did you say?"

She pressed the phone deeper into her ear. Leaned against an ATM machine.

"No, no, no, no. I—I don't believe that. Put Lauren on the phone."

I looked at her, but she wouldn't look at me. She just sighed hard and loud, then said, "Oh, I see."

Her face fell.

She hung up.

"What up, Trace?"

"This is *sooo* weird. Lauren told Derrick she doesn't want to live with me anymore. She's moving out."

35
Tracey

It was Sunday, the day after I was informed about Lauren's moving out. I got no sleep that night; instead, my hours were used up in pacing through the apartment, and in trying to get in touch with Derrick, but not being able to reach him by phone.

That afternoon I called Aaron and begged him to swing by. When I first noticed his Legend pulling up outside my apartment, I practically leaped across the balcony, my legs powered by my fears, motivated by my hopes.

I ran down the stairs two at a time, and was tapping Aaron's window before he could turn off the ignition.

"Aaron," I gasped, feeling like I could hardly breathe, "you gotta help me, please tell me what to do."

"Dang, Trace, it's forty degrees outside. Where're your shoes?"

"What do shoes have to do with this, Aaron?"

"Okay, okay. Let's go upstairs."

As soon as we burst through the front door, I pulled him by his shirt collar.

"Aaron, you need to talk to Lauren. She can't move out. She can't move out."

"Tracey, of course she's not moving out, she just wants to see how you'd react. Where's she gonna move, anyway?"

"With Derrick. I know he put her up to this."

"Now, why would he do that?"

"Hello? To get out of paying child support. If she moves in with him, he won't have to pay child support."

"Nah, that doesn't even sound right. That man has been paying child support for years, why would he stop now? Think about it."

"Well, what else could it be?"

"It's not that, Tracey. It's not that."

I lifted my open hands to the ceiling and shook them incessantly, "Oh, why am I even asking you? You don't have any kids."

I went into my bedroom and slammed the door.

Came back out ten seconds later.

"And another thing, since you know so much—"

The front door swung wide open like it was announcing something important. Lauren entered the living room first, Derrick right behind her, his eyes crinkled, his face ashen.

I rushed to her.

"Lauren—"

She held up a hand.

"Mom, don't have time. Gotta ton of stuff to pack," she said, and ran to her bedroom, slamming the door behind her.

Aaron went to sit on the coffee table and folded his arms across his chest.

"Tracey, how are you? Aaron." Derrick nodded.

"What do you mean how am I? What difference

does it make, Derrick? How are *you*? I'm sure you want to turn cartwheels right about now, huh?"

"What?"

"Oh, don't 'what' me, Derrick. I can't believe all that big talk you did the other day. If it weren't for you, I wouldn't be going through this."

"Excuse me? Tracey, I hope you don't think I asked Lauren to move out. Because I didn't."

"Well, why else would she make this decision, Derrick? She's not the type to make this kind of decision."

"Look, Tracey, when you called me yesterday, that's the first time I heard of her wanting to move out. I didn't know. You have to believe me."

"I don't have to do anything except pay off Master-Card and die."

Derrick sighed real loud and massaged his forehead.

Lauren walked calmly from her bedroom, snapping her fingers at her dad.

"Daddy, I could use a hand. Can you help me out, please?"

He looked at me and hesitated, but then said, "Sure. Be right there."

Before leaving the room he repeated, "Tracey, I honestly didn't know."

"He honestly didn't know," I said to Aaron. "He honestly didn't know."

"Tracey, would you calm down? You act like it's the end of the world. Lauren's almost a senior. She'd be moving out to go to college next year anyway."

"Oh, Aaron. What are you even talking about? If the things you're saying don't make sense, then don't say anything. The last thing I need is for you to be critical and unhelpful. What are you doing here anyway?"

Aaron threw up his hands in exasperation, and

snatched up an old copy of *USA Today* that was sprawled on the floor.

My hands jittered and my legs did too. I couldn't believe all this was happening, that even after things had started to look up, life had gone and changed on me again so quick. I felt like things had gotten totally out of control and that, like times before, I was again on the losing end. I hated, hated, hated having to choose between my daughter and the guy I wanted to be with. I honestly felt we could make it work somehow, that things really didn't have to get to this point, if we could all try and make this work. As far as I was concerned, the attraction that Aaron and Lauren had could never, ever be again, so to me, if she just let go of her anger and accepted my decisions, we could do this. Couldn't we?

Derrick entered the living room hauling two wicker baskets laden with pajamas, socks, and underwear. Then he went back and got tons of my daughter's clothes, which were hanging on plastic hangers, looking like they were being taken against their will. I reached out toward her clothes, but Aaron stepped in my path and held me back. Speaking softly in my ear. Rubbing my shoulder with one strong fingertip.

When Derrick had carted the majority of Lauren's belongings into the living room, there was a knock at the door. Aaron left my side and answered.

"Hey, what up?" I heard him say.

This tall, muscular-looking guy with a crooked Afro walked through the door looking disheveled, as if he had just survived the bombing of a building. He had a metal pick in his hand and backed up until he was sitting on the edge of the couch. The guy didn't even bother to speak to me; just looked at the floor.

Derrick entered the room lugging a suitcase with

Lauren right on his heels. She brightened when she saw the fidgety young man.

"Hey, there. Thanks for coming."

"Uh, yeah," he said and turned red.

"Who is he, and what's he doing here?" I asked Lauren.

"Hey, Brad. Go help my dad carry some of my stuff," she ordered, and whisked right by me out the door.

I looked at Aaron, but he just shrugged his shoulders and shook his head.

Brad obediently picked up a box filled with books and followed Lauren.

"Hey, let me pop open the trunk," yelled Derrick, rushing behind Brad and Lauren. Aaron and I followed everyone outside. Instead of hauling her bags to her dad's car, Lauren set a laundry basket next to Brad's Nissan Sentra. He fumbled with his keys so long he finally dropped them on the ground and took the longest time rising back up.

"Wait a minute. Lauren, what's he doing here? Who is he?" asked Derrick.

"Aha. I thought Derrick knew everybody that Lauren hangs out with," I mumbled to Aaron.

"Daddy, this is Brad McMillan. He's Aaron's roommate. And I'd . . . I've decided to move in with him."

"What did you say?"

"Daddy, bring the rest of my stuff over to Brad's. This is just temporary and I—I—I'm going to be living with him."

"Like hell you are."

"Daddy," Lauren said, the volume of her voice rising toward the sky, "I've already made up my mind and I'm not gonna live with Mom or you."

"Well, isn't that just too bad, because I don't care if

you don't want to live with us, Lauren, you—you—you are not moving in with this—this young man. I don't know him."

Lauren blinked back tears and shot a desperate look at Brad.

He squirmed and refused to look anybody in the eye.

Aaron walked up to Brad and stood directly in his face.

"What up with this, man? Why is it that Lauren wants to get with you? Last time I checked I still lived there, or are you trying to tell me something I don't know?"

"Hey, Aaron," he said in a low voice, "Lauren said she just needed to crash at our place for a minute. I thought it would be cool, but I didn't know her peeps weren't down with this."

The more disdainful Derrick was, the more Lauren looked like she wanted to explode from frustration. She muttered and groaned, her bottom lip quivering. She rushed and grabbed her father by his elbow and started shaking it.

"Look, Daddy, please, *please* just let me do this. I know what I'm doing and I know what I want. I *don't* want to live with her anymore, and I feel if I were to move in with you, it would still be like living with Tracey Davenport."

"But see, Lauren, what you're saying doesn't even make any sense," her dad answered.

"Why?"

"The fact that your mom is still with Aaron should tell you that trying to live with his roommate is the equivalent of living with your mom, too."

Lauren didn't say a word. She just closed her eyes and threw back her head.

"Lauren, baby," I said stepping to her. "Don't make any rash decisions right now. You need to go back inside and think about what you want, what you're doing. I don't want you to do anything that you'll regret."

"Oh, Mom, *please*," she said, squinting at me in a way that made me feel very uncomfortable. "You don't want me to do anything that I'd regret? Well, why don't you think stuff like that before you make the kind of decisions you've made? See, that's what I hate. *You* get to do whatever you want, say whatever you want to me, just because you gave birth to me, Mom? Is that even right? Wait. You don't have to say anything. I already know what's up, and that's why I refuse to live up under your junk another minute. Brad, get your key and put my stuff in your car even if the shit gets broken in the process. I'm out."

"No, no, noooo. I am your mother and when you're under my roof—"

"I'm not under your roof, I'm under God's roof."

"You will do what I say. You are *not* moving out, Lauren. Now get your dramatic behind inside that house right now before I do something you really won't like."

"Tracey, don't threaten Lauren," Derrick said. "Y'all need to talk. You need to let Lauren tell you how she feels, whether you like it or not. And I think she's right. You can't just do whatever you want to do because you're her parent. You gotta think about her feelings, and I don't think you've done that at all."

"But, Derrick, you just don't understand," I cried. "I want to do the right thing, but I don't know what's right anymore."

Aaron stepped up to us. "Hey, maybe we can nip this in the bud right now, Trace. I—I don't want to come between y'all, so maybe we should—"

"Uh-uh, no, no, no. That's the last thing I want."

"But see, that's just what I'm talking about. Why is everything about what you want, Mom? Why does everything have to go your way?" Lauren's words echoed in the air. I felt embarrassed and my ears were tingling.

Lauren snatched Brad's keys out of his hand, opened the trunk, and began throwing shoes, books, clothes, and all the rest of her belongings in the back. Brad hesitated, but began helping her when he saw Lauren shrieking, wiping away tears, and talking to herself. I stood immobile, feet feeling like lead, my brain turning to useless slush.

My heart felt so heartless, so far removed from me, that I knew nothing would happen unless we all came to some sort of agreement.

"Okay, okay," I said, raising my hand, "hold up, everybody."

Lauren stopped crying and glared at me.

"Okay, Lauren. If you want to move out, move. If that's what you think you need to do, then I am releasing you . . . right now . . . to Brad McMillan."

A flash of dazed hurt spread across Lauren's face, and she gave Brad a wide-eyed look.

And within minutes, Brad and his new roommate were gone.

It was around six o'clock Sunday evening. Derrick and I had agreed to meet at Solomon's Temple. When he first suggested the church as a meeting spot, I felt reluctant and nearly backed out. But he assured me that this was a good atmosphere in which to meet, that being around a peaceful place might assist me in making a sound decision.

It had been so long since I'd been near the church grounds that I felt uncomfortable when I pulled into the parking lot. Even though only a few other cars were sprinkled here and there, I imagined that everyone and their mother could see me. But I shifted the car into Park and turned off the ignition. Saw Derrick waving at me and urging me to get out.

Adjacent to the parking lot is an octagonal gazebo that is available twenty-four hours a day for anyone who needs a place to come when they're troubled. The structure is made of cedar and includes padded seating and customized knee pads. I glanced at the gazebo, where Derrick was sitting, took a deep breath, and got out of the car. Gripping my purse, I took a seat next to him and watched the leaves on the towering trees flutter in the wind. It seemed as if the sounds of the wind were telling me that there was hope; that a resolution was possible.

Derrick was saying, "There's a mother-daughter retreat coming up the first weekend in April. If you come to services next Sunday, you can register and that'll be the first step in making a commitment for change."

I laid down my purse and thought for a few minutes.

"Okay, Derrick, what else is involved? What would I have to do?"

Derrick smiled. "I was on the committee last year, so I know it's a great program. You'll meet at the church that Thursday morning, and they'll transport the ladies in these deluxe air-conditioned buses that have television screens and really comfortable seating. A few hours later you'll arrive at the campgrounds for a four-day weekend. The mothers and daughters will do physical activities like canoeing, softball, and hiking, attend enrichment seminars, and you'll get to re-group and become reacquainted with yourself and Lauren . . . and God."

"Aha."

"Don't prejudge it, Tracey. This retreat will be a great opportunity for you to find out who you really are. You don't have to give an answer now, but could you just think about it?"

"Well, thank you, Derrick, for the info. Sounds interesting, but I—I just don't know. I mean, I know I need help, all the help I can get. I feel so stupid, you know, with me telling Lauren that she can move out. But at the time it seemed the right thing to say. I just didn't expect her to leave so fast."

Derrick said nothing. He closed his eyes for a moment and crossed his legs.

"And another thing. I've never told anyone this before, but it was never my first choice to be with Aaron. Okay, I'll admit I wanted him, but I knew getting with Aaron would hurt Lauren. So that's why I kept trying to get back with Steve Monroe. I hoped and hoped Steve and I could work things out, and if we did, I wouldn't have to deal with the attraction to Aaron," I sighed.

"But it was like I went from one bad thing to another bad thing, not realizing that just because I had another choice didn't mean it was the best choice. So I just did what I convinced myself was okay to do. And now everything is a complete mess."

"Tracey, I know it seems like things are out of control right now, but no matter what happens, everything, even bad things, must change. Nothing stays the same forever." Derrick laughed. "Remember when we were first going together? The way we wanted to be in each other's faces from eight in the morning to ten at night? We swore we'd never get tired of each other, that nothing could tear our love apart."

I lowered my eyes, stunned that guys could admit such feelings. Amazed that even Derrick could hold fast to old memories, things I would have sworn he'd long forgotten.

"But after Lauren came along," Derrick continued, "and when our lives radically changed, so did our feelings. All these new and complicated dynamics were thrown in the mix. Shoot," he chuckled, "some days I felt like I was caught standing on a tidal wave that made me lose my balance in a way I could never regain."

"Oh, you must be talking about how we are at each other's throats a lot, right?"

"You know just what to do to get under my skin."

I raised a skeptical eyebrow and cleared my throat.

"And vice versa," he rushed to add.

"Amen to that," I said. For a second I felt tense, as only another person's heartfelt declarations can sometimes make me feel. And the truth of Derrick's words was powerful enough not to be challenged. I couldn't believe a person I'd once felt close to was one I ended up clashing with just about every time we saw one another. And it tripped me out to realize that Derrick resembled a female version of me. Strong, dedicated, passionate, and not easy to back down from the things he believed. When I thought about all the hurtful, spiteful words we'd exchanged throughout Lauren's life, I felt ashamed. Wished I could retract the pain I'd caused in my life, his, and whoever else's. Seemed like in the big scope of things, what I wanted was not all that important. That other people's feelings counted just like mine.

"But see," Derrick interjected, "the fact that we

know the deal now, and that we've gained a little understanding about all this, it makes things seem less harried. Well, that's how I feel, anyway."

Useful words weren't mine to add. I felt all I could do was listen and hope his beliefs and attitude would penetrate my own.

"And," Derrick paused, choosing his words with caution, "I don't care what has happened, Tracey. Try not to be too hard on yourself. Even if you made mistakes, I'm sure you did the best you could."

I smiled and nearly fell out of my seat. But Derrick reached out and held me, tentatively at first, like a man who hasn't touched a woman in years. But the longer he held me, the firmer his grip became. And the tighter Derrick squeezed, the more the tears streamed from my eyes.

"Damn, female problems," I grunted and tried to wipe away my shame.

"Not female problems . . . human problems, Tracey. We all have 'em and we just gotta learn the best way to deal with them."

I dabbed at my eyes with my hand. "I don't know anybody who has problems like me."

"Thank the Lord you don't. He'd really be backed up, now wouldn't He?"

A faint smile broke through my weary-looking face. I didn't want to smile, but I had no other choice.

After getting on our knees and praying quietly, Derrick and I said our good-byes. On my way to the car, Lauren's welfare weighed on my mind. Was she all right? Did she feel she was a throwaway child, her life given up without a mother's fight? I shuddered away the unanswered questions, started the car, and began

driving through the church grounds. I traveled past a
sign that was erected near one of the parking lot exits.
The redbrick sign bore the name Solomon's Temple
in white lettering. The days and times of church services were listed as well as the name London P.
Solomon, the founder and senior pastor. I also noticed the monthly saying posted at the bottom of the
sign:

*Thinking beyond where you are will bring you out from
where you are.*

I read the sentence three times until I had it mem-
orized and then I drove off.

Sweet sleep was an unrealized goal that night. It
seemed I woke up every hour on the hour, listening
for the phone to ring and getting up to go press my
nose against the living room window. When that monotonous cycle played out, I crept to Lauren's bedroom and kept expecting to find a sprawled-out lump
underneath the covers, or to hear the obnoxious
thump of rap music. God, how I wished I could hear
Eminem, or Cypress Hill, or any noise at all coming
from Lauren's room.

The next morning was a no-brainer. I called in sick,
and I *was* sick— sick and tired of being sick and tired.
I didn't like how things had turned out, didn't like myself. I refused to look in the mirror when I went to
wash my face and brush my teeth. I wished I could run
and hide somewhere, in a place where no one would
ever find me, a place where pain didn't exist.

After sleeping through the morning, I got dressed
and went for a ride. I ended up going to Auchan
Hypermarket, not because I wanted to buy anything,

but because I felt it would be better to go among people rather than to be isolated, musing over problems. Auchan is like a Walmart SuperCenter: a retail store that sells groceries, housewares, electronics, and clothing. It was bustling with activity as usual, clogged with shoppers who represented every nation in the world, men and women shuffling their squeaky-wheeled shopping carts, pinching fruits and veggies and inhaling the aroma of baked breads. I eyed the cinnamon rolls, but pushed myself in another direction. After loitering for ten freezing minutes in the meat department, I decided to venture into a more temperature-friendly part of the store.

It was in the baby section that I noticed her. The last time I'd seen her was several months before, but I couldn't forget her form. I still remembered our last encounter. She was holding a pastel yellow sleeper in her hands. Her stomach had grown much bigger from the last time I saw her. She still had on way too much makeup, and her tits were as swollen-looking as ever.

"That's a cute sleeper. Do you know the baby's gender yet?"

Lelani looked up at hearing my voice. At first she grimaced, then she lowered her eyelids and kept staring at the fabric clutched in her hands. I walked closer to her. And as difficult as it was for me to do so, I began to rub her shoulder.

"It's okay, Lani. I'm not here to battle with you."

She peered at me from the corner of her eye.

"Believe it or not," I told her, "I feel—I feel we can relate to each other."

"What do you mean by that?" she asked, staring at my hand as I continued kneading her shoulder.

"Steve Monroe. He's not what I thought he was."

She laughed. "You have some nerve."

I wanted to remove my hand, but forced myself to continue rubbing.

"Lani, now you know Steve is not right . . . or maybe you don't know."

"All I know is, you don't know nothing."

"Oh, but I do, Lani, and something tells me you know, too."

Her sagging eyes told a story that I'd never want to witness, and right then she looked like she'd rather be anywhere but standing in that aisle facing me.

Old visions of Steve vanished from my mind and I smiled at Lelani and reached to embrace her. "Everything's going to be all right, Lani."

The second I touched her, Lani tensed, but I squeezed through her toughness, clasping her against my chest as if she was my dearest friend.

When I released her a few minutes later, a line of tears made its way down her cheek.

"Stupid bitch."

"Lani—"

"I'm not talking about you."

She turned away from me, but I could hear her moaning. Her shoulders were hunched over, weighted by things gone wrong.

I said a little prayer and made a quick left toward the electronics department. I started flipping through stacks of CDs. Not long afterward I detected an eerie presence behind me, a raspy breathing, then I felt a light rap on my shoulder.

I turned around.

Her face was a canvas of zigzagged streaks, white lines crawling like they had no other place to go. Her eyes were beady and red, reluctantly telling the story of a woman who'd seen more than she'd care to remember.

I gulped and raised my chin.

"You know, don't you?"

"Yep," she replied, lips trembling and forehead creased, almost looking like she'd burst into a fresh round of tears.

"Hey," I said, looking around. "Let's move to a more private spot. You wanna go sit in my car?"

She hesitated, but gave a slight nod. I returned the CDs to the bin and placed Lani's timid hand in my own. When we began walking, Lani moved with difficulty.

We stopped by the side of my car.

"He always wanted Hayden more than he wanted me," she murmured.

"That's her name? Hayden?"

"Yep. Hayden is all I know. He never revealed her last name. Anyway, they're common-law."

"Oh yeah?" I shivered. "Since when?"

"Since the beginning of the year, might've been even sooner."

"Well, who is she? Why her?"

"Ha! That's the unsolved mystery. All I know is they met at Memorial City Mall a couple years ago. Steve would date her off and on just like he did me. But late last year he got into the habit of being away from his place for days at a stretch. I'd ask him where he'd been, and it was always 'Working. Had some business to take care of out of town.' Always something. But the deal was, he'd started shacking with her. Hayden already had their baby. She and their daughter had more immediate needs. I guess Hayden had always been the one he'd kept in the background and decided to bring to the forefront. Hmmm! All that time I thought I was the one he'd want long-term. Boy, was I ever a fool," Lani said, staring into a world only she could see.

"Steve was the fool, the way he fooled everybody."

"Who you telling? I never knew the nigga was gonna be fruitful and multiplying all over the place."

I couldn't help but smile. "Nothing really surprises me anymore these days. So, what are you going to do about . . ." I bit my lip and nodded toward her belly.

She raised her chin. "Life goes on, and this one here is a keeper. His name's gonna be Dante August Thibodeaux. Yep, Thibodeaux."

I stepped back and appraised Lani like she was a strong black woman. I was impressed that, in spite of obstacles, she had the power to remain focused on what was most important.

"Hey, Steve Monroe is welcome to put his name on the birth certificate, but if he doesn't, fine with me. I don't know. Quiet as it's kept, I kinda got mixed feelings about this whole thing. I never wanted my son to grow up without a father, but how many of us end up having everything we want?"

I saw her swallow hard like all the cares of the world lived inside her soul.

"Well, Lani, if there's anything I can do to help . . . I'd like to. I know it sounds bizarre, but I mean it. My heart goes out to you."

She laughed and massaged the roundness of her swollen belly.

"How 'bout if you carry this load for me? That would help a lot."

I laughed. "Somehow, Lani, I refuse to believe you'd allow me to do that." I hesitated. "I could never take your place. No one could."

She cocked her head. "What you trying to say? There's only one Lelani, huh?"

"That's exactly what I'm saying. And you know it's the truth."

We hugged once more and I reached in my wallet and handed her a designer call-me card.

"That's my number. Let me know if you're having a shower or if you need anything. Even if you don't, I'm going to call you. We can hook up."

"That's cool with me, Tracey."

She smiled and waddled away, and I slapped my hands over my mouth and listened to the crash of my purse hitting the ground.

"Well, what do you want me to do?"

"I don't know. What do you want to do?"

"Aaron, that's not good enough. Don't you have a strong opinion about this?"

He didn't say anything.

"Please don't get quiet on me now. Just say whatever is rolling around inside that mind of yours."

Aaron squirmed in his seat. It was Monday evening around six o'clock. He and I were sitting in my car in the visitors' parking lot of Memorial Hermann Southwest. The windows were rolled down, and a cool breeze freshened the air.

"Look, I have a lot going on in my life, and right now my dad is the highest priority. I don't know how to put this, but—"

"You don't want us to be together any longer."

"I'm not saying that."

"You're not saying it, yet you are saying it, Aaron. You're afraid to hurt me after everything else I've been through. But if I can manage the other stuff, hey, I'm sure I can manage this, too."

"Oh, Trace."

"Don't, Aaron. It'll be cool. You go and look after your dad. I'll be around if you need me."

"I do need you, Tracey."

"Don't say that," I murmured, and buried my forehead against his neck.

"I do, I do need you. I want you . . ." he said, grabbing me.

"It's been real, Aaron, but . . ." I said, pulling myself away.

"Hey, we'll still be friends?" he asked, his eyes filled with suspense.

"Always," I told him. Then I unsnapped the locks and wondered what "always" meant.

"Hello."

"H-hi, Brad. This is Tracey Davenport. Is Lauren there?"

"Nope, she's not."

"What? Brad, please, *please* don't play games. This is serious."

"I *am* serious. Lauren's not here . . . she never was here."

"Look, you think I'm stupid? Put her on the phone right now."

"Lauren's not *here,* Ms. Davenport."

I stood up. "Then where is my daughter?"

"Look, I—I can't tell you where she is, but she's fine. She's in a better place."

I gasped for breath and pushed out, "And what's that supposed to mean?"

Brad hesitated. "She . . . I'll have her call you."

I hung up the phone feeling more confused than I'd been the past few days. I wanted to race over to Brad's and shake the hell out of him. It seemed things were going from bad to worse, and frankly I didn't know what to do.

But I steadied my nerves by going into my walk-in closet and lowering myself until I was on my knees. For the longest, nothing came out of my mouth. I felt ashamed, like I had a whole lot of nerve asking God for favors when I barely paid him respect through my recent lifestyle. But even though I may never be a finalist for a saint-of-the-year award, that didn't stop me from believing in him. And if God could see me and realize I had a need, I hoped he could hear me. So I took a chance and whispered, "Gracious Father, please help us. *Please.*"

I closed my eyes tight, eclipsing my surroundings and at first perceiving nothing but total blackness. But the longer I prayed, the more an image developed in my mind. Instead of seeing things as they were— confusion, separation, and hurt—I begin to see them the way I yearned for them to be: reconciliation, peace, and understanding. Even though in the physical realm, things didn't seem like they'd ever get there, I clung to a hope, an inner vision, that showed me something beyond what I could touch. Something that I knew could become tangible if I could only see past my present.

Thinking beyond where you are will bring you out from where you are.

Feeling a lot less burdened, I rose to my feet. I walked into the living area and looked toward Lauren's room. Standing as still as I could, I tipped my head and smiled.

"Turn that music down, Lauren!" I yelled.

The lack of response didn't bother me.

Instead of feeling discouraged, I went and set a table for two.

A few days later, I had fallen into a deep sleep on the couch when the phone rang.

I stood up and looked at caller ID. It was Indira. I felt relieved to be able to talk to my support line. It had been a while since we'd talked, and it seemed like a good time for me to unload and get those supportive strokes that I craved.

"Hey, Indy," my voice dragged.

Silence.

"Indy?" I said in irritation, not in the mood to play around even with my friend.

"Not Indy, me, Mom."

My knees buckled.

"Lauren?" I laughed, and put my hand over my heart. "Lauren? Where are— How are you?"

"I'm fine."

I threw back my head and gasped, sucked in a large amount of breath, and gasped again.

"What are you doing over at . . . at Indira's?"

"Mom, you think I'm dumb enough to live with both Brad and Aaron?"

I laughed and laughed, like an exhausted woman who'd just given birth after twenty hours of labor.

"Ahhh, my baby. You've been with—with Indira all this time?"

"All this time."

I threw down the phone and flung myself on my knees, not having any words, but raising my hands to the heavens.

* * *

Every night that week, I talked to my daughter. She was still moody, didn't really say much, but at least she allowed me to talk, let me ramble like an idiot, without hanging up in my face.

Derrick, who was just as shocked about Lauren being at Indira's, felt it was best that she stay there for a while. At first I disagreed, but eventually relented. I wanted what was best for everyone involved, and decided to take things one day at a time.

Two weeks later.

Lauren, Derrick, and I entered the two-thousand-seat sanctuary of Solomon's Temple. My hands were sweating so much I had to wipe them on my dress. The music was thumping, the choir was harmonizing, and the entire atmosphere was drenched with high-spirited worship and praise music. It had been a whole year since I'd last been there. I shivered, feeling as if I'd been swallowed up into another world.

When we walked down the sloped center aisle, I couldn't believe how many members smiled and waved, or came up and gave me warm hugs. "How you doing, Sister Davenport? We've missed you." I was embarrassed, shocked, and thrilled all at once, and was unable to mumble one suitable word. I just received the embraces with a grateful smile and remained in awe at the transformation in process. I was happy. I was home. And it amazed me to learn how things can happen in your life that make you stop going to church, but then something happens that makes you go back.

By the end of the service, I felt so invigorated, so

lifted with hope. I raised my head high, not because I felt arrogant, but because I felt I had as much right to be there as anyone else; that even though I had numerous flaws and didn't feel equal to the other devoted church members, God loved me enough to work with me, in the middle of my mess, just as I was. And when we passed by the administrative offices, I couldn't help noticing the banner:

SOLOMON'S TEMPLE PRESENTS
The 2nd Annual Mother-Daughter Retreat
THEME: NEW BEGINNINGS
Register Now for This Empowering Four-Day Weekend That Will Change Your Life
APRIL 6–9
Cost: $225.00 Mothers—$185.00 Daughters
RETREAT MOTTO: **Thinking beyond where you are will bring you out from where you are.**

I stood and stared at the banner for a long time. Looked at the hordes of women who were lining up to complete the registration and make payments. Looked at my daughter, who stood next to her dad with a stony expression on her face. I motioned to Lauren and we walked a ways down the hall, found a bench, and took a seat.

"So, I've been doing a little bit of thinking about this retreat stuff. Have you?"

"Not really," she replied, and folded rigid arms across her breasts.

"Okay, Lauren. I won't pressure you."

"That's nice to know."

"Look, Lauren, if you think I'm still involved with Aaron, don't bother. I haven't talked to him in almost three weeks."

The hardness of her eyes, forehead, and jaw soft-ened. And even though I could surmise she was prob-ably relieved that Aaron and I hadn't talked, a flicker of disappointment was still etched on her face. Her bottom lip trembled and her folded arms collapsed to her sides.

"Oh, Mommm."

I grunted and clasped my daughter in my arms, rocking her like she was a three-year-old, even though I knew she'd never be that innocent again. If I acted fast enough, maybe I could prevent what had hap-pened between me and my own mom; maybe I could regain my daughter by letting go of what I'd tried so hard to hold on to.

Sitting close to her, I moaned and buried my face in her hair and released the words that had been inside of me longer than I wanted to admit.

"Baby, there's something I have—I have to tell you, and it's hard for me to say this, but . . . I was wrong, I was wrong, I was wrong, Lauren. I know this, I know I hurt you, and I'm . . . I am so very sorry."

The reprimands and ugly looks I'd expected didn't come. Instead I felt my daughter trembling and con-vulsing as if she were fighting against some invisible force. She looked in my eyes, her legs, arms, and torso vibrating. With each jerk of her body, it seemed she was releasing a buried emotion. I gripped my arms around her, pressing her against me, transferring her burdens, and welcoming them inside my soul. We said nothing for the longest, and my ears belonged to her, if she would have me.

After what felt like a long tired day, and with her head now resting against my chest, I heard Lauren whisper:

"Me too, Mommy. I—I—I'm . . . sorry too." I couldn't believe she'd said that, and I wanted to scream. We rocked and held each other for so long it seemed like one long and awful experience had turned into a brand-new day—just like that.

36
Lauren

"Acceptance is one of the first steps toward healing," announced Miss Debbie, our unit's counselor. Miss Debbie, a voluptuous yet holy-looking woman, sat in the circle just like the rest of us: ten women with ten daughters ranging in age from thirteen to nineteen. I looked around the classroom, hoping we'd not have to say anything or make any confessions.

Miss Debbie held Mom's complete attention. Mom was holding on to my hand so tight I thought my bones would splinter.

"As we discussed last night, many of you are here not really by choice but by divine appointment. You are here because you're ready for a change; you're seeking a new beginning for your lives. And that new beginning is going to come again by . . ."

"Acceptance," we said in unison, as Miss Debbie pointed at the word written in bold letters on the presentation board.

"If you are not yet able to accept a situation that's

come up in your life—a job loss, a death, a separation, or a divorce—the healing process will be delayed. Now I don't mean that you should force yourself to accept a situation before you're ready, but be willing to acknowledge the reality of where you are, because that's what you're going to have to do to make that first crucial step."

"Okay, now who in this group needs to acknowledge something that's been difficult to face up till now?"

Half the women raised their hands. Mom's hand continued to clutch mine.

"I see. I guess only some of y'all have problems, the rest of you must be gliding through life, huh?"

That remark brought a few chuckles and shifting of tired legs.

Miss Debbie gave an example of what she's had to accept: because of cancer, she'd lost a lot of hair and had had to resort to wearing wigs and hairpieces.

"So you see, not every black woman is gung-ho about buying fake hair, but like comedienne Margo Hickman says, 'If you can't grow it, sew it.' "

"I can sew. Pass me some needle and thread," someone yelled, while the rest of the group laughed.

"Okay, I know there's someone else out here that has a situation that they've been unable to face. Maybe it's something so painful that it's hard to talk about. Is there anybody in the house today?" Miss Debbie asked.

Most of the women murmured "Yes" or waved their hands.

I saw Mom raise her hand and stand up. I was surprised when I heard her clear her throat.

"I've had trouble f-facing something that's bothered me in my life."

"You wanna talk about it, sweetie? Only if you want to," Miss Debbie said with a warm smile.

Mom sighed. Glanced at me. Looked at the women sitting in the circle.

"Yeah, I do. My problem is . . . I've had trouble accepting that I haven't been the best mother that I can be to my only child, my daughter who's here with me. For the past few months, I chose to live life in a way that, that, that *hurt* her," I rubbed Mom's hand, "and hurt me and other people, too, and I—I . . . well, sometimes it's hard to admit there are things about myself that I *hate*, but I'm trying . . . I'm trying," Mom screeched, pushing the words out of her mouth and her soul with a tortured vengeance. She gasped, closed her eyes, sat back down, and covered her face with her hands.

"Since you guys are out of McFlurries, may I get a rain check?"

I froze. Hadn't heard those words in so long, they brought back a flood of memories. He laughed at my startled expression. My shoulders loosened and my nervous laugh joined his.

"Hey, you got a moment?" he asked.

I looked at my watch. I had ten minutes to go before I was supposed to punch out, but I called out to my coworker and told her I was leaving a little bit early.

He met me right outside McDonald's, looking just as I remembered. Calm, happy-go-lucky, with his hands buried deep in his pockets. It was now the beginning of June and a few months since we'd seen one another—a bittersweet realization that things had changed just that fast.

"I was in the neighborhood and was thinking about you. Didn't know if you'd be here, but thought I'd take that risk."

"You always were a risk-taker," I said, even though that wasn't what I meant.

"You mean I always did stupid things."

I placed my finger against his lips, gazing at them far longer than what I thought I could ever do again. Like me, he noticed the charge in the air, but averted his eyes and pulled back.

"You guys are always in my thoughts, always."

"Oh yeah?" I said, and swallowed hard. "You seen my mother lately?"

He smiled and glimpsed at the sky. It was a muggy Houston afternoon, overcast, the sun hidden seemingly out of our grasp. I waited for his answer, expecting a denial or a confession, but he never said a word, just continued gazing at the sky like it held the answer to my question.

"Okayyyy," I said. "New business: What's Brad been up to?"

He scoffed. "Don't know. Last I heard, he might have relocated to Hotlanta."

"You're joking."

"Nope . . . we stayed roomies for a month or less after . . . uh, and, well, we've been out of touch."

"I see," I said, thinking about what never could have been.

"Hey," he said, face brightening, "how's old Mr. Hayes?"

"Same ole, same ole. Still doing his thing, except now he's with Big K." I giggled.

"Same ole, same ole," Aaron teased with a wink.

"And how is your father?" I asked.

He stopped laughing. "Well, Lauren, my dad went on to be with the Lord."

"Oh no," I said, covering my mouth with my hand.

"No, it's cool. I'm all right with it. He was suffering so much, and I didn't like seeing him in all that pain anyhow."

"That must've been awful to watch, Aaron."

"Awful is not the word. Yeah, it was tough, but we made it through, my mom, my relatives. Yep, his spirit left this earth on the second day of April."

He looked down at his hands and fiddled with his fingertips. I wanted to touch Aaron, rub his shoulder, anything, but felt too afraid. Like it would be too much, too late.

Aaron looked up, his eyes crinkled. "But you know what? The good thing about it is, a few days before he died, he . . . he talked. Dad had been in a coma for a while, but I actually got to hear him say some words, Lauren," he said, staring into space. "Anyway, what happened was a trip. As usual, my mom was in the hospital room and she heard my dad trying to say something. I happened to be down the hall, and she came flying out of the room looking like she'd seen the ghost of . . . whoever. And Mom couldn't even talk, just motioned with her eyes. I ran to the room. My dad's little body was shrinking in his bed. And I heard his voice weakened by the certainty of death, and he said, 'Khristian? Khristian. What's a five-letter word for, for, for . . .' I barely heard, yet I know I heard him and I was like, 'Daddy, what did you say?' And he took a deep breath and tried again. He answered me directly, Lauren," Aaron exclaimed, and hugged me around my waist, and I didn't mind him grabbing me like that.

"I always hated to be called Khristian, but you don't know how it felt to hear my dad call me that . . . I felt it was Dad's way of saying good-bye . . . him saying something that he knew would catch my attention. And these days I'm the king of crossword puzzles, if you can imagine that." He smiled.

"That's good to hear, Aaron." I smiled back. "At least you got to hear his voice one last time."

"Yeah, that means everything to me, and, well, I just . . . just had to tell somebody," he mumbled, and released me.

I nodded my reply.

He stood there for a moment, staring at me but not really looking at me.

"Lauren, would you—can I ask you to do me a huge favor? Will you tell your mom for me? Please? I think she'd want to know."

I gazed at Aaron, reliving the memories yet at the same time letting them go. No longer wondering what would have happened if I'd had a chance to let him show me what making love was about. The thing I used to dream about and thought should have been mine, well, now it seemed so far gone, so out of reach, that I had no other choice but to release those old feelings from my mind. As I recalled all that we'd been through, for some reason I felt an urge to shed a tear or two.

I pressed my eyes shut, thinking they'd produce moisture, but when I opened them, my eyes weren't wet at all.

Aaron looked at me intently, his eyes large, his body rigid. I smiled and replied, "Okay, Aaron. Mom and I are supposed to cook dinner together tonight. I guess she still doesn't trust my cooking—even though she taught me everything I've learned."

"Hey," he fussed gently, "you never cooked for me. Why was that?"

"You never asked me to cook for you, that's why."

"Well, maybe I could get a taste of your culinary skills tonight. Would you guys mind setting a table for three?" He smiled and buried his hands deep in his pockets.

I reeled back and stared at him. Shocked at even considering the prospect of Aaron, Mom, and me being together again. It had been months since we were together last, since that day Brad came over to pick me up and rescue me from the madness.

Mom had made such progress. I mean, she still had her ways, and could be stubborn many days. But now she tried to listen to me more, and she compromised or considered how I felt about things. And I felt very hopeful about how much the retreat had helped us, and didn't want anything to interfere with that.

Yep, things had changed, and it seemed like it had taken far too long for us to even get to this point.

I looked up and noticed this amused expression on Aaron's face. He stared at me, then tipped his head toward his car and aimed a finger at Pudgie, who stuck his head and tongue out the window, to savor some fresh air. I assume Aaron thought that gesture would lure me back into a once-forbidden zone, a zone I'd been desperate to abandon.

I gave a tiny smile. Aaron walked away and approached his Legend, readying himself to be my happy little escort.

"Hey, Aaron," I yelled.

"What up?" he turned around.

"Not going home right now. Sorry."

"Oh," he said. "Well, what if I just meet you guys

there later tonight? I have no special plans." He raised his eyebrows and smiled once more.

I lifted my head and smiled, too.

"No, Aaron. I don't want you coming back to our place. Mom and I are okay. Last April we went to a retreat, a mother-daughter thing, and started the long process of getting healed. We've made great improvements, and we don't need you riding in on your white horse to sparkle up our lives."

He furrowed his brow and leaned against his car.

"Damn, Lauren. It's been a while since all that drama-club stuff happened. Hey, I know things probably hurt, but I thought you were over it. I didn't know you were bitter."

"Not bitter. Just better. Better off without you in our lives. And neither of us is planning to go back to that place where we were. We've moved on and I wish you well in doing the same. So, if you'll excuse me, I gotta break. 'Bye, Aaron."

I turned my back and made my way toward the bus stop, made my way toward a new method of thinking, a new beginning.

ACKNOWLEDGMENTS

I am grateful for the following:

Thanks to the Lord for giving me the writing ability, for sticking with me through life's most trying moments, and for letting me find out what it feels like to be an author.

Thanks to my friends who encouraged me and believed in my writing (you know who you are).

Thanks to my mom, my sister Adrienne, Darryl, Brandon, Carl, Lula Phillips and family, grandmother, great-aunts, aunts, cousins, uncles, niece, nephews, and the whole gang of family around the USA.

Thanks to my agent, Claudia Menza, for representing the novel, and to my editor, Rachel Kahan; your input made the novel much better. I hope we can do this again.

Thanks to all the wonderful people, including the FP&C folks, who would ask about the status of the book (especially Deedie Gentry Phillips, Lori Lawrence, William Wade, Kim Barras, and Dilip Anketell). Your faith and interest motivated me. And I can't forget Candy Wirt of UH-CL.

Thanks to the various ladies who gave input after reading my online excerpt and encouraged me to go for it: Delores Thornton, Nancey Flowers, KaTrina Love, Pam Williams (Kendari), Missy, Simone Hawks, Shaye Luv, Nick Lancaster, Danielle Dixon, Dawn Reeves (Tamardi), Linda Dominique Grosvenor, Jeanette Wallington, Michelle McGriff, Gayle Sloan, Jacqueline Battle, and many others.

Thanks to the many, many authors who answered my questions and provided encouragement either online, in person, or at various literary conferences, especially Margaret Johnson-Hodge (Cuz, whassup? You keep a smile on my face), Marissa Monteilh (my play sister and kindred spirit; thanks for everything), Timmothy B. McCann, William Fredrick Cooper, Brandon Massey, C. Kelly Robinson, Trisha R. Thomas (thanks for the suggestion to send the manuscript to Rachel), Vanessa Davis Griggs, Kim Roby, the always encouraging Victoria Christopher Murray, Zane, Evelyn Coleman, Venise Berry, Lois Lane, Alex Hairston, Nane Quartay, Tanya Marie Lewis (prayer warrior), Renee Swindle, Franklin White, Lori Bryant-Woolridge, my "twin" Cheryl Robinson, Mary B. Morrison, Nelson George, JD Mason, Rosalyn McMillan, Michael Baisden, Curtis Bunn, J. J. Murray, Wanda Moorman, Evelyn Palfrey, Elyse Singleton, Eric Pete, Andrea Smith, Gayle Sloan, Shá Givens, Preston Allen, Pam Jarmon, Marcus Major, and Freddie Lee Johnson.

Thanks to Carl Weber for the surprising and unselfish gesture that helped me immensely.

Thanks to Marie Hoke, AIA, for the Spanish translation.

Big shout-outs to Sheila Lindsay (future author), Lisa R. HammAck of Baltimore, and my birthday twin Marla Jennings (another writer)!

Thanks to the people who agreed to read parts of the manuscript while it was in its early form: Chris

Brand, Tee C. Royal, Bill McKinney, Glendon Cameron, author Marissa Monteilh, Deedie Gentry Phillips, Cynthia Holsome, William Dailey of St. Louis, author Trisha R. Thomas, author Thomas Green, and my hilarious pal Verde.

Special thanks to one wonderful, strong, and supportive lady, Ms. Christina Pattyn, who has been with me since the beginning, through thick and thin, to listen to my joys and sorrows, and who gives loyal support and positive reinforcement no matter what.

Also shout-outs to my supercool online buddies: Margaret Johnson-Hodge (thanks for your counsel), Marissa Monteilh (you are the best in the world), Cheryl Robinson (thanks for the friendship), Djuanna "BKDiva" (thanks for the laughs), the generous and thoughtful Trina "Miss Love," Simone Hawks, Dera Williams, Ms. aNN (Loretta) Brown, Verde (thanks for your expertise), the incomparable Brian K. Walley (Eat Wheaties! LOL!), and Chris Brand of Detroit.

Special, special thanks to another online friend and colleague, Tee C. Royal, a hard worker who is giving, sweet, funny, and helpful. You've done so much I can't name it all. Tee is also the greatest author advocate that I know. Believe that!

Shout-outs to RAWSISTAZ, The Nubian Chronicles, The Sistah Circle Book Club, Shades of Romance, Black Writers Alliance, TimBookTu, The GRITS, Alvin C. Romer of The RomerReview, and the other online organizations that have supported me.

Thanks also to Donnie E. Howard, my crazy but cool "play-brother," who in 1998 refueled my interest in books written by African-American authors. Thanks for the friendship and the laughs, D.

Thanks to Mike Silvers because I said I would.

And thanks to Howard of Delta Steel, who'd ask

"when's the book coming out" before I ever wrote one word (and I don't even know what Howard looks like).

Thanks to Dale Cornelius of *Pages* magazine for the outstanding advertisement.

Thanks to the Crown Publishing Group people: Jason Gordon, Cindy Berman, and David Wade Smith for doing your part regarding the novel. Huge thanks to cover artist David Tran and designer Karen Minster for doing a fabulous job on the book. You've both made me very happy.

And huge thanks to Conrad Murphy of UH, who went out of his way to help me find my "lost" copy-edited manuscript when no one knew where it was.

I cannot end this without saying thank you to the wonderful supporters of the Book-Remarks.com Web site. This appreciation includes the authors, site visitors, publicists (especially Julia Bannon of Harper-Collins), and anyone else who has cooperated to make the site successful.

Thanks to everyone who did anything to help me with this project. I hope you enjoy the novel.

Cydney Rax
August 19, 2003

Turn the page for a preview of

GROOVE

by Geneva Holliday

On sale now

ɢeneva Holliday

In my bed that April night, my mind everywhere but where it should have been, which was on my ex-husband's tongue as it slid across my stomach and down my side.

Instead, my mind was on how hard my life was. How hard it was in so many different ways. Hard like a stone when you're black, female, and a single mother holding a GED instead of a high school diploma.

I wasn't thinking about how good it felt when he pushed his fingers through my hair and moved his tongue in circles around my navel. No, my mind was on the fact that I had missed three weeks of Calorie Counters meetings and how in that time I had stopped counting points, calories, carbs, and everything else.

Now my size-sixteen skirts and pants were giving my size-eighteen hips hell! Every morning it was an out-and-out fight. And I was steadily losing. Not the weight, of course. And on top of it, my Calorie Counters sponsor, Nadine Crawford—a former soda-guzzling, pound cake–eating accountant and mother of three, who'd joined the program three years earlier, had shed half her body weight and was now a size six and Calorie Counters' biggest cheerleader—was now calling my house every other day like a goddamn bill collector, talking about "When are you coming back, Geneva?" and "I'm here for you" and "Let's get together for an eight-point lunch and talk about it." I know I should have followed my first mind and joined Weight Watchers!

My mind was everywhere but in that bedroom where it should have been.

It was on my two-decade-old secondhand Cold Spot refrigerator that was humming so loud, it sounded as if any moment it would hack up something green, cough, and drop dead.

If that was to happen, it would take Housing a whole month to get me another crappy refrigerator in this apartment, and then how would I keep the milk cold for my sixteen-year-old son's morning cereal?

And he was another problem—my son, Eric Jr., who we all lovingly refer to as "Little Eric."

Little Eric hasn't been little since he was ten years old, and now he's a sophomore in high school, towering over me at a staggering six feet, and that boy still has years of growth ahead of him. Just trying to keep him in sneakers is going to send me to the poorhouse.

He was a good kid, even though I knew he was sampling weed. I mean, do these kids think we weren't kids once too? Do they think we were all born big?

The other day he strolled into the house, smelling like he'd been rolling in a field of reefer. I snatched him by his collar and dragged him through the living room and into the kitchen where the light is better and looked him in his eyes and asked him if he'd been smoking. Of course he lied and blinked those big brown eyes at me and said, "Look them, they ain't even red or nothing. I was with these guys that was smoking it, bu

I said, "Fool, I know Visine gets the don't take the scent out of your clothes your breath!" And with that I popped him upsid his head and sent him on his way. I told him that if he came back in my house smelling like a pothead, I was going to call the police on him my damn self!

O*hhhhhhhh,*" I moan, just so Eric can feel like he's doing all of the right things even though my mind has skipped over to my best friend, Crystal.

Not only is she my best friend, but she has been on many occasions a godsend as well.

I've had some rough times, and Crystal has always been there. Like the time when I was still on welfare and I had just collected my money and food stamps for the month and was on my way downtown to buy Eric, who was just about four years old then, a new pair of shoes. I hadn't even stepped off the bus good when two young boys rushed toward me, ripped my pocketbook from my hands, and then took off across Union Square.

I didn't even have a token to get home. It was Crystal that I called, and she left her job and came downtown and got me and then took me to the supermarket and filled up my refrigerator and cupboards with food. When I collected again the following month, she wouldn't even let me pay her back.

Crystal is also the one who saved me from the cosmetics counter at Macy's and got me a job as a receptionist at the Ain't I A Woman Foundation. Ten dollars

ur is certainly better than seven-fifty and stand-
g on your feet for eight to ten hours a day. Much better, and I will be forever grateful to her.

But lately Crystal just hasn't been herself. Something is bothering her; I see the sadness lurking behind that phony smile she walks around with all day.

I keep asking her what's wrong, but she just says,
"Nothing."

I guess she'll tell me in her own good time.

That feel good, baby?"

"*Ooooooooooooooooh* yeah, baby, real good."

Okay, now where was I?

Oh yes, my mind being on everything outside of
this here bedroom.

Well, I've also been thinking about Chevy. That's
another friend of mine, who is just . . . just—I don't
know—just crazy is the best way to describe her. Crazy
and a chameleon. You can never tell what Chevy was
going to look like the next time you met up with her.
She could be sporting a long weave, short weave, hazel
contacts, red weave, blue contacts, blond Afro puffs,
green contacts. Who knows!

Dr. Phil said that a person who needs to change her
appearance as many times as Chevy did is unhappy
with herself.

I believe that. But what I want to know is, what does
it say when that same person can always find money
for a new pair of La Blanca stilettos or a slinky thong
from La Perla but ain't never got enough money to
pay her light bill or rent?

She's making at least twice my hourly rate, for chris-

sakes! And don't have chick nor child to worry about.
Not a dog, goldfish, or hamster, just her! As my mother
says, "When she eats, her whole family has eaten."

Crazy is all I can think to call her. Oh yeah, and
selfish is another word that fits too. It's all about Chevy,
all of the time.

You want it, baby, you want it?"

"*Ooooooooh* yeah, baby, I want it *reaaaaaaaaaal* bad."

Now finally, there's Noah.

A dead ringer for Howard Hewitt, except fairer
complexioned. A successful merchandising manager
for the high-end casual clothing company QV, and a
Cancerian, so he can be a moody something.

When we were younger, Noah was the best double
Dutch jumper in our building and could corn braid
better than any of us. The highlight of his year was the
Miss America beauty pageant, which we had to watch
with him. Afterward he'd reenact the last fifteen minutes of the pageant—the surprise on the winner's
face, the tears, the halfhearted hugs she shared with
the losers—then he'd plop a lampshade on his head
and tie a bedsheet around his neck and prance back
and forth across the living room, demonstrating the
proper way the new Miss America should have strutted
down the catwalk.

Do you see where I'm going with this?

We've known Noah was gay since forever and have
always accepted him. His Jamaican mother, on the
other hand, is still in denial and even to this day still
tries to fix Noah up on blind dates with her friends'
daughters.

Noah is about the only one that I'm not really worried about. He seems happy with his career and has met some new man who lives in England, so he's always flying back and forth to London to be with him.

Yeah, I think that Noah should be the least of my worries right about now.

Now me; besides the war with my weight and a pack-a-day cigarette habit, I guess I don't have any real pressing concerns. Well, not that living in the projects is a great joy, but at least I'm not on the streets.

I'm thinking about going back to school. College. To major in what, I have no clue, but I think a college degree is something I should have. Well, I know it's something I need if I don't want to be a receptionist forever. And besides, maybe it will motivate that son of mine to do the right thing with his life.

Okay, enough of that, Geneva—try to concentrate on all of the kisses Eric is covering your body with, I tell myself, and I try, but my mind won't stay put. It keeps straying to the load of clothes that needs to be washed, the pile of unopened bills sitting on the kitchen table, and that goddamn pervert with the chiseled good looks and expensive suit who flashed me on the C train this morning when I was on my way to work.

"Turn over," Eric says, and I do and so do my thoughts.

He enters me from behind and I grip the headboard, not because it feels good—it does, though—but to hold on tight to try to keep it from banging too hard against the wall. Little Eric should have been asleep hours ago, but I don't want to take any chances.

Eric stops, his body shudders, and he withdraws.

This is his control method. It's been the same for years. Our sex life should have ended when I caught him cheating, moved out of our Queens apartment, and signed the divorce papers, but it didn't. It went on through all of it and still goes on.

Why? I don't know. Stupid, I guess. Or just plain horny.

"Where are you, Geneva?" Eric coos.

"I'm here baby, I'm here," I assure him and push my behind up into his chest.

He starts kissing my back while his hands massage my shoulders.

He begins to ease his penis back inside me. "You like it? You like it, baby?" he whispers in my ear.

"Uh-huh," I say, and in my mind I start to separate the white clothes from the dark, flip through the mountain of mail on my kitchen table, and clip coupons.

Eric's body trembles with excitement and then he whispers, "You want me to put it in your ass?"

My mind comes to a sudden and complete halt.

I've allowed him there only twice in my life, and both times we were still Mr. and Mrs. and I was really in love then. So in love that all I wanted to do was please him. But now I just wanted to be pleased and had no desire to have my asshole stretched out of shape. And besides, anal sex is notorious for leaving one unable to control the passing of air, if you know what I mean.

"Uh-uh," I say and start to turn back over and onto my back.

"Oh, c'mon, please?" he begs and gives me that puppy-dog look of his.

"Uh-uh," I sound again and shake my head from side to side.

After the day I had I thought some sexual healing was in order, but my mind won't let me concentrate on it, which means I'm dry as a bone down between my legs. Really and truly, all I want to do is just have a beer, maybe some chips, and a couple of spoonfuls of ice cream.

"Turn back over," Eric presses. "I won't put it in your ass."

Now Eric is one who cannot be trusted. He's a liar, cheater, and all-around crooked cop. Oh yeah, he's one of New York's finest. And I do mean *fine!* Six foot four and chocolate-colored. He'd been working out a lot lately and so was cut and as solid as a rock.

"You know, Eric, I don't think I want to do this," I say as I clamp my legs closed and reach for the sheet.

Eric looks surprised. His erect penis looks even more astonished than he does.

"What?" He half laughs.

"I said I don't think I want to do this," I say again as I catch hold of the sheet and try to pull it up and over my naked body.

"You're fucking kidding me, right, Geneva?" His rock-hard dick gives me an accusing look. "What the fuck am I suppose to do about this?" he says, indicating his stiff member with his index finger.

"Whatever you do when you're alone," I say and try not to smile. "I'm just not here. I'm sorry."

Eric looks down at his penis and then back at me.

I could tell he was having a conversation with it in his mind. His dick was his best friend, and any woman who had ever been with him knew it.

Suddenly his features softened and a mischievous smile spread across his face.

"How about a little licky-licky, then?" he says, and sticks his long pink tongue out at me.

I think about it for a minute. If I let him eat me out, it would release some tension. No effort on my part. It seems like I win all the way around. But then I remember who I'm dealing with and say, "What do I have to do to you?"

"Suck my dick, of course," he says proudly and thrusts his hips toward my face.

"Nah," I say and pull the sheet up to my chin.

"You're so fucking selfish," he hisses and sticks his lips out like a two-year-old.

"Then leave."

"Aw, c'mon, Geneva." He laughs.

"Nope."

Eric lets out a long sigh and looks around the bedroom for a moment. "Okay. You win."

Wow, I think, this is a first.

He pulls the sheet away from my body and gently separates my legs before moving into "eating" position.

Eric loves to eat pussy; always has. It's like a delicacy for him.

He begins by teasing my clitoris, rolling his tongue across it and then darting it in and out of my hole, bringing me to the point of orgasm seven or eight times before I finally scream, "Please, please!" when I know I can't take much more.

"Okay, baby, okay," he pants and takes a deep breath before moving in for the kill.

"Motherfucker, motherfucker!"

The firecrackers go off behind my eyes and bells ring in my head, and how it is that my behind and the heels of my feet are able to levitate above the sheets for a moment is anyone's guess, but they do.

That's how Eric makes me come: cussing, screaming, and levitating, which is why even after all of the low-down shit he's done to me and the half-ass child support he pays I'm still fucking him.

I don't have any excuse and won't even try to make one up. All I know is, a good dick is hard to find and an orgasm that can shoot you to the moon and back is even more elusive.

After my body stops shaking and I begin to feel uncomfortable in the wet spot, he lifts his head off my thigh, looks up at me and asks, "You sure you don't want me to fuck you?"

"N-no." I can hardly speak, and I lock my hands around his head and guide his mouth as far away from my vagina as possible.

Even if I wanted to fuck, I wouldn't allow it—shit, my pussy might explode!

Eric looks up at me and smiles. "I am good, ain't I?" he gloats and moves up beside me.

All I can do is shake my head in agreement and turn over onto my side.

Eric kisses my shoulder and then tries to put his arms around me, but I don't want that part of it. That tenderness belonged to us a long, long time ago. What we do now is primitive and carnal and that's the way I want it to remain.

"What's up with you?" he says and sucks his teeth in disgust.

"Shouldn't you go home to your wife now?" I say before punching the pillow and readying myself for dreamland.